Praise for Marion Zimmer Bradley's Previous *Sword & Sorceress* Anthologies

"Together with nineteen other tales, this latest collection featuring women who excel in their talents for magic and war presents a varied and entertaining sampler of current fantasy storytelling." —*Library Journal*

"Solid writing and an engaging range of themes . . . a series that is gaining in popularity." —*Booklist*

"Typical example of this anthology series—good to great stories emphasizing women/girls as strong females." —*Science Fiction Chronicle*

"A rich array of the best in fantasy short stories." —*Rave Reviews*

"Female warriors, witches, enchantresses make up this wonder-filled brew of horror and magic." —*Kliatt*

"Each tale is extremely well written, holding the reader in the grip of belief until the very end. A better collection of fine writing would be hard to find." —*Voya*

MARION ZIMMER BRADLEY
in DAW editions

SWORD AND SORCERESS I–XIX

THE DARKOVER NOVELS
The Founding
DARKOVER LANDFALL

The Ages of Chaos
STORMQUEEN!
HAWKMISTRESS!

The Hundred Kingdoms
TWO TO CONQUER
THE HEIRS OF HAMMERFELL
THE FALL OF NESKAYA

The Renunciates
THE SHATTERED CHAIN
THENDARA HOUSE
CITY OF SORCERY

Against the Terrans—The First Age
REDISCOVERY
THE SPELL SWORD
THE FORBIDDEN TOWER
STAR OF DANGER
WINDS OF DARKOVER

Against the Terrans—The Second Age
THE BLOODY SUN
HERITAGE OF HASTUR
THE PLANET SAVERS
SHARRA'S EXILE
THE WORLD WRECKERS
EXILE'S SONG
THE SHADOW MATRIX
TRAITOR'S SUN

SWORD AND SORCERESS XIX

EDITED BY

Marion Zimmer Bradley

DAW BOOKS, INC.

DONALD A. WOLLHEIM, FOUNDER

375 Hudson Street, New York, NY 10014

ELIZABETH R. WOLLHEIM
SHEILA E. GILBERT
PUBLISHERS

www.dawbooks.com

First Printing, January 2002
1 2 3 4 5 6 7 8 9 0

DAW TRADEMARK REGISTERED
U.S. PAT. OFF. AND FOREIGN COUNTRIES
—MARCA REGISTRADA
HECHO EN U.S.A.

PRINTED IN THE U.S.A.

ACKNOWLEDGEMENTS

The Curse of Ardal Glen © 2002 by Laura J. Underwood

When the King Is Weak © 2002 by Barbara E. Tarbox

The Sign of the Boar © 2002 by Diana Paxson

A Matter of Focus © 2002 by Penny Buchanan

Inner Sight © 2002 by Susan Wolven

Familiars © 2002 by Michael H. Payne

Ordeal © 2002 by Robyn McGrew

Grain © 2002 by Esther Friesner

Gifts of the Kami © 2002 by Carol E. Leever

One in Ten Thousand © 2002 by Aimee Kratts

Lord of the Earth © 2002 by Dorothy Heydt

Lady of Light © 2002 by Jennifer Ashley

All Too Familiar © 2002 by P. Andrew Miller

Artistic License © 2002 by Deborah Burros

Earth, Wind and Water © 2002 by Bob Dennis

Fire for the Senjen Tiger © 2002 by Stephen Crane Davidson

Fighting Spirit © 2002 by Karen Magon

Pride, Prejudice and Paranoia © 2002 by Michael Spence

A Simple Spell © 2002 by Marilyn A. Racette

Sword of Queens © 2002 by Bunnie Bessel

Better Seen than Heard © 2002 by Emily C.A. Snyder

Openings © 2002 by Meg Heydt

A Little Magic © 2002 by P.E. Cunningham

Eloma's Second Career © 2002 by Lorie Calkins

Sylvia © 2002 by A. Hall

CONTENTS

INTRODUCTION

by Elisabeth Waters

If this volume of *Sword and Sorceress* has a theme, it's learning about magic. Nearly everything I learned about magic I learned from Marion Zimmer Bradley. The part I didn't learn from her was what she and I had learned in the same place: our church. She was, and I am, an Episcopalian, and if you think Christianity doesn't have magic and ritual, you're wrong. The research for her historical fantasy novels (*The Firebrand* and the Avalon books) was decidedly ecumenical, but at least we got to keep our clothes on. Berkeley is too close to the ocean for "skyclad" to be comfortable.

Marion was a born teacher, but what she probably taught best was writing. Except for grammar, which I was lucky enough to learn in grade school, I learned about writing from Marion. Every time she gave one of her weekend writers' workshops, I took it, and I produced a salable short story every time. And while I was certainly happy that she thought my stories were good enough for her anthologies, I got more of the "first sale thrill" feeling the first time I sold a story to someone who didn't know me personally.

Marion was strongly influenced by Henry Kuttner, C.L. Moore, and Leigh Brackett; she loved their writing and admired them as people, and they encouraged her in her early career. So, in the best tradition of paying it forward, she taught the craft of writing to everyone who came near her. (The only member of her extended family who never had anything professionally published was a literary agent.) It wasn't enough for her to write herself; she had to become an editor and encourage all the new writers she possibly could. When *S&S* didn't let her buy all the stories she wanted to, she started her own magazine, funding it with the royalties from her novels. The magazine was never, alas, a commercial success, but it had a loyal, if small, following, started the careers of still more writers, and gave Marion something productive to do as her health failed and producing an entire novel by herself became too much work for her.

By the time she was reading for *S&S XVIII*, her health did not permit her to read the quantity of slush that *S&S* generated, so she made *S&S* by invitation only. She then invited almost everyone who had ever sold her a story, so the invitation list contained over 500 published writers. She was still reading the manuscripts on a daily basis the morning of her fatal heart attack, and, as always, she had enough for three anthologies.

This is the second of them. I hope that you enjoy it.

If you want more information on MZB's life and work, the Marion Zimmer Bradley Literary Works Trust maintains a web site at http://mzbworks.home.att.net.

THE CURSE OF ARDAL GLEN

by Laura J. Underwood

As of this story, Laura J. Underwood has sold thirty-nine short stories of fantastic fiction. Her work has been featured in numerous publications including *Marion Zimmer Bradley's FANTASY Magazine, Catfantastic V, Pulp Eternity* and *Adventures of Sword & Sorcery,* as well as several volumes of *Sword and Sorceress.* In her more mundane life, she's a librarian, a hiker, and a fair harpist, owner of the real Glynnanis.

This story was born from her love of Scottish folklore and archaeology. She tends to mutter in a strange accent as she writes Keltoran tales, which greatly confuses the family cat. She's a former state fencing champion and an active member of SFWA.

She would like to dedicate this story to the memory of Marion Zimmer Bradley whose encouragement and kindness over the years will never be forgotten.

Though Etney was but five at the time, and unaware of her mageborn legacy, she still knew the smith was coming to Ardal Glen days before he arrived. As a forthright child, she said so to all who would listen, noticing how their eyes grew hollow with pain. She also told her Auntie Bidina, who was long-lived like all mageborn and said to be older than anyone else in the village. The old woman, who had taken Etney to raise when her mother passed on, warned the child to mind her tongue and not fill folks' hearts with such grief. But the day the smith arrived, riding a black horse that some swore carried the fire of his forge in its eyes, there were those in the village who recalled Etney's words with a shudder of dread.

Etney was twelve the next time the smith came. By then, she had learned his name was Dougal, though Black Dougal the Lost was what the villagers whispered as they made warding signs. Etney watched him from the small window of the loft room where Auntie insisted the young girl stay. By then, Etney's mage-born powers had blossomed, and as the smith rode by, his blue eyes flashed up from under the shag of black hair that surrounded his handsome face, revealing a mixture of rage and remorse. Etney saw then with the two-sight of her mage eyes that two hearts beat within this man. Two souls were woven into his brawny flesh, one warm as bronze, the other dark as death.

His black hair fluttered like a cape in the wind as he looked away from her. With mage senses still sensitive to the world at large in their blossoming, Etney felt a wash of pain and sorrow. But the dark that was in him quickly hid it from her, and he set his face in an angry scowl and rode on.

Etney told Auntie Bidina what she had seen. The old woman shook her head. "Pay him no mind, lass," Auntie said as she drew out her old corrie, the only kettle in the village that never needed the smith's attentions, and prepared a stew of rabbit and carrots and barley. "Black Dougal will not have you nor I for what we are. That's the law. We, at least, are safe from his dreadful lottery."

That Auntie's eyes grew a little misty did not puzzle Etney half as much as the old woman's words. Now, she was old enough to know that the folks dwelling in Ardal Glen feared the smith, for when he came at the Spring Solstice once each seven years, there was a lottery. All lasses of purity who had attained marriageable age had their names tossed into a newly repaired corrie. One name was drawn, and that lass went, weeping, with the smith.

Only the day after his departure did Etney learn

the girl's true fate. Etney was wont to wander the glen beyond the village boundaries, giving in to the ancient call that sang in her blood like a fire. There was much magic in the world in those days, and with her mage eyes, she could see it in nearly everything. She loved to go wandering the moors for she knew every tree and stone and wild hare among the sedge like her own name.

At the mouth of the glen sat a circle of stones and a cromlech known as Annwn's Gate. It was there that Etney found the lass who had left with the smith. The girl was cold as the stones and wet with the dew. Her eyes were wide open, as was her mouth, and her hands were knotted into claws at her throat, giving the impression she had died unable to draw breath. Except for that, there was not a mark on her. And when Etney scried the dead lass, she found that the girl's soul had been sundered from her as well.

Half stumbling, half running, Etney returned to the village, sick with grief over the terrible sight. She cried as she told Auntie Bidina what she had seen, and was given comfort tea of blackberries and sage, sweetened with honey, while Auntie sent some men from the village back to deal with what lay beneath the stones. They wrapped their plaidies over their heads and wandered out into the spring chill, faces grim.

"Why?" Etney wailed as she leaned into her Auntie and shed tears.

"Because it has been so for several generations," Auntie said.

"But why does he do it?" Etney insisted. "Is it because he carries two souls?"

Auntie Bidina stiffened. "You have seen this, child?" the old woman asked, and her face seemed to grow pale with some memory.

"Aye," Etney said. "One black as death, the other good bronze. What does it mean?"

The words drew long silence from the old woman before she spoke again. "Forget it, child," she finally whispered. "There is nothing your magic nor mine can do for him. Now, I have mending to do and you've hens to feed and eggs to gather. Go."

But Etney could not forget the girl's face, nor the terror in her eyes. And, as the next seven years wound past, she made a vow. She would solve the riddle of the smith with two souls the next time he came to Ardal Glen, and put an end to the dark pall he had laid upon her village.

Folks spoke to her more freely of Black Dougal as she grew, as freely as they complimented her raven hair and cerulean eyes. Those who could remember far enough back said he had been coming to Ardal Glen every seven years for thrice seven times seven. That he always rode the same ebon horse and never seemed to age or change.

When the time of his coming was at hand, every bit of his old work on their kettles and knives suddenly went awry, so there was never a lack of need for his skill. Ardal Glen was forced to keep the bargain made long ago, to pay the smith whatever he desired. And always, he asked for a maiden pure of body and soul, a maiden who was never seen alive again.

"Why do you not fight him?" she asked. "Why do you give in to him like cowed dogs?"

They shook their heads at her youthful disdain. One year, an elder assured her, they had refused the smith's demands, and in that year seven children disappeared, only to be found dead at Annwn's gate. After that, they dared not refuse.

"But who made this ill bargain to begin with?" she said.

That tale, they told her, was lost before their time, and refused to say more.

A fortnight before the smith would come, Etney saw her nineteenth birthday. And it was on that day that a young bard strolled into Ardal's Glen. "Master Garan has come again," she heard folks whisper, and she vaguely recalled that he had come the last time before the smith arrived. But then, she had been younger and ignored him while other lasses flocked about him, hoping for his favors to save them from the dire fate of the smith's bargain. It was well known in Ardal Glen that young maids sought marriage and children most hastily in the year the smith would come. But the bard always teased them as he sat in the square and sang his songs.

On market day, he came, seating himself on the steps of the well and setting out his tam to collect coin. He was a strange sight with his eldritch features. His lengthy hair was almost white and his eyes were the color of bronze. He carried a lute of Keltoran black walnut on which he played many a wistful tune. Before, Etney had always ignored his song, but on this day, as she wandered from merchant to merchant to study their wares, she listened.

> *"A blacksmith came to Ardal Glen*
> *His hammer boldly in his hand.*
> *He filled the braes with metal's din*
> *Until the end of day.*
>
> *But then he made his price well known,*
> *A maiden pure to call his own.*
> *Each seven years he set this boon*
> *And took the maid away."*

His sweet voice was unearthly as he continued to sing, and Etney was drawn closer by the sound of it.

> *"So bar yer lass,*
> * Behind the door,*
> *And give yer lad*
> * A mighty sword.*
> *The blacksmith's come*
> * To Ardal Glen*
> *To clout yer daughter's*
> * Cauldron."*

Garan froze when he saw Etney staring hard at him with her blue eyes glowing like glims, and a rich flush wandered across his cheeks as he looked at the ground.

"That's not a very nice song," Etney said.

"Ah, well, I fear I quite forgot myself, lady," Garan said and smiled. "I do ask that you forgive me."

" 'Tis not my forgiveness you should seek, Master Garan, for I've no fear of your randy song or its subject," she said.

"Have you not?" he said, looking more cheerful.

"No," Etney said, "And I know that you've come to Ardal Glen each seven year as does the smith about whom you sing. Why?"

"Ah, well," Garan said. "It has always been my hope that one day I shall be able to finish my song about the demon smith whose curse falls on this place."

"He's no demon," Etney said. "He's but a man with two souls in him, though I have sensed that there is mage blood in him as well."

"Really?" Master Garan angled his brows in a questioning manner. "And how do you know this, my pretty lass?"

The words dripped with a bitter honey that set Etney ill at ease. She drew a deep breath and quietly called on the magic that was in the ground beneath her to build a protective wall around her mage soul. "I can see his two souls," she said, "as clearly as I can see that you have none."

Garan looked as though she had slapped him. His mouth fell open. Frantically, he began to gather his belongings into his satchel. Tossing the lute by its strap across his shoulder, he met her persistent gaze with one of his own.

"Stay clear of the smith, then, lass, for there's nothing you can do to save him," he said in a soft voice that only she could hear. "There are dark powers afoot here, and while you may have the blood of the Old Ones in you, even that will not save you should you interfere in matters you know nothing about."

He turned on his heel and pounded up the road

from the village at a fierce pace. Several folks milling about the market made warding signs and looked relieved to see him go. Etney crossed her arms and watched Garan follow the road that would lead him to the stones of Annwn's Gate.

This was a mystery indeed. She headed straight way back to Auntie Bidina's cottage, fire burning her thoughts. Auntie was filling her corrie with water to set upon the fire to boil when Etney blustered into the cottage like a bogie wraith.

"Child, what has you walking like the wind?" Auntie asked with a frown. "The cottage is still trembling from the way you slammed that door."

"Today, I spoke to the bard they call Garan," Etney said, hands to hips as she paced the floor. "And when I looked at him, I saw that he had no soul, and the smith has two, and I want to know why."

Auntie Bidina shook her head. "I suppose there's no keeping the truth from ye, lass."

"What truth?" Etney insisted.

Auntie Bidina sighed. "Black Dougal is my older brother, your great uncle by blood."

Etney sank to the chair as her legs weakened beneath her and the blood rushed from her skin, leaving it clammy and cold. "The smith is my great uncle? But how?"

"Long ago, when my brother was a young man and I was still but a lass yet to find my powers, he fell in love with a Unseelie woman as old as the world and as fresh as spring, and though I warned him that courting such a creature could only lead to harm, he did tryst with her beneath the stones of Annwn's Gate. But one night, he did not return, and so I went in search of him. I found him there, weeping like a child, and when I tried to comfort him, he pushed me away.

"I begged him to tell me what had happened, and he could do no more than rant and rage. But then, he looked at me and said, 'I am doomed, dear sister, and so are the women of Ardal Glen, for I have made such a terrible bargain with a Lord of the Dark Ones.

The lass I loved was his sister, and when he came upon us here, he sought to slay me for daring to touch her. Only she did love me enough to step into my path and take the blow of magical death he meant for me. She died in my arms, and in anger, he cursed me and said that I owed him a boon in exchange for his sister's life. That by my love and his act, her soul was now damned, and that unless I wanted all who dwelled in Ardal Glen to suffer, I would tie myself to him as he willed, and bring him a maiden pure each seven years to keep his sister from Arawn's grasp.'

"And since that day, every seven year, my brother comes to mend our kettles, and takes with him a maiden pure to give her soul to the Unseelie Lord so that his Unseelie sister might stay in the Summerland."

"But that goes against all that we are taught," Etney said. "For if the Dark One Lord is the one who killed his own sister, should his soul not be the one that takes the brunt of the curse?"

"Aye, so I thought when I tried to take the darkness from Dougal and set him free," Auntie said. "I even opened Annwn's Gate and sought to give that wretched soul to Arawn in the maiden's place, but the Dark One came upon me clothed in shadows so I could not see his face. I had not the strength to fight his evil power, and he in turned, caused my brother such pain with the rending of his soul from my brother's flesh, I had stop fighting to end Dougal's screams. The gate closed, and the Dark One mocked me before giving the lass to Arawn and fleeing with Dougal under his command."

"And what of Master Garan?" Etney said. "How does he tie into this tale?"

"Him?" Auntie said and made a warding sign. "None knows from whence he came, except that he arrived the year the villagers tried to resist Dougal's bargain, and started to sing that wretched song of his. Now, every year, he comes to mock us in our grief, and not one man dares to raise a hand against him, for all know it is bad fortune to harm a bard."

"He's no bard," Etney said as she frowned and crossed her arms. "He has no soul, Auntie, and any man who has no soul cannot be mortal but faery. And if what you say is true, he could well be this Dark Lord come to make certain the bargain is kept. Which means there must be a way to stop him and break this curse on Ardal Glen."

"But I tried to break the curse to tear the darkness from Dougal and set him free," Auntie Bidina said, shaking her head. "I failed and nearly killed my brother. Just what makes you think you can succeed?"

"I must try," Etney said.

"But all know that a Dark One cannot bear the full light of day," Auntie argued, "and that the bard always comes when there is light. How can the bard be as you claim?"

Etney made a face, twiddling with the hem of her shawl. True. Still, she could not sit idle with this new knowledge in her thoughts. She had to try something to break this terrible bargain.

She said nothing after that, merely took her basket and went for the eggs, holding each one in hand and studying the shells to see which held new life and which could be eaten. But all the while, as her fingers slid over the smooth surfaces, her mind raced with a plan.

The bard did not return for the rest of the fortnight, but the smith came to Ardal Glen came as always on the Solstice Eve, setting up at the old forge. Etney was of an age now that she could do as she pleased, and she went straight to the forge to watch the smith work. He was handsome, this great uncle, with fine features that belied his strength and age. Only a bare hint of a black beard edged his face, and his eyes seemed to glow like his forge as he worked on mending all that was brought to him. Once, he looked up at her, standing in the door of his forge, watching him with eyes not unlike his own.

"What is your need?" he asked.

"Nothing, Uncle," she replied, and saw him wince with recognition that briefly drew remorse into his eyes. "What is yours?"

He set a black look upon her then, and she noticed that his hand trembled on the iron he worked, as if its touch had suddenly grown painful to him. But then the darkness faded back, leaving the bronze to glow through, and he took the iron with the surety of a man who knows his trade and set to mending the pot hooks one woman had delivered.

Iron, Etney thought. The Dark One's soul was Unseelie. Cold iron and steel, forged from the bones of the good magic that lay in the earth, were the enemies of all its kind. Perhaps, there was hope for her great uncle yet.

Satisfied with this knowledge, she went home and rummaged among the effects left by her father, who had parted this world in a bandit raid just after she was born. There was a dagger of steel that never seemed to rust, and as she held it in her hand, she felt the faint course of magic that had been laid upon it to protect it from nature's destruction by Auntie's own hand. Etney carefully wrapped it into a bit of her father's old plaid to hide it from prying eyes as she slipped out of the village.

Etney had little time, but she knew now what must be done. With the dagger, she went up into the braes that overshadowed Annwn's Gate, and sought a private place she knew of where a spring of water flowed out of the rocks. There, she started a white fire, and thrusting the blade into its depths, she sang a song with her mage tongue.

> *"Fire of White Light, gift of the gods*
> * Gift of the Silver Wheel Lady of Old*
> *Give power to this blade to cleave immortal flesh*
> * And sunder the Dark One's soul"*

The blade turned a brilliant rainbow hue, and draw-

ing power from the air, Etney lifted the blade as
though it were in the grasp of an invisible hand. She
floated it over to the heart of the stream where the
water was sweetest, and there she magically thrust it
into the rapids. There was a hiss and a cloud of steam
as the dagger sank into the shallow depths. Etney
waited until the steam vanished before she slipped off
her boots and stepped barefoot into the cold water.
When she lifted the dagger from the stream, it took
on a wondrous glow of magic. Pleased to know the
smith's skill was in her blood, she hid the glowing
dagger in her plaid and made her way to the circle of
stones to wait.

She had barely arrived when she saw movement at
the mouth of the cromlech. The air stirred before her
mage sight, revealing a wispy form that convulsed like
mist. Slowly, the form grew solid and became Master
Garan the bard. His bronze eyes were now hard as
diamonds and glittered with an evil light as he stared
out at the moor road. Etney hid herself in the shadows, whispering a cloaking spell, and crouched to wait
as the bard approached the central altar stone.

The clatter of hooves on the road alerted him and
Etney to the smith's arrival. Black Dougal charged
into the circle on his ebon steed, and behind him sat
a weeping lass, the innkeeper's daughter Megan.

"Right on time," Garan said and approached the
horse. "Give her to me."

Hesitation filled Dougal's eyes, as though he did not
wish to obey, but his will was not his own. From her
shadows, Etney saw his eyes grow dark with the power
that controlled him, and he seized the girl roughly by
the arm and flung her from the horse. She gave a
terrified shriek as she landed on the ground and
looked up at the bard.

"Help me, Master Garan," Megan pleaded.
"Please."

"But of course, I will help you child," Garan said
with a wicked smile and started to lay hands upon
Megan, to draw her from the ground.

Etney chose that moment to spring from behind the stones and charge at Garan's back. Still, the bard heard her and turned just as she jerked the dagger from beneath the bit of plaid. At the sight of it, his eyes widened, and there was naught he could do quickly enough to keep her from thrusting it into his chest all the way up to the hilt.

But Garan did not fall. Instead, he struck out hard with the back of his hand, and the blow flung Etney to the ground. Stunned, she shook her head and stayed there but a moment, long enough to keep his eyes on her as Megan bolted toward the village like a frightened hare. Garan sneered at Etney, his eyes glowing like glims.

"Foolish creature," he hissed. "What made you think this steel could stop me."

A hand seized Etney from behind, pulling her upright and holding her tight. She smelled the sulfur and sweat of a man whose life was spent at a forge, and turned her head to see that it was the smith who held her now. His face was set in a dark scowl that matched the one on Garan's face as the bard carefully drew the dagger from his chest and waved it before her.

"Clever, wench, but not clever enough," he said and let the dagger fall so it stabbed the ground at her feet. She struggled in Dougal's powerful grasp. "Your magic steel would have worked, but you chose the wrong heart for it, my dear, and now you shall die. Arawn will be more than pleased to be given the soul of so bright a young mage, as the Dark Lord of Annwn cares naught for Keltoran law."

How could she have been so foolish, she thought despairingly. He had no soul, and that was what protected him from the steel and the sun.

He smiled and turned toward the cromlech, waving a hand, and she saw darkness swelling there.

"Come, Arawn, and claim this one in exchange for my debt," Garan said and laughed. "Let me be free another seven years of penance for my sister's death."

The dark became slashed with fiery gouts that licked

the air like flames. It was as though the world was tearing apart in that place, and opening a path into the pits of Annwn. Etney stiffened when she realized a figure was forming in the dark, one wrapped in the plaid of night with bits of blood and bone in its weave. Arawn himself was coming to Ardal Glen to claim Etney's soul.

The darkness grew as the winds of Annwn poured from the gap to buffet Garan. But as the Dark One danced like a child in his mad joy, Etney felt Dougal's grasp lighten on her arms. She turned and looked up at the smith's face, and saw that he wept. The warm bronze of his aura reached out to her like a hand.

"The Dark One cannot die unless the dark in me is killed . . ." a voice whispered to her mind.

The hands that bound her let go. Sensing that she was free, Garan turned back, face tight with fury as he shouted "NO!"

Etney dropped to her knees and jerked the dagger out of the ground. Its blade glowed like moonlight, soft and blue white, as she turned toward the smith. For one brief moment, she saw his pain flare, before she sprang to her feet again and plunged the dagger into Dougal's heart.

He shrieked, the sound echoed by Garan, who fell and writhed upon the ground. Darkness began to rip out of the smith, separating from the warm bronze as good steel from slag. Dougal sank to his knees before Etney as the shadowy soul of the Dark One was torn from him and went flitting toward the gate. Desperately, Garan flung himself at it, trying to wrap arms about it in vain, but there was no power in the mortal world that could stop Arawn once he drew a soul to him. Screaming, Garan followed his soul through the gate. The wild wind of Annwn faded, and the gate closed, leaving only the indigo outline of the braes in the dark to Etney's mage eyes.

Frantically, she whispered "Solus," to call forth an orb of mage light, and turned back to the fallen body of the smith. She was startled to see that his black

hair had gone silver, and that his brawny frame had
shrunk to that of a wizened old man. Kneeling at his
side, she gently supported his head with her knees and
pulled the glowing dagger from his flesh. He gasped
and his blue eyes flickered open, and he looked up at
her with a feeble smile that trickled blood.

"My thanks to you, dear niece," he whispered.
"You have broken my curse and set me free. At last,
I may join my beloved in the Summerland."

There was naught she could do to save him as his
head sagged and the last breath slipped from him. She
closed her eyes in a brief moment of prayer to the
gods who guided good souls to their rest, then eased
him to the ground as she rose, taking the dagger in
hand.

There were torches on the road, lights bobbing like
hob lanterns across the moors. The innkeeper's daughter must have rousted the whole village with her unexpected return. Etney sensed that Auntie Bidina was
at the head of the party of plaid-wrapped men hur-
rying toward Annwn's Gate. The lass smiled wistfully
as she wondered if any of them would venture to finish
Garan's song about the curse of Ardal Glen.

WHEN THE KING IS WEAK
by Barbara E. Tarbox

Barbara E. Tarbox was born just months before the turn of the half-century in New York state and has lived there ever since. She has a Master's in Education and is certified to teach high school English. She works as a substitute teacher, which leaves her time to write and take care of her menagerie: three horses, two dogs, and assorted goldfish. She sold a story to *Marion Zimmer Bradley's Fantasy Magazine*; it appeared in issue 42 (Winter 1999).

Education is a funny thing. You pick up all sorts of bits and pieces, and what you *think* you are learning isn't always what you are *really* learning.

Red crept down Dohanna's sword, not the rich blood of man or beast, but the thin blood of iron.

Just yesterday she had felt the sickness and drawn the blade to watch it bleed. Just yesterday, two of its forge-mates had lost their masters. Just yesterday, she had lost two of her friends and fellow Guards.

Today the last was gone. Distance meant nothing to the magic that bound the swords together, but Kalea had not been far away when she fell. They had parted only last night, grasping at the poor chance of keeping the last two sections of the Book of Findings separate; of keeping at least one from the hands of The Ten.

She looked through the age-separated boards of the deserted cowshed where she had spent the dark hours. It was not far past dawn; clear sun made the early autumn leaves glow. A beautiful day.

Had Kalea seen it?

How many of those vermin magicians had she taken with her?

Sorcerers, they called themselves. They had dazzled the king with their tricks and fire-shows. Hannish was a good enough king, if you measured by intention, but to say he was far from wise would be putting the matter kindly. He let The Ten stay at the castle, turned a deaf ear to his True Sorcerer's warnings, and shed a sincere bucket of tears when that True Sorcerer was found with a pike through his chest.

But he never thought to blame The Ten.

Her horse sneezed and coughed behind her. "I told you not to eat this hay, Acorn, old boy," she said as she picked up a handful of the summer-dried stuff to polish the orange-red stains from her sword. "It's not fit." She held her breath as a cloud of mold-dust rose from her rubbing. He snuffled into her hair. "Don't try that either," she said, and reached over her shoulder to rub the big dun nose.

She wondered what would happen to him when she died. He would probably find his way back to the castle; he had been trained to do that in an emergency. She hoped it might be safe there for a horse. Once The Ten had the last section of The Book—the section that she carried—no place would be safe for a human.

The Ten would rule the kingdom.

At *least* the kingdom.

As miserable a lot as they were, once they had The Book, they would be able to call enough power to be dangerous to the True Sorcerer of every kingdom. She stopped polishing the blade, held the edge up to the light coming through the boards, and shook her head bitterly. They had been dangerous—deadly—to a True Sorcerer even without The Book. How had such charlatans overcome old Sestal's defenses, how had they even come within a pike's length . . . ?

She didn't want to think about the king's True Sorcerer, didn't want to think about how she and the other seven of the Sorcerer's Guard had been drawn away by the illusion of a threat outside the castle walls.

She tried to shut the memory away where she was keeping the memory of Tonno and Wen and all the others—and Kalea.

She and Kalea had applied for apprenticeships with Sestal within the same month. They had tested together, been told, together, that their talents were not great enough for acceptance, and were offered training for the Sorcerer's Guard—together.

They had almost died together.

Now The Ten had seven of the eight pieces. The Guard had divided the Book of Findings, the book that Sestal had used to record years of refinements to basic spell-casting. They had scrambled the pages between them before they fled the castle. They had scattered in pairs; trying, by separate routes, to reach kingdoms to the south and east that had True Sorcerers Sestal trusted.

They had all failed. She and Kalea had almost made it to the eastern boundary and the protection of Cosilla, Sestal's niece and True Sorcerer to the Queen.

Almost. Almost wasn't good enough.

She slipped her sword back into its scabbard. She had practiced long hours for her skill with the weapon, and her talent for magic was probably as great as most of The Ten who dared to call themselves sorcerers. But the same could have been said for Kalea and all the rest.

All the rest who were now dead.

Funny how she still thought of her enemies as The Ten. It had never been a real title, just what the guards had called them in tones half-mocking, half-anxious.

There would be fewer than ten now. To be accepted for the Sorcerer's Guard, a gift for magic was basic, but you also needed the strength and will to become a warrior. Lack either, and you were sent home to hoe turnip fields.

She wished she were hoeing turnip fields.

No. Not true. She knocked old hay from her tunic as she stood and stretched the earthen floor's cold from her muscles. Not true at all. She didn't know how many of The Ten had survived, but she promised herself there would be fewer before she joined Kalea and the others.

A corner of the shed made a poor privy, and a hard slice of bread made a poor breakfast before her horse whickered softly and shifted the weight on his front hooves from side to side.

"What is it, boy?" she whispered as she buckled on her sword belt. "Have they found us already?"

She slid along the wall, taking advantage of whatever view the boards would allow her. There—on the eastern side—trying to move silently. Three. One, she didn't know by name; the second was a braggart called Naffic; the third . . . The third wasn't one of The Ten. He was a servant in the castle, one of those appropriated by the magicians as they took over more and more of the household. Gran, she thought he was called; yes, Gran.

Two, then. She invested another minute in studying Gran. He wasn't armed, so he probably hadn't joined the dwindling forces, but from what she remembered, he wouldn't be likely to rush heroically to her aide either. Gran was a mouse that none of her magic could turn to a lion.

But two . . . Two was good.

"Come out of there."

It was the one whose name she didn't know. She was surprised that he would speak first. He had been the quietest of The Ten; the one easiest to ignore.

"Come out," he repeated. "Come out and give us the pages you carry. Join us. There is power enough to be shared."

It was pointless to pretend they hadn't found their quarry. She tried to sound uncertain. "Have the other guards joined you?"

"Of course. Their talents will be rewarded by the new order."

Rewarded. The Quiet One must not know her sword had shed sympathetic blood seven times or he would not have tried so transparent a lie. "Have one of them come and argue for your side," she called out, "and I will accept your offer."

Neither he nor Naffic reacted at all, but Gran took to studying his toes.

"They are busy at the palace, assembling the book. Ride back with us and speak to them there."

Walk out and be slaughtered. Not likely.

"I don't believe you. I believe that they are dead."

"Have it as you will, woman." He made *woman* sound like a word not fit to speak. "The pages you carry are mine."

Mine. Not ours. *Mine.*

"Which one of you will die to take them?"

"You're a fool, woman." His hands caressed a sphere of air. "A fool and a coward. The others defended what they had; face-to-face."

The others had followed their training as warriors.

The others were dead.

The Quiet One's hands opened toward the shed as though he were tossing her a ball of yarn.

Something stung the back of her nose, something burned her throat. Her horse snorted and tried to pull loose from his tether. She fought her own panic. Spells against noxious air. What were they? She had learned them, as she had learned to parry with a sword, but she had never used them. To remember them now . . .

There was a deep grunt behind her. Acorn was down, his front legs making circular running motions in the hay.

Her eyes watered and her lungs strained in the thick poison. She dropped to her knees by the horse's head. Counterspell. Counter . . .

The air around her was thinning, losing its sting. Words were running through her mind so quickly she could barely recognize the spell reeling itself off over

and over. She blessed old Sestal for the endless drills
that had written the words into her mind in ink so
dark that even the face of death couldn't erase them.

Acorn's breathing eased, but he didn't try to get up.

A bad sign.

But good strategy.

"Thank you, boy. Quiet now. Please be quiet." She
stroked the sweat-dampened neck beneath the black
mane and crawled back to the eastern wall.

They were still there, the three of them. Gran still
watching his toes, the no-longer Quiet One still watching the shed, Naffic twirling the hilt of his sword between his palms.

The air was fine now, but she barely breathed.

"Woman!"

Silently, she pulled herself up behind the door.

"Woman!"

Carefully, she drew her sword.

Naffic, left hand holding a cloth over his nose, right
holding his blade ready, burst through the door.

She struck hard, two-handed.

The leather brace he wore kept her sword from sev-
ering his wrist. Still, bone fractured nicely and he
howled, fallen weapon forgotten, and spun to face her,
clutching the deep wound with the cloth in his left
hand.

She pushed the door shut behind her. "You'd better
tie a bandage above that," she said. "I think you
would be more useful alive."

He grimaced and the tendons on the back of his
left hand stood with the grip he was using to try to
stop the steady flow of blood. "I'll destroy you with
a spell!"

"Destroy me? You can't even save yourself."

It was true. Naffic's face had gone pale, his knees
swayed like stream grasses, and still the blood flowed.

"Sit down," she said, "or fall down. The choice is
yours"

He stood for a moment, defiant in defeat, then
folded to the floor.

She tore a strip of cloth from his short cloak, used it to slow the flow of blood then recited a simple coagulation spell.

He blinked at her. "Are you a True Sorcerer?"

"There's only one True Sorcerer in each kingdom, and you killed ours—remember?"

"It wasn't me. I—"

She pushed him down with her foot. "Save it for the king—if we live that long."

True Sorcerer. She hadn't even aspired to the ancient title. Just an ordinary, everyday sorceress was all she had wanted to be. Even the Guard was close enough.

"Naffic!"

She stopped the magician's answer with a warning look as she bound his feet together with Acorn's tether rope. He was so weak that the precaution probably wasn't necessary, but she wasn't going to risk the kingdom on *probably*.

"Naffic!"

The One was pushing Gran toward the shed. Gran was a big enough man to resist, but his fear of the magician was clearly stronger than his fear of what was in the crooked old building.

Cowardice—or good sense?"

The magician gave Gran a final shove and retreated.

She hid behind the door as it creaked open. Gran crept inside, casting about with his eyes like a hound searching for a scent.

"Lady?" his voice was as hesitant as his steps. "Lady guard?" He crept farther and froze when he saw Naffic.

"Hello, Gran," she whispered as she pushed the door shut behind him and lifted the sword to his neck. "There's something I'd like you to do for me. I'd like you to scream."

The sound that came from Gran's throat was more raspy gurgle than scream.

"Not good enough," she said.

"Please, lady . . . They made me come; two other

servants, too. They're dead. I didn't hurt anyone. Please . . ."

Poor fool. "I believe you," she said. "I believed you before you told me. That's why I asked you for a scream instead of cutting one from you. I'm not going to hurt you if you do what you're told."

"Thank you, lady, thank . . ."

"Don't go faint on me, man. I need that scream— better make it two or three. Come on Gran, put your lungs into it."

By the third try, he had it right.

"Good," she said.

"Can I leave now?"

She looked through the boards. The One was pacing. "Of course not. You're dead."

"I . . . Oh."

"That magician," she said. "What's his name?"

"Lesteg—and he's a *sorcerer.*"

"He's no more a sorcerer than I am."

"He said you were. Said you all were—or could be. Everyone in the Guard."

"He told you that?"

Gran's mouth turned down. "Not him. He just gave me orders and cursed me when I wasn't fast enough following them. It was the others he talked to. Big talk about how when they had the book and the competition was dead, they would have all the power and the riches that went with it."

"Competition? The Guard?"

"That's what he said, lady. He laughed at the old True Sorcerer for teaching his apprentices to be warriors; said it was a stupid way to choose a successor."

She kept an eye on Lesteg. He had stopped pacing. "One of the Guard was supposed to be the next True Sorcerer? But we all failed the tests."

"That's what he said, lady. That's all I know. I never even worked in the sorcerer's hall. I don't know what the old True—"

She waved him silent. She had to think, but not

about what Gran had revealed. Not now. If she let herself be distracted . . .

A dead potential sorceress was just as dead as a dead guard.

"Gran!" Lesteg shouted. "What's going on in there? Answer me, you miserable slops hauler!"

She looked sharply at Gran. He pressed his fingers to his lips in a promise of silence.

"You out there!" she called to Lesteg. "You've run out of men you can send to do your fighting for you. If you want the last part of the book, you'll have to come for it yourself."

He threw a ball of fire. She raised her hands to counter it, but it snuffed out of existence just short of the wall.

Odd.

She looked at her hands as she lowered them. She had never realized just how much magic Sestal was slipping into their training under the guise of things useful to them in battle.

But she hadn't stopped the fireball. It had stopped itself.

No. Lesteg had stopped it. It was a bluff. He was trying to frighten her into doing something rash. He wouldn't dare use fire against the shed.

The book would burn.

She whispered instructions to Gran and shouted through the space between door and wall. "I don't know who you are; I don't know where you came from. I don't know why you chose King Hannish's court as the place for your ambition and murder. None of that matters. You will not become True Sorcerer of this kingdom."

She hadn't practiced much with fire, couldn't have thrown a ball of flames, or extinguished it in mid-flight; but she could cast a line of tiny golden flickers along the base of the tinder-dry wall.

The old hay sparked and caught.

A sprinkle of water droplets materialized and turned

to steam without discouraging the spreading blaze. Dohanna smiled, mouth tight. He was no better at Water than she was at Fire. He had strengthened different aspects of his gift, but he was no closer to the power of a True Sorcerer than she was.

Unless he completed Sestal's Book of Findings.

"Woman! Sorceress!"

She grabbed a dry-rotted board and used it to sweep burning hay to the north wall.

"Gods and demons," Naffic whined and started inching like a caterpillar toward the southwest corner where Gran was urging Acorn to a wobble-kneed stand. "You're going to roast us all!"

"I don't think I'll roast Gran," she said as she pulled him the rest of the way to the corner, "and I'm very fond of my horse. You, however . . ."

She left Naffic to finish the sentence any way he wanted and kicked a path to the door through hay that was not yet burning. Breath held and shielding her face against the heat, she peered out through the gap between the hinges.

Lesteg was still trying to conjure water, this time around himself.

His lack of success was no reason to underestimate his sorcerous gift, or to underestimate the danger. This was the man who had killed, or ordered killed, all of her friends. She was sure he was the dark heart of the plot; that he had fed his own followers to the furnace of his ambition; that he was the only one who could have come close enough to Sestal to drive that steel pike head—

She stopped herself, loosened the tension in her jaw. A warrior needed a clear head, a sorceress needed poise under pressure. Training for one—training for the other. Sestal told them that a weak king needed a strong True Sorcerer. Sestal had been no fool.

Acorn snorted, the first recognition he had given the fire. His eyes showed white and he fought Gran's hold on his bridle.

"Easy, boy," she said. "It won't be long now." She

took the reins and moved him forward and back until he was steady on his broad hooves.

The west wind was drafting most of the smoke away from them, but she used the newly remembered spell against noxious air anyway, forming a clear bubble around them.

"When I tell you," she said to Gran, "slip off his bridle."

"He'll trample us, lady!"

"Don't worry about him, he's a wise old boy. Do I have to worry about you?"

Gran shook his head gravely. "No, lady."

"Good."

She kicked burning pieces of roof thatch from the path she had already cleared and looked out again. Lesteg had given up spell casting and doused himself from a waterskin.

He drew his sword.

He came closer, slowly, appraising.

She bunched the hem of her tunic to grasp the hot iron of the latch. "Now, Gran."

Lesteg lowered his head, turned his shoulder, and charged the door.

She swept it open.

"Home, Acorn!" she shouted. "Home!"

The horse bolted, massive hindquarters driving him away from the flames and through the door; heedless of his collision with the sorcerer.

Lesteg lay sprawled on the ground, gasping for air.

Her hand went cold on the hilt of her sword. A fight was one thing, an execution another.

When the king is weak, Sestal's voice echoed in her memory, *the true Sorcerer must be strong.*

But . . .

Lesteg's hands had moved together. Something dark and vile, oily and winged, was materializing between them.

The True Sorcerer must be strong.

Her sword went through the conjured thing, scattering it into dissipating wisps.

Through the creation to the creator.

She turned away. Lesteg was the first man she had ever killed. She asked every goddess she could name that he would also be the last.

But when the king is weak . . .

"Lady? Lady? The fire?"

She helped Gran drag Naffic to his feet and out of the shed, then returned for Acorn's saddle.

The leather was warm to the touch, but the precious pages rolled inside one of the heavy saddlebags were safe. She pulled them out and held them in front of Naffic's face.

"Do you know where the rest of these are hidden? The truth!"

"Three places—lady. Hidden by spells. Lesteg . . ." He looked at the dead sorcerer and swallowed.

"You will show us where they are." It wasn't a question.

"Yes, lady."

"When you have shown us where they are, we will take you before the king. King Hannish has a kind heart. If you tell him all you know, he might let you live, not that you deserve it.

"Gran is a witness, he will judge the truth of much of your story. I will judge the rest. If you lie to the king, if one word is false . . ." She grabbed the tether-rope Gran had moved to Naffic's neck and pulled him close. "My horse is old, he needs rest. I will use the book to transform you into a replacement—and I have a preference for geldings. Do I make myself clear?"

The color that his face had started to recover drained away. "Yes, lady."

Flames from the crumbling shed were igniting piles of fallen leaves, threatening a spread to the wood-land beyond.

The words for water came easily.

She turned. Naffic was watching her. "You are the True Sorcerer," he said. "You could do it, couldn't you? You could change me into a horse."

She smiled grimly. Horse? The first person to acknowledge her as True Sorcerer was someone she would gladly change into a worm. "You're not stupid enough to test me, are you?"

"No, lady, every word will be true."

"Good."

She picked up the saddlebag, settled it over her shoulder and pushed him into the first slow steps of the long walk home.

THE SIGN OF THE BOAR

by Diana L. Paxson

Diana L. Paxson is MZB's sister-in-law and one of the people who caught the writing habit from her. I've never been certain whether being close enough to Marion to "benefit" from her personal criticism was a good thing or not—Marion's first-hand criticism was apt to reduce one to tears in the cause of producing a better writer. She also tended to demand more rewrites of those of us who were conveniently accessible. We can only be thankful that she refused to use a computer for anything but word-processing. Imagine what she would have been like with e-mail! Diana has written over 20 novels, as well as collaborating with Marion on the later Avalon books, and she has sold a story to every anthology Marion ever edited. She lives in Berkeley with her son and daughter-in-law and three grandchildren.

Northumbria was a gray blur, half-seen through shifting veils of rain. It was turning now to sleet as the steersman leaned on the side-oar and the ship heeled round toward the narrowing opening where the river Ouse came down from Jorvik to the sea. Bera huddled beneath the skin tent the sailors had stretched beside the mast to shelter the passengers, tucking her fingers into her armpits for warmth and wondering why she had ever consented to journey away from her own land.

The reason lay beside her, pale as whey and groaning faintly as the tubby trading ship bucked the waves. Six months before, Bera had won Achtlan's freedom, and taken oath to go with her back to her home in Irland. A week at sea had leached the Irishwoman's high color and gaunted her cheeks, but Achtlan was still a big woman. Bera's compact body had the strength of the bear from whom she got her name, but despite her thirty years, she looked like a cub beside her companion. Yet for all their differences in appearance, they shared a deeper likeness, for both had walked the ways of the spirit and wielded its power.

Bera straightened, checking, with a concern that had become habit in the two weeks since they had left Norway, the location of the rest of her little band. The twins, Alfhild and Alfhelm, were clinging to the rail at the bow, straining for a sight of land. At least, thought Bera, on board the ship she could keep track of them. She trembled to think of the mischief two eight-year-olds might get into once they were running free on land. But perhaps their high spirits were natural. For the first time in their lives they and their Irish mother were safe from the malice of their father's wife, from whom Bera had won their freedom.

Taking ship in Nidaros, it had seemed a great adventure, but Achtlan had been sick from the moment they left harbor, and this first sight of the British Isles promised little welcome. Admittedly this was the north of England, and Jorvik, a Norse enclave carved out of the kingdom of Northumbria, not the milder country Achtlan had promised her in Irland—but Bera was not encouraged by her first sight of this new land. She wondered if Devorgilla and her children would still feel so safe once they had encountered the dangers here.

Wood banged and rattled as the long oars were run out and the ship moved into the channel. Achtlan lifted her head as the chop of the sea gave way to the regular surge and pause as the rowers pulled.

"Ja—it is land at last," said the captain, laughing. Anlaf was half Irish himself, and had treated his passengers with courtesy, although, as a good Christian, he tended to avoid Bera's gaze.

It was said that most of the folk in Jorvik followed

the White Christ these days. Even Eric Bloodaxe and
Queen Gunnhild had accepted baptism, though neither seemed a likely follower for a god whose totem
was the lamb. But five years since, Eric had been
driven from his high seat in Jorvik and killed at
Steinmore, and Jorvik was ruled now by a jarl who
answered to the Northumbrian king. Bera supposed
that the Christians had their own wisewomen, but perhaps if they had need she could earn her keep as an
herbwife. Their god might save souls, but she had
heard that their bodies fell sick as easily as those of
other men.

The briny tang of the sea warred now with the
softer breath that was coming from the land. Bera
recognized the scents of cattle and woodsmoke and
the good earthy smell of rain-soaked soil. Beyond
reedy banks, the countryside rolled away to either
side, fading to gray distances beneath the low clouds.
To one used to the toothed coastline of Norway it
seemed tame and tilled, but to the west she sensed
greater heights, and thought that this surface gentle-
ness might yet conceal a grim soul.

Such a land might have powerful spirits. When
Bera's people went raiding, they fixed fierce dragon
heads to the prows of their ships to frighten the land-
wights, and took them off again when they returned
lest they upset the spirits of their homes. But she was
coming in peace. How, she wondered, might she reach
out to the wights of this place and persuade them to
help her?

She peered across the gray waters, shading her eyes
with her hand. Now the banks showed signs of habita-
tion—an occasional shack, a small girl tending a flock
of geese at the edge of the reeds. Ahead, a tumble of
shapes was resolving itself into larger buildings and a
gray strip of wall that curved around to the north.

Achtlan pushed lank black hair back with a
trembling hand and struggled to sit up.

"Look—" Bera said with determined cheer, "I can
see walls, and the masts of ships drawn up at the riv-

er's edge. Very soon we will be on solid ground once more."

She looked again. From beyond the walls, a drift of black smoke was rising.

"What is that? Is the city burning?"

The captain followed her pointing finger and frowned. Then the wind shifted and the harsh reek, with a hint of burning meat in it, caught in her throat. The captain sniffed as well, and signed himself with the cross.

"It is not the buildings . . ." he said harshly. "There must be plague in the city. They are burning men. . . ."

Achtlan groaned and subsided against the side of the boat once more.

"It is ill to death I was upon the sea. So that we come safe to land, I will take my chances upon the shore."

They found lodging in an inn on the southern bank of the Ouse, near the landing where the ships from Dubhlinn came in. The house had been cobbled together from old ships' timbers and stones from the ancient Roman town. Behind it was a garden where a few vegetables and pot herbs struggled to grow, and a muddy pen where a dispirited looking pig fed on scraps from the inn. There was enough dirt in the inn itself to offend Bera's Norse soul, and her first act had been to wash the sheet on the bed she and Achtlan shared, but the woman who kept it spoke Irish, and her mother had come from the same district as Devorgilla, which made them almost kin.

Better still, it was cheap, and if they were to make their money last them to Irland, they would need to hoard every coin Bera's worn purse held. Dubhlinn was still far away, and as Achtlan absolutely refused to set foot on a ship again until the Irish Sea lay before her, they must find some pack train or a group of travelers making their way across the neck of Britain with whom they might make the journey, and purchase supplies and ponies to carry them.

The southern side of the river had once been the Roman colonia, while the higher ground on the northern bank held the ruins of the legionary fortress and the hall of the Norse kings. Erik might be gone, but in all but allegiance it was still a Viking town. Bera had been used to think of Nidaros as a bustling city, but Jorvik was much larger. She had never seen so many houses all together, but the sailors had said that London, to the south, was greater, and the cities of the Continent larger still.

But such a concentration of folk brought more than trade. The innwife had confirmed the captain's word. There was sickness in the town. It seemed to Bera that a shadow lay on the faces of those she passed, and she shivered despite the morning sun as she passed the body of a pig, dead by the side of the road. The sooner they found a way out of this city, she told herself, the better she would feel.

But the life of Jorvik continued, despite men's fears. The clink of a smith's hammer and the complaint of a goat tethered where it could crop the long grasses at the verge of the road sounded as they did at home, and so did the squalling of babies and the calling of fishwives, From every lane, she heard the sing-song lilt of the Norse tongue. A long tailed gray-and-black-spotted pig that could have been a litter mate of those she used to feed on her father's farm shouldered past, flat snout quivering as it rooted in the gutter.

In the old days, warriors had worn the boar on their helmets because of its fierceness, but she supposed that the traders of today would rather praise the beast for its ability to locate food. Her own belly growled as if in sympathy. The innwife's cooking was not much better than her cleaning. Perhaps in this town where the speech was so like that of Nidaros she could find a stall that sold food with the taste of home. It might tempt Achtlan, who had still not recovered from the journey.

From one of the lanes came a tantalizing whiff of hot sausage. Bera turned toward it, pulling the pouch that hung around her neck from beneath her gown so that she could count the coin there and see if she had a piece small enough to spare.

When she returned to the inn, Achtlan was lying on the straw mattress. Her face was the color of whey, and when Bera offered her the sausage she turned away with a groan.

"My guts have been heaving as if I was on the sea once more . . ." whispered the Irishwoman. "The inn-wife is sick as well, and so is Alfhelm."

Their eyes met. *Plague* . . . thought Bera. *The spirits of this place are evil, and Achtlan was too weak to resist their spells. . . .*

"You must drink water," she said aloud, "even if it only comes up again. I will look for healing herbs. I have not come all this way with you, woman, only to lose you now!"

But it was not so easy, despite her resolve. Alfhelm was strong enough to cast off the contagion, but with each hour, Achtlan grew more gaunt, muttering in Irish as her fever soared. Now there were several in the inn who were suffering, and one had already died. Bera needed herbs to go with her prayers.

Night was falling, but perhaps, she thought, she would find some useful plant in the garden behind the inn. She walked along the rows of turnips, examining the weeds and pulling those that were of no use. The pig in its pen at the back was a pale lump against the dark earth. It was lying on its side, breathing in harsh gasps.

Bera reached in to touch the bristly head. The white sow opened one eye, and she moved its water pan closer. Was the beast sick, too? What illness was this, she wondered, that struck with equal power at pigs and men? When she saw that the animal was drinking, she returned to the garden, stooping and weeding as she went along.

As she dug into the moist soil, her fingers scraped something harder. Biting her lip at the pain, she jerked out the dandelion she had been pulling and sat back on her heels as a piece of stone came with it. In another moment she would have cast it on the pile of weeds, but as she picked it up she saw carving and shifted it to catch the rays of the setting sun. It felt like sandstone, its natural ruddy color deepened by the light. As she brushed earth away, she saw weatherworn Roman letters—"LEGIO IX"—above the outline of a boar.

The Anglians, like her own people, worked mostly in wood. But the men of Rome who had once ruled here built in stone. The innwife had said that the name they gave the place, "Eboracum," came, like the Saxon "Eoforwic" and "Jorvik" itself, from the British name for the boar.

"So, old tusker, are you the wight who rules here?" Bera carried the stone to the edge of the garden and set it against the trunk of a holly tree. "If that is so, I am sure you do not like to be trodden on."

She paused, her fingers still covered with the mud she had scraped away to settle the stone, for the first time since their arrival opening her awareness to the spirits of this new land. In the next moment a complex mix of impressions assailed her—the familiar Norse and others, left by the many peoples who had lived here. But strongest of all came the irascible vitality that she identified as the spirit of the Boar. She remembered the sick pig and frowned, still gazing at the stone.

Had that been pure chance, or was there a power active here that might work for her, if only she could understand? "What do you want, Old One?" she whispered. Achtlan had called on Brigid, and once Bera had seen the Norse goddess Gullveig, whom some said was also Freyja, emerging from the same fires. "My goddess also rides a boar. Do you know her? Do you desire an offering?"

When the warrior Ottar sought Freyja's help, he had reddened the stones of his altar with blood till they shone glassy in the sun, and the goddess had turned him to a boar to ride to the cave of the giantess who gave them counsel. Bera had no beast for sacrifice, and no coin to buy one. But there was one source of blood which she had both the means and the right to give. Bera pulled out the little knife that hung from her shoulder brooch and slashed it across the soft flesh on the inside of her forearm. As she bit her lip against the sting, she saw a line of crimson start up on the white skin and turned her arm so that it would drip onto the stone.

"Thus do I redden the sacred stone. As my blood flows, I become part of this land. O ye wights who rule here, accept my offering and grant me your protection!"

A wave of vertigo made her head swim, and she clutched for balance at the stone. Was it blood loss that made her vision darken and then blaze red, or the last light of the setting sun? *Gullveig! Brigid! Lady of Flame! Freyja who rides the Boar, hear me!* her heart cried, and through her blurred eyes, she saw the boar on the ancient stone outlined in fire.

Taking a deep breath, Bera sat back on her heels. In the next moment, the vision vanished. Blinking, she looked up and saw that the sun had sunk behind the trees. Carefully she pushed the stone deeper into the shadow of the holly, where it would not be seen by unfriendly eyes, and got to her feet. Night was falling, but in her heart the fire of hope was burning once more.

When Bera came back into the inn, a stranger was sitting by the bed where the innwife lay, next to the hearth. At first she thought him a new guest, though as the plague spread, commerce had nearly halted in the town. Then she noted the shaven circle in his graying hair and realized that she was looking at a priest of the White Christ. This one, she thought with inner amusement, would never tempt Viking raiders. The rusty black wool of his tunic was worn, and the cross that hung at his breast was of polished wood, not gold. And he was thin.

She drew back politely as he finished drawing his own runes upon the sick woman's eyelids with scented oil and bent over her, murmuring in the sonorous tongue the Christians used for their magic. When the priest was done, the inn's two servants knelt for his blessing.

Then he turned to Bera. "I have shriven all those on this floor. The maids said I should wait to take care of the woman upstairs until you returned." Now she could see the shadows beneath his eyes, and in them the desperation of a man who like herself grieved to see folk suffer whom he could not save.

"I thank you for your concern," Bera said carefully. "But my companion and I are newly come to this land from Norway, and we are not of your faith."

The priest's eyes widened and Bera suppressed her amusement. Had he never seen a heathen before?"

"All the more reason to take me to her," he said then. "For if she dies unbaptized, she will surely burn in hell."

Bera shook her head in confusion. "Hella's land is the home of our fathers and mothers who have gone before us, and the only fires there are the torches that burn in Her hall."

"My child—those are tales with which your lying sorcerers seek to delude you—" the priest said kindly. "Let me teach you the true faith."

"Why should I believe *you*?" Bera drew herself up proudly. For the first time, she regretted having given the thrall Haki his freedom and leaving him in Norway. He would have supported her claim to standing now. She knew she cut a poor figure in this sea-stained shawl and muddy gown. She took a deep breath, pulling power around her like a garment, so that this man would no longer see the mended places in her shawl and the smears on her skirt, but only the Voelva, the Lady of Wisdom, whose word no sane man would deny.

"I am Bera, daughter of Steinbjorn, and I have walked in the Other World. Can you say the same? I was trained by Groa of Raumsdale and have served the people as a Voelva in my own right for three years now."

The priest held his ground, but she realized with unease that the maids were backing away, signing themselves with the Cross. "Wicce . . ." "Troll-kvenna," "Seidhkona . . ." From among the whispers she made out the words in Saxon and Norse for a witch or sorceress.

"Nay—I work no ill," she said quickly. "I walk between the worlds and stand before the gods themselves—how should I dare to lie?"

"Those are no gods with whom you are consorting, but demons!" said the priest, gripping the cross that hung at his breast.

"Poisoner! She brings the sickness!" said one of the maids.

"Nay, how could I? When I arrived, there was already sickness in the town!" Bera exclaimed, but their hostility was like a stench in the air. She saw Devorgilla hovering anxiously in the doorway and shook her head. The Irishwoman could not help her, and she and the children must not risk becoming a target too.

"Whether you are a demon or only deluded I do not know . . ." the priest said, starting toward the stair. He was still holding up his cross. "But it is my duty to save that woman's soul!"

"While she is too weak to deny you?" Bera took a quick step to bar his way. "I will not allow it! Her soul is in no danger—it is her body I fear for, and to save it, I will use all my skill!"

"All your sorceries?" spat the priest. "Then beware, for if that woman dies a heathen I will have you before the eorl for *maleficium*. We will see if your gods come forth to save you then!"

Bera was still shaking with reaction when she reached the upper room. The priest had left at last, still threatening, and she knew she would get little help from the maidservants now. She and Devorgilla

would have to take turns at nursing Achtlan. The sick
woman roused a little as she entered, muttering, and
Bera began to sponge her feverish body.

"Please Achtlan, you must drink," she whispered,
pouring a little mint tea into the cup and holding it
to her lips. "Fight, woman! Both our lives are at stake!
If you die of this illness, then they will drown me as
a witch for sure!"

That night, as she sat dozing by Achtlan's bedside,
Bera dreamed. She was out in the garden once more,
but this time the gate to the pigsty was open. As she
gazed around her, she saw the white sow making her
way across the open land beyond. Her first response
was relief that the gift of water had revived the beast,
but the innwife would not thank her for letting the
pig go.

Picking up her skirts, Bera began to pursue it, but
as is often the way in dreams, no matter how she
hurried, the sow seemed to maintain the same ef-
fortless lead. Now they were far from the city and the
farms that surrounded it. Bera toiled upward through
a waste of gorse and heather, and realized that she
had come to the moors. The dream was losing all pre-
tence of reality, for she knew she herself could not
have come so far so quickly, even if the sow had made
such a speedy recovery.

It was time, she thought, to remember who and
what she was.

Bera stopped, willing the pounding of her heart to
slow.

"Hvitsyr! White Sow! I command thee to halt in
Freyja's name!"

It seemed to her then that the pig slowed. Now it
was turning, changing shape before her eyes, until it
was a human female, not the white sow but Freyja
Herself, who stood there.

"Why did you make me run after you?" Bera said
breathlessly.

"Why did you never ask me to wait for you?" came

the reply. With relief, Bera realized that the goddess sounded amused.

"Shining One, I salute you," said Bera, remembering her manners. "I call to thee from my fear and my need—the people are dying, my friend is losing her fight against this illness. What can I do?"

"The pigs are dying, too—" came the answer. "Do you ask My aid for them as well?"

Bera nodded. "If there is something that is in my power to do."

"The pigs were the first to fall prey to this evil. The health of the swine cannot be separated from that of the men."

"Lady! I am one woman and alone. What I can do I will, but I am a stranger, and the people of this place will not welcome my interference."

The goddess sighed. "In My world, what is done for one is done for all. Tend the sow that you thought you were following and the folk in the house where you lie. Healing will flow from that place like the underground waters of a spring."

The image of the goddess was beginning to shimmer. Lost in wonder, Bera fought for the focus to speak again.

"But *how,* Lady? What is it that I must do?"

"Healing comes from the earth . . . the wights of the land will show you which herbs you must use. . . ." The figure of Freyja became a blaze of light.

Lost in contemplation of that glory, Bera knew no more until she opened her eyes to the pale illumination of the dawning day. For a few moments she knew fear, for she ached as if she had been chasing the goddess in body as well as in spirit, and wondered if she herself were sickening with the plague, and her vision no more than a fevered dream. But once she was up and moving, she realized she had only grown stiff from sitting still too long.

When her muscles were limber once more, she left Alfhild to watch with Achtlan and went out to the pigsty to tend to the white sow. The animal was weak, but still alive. Bera stroked the sow's sides, murmuring softly of what she had seen, and when she left, it seemed to her that the pig's eye had brightened and she was breathing more easily.

Humming softly, Bera took up her basket, wrapped her shawl around her, and set out for the open fields beyond the walls, Alfhelm at her side. This was not her own country, but she hoped that the goddess would lead her to some plants she knew.

It was still early, and dew lay heavy on the grass. Soon the hem of her skirt was flapping damply about her ankles, but Bera strode forward, glad to get the stink of the city out of her nostrils and breathe in clean air. Norway was a land of scattered farmsteads. It did not seem to her that humans were meant to live cooped up so closely. No wonder they were easy prey to whatever illness evil wights might send.

At the edge of a stream that flowed toward the Ouse, Bera recognized the bunched white flowers and jagged leaves of a plant that was called after Frigga at home. With a prayer to the goddess and the spirit of the flower she cut a goodly number of blossoms. Mint grew here as well, and with another prayer she showed Alfhelm how to gather the sweet-smelling stems, being careful as always to leave enough to grow another year. Beyond, the ground rose, supporting scrubby oak trees beneath which she found bramble and bilberry, both bearing fruit, though she had scarcely dared to hope for it so early in the year. As they moved through the countryside she was beginning to understand that summer came earlier in this land. She could see why the men of the North, tired of winter darkness, had been eager to settle here.

By the time they turned their steps homeward, the sun was high. Her basket was full, and she was no longer searching, and so it was with some surprise that she found herself staring at a patch of thistle that seemed to have sprung from the ground of a purpose to bar her way. It was not yet in flower, but the narrow toothed leaves jutted like the blade of a spear, or, she thought suddenly, the tusk of a boar.

The plants that filled her basket had been chosen for their healing virtues, but this thistle seemed to shimmer with magic.

"Thistle, thistle, sharpest of thorns," she whispered, "Boar tusk baneful to evil beings, Wild One I summon now to ward against attack by all ill wights."

Alfhelm widened his eyes but dared say nothing as she wrapped her shawl around a large clump, and resolutely ignoring the spines that pricked her hands through the coarse cloth, sawed through the stems with her knife. By the time she was finished her hands were aching from the sting of the spines, and bleeding, but this too, she knew, was an offering. Triumphant, she made her way back to the inn.

The maidservants scuttled out of Bera's way when she came in, but at least they did not interfere as she filled the cauldron with water and set it over the fire. Leaves and flowers and berries went into a net bag which she set to steep when the water was boiling, all the while murmuring spells to bind into the brew the healing virtues that were needed now.

The first, fresh liquid she took up to Achtlan while the rest boiled down into a decoction that could be diluted later on. But the contents of the net bag she carried out, still steaming, to feed to the sow. Assisted by the children, she festooned lengths of boar-thistle around the pen, set some above the inn's doorway, and took the rest upstairs to ward the room where Achtlan lay.

That done, Bera could only wait. Every hour she would make the sick woman drink a little more, and gradually, it began to seem to her that Achtlan's cramps were easing, her sleep was becoming more restful, her fever going down. Some time after midnight the fever broke, and when Bera had changed the sick woman's sheets and gown, she lay down herself beside her, and slept dreamlessly until the dawn.

The next day, though Achtlan was still weak, it was clear that she was on the mend. Bera began to feed her small amounts of bland porridge, adding a jelly of crab-apple as she grew stronger.

That evening, the Irishwoman was well enough to come down and sit by the fire, and it was there, as the innwife lay in her stupor and the two maids watched wide-eyed, that Bera told her about the priest and the threats he had made.

"Oh, my dear one—" Achtlan shook her head with a smile. "You'd no need to be risking yourself for me. In my country the folk, even the Druids, accepted Christianity long ago. I was baptized into that faith, and the man's mutterings would have done me no harm!"

"But you are a wisewoman—a priestess of Brigid—" stammered Bera.

"Indeed, and is not the blessed Brigid Herself a saint of the Church in my own land? Ah, well, perhaps it is only in Eriu that the wise ones know that there is one truth behind all men's creeds." Achtlan laughed. "If the Christ-priest comes again, you must have him talk to me. I will soon set him right."

Bera shook her head. "I do not understand . . ."

"And how should you?" Achtlan's face grew grave. "You were a person of worth in your own country— now you see how it was for me, when I was suddenly come among a people for whom the name of Brigid meant nothing!"

Bera sighed, remembering how her father's wife had treated her when she was no more than the master's daughter by his Irish thrall. But it was true that the past fifteen years, first as Groa's student and then as her heir, had accustomed her to respect.

"So that you keep that priest from my sight, I do not care," she said with a sigh.

"Lady—" One of the maids got up the courage to come forward at last and speak to Achtlan. "If you are a Christian woman, as you say, then will you help our mistress, who lies there?"

One eyebrow lifting, the Irishwoman looked at Bera. "You will not be needing my brew much longer. Use the rest for the people here . . ." she replied.

"You will not use any heathen spells?" asked the girl.

"The people of this land swore by Brigid once, when she was called Brigantia," Achtlan answered her. "I will pray to her, and she will grant us aid!"

I have already prayed to a goddess who, in certain moods, is Brigid's sister, Bera told herself ruefully, *and She has replied!* But she did not say so aloud. At least, with the Irishwoman taking over the nursing inside the inn, she would be free to give her attention to the white sow in the garden outside.

Bera was in the garden, cleaning the pigsty, when the Christ-priest came back to the inn. Achtlan had recovered quickly, and the other patients whom she was now tending were making good progress. Indeed, the power of the plague seemed to have been broken. When Bera went out to the market to shop for food, there were more people in the streets, and the black columns of smoke no longer stained the sky.

She had finished shoveling out the rotted vegetation that littered the pen and was working on digging a hole that would drain the sty and give the pig a clean place to wallow when she saw the black robe of the priest coming past the holly tree. Suddenly she was very glad that she had hidden the boar-stone.

The sow, who had been basking in the sunlight, heaved to her feet as the priest approached, grunting softly. She was still thin, but her white bristles glistened, and her eye was bright with interest.

"Humble work for a great sorceress—" said the man. "I see the good Christians inside have rejected your deceptions, and now, as Our Lord said, you cast your pearls before swine. . . ."

Bera straightened, flushing. "Does not your own faith teach humility? I see no dishonor in tending the beasts, if men do not wish my care." In fact, several of the neighbors, no longer fearing for their lives, had asked her to help with their livestock. The sow leaned against her thigh and she began to scratch along the bony ridge of her back.

"Your friend says you did not know she was a christened woman," he added reluctantly, "and since she has survived, I cannot accuse you of witchcraft. But Jorvik is not a good place for you, and you would do well to leave it soon."

He knows that it was my herbcraft that saved those people, Bera realized suddenly, *even if they attribute it to Achtlan's prayers. He is afraid of my power.*

"In five days a pack train will be leaving," she said agreeably, "and by then Achtlan will be strong enough to ride with it." The innwife, who was now mending rapidly, had paid them generously, and they now had enough for the fee. Bera gave the pig a final pat and drew herself up, putting on the glamor of a priestess once more. "Do you think I would stay in this place one day longer than I must? The swine of Jorvik have shown me more gratitude than its human inhabitants have offered, and it is with the pigs that I will leave my blessing."

But before she departed, Bera thought as she watched the man making his way back to the inn, she would make another offering to the boar stone and then rebury it in the pigsty to guard the white sow and all her kin.

A MATTER OF FOCUS
by Penny Buchanan

Penny Buchanan sold a story to MZB for *Red Sun Of Darkover* in 1986. When she got the invitation to submit to *S&S*, however, she hadn't written anything in a while, and she was in the hospital recovering from surgery. She wasn't terribly enthusiastic about the idea of writing a story (one generally isn't enthusiastic about *anything* right after surgery), but her best friend, Debbie, decided that writing a story for *S&S* would be great rehabilitation and nagged her into it. Penny describes Debbie as "the midwife for the birth of this tale" and wishes to thank her. Penny lives in San Diego with two cats: Tatiana and Merlin.

There's a concept called state-dependent learning, which holds that you perform a task better in the same conditions under which you learned it. But if you can perform magic only while drunk, you may have just a bit of a problem. . . .

The tavern "The Addled Pate" rang with raucous catcalls to the serving wenches and the bustle of a thriving establishment. The air was redolent with the smell of wood smoke, sweat, and ale. No one seemed inclined to crowd the disheveled redheaded woman sitting at the corner table.

Siobhan was hunched over the scarred table clutching her tankard in one hand while the other absent-mindedly traced symbols through the ale puddles. She jumped at a touch from the serving girl. The wench pointed to the most recently drawn symbol. "Oh, that's a pretty one that is! It looks like a horned mouse. It's an odd taste in creatures you have, Ducky!

Oh, yer mug be 'bout empty. There you go, a bit of ale will perk ya up a bit."

"Why do you keep calling me 'Ducky'?" Siobhan asked.

"Because ya've had enough ale to swim in, Ducky," the bar wench tossed over her shoulder as she swished away to serve more ale.

"Ducky, Ducky!" Siobhan mumbled. "No one would call a fully fledged mage, 'Ducky'!"

She sighed despondently. Her expulsion this morning from the premier magic school, Ars Magica, seemed to doom her life's dream. Siobhan had never before felt her goal to be so far out of reach. A spark of anger ignited.

Siobhan began to smolder as she considered the injustice of her expulsion. Her finger traced symbols a bit more rapidly as she gulped more ale. The tankard shook a little in her hand.

"Master Vadin just refused to understand the real problem. Blowing up the Alchemy Lab was not such a big deal. He should have understood the importance of what I was doing!" Siobhan mumbled aloud between gulps of ale. A tankard at a neighboring table gave a little hop and a skip.

"No, that's not quite right," Siobhan muttered as she passed her hand over the symbol. She squinted at the tabletop, "Now if I were to add a bit of a hook, here, it would be more effective." A thin glow briefly flickered through the symbol as Siobhan passed her palm over it. Her tankard lurched in her hand unnoticed as she took several rapid swigs of ale.

All around Siobhan arose sounds of consternation, " 'Ere now! I'm not paying fer ale that won't sit still to be drunk!" "I'm swearing to ye! I saw that tankard jump off the table and into yer lap!" "Do you think I'd be wastin' good ale by throwing it on the ground? I saw the mug hop off the table by its own self!" "Catch that tankard!"

Pandemonium broke like a wave around an unnoticing Siobhan. A heavy hand thumped her shoulder. It was the tavern keeper.

"That will be enough from you, my little hedge mage! You've got all my customers in a stir! A bit of excitement's good for a business, make no mistake! But an alehouse where the tankards run away with the ale is no good at all! So, we'll have no more of your magicking in here!"

Siobhan found herself deposited gently, but firmly, in the street. She blinked confusedly at the sudden change in scenery. She finished the last of her ale and carefully set down the now quiescent tankard. "Well now, this is a fine state for a budding mage. Top of my class! More magic in my big toe than most of those ninnies at Ars Magica! Now I'm expelled from school, homeless and tossed into the street. I can't return to my clan as a failure." Siobhan mumbled disjointedly as she made her way down the street.

It was just as Siobhan passed the alley mouth that she heard a scuffle and a cry of pain. Curiosity nudged her into the alley. There she found a trio of humans belaboring a she-troll with clubs. Although she was bigger than the three bullies who beat and taunted her, the troll stood quietly with her arms wrapped about her head waiting for them to tire of their sport. Around her feet lay baskets and bundles of herbs, crushed and trampled by her tormentors. Siobhan had seen enough. Although she was no great lover of trolls, she didn't much like to see anyone abusing another. Three on one smacked of cowardice and needed to be evened up a bit. To announce herself, she fired off several small balls of mage fire. The balls ricocheted and careened down the alley, hissing and spitting like a sack of cats. One bounced off the wall, dropping into the trouser seat of its intended bully. Another fire ball nestled in the straggly beard on one man, setting it aflame. The last bully ran screaming from the alley as mage fire stuck persistently to his hose, dropping hot cinders in his shoes. The men forgot all about the she-troll and fled, hardly noticing the slight red-haired woman lounging against the alley wall with her arms folded across her chest.

The troll kept her protective stance until the hissing and spitting died away. Unwrapping her arms from around her head, she cautiously looked around. The alley was clear. Slowly and carefully she gathered up what was left of her baskets and herbs. She ached a bit, but, as beatings went, it had not been a bad one. The troll had received far worse at the hands of humans before this latest assault.

Gurda approached the woman at the alley mouth, "Magic woman, you did me a good turn against your own kind. Why?"

Siobhan shrugged. "Three on one was a bit lop-sided. Three on two had a nicer balance. I like balance." Siobhan studied the troll. This was truly the homeliest troll she had ever seen. The she-troll was six and a half feet of greenish, pitted, and warty skin. The creature wore a shapeless tunic from which stuck overly long arms and bowed legs. The head was pear-shaped and topped with black dreadlocks. Her face was dominated by a large bulbous nose, over which two watery yellowish eyes peered anxiously. Beneath the nose, a mouth armed with a full set of troll teeth and bluish lips worked nervously.

The troll's splayed feet shuffled the alley dust. "Thank you for your help." Her voice rasped off the stone walls. "I am Gurda, the herbalist and healer."

Siobhan raised her eyebrows, "A troll herbalist and healer?" she asked. "I thought trolls were bandits and bridge keepers."

"Oh, to be sure, many of us are bridge keepers and such. But I have always had a way with plants and healing, a talent that would be wasted guarding a bridge!" Gurda proudly replied.

"I am Siobhan, and until this morning, I was learning mage craft at Ars Magica. Now I am footloose, with no prospects except for finding a way back to the mage school." She shrugged and turned to continue her progress down the street.

"Wait, wait!" Gurda hastened after Siobhan. "I believe that we can help each other!"

Siobhan stopped and turned. "Now that is an interesting notion! Just how could we help each other? I cannot imagine a more unlikely pairing."

Gurda planted herself firmly in front of the young mage. "I need a protector and could pay you for your services. If you would protect me while I sell my herbs in the markets, I will provide you with a place to stay and wages."

"I won't live under a dank bridge!" Siobhan stated unequivocally. "I hate the damp! No, no, I don't think it would work. You see, my magic is focused by hard spirits. In short, I have to be drunk to work magic with skill. I would have to spend all my wages on drink. That is why I was expelled from school. For working magic under the influence of spirits! I blew up the Alchemy Lab trying to find a new focus for my magic. I can't return to school until I can do magic without drinking."

Laughing, Gurda replied, "Not all trolls live under bridges! I have a lovely cave not far from town. It's dry, light and airy. I think you would like it."

"You don't understand! My magic is very erratic unless I drink! Do you want to be protected by a drunken mage? If I protect you, I will be drunk everyday! Besides, no respectable mage practices drunk!"

Plunking herself down on a boulder at the side of the road, Gurda pondered. "I don't understand why it is unacceptable for you to do magic in the manner which is most natural to you."

Siobhan explained, "Great harm has been done by out-of-control magic. Among most magic-using societies, the mixture of magic and hard spirits is banned. These who do mix them are called 'rogue mages.'"

"But surely if this process of working magic is how the magic works in you, it cannot be so very wrong," Gurda stated emphatically. "That is your nature and surely must be right for you."

"I wish the governing council of mages shared your

opinion," Siobhan said ruefully. "My people are the
only ones I know of who understand. Many of our
best mages have the same problem. They've had to
conceal it to get their training and still be sure that
the council gets no wind of it. There are no magic
academies among my folk, so we have no choice but
to abide by the rules of others."

Gurda's brow wrinkled as she considered the matter. "Through the study of natural processes, we trolls
have learned that there is always more than one solu-
tion to any problem. You can protect me and use your
spare time to search for another path. Maybe you
could even learn to work sober if you used yourself
as the focus."

"Listen," Siobhan said, "empathy is one of the un-
derlying forces of magic. All mages have an empathic
bond to something that amplifies and focuses their
power. For some it is a crystal, or a wooden object.
For others it may be a living creature. Cats are quite
common, though I did once meet a mage who was
bonded to a fish that he had to carry about in a bowl.
It was difficult for him to attend a mage convention
with all those cats around. He has held up quite well
given his circumstances. But to use myself as the focus
would create a destructive resonance quite uncontrol-
lable. Prideful mages always try this and usually blow
themselves up or turn themselves into trees or rocks.
I must find something else besides hard spirits."

The troll shook her head. "It still seems wrong to
work against the natural forces within you. I have seen
the effects of such workings. No good can come of
creating strife between the inner and outer selves."

Siobhan lost patience with the discussion. "You
don't understand! My magic needs a new focus, or I
cannot practice except as a rogue! Nobody in my clan
has ever been a rogue. Without spirits, I blow things
up, my transmutations go awry, and my most basic
spells become chaotic. Even my fire elementals dance
a frantic jig abrim with disobedience. Once I was

asked to turn a plow horse into a fine Araby steed. Squire DuChamp believed I would create a better horse if I was sober. The spell went amiss. That unhappy squire had no use for fifteen hundred pounds of cabbages!" Siobhan picked up a rough shard of stone from the road, "You just watch what happens when I work magic sober." She held up the stone for the troll to see. "I'll try to create a beautiful crystal from this bit of rock."

Gurda nodded and folded her hands in her lap and watched expectantly. Siobhan clutched the rock and closed her eyes. Her face tightened with the strain of concentration, her lips muttered syllables to low to be easily heard. Siobhan felt a flash of heat, followed by a numbness that flowed from her wrist to her fingertips. At the same time she heard a tremendous clap of thunder that nearly deafened her.

Well now I've done it, she thought, *I've gone and blown off my own hand.* Slowly she opened her eyes. She still had two hands. Fighting the numbness, she opened her fingers. There in her palm lay the most beautiful blue crystal she had ever seen! Never before had she accomplished even the merest spell correctly while stone cold sober. "By the Goddess! How did I do that?" she exclaimed. Looking down she saw a charred circle around her feet with a trail still smoldering leading to the rock where Gurda had been sitting. The area around the rock was charred and smoking and the troll was nowhere to be seen. Siobhan ran to the boulder fearing the worst. To her great relief she found Gurda knocked flat on her back behind the boulder. The troll was groggily trying to sit up.

"What happened?" Gurda mumbled as she struggled to sit up. Her blinking eyes had a glazed look and the black dreadlocks were standing up at all angles. Wisps of purplish smoke were rising off the greenish skin and the shapeless tunic was charred around the hem. "What hit me?"

All of a sudden Siobhan started to giggle. The nervous tension had become too much for her. "I, I, I think just found my new focus!" Siobhan laughed and held out the blue crystal to the troll.

Gurda flinched and looked totally aghast. "That can't be!" she sputtered. "Who ever heard of a troll being a magic focus?"

Siobhan shook her head, "I don't know how it works. But you are indeed a focus for my magic. Remember what you said about natural processes? Your nature has empathy with my magic! You were right all along. We must be a team!"

Gurda nodded reluctantly and looked at the scorched boulder. She sniffed the air; the odor of singed troll still lingered. "Am I going to get knocked flat every time you work a spell?" Gurda asked plaintively.

Siobhan shook her head. "Oh, I'm sure it's just a matter of focus."

The still-smoking she-troll and the magic woman looked at each other and began to giggle.

INNER SIGHT

by Susan Wolven

Susan Wolven says, "I received this story's acceptance letter on December 30, 1999, a truly wonderful way to usher in the year 2000. I consider it an especially favorable omen since three months ago I quit my copy-writing job of 13 years in Los Angeles and moved to a little house in the San Bernardino Mountains. After years of saying, "Someday I'm going to take a year off and concentrate on my own writing," I thought the new millennium would be a fine time to do just that. So now I'm living in Sugarloaf, California, with my two cats, Jessie and Guinevere (named after you know who), and writing away like mad." This her second story to appear in *S&S*; her first was in *S&S XVI*.

In a small turret room high above The Citadel's main practice yard, Endra sat in silence as she cleaned the sword of a recently fallen comrade. She sat next to an open window in the warmth of the late afternoon sunlight. With long, rhythmic strokes, she rubbed the blade until it shone. A recent battle had reduced her sight to shadowy images and brilliant flashes of light, and she looked longingly at the bright reflection the sunlight made as it danced along the sharply honed length of deadly metal. As she slowly turned the blade, a bright beacon moved crazily over the room's walls and ceiling.

With a small sigh, she tucked her cleaning cloth in her shirt pocket. Although she could not see small details, she could feel, could sense, that she was done. She stood and slipped the unfamiliar sword back into its sheath, pleased she had gotten it in on her first try.

63

But then she had learned years ago, and unfortunately the hard way, that it is best to sheath your sword without looking down. Some opponents who admit defeat are not always eager to fully embrace it, and the victor must always be ready for this unfortunate change of heart.

Then she froze as a faint hum filled the room. An instant later she turned toward the far corner and in two strides crossed the room and pulled the humming sword from its scabbard.

Luna!

A sword with a blade the silvery color of the full moon, its previous owner had been cut down by treachery a mere two weeks ago. It was said the swordswoman who first wielded the sword had given it its name after the shining blade had magically guided her back to The Citadel on a stormy, moonless night many years ago. As Endra waited for the arrival of Luna's new partner, who would be summoned to the tower room by the sword's call, she felt another twinge of worry that her own sword had not called to a new swordswoman.

"Six months it has been," she whispered, drawing her soft cloth down the length of Luna's blade for the last time. Does everyone who must give up her sword feel this way—somehow less, somehow suddenly unworthy?

Endra turned in a slow circle. To her damaged eyes, the swords fanned out around her in a blur like the petals of a sunflower undulating in a summer's breeze. *Are these four walls to be my future?* Endra breathed deeply and halfheartedly began a routine calming exercise. But it was for naught. "I am too young for this!"

The agony of the last few months washed over her anew. A month of healing had saved her life but, in the end, not her sight. Now her life revolved around evenings spent gathered at the great hearth in the main room, drinking red wine and listening to tales from The Citadel elders, some whom had lived through many generations of swordswomen. They talked of battles gone by, not of battles yet to come. Endra listened and slowly learned each sword's history, something she never had time to do before.

Nor had I wanted to. Endra slowly crossed over to where her sword, Mer, hung on the wall. *I was too busy trying to write my own piece of history with my own sword.*

Reaching up, she grasped Mer's scabbard and lifted it down. With one swift movement her hand closed around her sword's hilt, and with a fluid motion she drew her sword out and held it high above her head. A sweet ringing reverberated between the room's ancient stone walls, and for a moment Endra's vision seemed to clear. She felt the thundering of her horse's hooves beneath her, the chill mountain winds on her face, smelled the tangy sea air from her last coastal post. For eight years Mer had hung by her side, a comforting weight on many a long, dark night. Now it hung on a wall.

"It is not fair," Endra whispered, clutching Mer to her chest, "for either of us."

Looking around, Endra felt the tangible sense of history that filled the room. Here were swords that magically never weakened, passed down from generation to generation, a priceless heritage, a vivid reminder of the constant battle between good and evil. A battle Endra prayed would someday end. But she knew there would always be someone, or something, rising up in evil against a peaceful land that wanted no part of war—and someone needed to defend the land and its people.

Suddenly, the floor rose beneath her with a great heaving motion. An instant later it fell back into place with a deafening crash. It was as if a huge hand were trying to pluck the tower out of the ground like a flower. Endra cried out as an intense and nauseating sense of vertigo swept over her. She fell against the wall, her sword torn from her hand. A suffocating heaviness pressed down on her, and as she struggled to breathe, panicked cries echoed up from the main courtyard.

A pitch-black shadow fell from the sky.

Groping in the sudden darkness, Endra reached out for her sword, her left hand skimming over the floor. Her fingers brushed against the blade, and she cursed softly as its razor-fine edge sliced her palm. But her sword hand was uninjured, and she grasped her sword and lurched to her feet. Stumbling out of the room, she threw a quick order over her shoulder at the two guards crouching on either side of the door, their swords aglow in the strangely dimmed torchlight of the hallway.

"Hold your post!"

She charged down the stairs, raging against her half-blind state. At the bottom, mayhem washed over her as she stepped out into the lower hall.

"What is happening?" she cried at the shadowy images rushing past her.

"Bonstrell!" came a shouted reply.

Endra staggered back as if struck. The name alone was enough to conjure a vivid image of the evil sorceress who had once been a member of The Citadel. Cast out years ago for dabbling in ancient arts best left in the past, she had often railed of revenge. But no one believed she would ever be powerful enough to go up against the combined power of those loyal to the peace-loving members of The Citadel.

Her gray world a jumbled collage of dark shadows and flashes of light, Endra plunged into the melee toward the calm circle of swordswomen she sensed gathering in the center of the main hall. Then she saw it out of the corner of her eye. A subtle blurring of light and shadow, a quivering disturbance in the air. It wove between the torches lining the narrow hall, there one moment, gone the next, bending the light in unnatural ways.

Endra turned back, following the strange, shadowy movement as it flowed quickly down the hallway, passing unobserved around and through the swordswomen running toward the main hall. An evil chill trailed behind it, leaving a stench akin to burning sulfur. Then a group of elders rounded the far corner, their blazing torches rendering the shadow invisible. Endra cried out, rushing toward the burning torches even as the women holding them rushed toward, then past, her. Though the returning darkness gave no clue to where the evil had gone, Endra knew one thing for certain.

"Bonstrell is inside! All else is illusion!"

Her voice drowned in the rising chaos, Endra stumbled back toward the main hall to warn the others. But as she passed the stairway, a cold wind whipped down from above, raising the hairs on her neck and arms.

The swords!

She took the stairs two at a time, closing her eyes so her faulty vision would not cause her to stumble upon the passage her feet knew so well. Not stopping to ask the guards if they had seen what Endra knew their perfect vision could not, she burst into the sword room. Blades and hilts formed crosses of shimmering light as they slowly floated upward toward a dark cloud descending through a gaping hole in the ceiling. Endra gagged as Bonstrell's evil washed over her, an evil growing ever stronger as the sorceress' shadowy essence wove around the swords, drawing on their power as she gathered them together.

Endra fell into a tucked roll as two swords flew toward her. "Forge your own weapons, traitor!"

A soft laugh echoed down to where Endra lay. The two swords next to her began to vibrate against the stone floor, then abruptly shot upward. The nightly stories still fresh in her mind, Endra immediately recognized the swords as Artesa and Flame. An instant later the shattering realization struck her.

It is not just the physical swords Bonstrell is after!

Endra stared at the sword that hummed in her hand, its calming vibration sending strength to her limbs, a vibration that suddenly buzzed faster in tune to the beat of her heart.

Their history, our history, is our greatest strength!

"Therein lies the real power," Endra whispered. She jumped to her feet, thrusting Mer high over her head. "And it is our power, Bonstrell!" She reached her left hand upward and cried, "Luna!"

A white flash illuminated the core of the dark shadow above her, and an instant later Luna flew into Endra's hand. The ominous cloud roiled and lowered, but Endra stood her ground as joy surged through her. Holding both swords high, she sang out, "Rose, Diamond, Sapphire, Forest!" The swords responded to her call, twirling and calling back with a song of their own. They danced through the dark cloud, cutting it to wisps. "Amethyst, Lilly, Sol!" More blades sang out, and as the room reverberated with their songs, a shrill cry rent the air. The darkness lifted with a flashing brilliance that blinded the eye. An unearthly silence fell over The Citadel.

A moment later a blue jay began to sing.

Two days later Mer called out to its new partner.

"So it was this last battle that kept you at my side," Endra whispered, as she polished her blade one last time. She took a deep breath, forcing her joy to overcome her sorrow. After all, how many swordswomen have the honor of personally passing on their swords?

Hearing quick steps coming up the stairs, Endra wiped away one last tear and turned to face the doorway. The shadowy figure that burst through the door couldn't have been more than five feet tall. Endra grinned at the thought of how many men and women foolish enough to cross swords with the young woman before her would quickly learn their greater height was not necessarily an advantage.

I eagerly await her first tale from the road.

And with that surprising thought came an unexpected acceptance, and an easing of pain. Endra straightened her shoulders and as she reached out, Mer cradled in her arms, the young girl took a stumbling step forward. Although Endra could not see the young woman's face clearly, she could tell by her rapid breathing that it must be flushed by the long climb upward and the excitement of the moment.

"I am Naniam, come to—to claim my sword," the girl stammered.

"This is Mer," Endra said solemnly.

There was a soft gasp. Then a voice full of wonder said, "Your sword?"

"No," Endra said with a shake of her head. She stepped closer and handed Mer to Naniam. "Your sword."

In the ensuring silence, Naniam's hand closed over the hilt of her new sword, and for a moment, Endra felt Naniam's heart beat. Then as Naniam took the full weight of the sword, Endra's link with Mer was broken, and she stood in numbing silence.

"I am honored to receive your sword," Naniam said softly. "I know all about you and your—my sword."

"Ah!" Endra stepped back and sat down in her chair. "But do you know that before this sword fought at my side, it traveled with a great swordswoman from the northern desert?"

"No," Naniam breathed. "What was her name?"

Endra smiled as a telltale creak told her Naniam had sat down on the room's other chair. Her smile widened as she heard the guards outside the door shuffle closer so they could overhear.

"Her name was Claireine, and it's said she fell under the attack of sixteen enemy soldiers," Endra began, as silence once again filled the small turret room high above The Citadel.

FAMILIARS
by Michael H. Payne

Michael H. Payne's stories have appeared in places like *Marion Zimmer Bradley's Fantasy Magazine, Tomorrow Speculative Fiction,* and *Asimov's Science Fiction.* His first novel, *The Blood Jaguar,* made the preliminary ballot for the Nebula award. He lives in Southern California, sings and plays guitar at a local church, clerks at a local library, hosts a Saturday morning radio program at a local university—check www.kuci.org/~mpayne for more info on that—and sometimes has to write about himself in the third person.

Here is a story about a pair of students who don't quite fit the normal pattern, something I suspect that a lot of us can understand. After all, if we were "normal," would we be reading—and/or writing—science fiction and fantasy?

The stink of Crocker's fear hit Cluny like an acorn dropped from the top of an oak tree, made her tail jitter, and her claws dig into the desk top. She forced them loose. "All right, Crocker. I'm breaking the link now."

Kneeling on the carpet across the room, Crocker nodded, his eyes fixed on the ball of blue fire spinning between his hands. With a quick prayer, Cluny lowered herself to all fours and backed away along the desk, her fur prickling as she mentally stretched the link between them till she felt it pop.

Immediately, sparks began crackling through the fireball. "Hold on," she breathed, but he was already trembling, sweat now visible on his forehead. "Hold on, you little—"

The ball exploded, fire engulfing his hands, and Cluny leaped to the floor. "Idiot!" She scrambled toward him, pushed her power into his, and water congealed around his arms, the flame dousing and the healing spells they'd set up rushing into place. "You're not feeling the flow!"

"Tell me about it." Crocker fell back onto his calves, ran a wet hand through his hair. "You snap our link, and I don't feel *anything*."

"Oh, come on." She glared up at him. "You do healings and make light and work doubling magic, so don't tell me—"

"Sure, small stuff." He waved an arm, drops spattering Cluny's fur. "But I can't even evoke a Chapter One fireball, and with finals next week . . .." He sighed, his chubby face lost in the evening shadows coming through the dorm room curtains. "The magisters are gonna kick me outta Huxley for sure. You'd better request a transfer to another novice."

Stomach tightening, Cluny turned away. "I have. Every week all semester."

"You have?" The shuffle of his robes made her ears fold back. "Then . . . then why hasn't someone asked you to—?"

"Because I'm a squirrel!" She whirled back. "Never mind that I've memorized the whole freshman spell book! I'm not a cat or an owl or a fox, so forget it! And the magisters say I don't have the right attitude to be a familiar, that I'm not deferential enough!" She bunched her paws into fists and scowled up at him. "They only assigned me to you, I'll bet, so I'd get sick of nursing you along and drop out!"

Crocker rubbed his ear. "Actually, I requested you. After we met during orientation week."

"What?" A vague memory, Crocker talking to her at one of the mixers for maybe two minutes. "You . . . requested . . . ?"

"Yeah." He gave another sigh and shook more water from his sleeves. "Well, if you're stuck with me, I guess we'd better try this again."

Staring another second—he'd *requested* her?—
Cluny shook her head to clear it, scurried across the
floor, and jumped back onto the desk beside his book.
"Well, since the textbook way isn't working for
you . . ." She closed it with a thump and tapped the
cover. "How about you make some light, just a little
in your hand. You won't need me for that, right?"

Silence, then a bubble of light began to grow ahead
of her, the room brightening, Crocker's eyes narrowed
and fixed on the glowing ball in the air above his palm.

"That's it." Her whiskers didn't twitch, so he wasn't
using her power. "Now, can you make it bigger?"

"Sure." He blew on it, and the ball pulsed into a
good handful of light. "Just like . . . blowing up a
balloon . . . only with light." His eyes darted up from
it. "Now what?"

"Now?" She rubbed her whiskers. Evocation was
mostly a mental discipline, so maybe she could get
him to . . . "Picture fire in your mind, lots and lots of
fire." She spread her claws. "Then just blow *that* into
the ball instead of light."

A puff of his fear wafted against her whiskers. "It's
easy," she said, trying to keep her voice calm. "Focus
on the fire in your mind. Then blow just like you
did before."

Several blinks, and he nodded, his eyes narrowing
even more. He took a deep, shaking breath, puffed
his cheeks . . .

And Cluny's whiskers sprang straight out, Crocker's
spell grabbing her power and sucking it in. She tried
to snap the link, but the light in his hand exploded
into a huge pillar of fire, knocking her back into the
wall before she could do anything.

"Who dares?!" a voice thundered, and Cluny
looked up from where she was sprawled to see the
pillar flowing into a fiery female humanoid figure, hair
like lava around her broad shoulders, eyes fiercer than
the sun at midday.

An ifrit. High Clan, too, Cluny was sure, with
those—

"I haven't got all day!" the ifrit roared. She swirled around to fix on Crocker, groaning as he pushed himself up from the floor in front of the closet. "You! Human! Why have you disrupted my schedule?!"

Crocker's eyes widened as his head tipped back, his mouth dropping open. "Well?!" the ifrit shouted.

The briefest of seconds, and Cluny leaped from the desk, rushed across to stand in front of Crocker, bowed down all the way to the carpet. "Uhh, forgive us, spirit, we meant no disrespect. We were just—"

"Talking animals?! I haven't got time for this!" A hand like a burning tree branch slammed into Cluny, knocking her sideways into the tangle of blankets on Crocker's bed. "You will learn the error of your ways, human!" Cluny heard, and she clawed her way free just in time to see the ifrit grab Crocker from the floor. "You will await me in my realm! Upon my return, I will deal with you properly!"

Flames burst from the ifrit's other hand, hit the wall, and spiraled open to a blast furnace beyond; a smile sharp as lightning bolts, and she flicked her claws, Crocker flying into the furnace, his eyes still wide with terror. The whole room flashed, and the creature was gone, Cluny blinking, the fiery hole in the wall beginning to wheel shut.

For half a heartbeat she hesitated; then she leaped for the hole, tucked and rolled, and smashed right into the flames roaring over her, tumbling her headlong into boiling liquid pain, her mouth opening to scream—

And relief surged through her, the breath she drew cool and damp. A moment to get her paws under her, and she rose to find herself standing in a pit of molten rock, the lava sloughing off the water coating her, her charred fur growing back as she watched.

The spell, the dousing and healing one she and Crocker had set up in case fireball practice got out of hand. Yes, her fur prickled under its watery coating, his power drawing on hers, so their link was intact. But where was he?

Squinting against the blazing whites and reds, she

could see that the lava pool she stood in was surrounded by walls of magma. She poked at the stuff,
steam hissing from her claw, and frowned. Like glowing red pudding, nothing to dig into, no way she could
climb out.

Unless . . . If this really was molten rock—she
cleared her mind, concentrated on the flow of her
power, focused her thoughts on the cold spells from
Chapter Six of Crocker's textbook—maybe she could
firm it up a bit.

The motions and phrases came easily, and she felt
her watery coating get colder and colder. The viscous
ground began to seize up beneath her, and when she
pressed her paws into the glow ahead, the lava crackled, turned gray and craggy. It still jiggled, but it
wasn't much worse than the half-dead trees she'd
played in growing up. A quick scramble, and she dug
her paws into more of the magma, which was solidify-
ing under her touch and letting her climb higher.

At least the water spell told her Crocker was still
alive, and he'd have the same protection as long as
their link didn't break. Unless he'd sunk into the
magma: he sure didn't know the Chapter Six cold
spells.

"Idiot." Her breath coming faster now with the effort of holding the cold spell in place, she reached the
crest of the flow, grabbed it, froze it, pulled herself
up, and looked down to see water, a lake lapping
against the molten rock walls.

And bobbing out in the middle, his dark curly hair
and chubby face unmistakable even through the curtains of steam—"Crocker?" she called.

"Cluny!" He sloshed around and started swimming
toward her. "Where are we? What was that thing?
How did we—?"

"You summoned a High Clan ifrit, you idiot!" She
struggled to keep on her paws, the magma pushing
against her cold spell and against the water rising in
the—

Rising? Cluny squinted, saw the lake was expanding

up the sides of the pit, felt it draw on her power every time it sloshed higher.

"It's our watery healing spell." Crocker had paddled to just below her, the water bringing him closer and closer. "I used some doubling magic on it, figured I could swim in water easier than lava, and now, well, now I can't get it to stop." He was almost level with her now, the water lapping at her paws, steam geysering up even as ice formed around them.

Crocker stared at it. "How . . . how are you doing that?"

"Chapter Six cold spell." She tried to back away, but she was already at the top of the lava flow.

"What?" Crocker blinked up at her. "But . . . you're a familiar. You can't cast spells."

The water topped the ridge then, rushed past Cluny into the pit she'd just climbed out of. Quickly she cut the cold spell and jumped forward to Crocker's shoulder. "What I *can't* do, Crocker, is swim."

"Uh-oh," she heard him say, then the current pulled them over and sucked them down. Water in her nose, eyes, ears, Cluny dug her claws into Crocker's hair, his shoulders swinging beneath her. She had to get out, had to breathe, had to—

She grabbed the flow of Crocker's power, added it to her own, let their combined force roar into her mind. Directing it downward, she smashed at the water, hot air rushing past her whiskers, her stomach yawing; she pushed her face away from Crocker's hair, gasped for breath, and saw Crocker looking down, his eyes wide and staring. She followed his gaze, the lake spreading below, several dozen empty yards between his feet and the water. "We're flying?" he whispered.

"Can't be." The power burning through her made her pant. "Flying's not . . . till sophomore year. I haven't learned—"

"What's going on here?!" a huge voice thundered around them, and Cluny's stomach clenched, light exploding to reveal the ifrit, her eyes blazing down over the lava field. "Who put all this water on my magma?!"

Her gaze snapped up, an even greater heat slapping against Cluny. "You again?!"

"Uhh . . ." Crocker swallowed so convulsively, Cluny could feel it. "I . . . I'm real sorry about that, but—"

"I will not have this!" The ifrit loomed through the mists, grabbed Crocker with one clawed hand. "I should have done this to you the first time!" She blazed brighter and hotter than before; then darkness crashed in, and Cluny felt herself falling. She still had hold of Crocker, though, so when they hit the flagstones, he took the brunt of it.

Flagstones? She raised her head and blinked as a flood of firelight showed her the main quad of Huxley College.

"Gollantz!" The fire towered into the shouting ifrit. "Gollantz, get out here!"

A dark puff of cloud, and Master Gollantz appeared. He blinked at the ifrit, then bowed. "Your Majesty, it's an honor to have the Ranee of the Ifriti grace our—"

"Never mind that!" Everything spun, and Cluny found herself dangling from Crocker's neck as the ifrit thrust them into the face of the school's Magister Magistrorum. "This is one of yours, isn't it?!"

"Uhh, yes, Ranee." Master Gollantz cleared his throat, his glare making Cluny's hackles rise. "I believe he is."

The world shook again, Cluny jumping away and landing on her paws this time when Crocker thudded to the ground. "He *summoned* me, Gollantz!" the ifrit bellowed. "In absolute defiance of the agreements you have with the elemental houses!"

"Ranee, I am shocked." Master Gollantz bowed once again to the ifrit. "Rest assured: he will be dealt with."

The ifrit flared up into a huge gout of fire. "See that he is!" And with a burst that Cluny saw even through her clenched eyelids, the creature vanished.

Things got very quiet then, and when Cluny opened

her eyes, she saw Master Gollantz, his arms folded, standing above Crocker. "One thing, Crocker," the magister said quietly, but his voice bit at Cluny's ears. Crocker's eyes shot open, and he scrambled to his feet, his robe charred and stained, his face sooty, his hair dripping, his mouth opening.

But Master Gollantz held up a hand. "Just tell me how my lowest ranking novice summoned the Queen of the Ifriti?"

"Uhh . . ." was all Crocker managed to say.

Cluny scurried forward, grabbed the back of Crocker's robe, climbed up to his shoulder. "It's my fault, sir." She bowed, then straightened to meet Master Gollantz's glare. "Crocker's been having trouble with fireballs, so I, well, I was trying to find another way for him to approach the spell."

"You?" Master Gollantz's brow wrinkled. "A familiar designing a course of study for a student of wizardry?"

Cluny's mouth went dry, but Crocker spoke up. "I'm barely a student, sir. And Cluny's sure not just a familiar."

Master Gollantz's brow wrinkled even further, and Cluny tried to think of something to say. But Crocker went on, his eyes moving back and forth between the ground and Master Gollantz. "See, sir, at the first mixer during orientation week, well, all the other novices and familiars were laughing and talking, and I . . . I knew I was a fraud, knew I shouldn't be here no matter what the tests said. And then, bam!"

He turned his head toward Cluny, a big smile on his face. "I saw Cluny sitting in the corner all by herself, and the flow of her power, it was like . . . like I was seeing the sun for the first time. I'd never really felt magic before I saw her, and, well, I knew the only way I was gonna get through Huxley was with her as my familiar."

She blinked at him, the moment rushing back: her frustration that night when the novices wouldn't do more than glance at her and smirk; the sudden wonderful tingle at her whiskers; the short chubby human crossing the room, a goofy grin on his face. All the trouble he'd been since, she'd forgotten how . . . how *right* she'd suddenly felt.

"I'm really sorry, Cluny." Crocker swallowed and looked away. "You deserve a real wizard to be partnered with, not an idiot like me." His eyes flitted toward Master Gollantz. "So please don't blame her, sir. She was only trying to help me."

Silence fell, Cluny's throat too tight to speak, until Master Gollantz blew out a breath. "I can see that you are both determined to make my life difficult."

"Sir?" Cluny and Crocker both said, Cluny's ears folding.

Master Gollantz pointed a long finger at Crocker. "Your familiar will accompany you to all your regular classes from this moment on, Novice. Your record will show that you are a remedial case who cannot function without the constant boost that a familiar provides."

Crocker swallowed and nodded. Master Gollantz's finger didn't move. "Further, you will accompany your familiar to all *her* classes. Your record will show that this is a punishment designed to teach you the vital difference between what a familiar does and what a wizard does."

"Sir?" Crocker's jaw dropped. "But . . . I can't handle that many classes! How'll I—?"

"Shut up, Crocker." Cluny covered his mouth with a paw and looked across at Master Gollantz. "So, in effect, sir, I'll be taking the wizard classes while Crocker here learns to be a familiar."

"Nonsense." Master Gollantz scowled. "The record will show that this is Novice Crocker's punishment. And if I hear even a whisper on this campus about animal wizards and human familiars, you two'll be cleaning bathrooms till graduation. I'll be your advisor from now on, by the way." He stroked his beard. "I find myself becoming interested in you."

Cluny nodded, a thrill sparking her fur. "Of course,

sir." She leaned back and whispered into Crocker's ear, "I'll explain when we get back to the room."

Crocker opened his mouth, blinked, closed his mouth, nodded, and started across the quad toward the dorms.

"Novices?" Master Gollantz's voice made Crocker stop and turn, Cluny blinking at the old wizard still standing with his arms folded. "Where do you think you're going?"

"Uhh . . ." Cluny looked at Crocker, then crooked a claw over her shoulder. "To sleep, sir?"

Master Gollantz pressed his fingertips together. "I rather think you'll be accompanying me to the realm of the Ifriti Ranee; there's still the matter of your *actual* punishment, after all." He nodded. "You will perform one task of the Ranee's choosing, and I'll be along to make sure you don't make any more of a mess of things than you already have."

"Back . . ." Crocker's eyes went wide. "Back to . . . all that lava and everything?"

Master Gollantz nodded again, and Cluny patted the side of Crocker's head. "Don't worry." She drew a breath, felt their joined power flowing through her. "I think we can handle just about anything right now."

ORDEAL

by Robyn McGrew

Robyn McGrew is a writer and editor currently living in the Southeast. Her fiction has appeared in *Sword and Sorceress* and *Relics and Omens,* and in various fantasy magazines.

She describes herself as a "lifelong student," so it's not surprising that she would choose to write about the study of magic—and the things that can go wrong with such study.

Jena rushed through the Temple District. The towering stone and marble buildings allowed little light between them. She had tarried too long with the priests.

"Jerana." A man's deep gravely voice called from behind Jena. She glanced over her shoulder at the tall, dark-cloaked man and cringed, remembering the previous encounters. Jena could not let him catch her, not today. Not if she would have the energy to find work. She increased her pace to a run.

Jena cut around the corner where Fidelity Circle met Temple Road and slipped on the frost-covered cobblestones. She made her way toward the Merchants' District. The thickening crowd slowed her. Gods' willing, it would slow her burly pursuer even more.

Darting through the large stone arch that marked the entrance to the Merchants' District. Jena cast an imploring glance at the cloudy sky. "Lord Tier, God of Mercy, please do not let this happen again. I beg You, put an end to this madness."

"Jerana, wait."

Ignoring him, Jena sprinted between two heavy-cloaked pilgrims and melted into the midday tangle of the Holy City's market. Slowing to a fast walk, she ducked inside the door of Barton's Sundries and searched for a place to hide. To her right stood a rack of small kegs and to her left a stack of barrels. She hunched down next to a large barrel and pretended to inspect it. The wide brass band on the barrel reflected a distorted image of her thin, pale face. Long strands of wavy auburn hair hung loosely over gray eyes focused more on the door than her own reflection. Had he seen her come into the shop?

Out of habit she ran her fingers along the gold chain at her neck. The warped onyx and gold medallion at the chain's bottom bit into her skin. She ignored the pain and twisted to her left so she could see better.

"Barton," Jena whispered to the brawny man who owned the sundry shop. "Don't let him know I'm in here."

"He's back?" Barton did not look at her when he spoke, but she saw the lines of worry form between his bushy eyebrows. "Where?"

"By the temple arch."

"Not anymore. He's heading this way. You'd better go out the back."

"Thanks." Jena crawled across the floor using the barrels as cover. At the back of the shop she crept silently under the door's heavy blanket and escaped into the alley.

Staying to the back wall of the store she skirted the building and risked a look around the corner. A quick glance in each direction showed the back street was empty. Relieved, Jena crossed to the shadowed passageway between the chandelier's and the glazier's shops. Half-rotted leaves squished under her feet as she worked her way through the alley to the front of the buildings.

Jena scanned the area between her and the northern market gate. She did not see the tall man in the black cloak. Once through the gate she could escape into the docks and escape him.

"Jerana, it's me, Tor. Stop this foolishness."

Her thin fingers trembled, and she clenched her hands into fists, in an attempt to stop the motion. The man still held her shoulder. A quick jerk forced him to relinquish his hold. Once free, she fought off the urge to flee. Bracing herself for the inevitable, Jena gripped the twisted medallion and turned to face him. "Why are you doing this?"

Startled by her sudden movement, Tor's left hand unconsciously moved to the hilt of the scimitar resting on his right hip. The maddening pattern unfolded.

The medallion turned cold in her hand. A tingling, burning sensation radiated from it. Energy drained from her like water being drawn from a well, and the bitter taste of salt filled her mouth. Tor's weathered face lost its reproachful expression and took on a dazed look. He inhaled sharply as if waking from a broken dream. "Sorry," he mumbled, "I could have sworn you were somebody I knew." One corner of his mouth lifted in a lopsided grin. Embarrassed, he turned to leave.

"Wait." Jena winced at the desperate tone in her voice. Tor stopped and looked over his shoulder. "Yes?"

"This is not the first time you have mistaken me for this woman. Who is she?"

The big man looked down at her with sympathy etched on his face. "This time you're the one who is wrong, little lady. I never saw you before today."

"Please," Jena insisted. "I don't remember anything before two years ago. Who did you think I was?"

"When I saw you from behind, I took you for a lady who once lived here. You have the same auburn hair and are small like her. You have about twenty years, like Jerana, but I can see now you're not her. You don't even dress like her. She would never wear the homespun robe or the over-tunic. I'm sorry." He nodded his head politely and walked briskly away from her.

Jena sagged, weakened by the encounter. The old

anger fought for supremacy. Other than the exact words, nothing differed from previous encounters—the burn, the energy drain, his change of demeanor and denials, all the same. She seized the twisted medallion in an attempt to cast it away from her. As always it wouldn't move, preventing her from ridding herself of it. Even the priests couldn't remove it. They refused to tell her why. The second wave of weakness hit her. Jena stumbled the few steps to the shelter of the alley and collapsed. The third wave engulfed her in harsh, unforgiving blackness.

Jena woke still lying in the alley. Her whole body felt stiff and cold. Dark clouds threatened with an immediacy given them by the hours she had lost. Mourning the lost time, Jena moved deeper into the Merchants' District.

Large crystalline flakes dropped from the sky as Jena left Slorin's small shop. The apothecary sniffed at the tang in the air and scowled at the darkening clouds. "I think I'll close early and head home. First storm of winter and it's going to come in like a bad temper. If you had come earlier, you could have made some deliveries for me. Maybe I'll have something for you tomorrow. You should find shelter soon, or there may not be any left for you."

Jena nodded agreement and wrapped her threadbare cloak around her shoulders.

As the snow began to stick to the ground, the people of Templeton rushed to complete their business. She watched them scurry about with their purchases and suppressed a pang of longing. If she had a home, she, too, would finish her business and rush to its welcoming hearth fire. She didn't have that choice. She had to keep looking for work. No work meant no funds, which in turn resulted in no food or shelter.

The shopkeepers' responses remained the same through the afternoon. They didn't have work for an unskilled laborer. If she could retain what they taught her, then she could apprentice with one of them. Jena simply couldn't remember. New knowledge fled with the night. Even forgoing sleep did nothing to help her retain what she had worked so hard to learn.

The storm grew rapidly worse, and her hope for work dwindled to nothing as the day waned. Even the shops in the shadow of the temples closed before evening prayers. By nightfall a hand's span of new snow lay on the ground and buildings.

The city's inhabitants closed themselves inside with hearth fires. The wind gusted, piling the snow in drifts against buildings and walls. Jena left the Merchants' District and made her way through the snow-padded streets. Gods willing, she might still find an inn or hostel in need of help. Failing that, she would have to shelter in a woodpile.

Surrendering to necessity, Jena trudged toward the western gate where the majority of the hostels were located. On Pilgrims' Row, a square wooden plaque stood lone watch duty before a two-level building. The snow frosted the image of a robed pilgrim praying before a bed and almost obscured the bold black letters spelling out "Seeker's Haven." Jena made her way up the scraped pathway and kicked the snow off her worn boots before entering the building.

The aroma of fresh-baked bread, mixed with the smell of burning wood permeated the inn. Jena's stomach lurched and rumbled a plea for nourishment. She firmly ignored it. Lewin Merdith, the hostel's owner, nodded his silver head at her. She returned the greeting and looked around the room to see how many patrons had braved the weather. Only one heavily cloaked figure huddled near the large crackling fire in the center of the common room. Jena exhaled sharply, no work here. Gathering her worn cloak about her, she turned to face the night.

"Wait, Jena, I could use your help tonight," Lewin's smooth baritone called from the kitchen door.

Jena closed her eyes, necessity battling with shame. Lewin could ill afford a helper on such a slow night.

Yet, if she refused, daybreak might find her half frozen and unable to seek employment. Even if she could overlook the fact she had not eaten in two days and felt weak, she dared not ignore the cold burn in her fingers and toes. She forced a smile onto lips stiff with the cold and joined the tall old man at the kitchen door. "Thank you, Lewin. I accept, but I insist on making it up during the busy season. This summer I'll work one night for free."

Lewin lifted the sopping cloak from her shoulders and handed her a leather apron. "If that's the way you want to do it." Jena knew that smile he wore. It said, *if things work out for you, otherwise forget it; I have.* He hung her drenched wrap on a peg by the hearth and retrieved a blanket from the warming bar.

"This should be toasty by now. Take it to our customer and see if he wants something to eat."

Jena folded the warm blanket over her arm, smoothed her wet hair into place and moved toward the stranger. His heavy wool cloak dripped with melting snow.

When she approached the table, he turned to face her. Clear gray eyes like splintered gems greeted her from under the folds of his hood.

"The owner thought you might want to let your cloak dry. You can wrap yourself in this until the chill leaves you." Jena stretched the blanket toward him.

"Thank you." His voice matched his eyes, soft yet commanding. He reached for the blanket with a hand lacking hair or the marks of age. Jena caught herself staring. She had expected it to look old and gnarled. When he took the blanket, the stranger's long delicate fingers brushed her arm.

The medallion grew hot, then cold, on her chest.

A heavy haze enfolded her. The briny taste of salt filled her mouth. Memory returned in a gushing torrent. Fleeting images from her past spun around her mind in a vortex. Pictures of stone-floored rooms with wooden tables danced wildly in her head like a wind-driven fire. The images fled, leaving only a numb feel-

*ing and ashes in their wake; empty echoes of old unan-
swered questions. Jena jerked her arm away, breaking
contact with the man.*

Collecting her wits, she asked the stranger numbly,
"May I bring you something hot from the kitchen?"

"Bring the house stew and bread." The man's gray
eyes studied her. Did he know what had just happened
to her? Had he caused it? "Please also bring me
heated water in a tankard."

"Yes, sir." Jena weaved her way around the tables
and returned to the kitchen. Leaning against the wall,
she slid onto the server's stool by the door.

Lewin stood at the cooking grate with his back to
her. "What does he want?"

"Stew, bread, and a tankard of hot water," Jena
muttered.

"I think there's something like that around here."
Lewin chuckled and scooped two ladles of the onion-
spiced stew into a miniature pewter kettle. Turning,
he started to pass the kettle handle to Jena but
stopped when he saw her slumped on the stool. From
his reaction, Jena knew she must look terrible. A
frown replaced Lewin's grin. "What's wrong?"

"I had an episode." Jena pulled a serving rag from
a bucket of cold water and wrapped it around her
right hand.

"Like Tor?"

"No. Just images like a dream."

"Perhaps it means you are getting your memory
back." Lewin started to hand her the stew, but pulled
it back when she reached for it. "You look pale. Why
don't you rest a minute? I'll take this out to him."

"I'll take it. I need to earn my keep. You promised
me. Remember?"

Lewin's lips thinned to a flat line. "Aye, I remember. You wouldn't touch a bite until I promised to let
you work for what you couldn't pay for in coin." He
surrendered the steaming kettle.

Taking the stew Jena returned to the common
room. The stranger had moved through the maze of

tables to the one nearest the fire. He sat cocooned in the blanket on a sturdy wooden chair between the hearth and the table. His cloak rested in a crumpled, sodden heap on the hearthstones.

"The stew is hot," Jena set the kettle in front of him. "I'll bring your water and bread in a moment." She lifted his cloak and hung in on a drying hook near the fire and returned to the kitchen. She heard Lewin outside grunting over the supply of firewood he kept sheltered against the outside wall. He called to her through the open back door. "After you take the rest to him, come back to the kitchen and eat something."

The bread waited on a place next to a tankard of water with a heating iron in it. Jena removed the iron with her shielded hand and took the order to the common room.

Steam circled Jena's wrist when she set the water on the table. The stranger produced a worn leather pouch from under the blanket. Opening the bag he sprinkled a small measure of dried leaves and flowers into the water. The liquid darkened to a deep shade of rose and perfumed the air with a sweet floral scent. The hand and the pouch disappeared back into the blanket. "When you finish your work for the evening, come sit and talk with me."

Jena nodded, but did not commit to an answer. On the way back to the kitchen she passed Lewin, who carried a small brazier. He moved carefully up the stairs and disappeared into the first guest room. In the kitchen a liberal serving of beef and onion stew and a large chuck of brown bread awaited her on the table. The stew held a hint of marjoram, and the bread tasted of nuts and rye. In only a few moments, she wiped the bowl clean with the last of her bread.

Lewin returned to the kitchen, set Jena to cleaning dishes and the floor, then disappeared through the cellar door. He emerged a candle-notch later brushing flour from his apron and smelling of honey-butter.

"It's been a long day and I'd like to get some sleep." Lewin yawned prodigiously. "If you promise to keep the fire going for me, you can sleep by the kitchen hearth tonight. I'd appreciate not having to come down every hour just to add logs."

Jena knew Lewin did not keep a fire in the kitchen at night. She also knew better than to argue the subject with him. She never won. "Thank you, Lewin."

"The Gods guard your sleep, Jena." Lewin gave her a gentle pat on the back.

She squeezed his arm in return. "Yours also. Good sleep."

Lewin retired to his private loft, leaving Jena to her work, which she finished in short order. The time had come to talk with the strange patron. She had to force herself to take up the kettle of hot water and return to the common room. Setting it at the fire's edge, Jena faced the stranger. "You asked me to return?"

"Yes, I thought we could talk." He had finally uncovered his head to reveal long locks of silver-gray hair.

"About what?" Jena studied the man hoping to recognize him. Wavy locks surrounded a compact round face that looked smooth as if recently shaven. What few hairs had not turned silver looked striped with traces of brown, blond-white, and even a strand or two of black. The blanket covered everything but his sleeve bottoms; one black with silver trim and the other white with gold trim. He smelled of the forest and the pungent aroma of incense. She knew this should mean something to her, but it didn't.

"About you," the stranger smiled warmly. "How long have you worked here, for instance?"

"Off and on for two years."

The stranger sipped his tea. "Two years can be a long time, especially when one is alone."

"Or lonely."

The conversation stalled, and an uncomfortable silence filled the room. "Water for your tea?" Jena offered just to say something to fill the empty space. The stranger nodded, produced the worn leather pouch and added to the leaves in his cup. She leaned forward to fill his tankard and her pendant swung forward to clank against the cup's side.

"What an interesting pendant. May I see it?"

Jena moved next to him, coming close enough for him to grasp the pendant, and braced herself.

The stranger's fingers closed around the onyx and gold medallion. His gem-splintered eyes viewed the twisted piece critically. He nodded as if seeing something he recognized and then lifted the chain over her head. Jena gasped and stared at him. He held the pendant by the chain over the fire and looked at it as if reading something on it. "How did you do that?" She bit her lower lip, drawing blood.

"What?" He smiled pleasantly.

"Remove my pendant?" Beads of cold sweat formed at her temples and trickled down the edge of her face.

"Why do you ask?"

The words came pouring out of her like a confession. "I found myself wandering the streets of Templeton two years ago. That pendant is the only clue to my identity. I never could remove it, neither could anyone else, not even the priests in the temples. The mages refuse to touch it. How did you?" Jena pulled back from the stranger, suddenly wary. "What are you?"

"Let us say, I am one who would serve as a link between your past and future."

"You know me?" Fear expanded her senses. She could feel the fluctuating heat from the fire, taste the flower steam from the whips of tea vapor floating toward her.

"Of you." He corrected gently and leaned forward to ease the pendant over her head.

She would have pulled away if she could. The same thing that had held the pendant to her now held her to it. As the medallion dropped onto Jena's chest, the world spun around her. The room faded and velvety darkness claimed her. The last thing she saw clearly was the stranger's smile.

*   *   *

Jena woke to find herself by a banked kitchen fire. The blanket used by the stranger had been tucked snugly around her small frame. Casting the cover aside, Jena rushed into the common room. Empty. Racing up the stairs, she checked the room where Lewin had taken the brazier. The door stood ajar. The bed, neatly made, stood vacant. The now-dark brazier rested at its foot. There was no sign that the gray-eyed man had used the room.

She dashed down the stairs to the entrance. A gust of snow-laden wind slapped her in the face as she flung open the door. Shivering and staggering back a step, she shielded her eyes from the rising sun and looked at the walkway. The snow-covered ground leading from the hostel looked smooth. If the stranger had left any tracks, the falling snow had hidden them. Sighing, Jena fought the door closed and returned to the kitchen.

Leaning on the cutting table, she noticed for the first time two scrolls and a large purse lying there. The scroll next to the purse had Lewin's name on it. She ignored it in favor of the second scroll. An adverse combination of fear and hope made her fingers tremble as she unrolled the leather parchment. It smelled of forest and incense. Hardly breathing, she read:

Jena. If you truly wish to solve the mystery of your past, come see me in the spring. Follow the trail which begins at the Well of Chanze and travel south through the Forest of Tryne. Travel from dawn to midday and you shall find me.

It had no signature at the bottom, but she knew it must be from the gray-eyed patron. "God of Mercy, please do not let this be a cruel hoax."

"Good morning, Jena," Lewin greeted her as he descended from his loft. "Sleep well?"

She handed her scroll to Lewin to read. His thin lips pursed and he exhaled sharply as he set the scroll on the table. "No wonder you look like you spent the night with a restless spirit. What does the other scroll say?"

"I don't know. It's addressed to you."

Lewin opened the scroll and skimmed it. "According to this, there is gold in the bag sufficient to cover a small room and one meal a day for you until mid-spring." He untied the bag and spilled its contents onto the tabletop. His eyebrows arched toward his hairline as he counted the coins. "Twenty sentinels, that's more than enough to cover expenses. In fact, I think it could easily cover the room, three meals, and still have enough to buy you a new set of clothes and a warm cloak."

Jena fingered the fluted contours of the gold and said nothing. Only the temples used such coins.

Jena stood staring at the ebony and oak temple. A steepled roof covered the spherical building. Two small square rooms, most likely antechambers, were attached to either side at the front.

"Welcome Jena." The greeting came from the shadows just inside the entrance of the large building.

Jena went rigid. She knew that voice. Its smooth tones had filled her dreams each night during the winter. She crossed the few steps to the temple and faced the priest. He eased from the shadows, making no effort this time to hide his telltale robes; black with silver trim on the right side, white with gold trim on the left side. Only his sash broke the pattern. It held every color imaginable. The colors seemed to move constantly with none taking dominance. Though she had rarely seen one, Jena recognized him as a servant of Tier, the God of Mercy.

"Come in, Jena." He pivoted and led her through a short corridor to one of the square rooms. "Please make yourself comfortable." He gestured toward two oak chairs by the small room's fire pit.

Jena removed her cloak and sat on the proffered chair. "Thank you, sir."

"Please call me Brother Andrus." He sat in the second chair and smoothed the folds of his linen robes. "I asked you to come to the temple because it is here I can help you the most."

"Why would a servant of the God of Mercy want to help me? We never met before that night at Seekers' Haven. Did we?"

"No, my Master sent me to you."

Jena's stomach felt like it had dropped to her feet. "He sent you?"

"Think Jena. How many times did you cry out to Him for help? How often did you beg Him to put an end to your torment?"

"I don't remember doing it once."

"You have done so many times. The most recent was the episode in the marketplace when Tor Abandon found you. You called on my Master by name and begged Him to 'put an end to this madness.'"

"I guess I did. What does that have to do with my past?"

"Tor is touched by Lord Zerin, the God of Magic. The Lord gave him a strong resistance to magic so the mages can use him and his ship to transport their special projects. The resistance allowed him to remember you. The magic in your amulet cannot affect him unless he stands within arm's reach and faces you."

"I am this Jerana he seeks."

"Do you truly wish to know?"

The concerned look on the priest's face made Jena hesitate. "Is there a reason I wouldn't?"

"I am not certain. I can only tell you what my Master has revealed to me."

Jena's mouth went dry. "Please, tell me."

"You served Lord Zerin. The only thing greater than your skill was your insatiable desire for more knowledge."

Andrus paused and studied Jena as if trying to decide how much to tell her. Fearful he would not tell what she needed to know Jena urged him, "Go on, please."

"Your lust for knowledge brought you to your current state." He held up his hand to stop further questions. "I know nothing else about it. Lord Tier will show you more if you are willing to accept the consequences of your actions. Are you?"

Jena frowned. "What do you mean, consequences?"

"The God Zerin took your memory, hoping time would change you."

"Have I changed?"

"My Master did not reveal this to me."

Jena puzzled over the information. She had been a mage. That would explain much. Mages rarely learned anything more than basic survival skills—a fact hardly surprising since magic required many hours of intense study. She must have done something serious enough to cause the last two years to be considered an act of mercy.

"Would you like time to think it over?"

Jena did not answer immediately. Andrus waited. Finally she looked up at him. "I cannot avoid the truth forever, and I wouldn't even if I could. Not remembering what I did doesn't change the past. I want to know the truth about myself."

"Good. Come with me."

He led her back through the corridor to the large room in the building. High vaulted ceilings and arched alcoves gave the room a feeling of perpetual pleading. Pine-scented incense burned in each alcove before an icon representing one or another of the Gods. Jena looked from the green leaf of Zancha, Lady of Growing Things, to the golden sun of the Lord of Rebirth.

"Brother Andrus, why are there shrines to all the other Gods in a temple dedicated to the God of Mercy?"

"You called on my Master for mercy. Benevolence comes in many forms. Have you forgotten that Tier is also the Lord of Repentance? The temple in the city is dedicated to those who need only mercy. This temple serves others, who like yourself need something more complex."

The muscles in Jena's stomach clenched, the saliva in her mouth turned sour and she suddenly felt nauseated. What had she done?

Brother Andrus led her to a huge altar of onyx and marble. At his gesture she knelt and placed her hands on the cool surface.

"I'm frightened," Jena admitted, her voice sounding small in the vaulted room.

"You have no need to fear, Jena. Trust Lord Tier. Among the Gods, He alone knows what it means to make a mistake and serve penance for it."

Andrus moved to the opposite side of the altar and knelt. Lifting a bowl, he poured ground myrrh over the stone surface. Flames rose in the center of the altar's surface but did not move toward Jena's hands. Black and white smoke spread out, filling the room. Andrus' muted voice came through the smoke. "Lord Tier, I ask You to show Your mercy. Reveal the mystery of this woman's past to her."

The smoke rushed at Jena. Her muscles bunched, but she could not move. Jena plunged into her past.

The singsong of imperfect chants filled the Temple of Magic. High-Mage Jerana Natar smiled. The novices would practice until they could do the spell correctly one hundred times in sequence or until they fell into an exhausted sleep. She needed to concentrate on the work before her. Jerana passed through the silk-shielded alcove and into the High Sanctuary. Ebony pillars inlaid with golden runes supported the distant ceiling. Coils of incense set in giant urns sent whips of musky smoke across the forest of kneeling cushions.

Just beyond the great altar rested the Book of Knowledge. The tome contained every spell Lord Zerin had created for the world of mortals. The words of her mentor, the Arch-magis, came back to taunt her. "You are not ready to learn the final spells, Jerana." She would prove him wrong by learning them on her own. She would copy the spells at her cave and return the sacred tome by morning. No one would know. She could practice at her convenience and reveal her actions only when she had mastered the spells.

Jerana moved through the triangular room to the rune-inscribed altar and made a perfunctory obeisance. She had not come here to pray.

Settling onto the smooth onyx floor, Jerana removed a pre-cast spell scroll from her sleeve and set it on her lap. Carefully gathering the strands of energy about her, she began the complex chant to weave them into the intricate filigree patterns of her spell. Jerana meshed herself with the raw beauty of the energy's flow and the joy of the power. She opened her eyes and reached toward the tome, willing it to come to her. Slowly and with great resistance the book lifted. Sweat poured down the side of her face, but she maintained the spell. The great book floated toward her, gliding past the altar and the supplicant's kneeling bench, finally coming to rest in her outstretched arms. Jerana tucked the tome into the crook of her left arm and broke the seal of the transport spell with the thumb of her right hand.

Nothing happened.

Impossible!

She had cast the spell hundreds of time with complete success. It should work.

Immense power saturated the sanctuary. The angry God of Magic stood within the sizzling energies. He flicked His finger at Jerana. The tome, wrenched from her grasp, transversed the distance to its stand and settled gently into place.

Hardly able to breathe, Jerana bowed her head. "Lord Zerin, please don't be angry with me. They wanted to hold me back. I can . . ."

The God silenced her speech.

She cast herself on the floor before the God and silently begged for mercy. Her tears flowed unchecked from both eyes in a near constant flood.

The God's voice thundered and shook the foundations of the room. "*You sought to steal what you had not earned. You took the power I gave you and used it for selfish ends. My gifts and My blessing I withdraw from your life. Leave My house and do not seek Me again until you learn to value the knowledge you have."*

The God's shadow enshrouded Jerana. Her temple robes transformed and become the clothes of a common laborer. His hand still glowing with power, Lord Zerin grasped her medallion of faith. "Since you value knowledge above all else, I curse you with its loss and deny you the acquisition of new enlightenment. Your past shall cloud and vanish from your memory. No one shall recognize you or you them. Thus shall you remain cursed until the day you truly learn to value knowledge."

Jerana's memory faded to gray nothingness she would come to know too well in the two years that followed.

The vision faded and the smoke cleared the room Jena stared at the altar but did not see it. The vision had returned her memory only of the event. The rest of her past was still a blank.

*   *   *

Jena rushed through the icy cobblestone streets of the Temple District. If she hurried, she could catch the priest before the temple closed for the day.

"Jerana," a man's deep gravely voice called from behind Jena.

She glanced over her shoulder at the tall, dark-cloaked man. "Hello, Tor." She slowed her pace so he could catch her, but was careful not to face him.

"Long time since I saw you last, Lady Mage. More than three years ago."

"My studies have kept me busy. In fact, I go now to see if the results please Lord Zerin."

"I'll see you later, then." Tor waved and took the turn leading to the docks.

Two more turns brought Jena to the Temple of Magic. The rune-covered doors already stood closed. Mounting the steps she stood before the huge entry

and lowered her head. "Lord Zerin, I beg You to
admit me. I repent my foolish actions of the past and
seek Your forgiveness." Jena held her breath and
waited.

A long moment later the door opened.

GRAIN

by Esther M. Friesner

Esther M. Friesner is the author of twenty-nine published
novels and well over a hundred short stories. She holds a
BA in Spanish and Drama from Vassar College and a PhD
in Spanish from Yale University. A four-time Nebula Award
finalist, she has won the award twice for Best Short Story.
She has also been a Hugo finalist, as well as winning the
Skylark, the Golden Cauldron, and the Romantic Times
Award. She is best known for her humorous fantasy, including her work as creator and editor of the popular *Chicks In
Chainmail* anthology series. She lives in Connecticut with
her husband, two children, and two cats who do very convincing imitations of bowling balls.

The first day at a new job or new school is usually the
worst; if you survive it, things get easier. I'll bet the apprentice in this story hopes this will be true for her.

Kithi sat in the sunshine on the bench outside
Mama Nila's house and swung her legs, bored beyond bearing. All around her the delights of Agatash
beckoned—the smells of roasting meat and baking
bread to tantalize her nose, the sounds of distant
music and laughter to tease her ears, and all the rest
of the little walled city's marvelous sights and wonders, hidden just around the next street corner, only
waiting for a girl like Kithi to seek them out and be
dazzled. She could almost swear she heard the city
itself softly calling to her from every sunbaked brick
wall and dusty street, *Come away, child, come away!
Come away and play with me!*

It galled her to the bone to know she couldn't. It

didn't matter that she was twelve years old and clever enough for the village headman to have noticed it; here she sat and here she'd stay until fetched, like a forgotten basket. She kicked the bench leg, hard.

Inside the house behind her, voices rose and fell. There were no windows at street level—no sense in tempting thieves—but the door of Mama Nila's establishment was left ajar on account of the heat. If Kithi cared to eavesdrop, she could have heard almost all of the conversation. She didn't bother. As far as she knew, her fate was already decided, her body delivered like a sheaf of barley to the threshing floor. Inside the house they were having just one last squabble over the details.

"Probably Father kicking up a row over my bond-price because he thinks it's expected of him," she grumbled, staring down at the little cloth bundle between her feet that held all her belongings and at the brand new apron she wore, gloriously white, which her father had bought her only this morning. "Spent so much on this rag, he'll never change his mind and take me home again. I'm here to stay; he's just bluffing."

Sure enough, the high, sharp tones of bickering voices soon dropped back down to softer, more friendly levels, and soon after that Kithi's father appeared in the doorway.

"Come in and meet your new mistress, girl," he said, all smiles. "Look sharp! This is where your life lies from now on. Make a good impression on her, eh?"

Dully and dutifully she picked up her bundle and followed him into the house. Once over the threshold she blinked, trying to force her eyes to adjust from brilliant summer sunshine to the flickering gleam of a claypot tallow candle, the only light in Mama Nila's entryway. It burned on a wooden shelf set high on the wall, just beneath a clay plaque bearing the image of a woman, her arms filled with ripe ears of barley, her crossed hands holding a sickle and a flail. Kithi gave the image a skeptical stare: What was such a creature up to, masquerading as a field hand? She was far too richly dressed. Back in Kithi's village, the women who went out to harvest the grain never wore earrings like that, or so many heavy bracelets and anklets, or a skirt so tight that it would make bending over to reap the crop impossible.

I'd like to see you in a real *barley field,* Kithi thought, gazing into the image's empty eyes. *I'll bet you wouldn't be able to gather a single stalk without tripping and falling on your face, let alone—*

Oh, wouldn't I?

Kithi startled. Who had said that? Had her new mistress crept up behind her and overheard—? Kithi whirled around, but she was alone in the dark entryway. Even as she did so, she realized that she had spoken nothing aloud. She turned again to stare at the image. Was that a smirk on the white clay lips, or only a trick of the dancing candlelight? She brought her eyes closer to the plaque, straining to stand on tiptoe and know for certain, one way or the other.

"Kithi! Stop your dawdling!" Her father's voice broke the spell. Mama Nila's entryway was not so much an antechamber as a tunnel leading into the heart of the house. Kithi's father was waiting for her at the far end, the black outline of a man backlit by blazing light. Kithi gave the clay image one last doubtful glance and hurried after him.

The echoing passageway brought her out into a grassy courtyard. A sheltered blue tile walk ran all around the central area, and more glazed tiles set in swirled patterns adorned the creamy walls. The doors of many rooms gaped open along the walk, rectangles of darkness. In the center of the courtyard a fountain leaped and burbled, tossing glittering crystals into the face of the sun.

A small, plump woman stood beside the fountain, her brown fingers dabbling in the falling spray. She wore a citywoman's tiered dress, green as a lizard's back, with a sweep of shimmering white cloth draped over her head to keep off the fiercest rays of the sun. She didn't smile when she saw Kithi, but her face did seem to offer the girl an unspoken message of welcome.

She looks *all right,* Kithi thought as. her father took her by both shoulders and marched her over to where the woman waited. *I thought I was going to be given to a dragon-lady, all bones and brimstone, but this one's got kind eyes and a mooncake face. They say that means a sweet temper. Hunh! And it might mean nothing, when it comes to the proof of things. You can't trust looks. Anyway, here's hoping.* She put on a smile and ducked out from under her father's hold, turning her escape into a shallow bow.

"Peace in this house, honored mistress," she recited, just as the village headman had taught her while preparing her for her move to the city.

Mama Nila's expression chilled. She looked up sharply at Kithi's father, ignoring the girl, and demanded, "*This* is what I'm to teach? *This* is the strong back I was promised, the legs that can run my errands all day long without tiring, the arms sturdy enough to haul my heaviest beer jugs and brewpots? You fraud! You calf-eyed cheat! I ought to summon the city wards! You should be chained to the swindler's block in the marketplace with a board bearing all your crimes hanging from your neck!"

Kithi's father fell back several steps under the woman's assault of angry words. "What do you mean, good lady?" he gasped, one hand resting on his breast. "I admit she's scrawny looking, but it's all muscle and sinew, I swear! She's wonderful strong, the Field Lord be my witness. Just give her a task or two and you'll see."

"Oh, I will!" Mama Nila spat back. "Don't worry yourself on *that* score. A task or two? Or *twenty!* And if she shirks even one, you'll hear from me. Never mind how unkindly the gods look on oathbreakers, you'd be wiser to fear *my* wrath! I'll hunt you down in that wretched little pig wallow you call a village,

with your worthless cub panting at my donkey's tail,
and I'll throw her *and* your measly bond-price back
in your face in front of all your neighbors."

Mama Nila continued to harangue Kithi's father,
who continued to do nothing more than cringe and
stammer repeated assurances as to the girl's ability to
work and work hard. As for Kithi, at first she was just
as frightened as her father by Mama Nila's unexpected
eruption. Unlike him, she soon recovered and began
to feel something quite different. Her eyebrows lowered, her bundle dropped unheeded to the ground,
and her cheeks burned hotter than when she'd lived
through the same marsh-fever that had carried off her
mother. Her stomach churned and bubbled like a
stewpot left too long above a fire that blazed too high,
until at last her rage boiled up and burst from her lips.

"Be *quiet,* you awful old woman!" she shouted,
stamping her foot on the grass. "If you don't want
me, just say so and give my father his money back
right now. How dare you decide I'm too weak or too
lazy to suit you when you haven't even given me a
try?"

"Hush, Kithi, hush," her father said, but Kithi was
past heeding him.

"I *won't* hush!" She shouted the words at the top
of her lungs just to prove her point. "And I won't be
talked *around* like this. I'm not a wall or a cookpot
or a dog: I'm here and I can speak for myself!"

"So I see, so I see." Mama Nila chuckled into one
hand and used the other to seize Kithi's chin before
the girl could draw back. The older woman's grasp
was firm, gentle yet inescapable. She raised Kithi's
face and looked deep into her eyes. "I do believe that
I was mistaken, good man," she told Kithi's father.
"The child will do admirably as my apprentice after
all. You may go."

Kithi's father bowed low to the woman, then paused
just long enough to give his daughter an awkward embrace and one last whispered reminder to be a good

girl. That done, he hastened from the house without
so much as a backward glance at his child.

Kithi started after him, but a strong hand on her
shoulder restrained her. "Men like to think we don't
know that they cry."

"I know he cries," Kithi replied. "I saw him do it
when my mother died."

"No doubt you also saw him shed tears when he
dropped a tool on his foot or cut his hand with a
knife. There are no mysteries guarding that kind of
tears. All human creatures cry in the face of death or
pain; those occasions need no excuse. It is crying for
any other cause that men fear, and the weakness such
tears signify . . . to them. They say that if a mortal
sees a god weep, his strength trickles out of him with
his tears. That is why the rains of heaven come from
the eyes of the Lady, not the Field Lord."

Kithi stared at the doorway through which her father
had vanished and wiped away the tears now trailing
down her own cheeks. Mama Nila made a clucking
sound and used one corner of her headscarf to dry
Kithi's eyes. "I see that you and I know the truth, that
tears steal no power from us. You are still a strong girl,
even if you do miss your father already. I have a great
need for strength in this house, especially now."

"Was—was that why you carried on so, before?"
Kithi asked, rubbed away the last of her tears with
the back of one sunbrowned hand.

"Why I yapped at your father like a jackal?" Mama
Nila smiled. "Oh, yes. It was to provoke *you*, to test
your mettle. I never know how well a new pot will
serve me until I've set it over the fire. You, my dear,
will serve very well indeed."

A fresh scowl banished what was left of Kithi's
homesickness. "I told you: I'm *not* a cookpot."

"I hope not. Even the strongest shatter. But enough:
Your sleeping place is ready and the midday heat is
upon us. When the sun is high, the house and her
Lady rest and dream. Who are we to do otherwise?"

She drew the white headscarf a little farther forward, to shade her eyes, and led Kithi across the courtyard. As they walked, the girl said, "The Lady of this house . . . I saw her picture when I first came in. She's very pretty."

"She? Oh no, child; that one is only Tareth, the Lady's daughter. She has no power of her own, being half mortal, but her blessed Mother has given her the task of watching over the boundaries of herds and fields and houses."

"So if someone were to come into this house uninvited, Tareth would destroy him?" Kithi asked.

"Destroy him! How? I told you, Tareth has no power, and her authority comes solely from her Mother. When a house she guards is invaded, she is supposed to summon help, in her Mother's name, but it seldom comes fleetly enough to stop the thieves. Truth is, Tareth can barely help herself." She shrugged. "Still, it's a foolish householder who risks offending the Mother by slighting the child. I'm surprised you didn't know that. Didn't your village wisemen teach you anything of the gods?"

"Not of this one," Kithi replied. *And a good thing, too,* she thought. *Our village was poor enough without wasting offerings to a do-nothing goddess.*

Mama Nila stepped through one of the open doorways ringing the courtyard. "This will be your place," she told the girl. Kithi peered inside. The room was bigger than half her old home, yet she had the definite feeling that it was the smallest cubby in all Mama Nila's house. Daylight streamed in through a trio of narrow slits high in the wall and dust motes danced down the sunbeams to fall at last on a narrow bed. Kithi set her little bundle on the well-swept earthen floor and wonderingly stroked the carved wooden leopard heads standing vigil at the bed's four corners.

"Sleep well. Your lessons begin this afternoon, when it's cooler." With that, Mama Nila left the girl alone.

In the dusky room, Kithi seated herself on the edge

of her bed as if expecting to be chased off it the instant that the real owner returned. She was weary in all her limbs from the trek down out of the mountains to Agatash, yet too taut-nerved to rest. Her head spun with memories of the past few days, from the moment the village headman had summoned her and her father to his hut, changing their lives.

Your daughter is keen-witted, he'd said, speaking over Kithi's head to her father as though the two men were the only ones there. *Too much so. Only yesterday I received a complaint against her from Losh, the potter. He said that when he told her to fetch him a jug of water from the well, she did not simply obey, like a good girl, but laid hold of his own words and twisted them until he found himself agreeing to* give *her the same jug she used to do his bidding.*

So that's *where our new jug came from!* said Kithi's father.

The headman was not amused. *This is not the first such trick she's played, and it goes beyond mere women's cunning. In my opinion, she has been given abilities wasted on a female. Alas, it is not our place to question this. All gifts are from the gods, whose whims we dare not question. It doesn't matter: Our duty is not to ask* why, *but to ask* how *we may best employ what they bestow. In your daughter's case, we are in luck: I have just heard from an old friend of my childhood, Nila the beerwoman, now called Mama Nila of Agatash.* Here he gestured with the small clay tablet in his hand. It was covered with blots and squiggles that did not even pull themselves together enough to make pictures, yet he spoke of it as though it were important, somehow. Kithi smelled a mystery and burned to learn its secret. *She sends me word that she stands in need of a clever child to whom she might teach her trade. Clever, but also bold—she* insists *on that.* He shrugged. *Insists. To me! Too long living in the city has made her forget proper deference. I'll pardon her for that: She* did *send a generous thanks-gift for any help I might render. I will give you some of it so that*

*you can meet the girl's bond-price. It's little enough to
pay for removing her from our village. The gods may
have given her cleverness, but it's a well known fact
that they never favor lands that harbor clever women.*

Where did he pick up that *chaff-brained idea, I wonder?* Kithi thought. *Probably made it up to suit himself.*
She removed her new apron and folded it neatly,
kicked off her straw sandals, and lay down atop the
thin coverlet. She closed her eyes so tightly that her
temples throbbed, willing herself to sleep, yet no
sleep came.

Well, no sense just lying here, she thought, sitting up
again. *If this place is to be my new home, the sooner
I know it, the better.* Without bothering to put her
sandals back on, she crept from the room and out into
the courtyard.

The tiled walk was warm underfoot, even where it
lay sheltered beneath the colonnade. Kithi padded
softly around the edge of the courtyard, looking into
each open doorway she passed. Most were too dark
to yield any secrets, but one smelled of old olive oil,
bread, and onions, so she knew she'd found the
kitchen. Mama Nila's chamber wasn't hard to guess
either: The beerwoman's snoring sounded like the
steady turning of a mill wheel grinding grain. One
room was full of stacks and stacks of the same kind
of squiggle-covered clay tablets that the headman had
brandished. Kithi eagerly grabbed one after another,
doggedly trying to make head or tail of them. She
could not, and only just managed to keep herself from
smashing them all before storming from the room in
frustration.

She had gone about halfway around the courtyard
when she heard the weeping. It came from an open
doorway like all the others, only this one gave up a
strong, bitter smell along with the sound of desperate
sorrow. Kithi peered cautiously around the doorpost
and saw a large chamber, lavishly lit and scrupulously
clean, without even the shadow of dust or the hint of

cobwebs. The smell of beer in all the stages of its brewing permeated the room in clouds of yeasty incense. Wide-mouthed clay jugs and brewpots like the drinking cups of giants stood in orderly rows against the walls, as did a host of tightly covered reed and willow baskets.

At the place where the rows of jugs met the rows of baskets, the goddess sat huddled on the floor, filling her cupped hands with tears. That she *was* a goddess was unquestionable, to Kithi's mind: She was the living double of the image from Mama Nila's entryway, though her posture was hardly imposing and her flail and sickle lay carelessly discarded at her side. Despite this, the radiance of her face shone brighter than the many oil lamps decking the chamber walls, and even her harshest sobs sounded sweeter than birdsong.

This was *not* what Kithi had expected to find in Mama Nila's house. Back home in the village, the headman's tales always stressed how testy the gods could be, especially when mere mortals stumbled upon them doing anything less than completely dignified. Such accidental meetings between gods and mortals were supposedly behind the creation of at least seven different breeds of snake, all of them the unlucky humans who had seen a god as he did not wish to be seen.

I don't think I'd enjoy being a snake, Kithi reflected, her heart fluttering as she backed off from the doorway as silently as she could.

Stop that.

Kithi stopped. In fact, she froze where she stood.

Don't be afraid. Come in. Talk to me. I'm lonesome with only my grief for company.

The words sounded inside Kithi's head, but they never touched her ears. She found herself obeying, even the command that bid her not be afraid. On stiff legs she entered Mama Nila's brewing room and approached the sorrowing goddess.

*Oh, dear, *that's* not right.* The goddess regarded

Kithi's approach critically, one gorgeously beringed finger to her cheek. *If I release you to follow your own will, are you going to run away from me?*

"Not if you're not going to turn me into a snake," Kithi said through wooden lips.

Nonsense. The goddess was miffed. Her earrings, gold shaped like ripe heads of grain, flared for an instant and Kithi's mastery of her own body was restored.

The goddess stared at the girl intently, like a child studying a grasshopper. Kithi remembered being examined like that before, by the village headman. She hadn't liked it then, either.

"Now *you* stop that," she demanded. "I'm sorry if I saw you weeping, but I didn't steal any of your power. And if I did, you wouldn't get it back by staring at me like a constipated owl!"

The goddess laughed. "*I* know that, silly." This time the words came from her mouth, not her mind. "It's only the gods who believe such tales, not the goddesses. Besides, I haven't much power to lose. Do you not know me? I am Tareth, daughter of the Lady."

"I know," Kithi said. "I recognized you from your picture out in the entryway. Mama Nila already told me that you don't have—" She checked herself before blurting what the beerwoman had said about Tareth's half-mortal blood. A goddess was a goddess, after all, and it never did to offend one needlessly. "I mean— er— That was you in my head then, too, wasn't it?" she asked quickly.

Tareth nodded. "It was wrong of me. I am supposed to keep quiet while I'm hiding here, so that *he* can't find me, but when I heard you thinking those scornful things about me, I couldn't help myself."

"Oh." Kithi remembered all too well how she'd scoffed at Tareth's unwieldy and unsuitable garb and wished the goddess had not. "I—I'm sorry."

"Sorry for being right?" Tareth sighed. "How could I change you into a snake when I can't change my job

or even the way I'm dressed unless my Mother so
ordains? You laughed at my clothes, but I didn't
choose them—Have you ever tried striding across the
heavens in a skirt *this* tight?—any more than I chose
to be assigned the part of a guardian-goddess. I may
be powerless, but why must I be useless, too?"

Kithi was only half-listening. There was something
else the goddess had said that caught the girl's attention. "Hiding?" she now asked. "From who? Who's
not supposed to find you?"

"Obviously not you, child." The sound of Mama
Nila's voice behind her made Kithi jump. The beerwoman came into her brewing room, hands on hips,
and gave both girl and goddess a severe look. "When
I agreed to shelter you, O Tareth, it was as a favor to
your blessed Mother. I will not lose the Lady's favor
just because her daughter has no sense."

"It's not her fault, Mama Nila!" Kithi grabbed the
beerwoman's arm. "I found her by accident."

"And was her speech with you in the entryway also
an accident?" Mama Nila shook her head and gently
removed the girl's hold on her. "You are fortunate,
Kithi: The gods do not speak to every mortal because
not every mortal has the ears to hear them. Those
who do are also those whose hands hold magic."

"All that my hands are ever going to hold is the
beermakers' trade. Beermaking isn't magic," Kithi
objected.

"Some think it is," Mama Nila replied. "Some
thought the first bread was magic, too, and what are
bread and beer but yeast and water and grain? Yet
with those three stones I can build a palace that will
shelter all Agatash from hunger and thirst."

"Not if *he* finds me," Tareth said. "Zarik isn't famous for leaving one brick on top of another, let
alone three."

"Zarik!" Kithi gasped, knowing the name, feeling
her bones go cold.

"The Lord of War." Mama Nila nodded sadly. "The

bloody-handed, the vulture-winged, the shatterer of cities, the blind god. And he will find you, O Tareth, depend on it. It's only a matter of time now."

As if to prove the truth of Mama Nila's words, the air within the brewing chamber began to throb with a beat as regular as a healthy heart. The walls quaked in time, and the rafters overhead shook while the jugs and baskets jumped like fleas on a drumhead.

"The footsteps of the god," said Mama Nila dryly. "Zarik is coming to claim his own. Of all the gods he is the only one who has never reached into the minds of mortals."

"He can't," Tareth said. "That is the one power forbidden him. My Mother said it is because he does you poor little things enough harm by his words and deeds. If his thoughts invaded your minds as well, the land would be overrun with madmen and the gods would wither away, unworshiped."

"I wish you had a little of his reticence then, O Tareth. Or perhaps you truly want to become his bride. Why else would you have given away your hiding place by speaking mind to mind with this girl? I used my small arts to weave a spell of sanctuary over this house, but all I have is mortal magic. It baffled Zarik's questing senses only so long as you cooperated and kept still." She sighed. "Nothing shatters an eggshell better than the chick within."

"I was so *lonely!*" Tareth wailed.

"You'll have company enough when your promised husband arrives," the beerwoman said, offering no sympathy. "And I will have company in the grave, thanks to you." She put one arm around Kithi's shoulders and added, "I am truly sorry that your first day in my service will also be your last on earth. I meant to train you as the goddess' handmaid, to teach you to sing and dance for her, to keep her amused, to keep her *quiet* until such time as Zarik might turn his sightless eyes to other things."

"Is *that* what I'm to be here? A *handmaid?*" Kithi demanded, indignant. "That doesn't require someone

bold or even halfway clever! Why didn't you just buy
her a pet monkey in the marketplace instead?"

Mama Nila folded her arms. "A monkey is not
clever enough to learn the scribe's art, nor bold
enough to serve a goddess face-to-face."

"The scribe's art?" Kithi echoed. Her mind's eye
filled with multitudes of dents and scribbles marching
across an infinity of tablets, and her soul yearned to
know the intriguing, alluring, maddeningly inaccessible
secrets they contained.

"To preserve Tareth's silence, but to allow her still
to speak with you, you would have brought the goddess fresh clay on which to write her wishes and commands *in silence*," the beerwoman explained. Another,
heavier sigh shook her body almost as heartily as Zarik's ever-nearing footfalls. "Now that shall never be."

"Run, child, run away!" Tareth urged, her beautiful
eyes full of pity. "Perhaps you can save yourself."

"Too late," Mama Nila said. "Your essence clings
to her as thickly as to me, and you know Zarik's ways:
He will take the scent and hunt her down."

"Call on your Mother, Tareth!" Kithi cried. "Ask
the Lady for help!"

"My Mother whispers to the grain and makes it
grow, conjures fruit out of the seed, and fills empty
houses with the chatter and din of children. Zarik
howls at the moon and leaves fields in ashes and
houses desolate. If her creations cannot stand against
the Lord of War, neither can she."

"That was why the Lady came to me," Mama Nila
put in. "In all Agatash, mine is the only house that
keeps a proper shrine to Tareth. A goddess of borders
and boundaries isn't of much interest in a city where
good, solid bricks do her work for her. The Lady
asked me to conceal her daughter and I agreed, for
the sake of the love I bore her."

"Also because the Lady probably threatened to let
the barley lie unsprouted in the earth if you didn't,"
Kithi stated. "No more barley, no more beer. Don't
tell *me* that love doesn't follow fortune like a dog."

Goddess and beerwoman exchanged an astonished look. "She *is* clever, this one," said Tareth.

"If only she were clever enough to— *Oh!*" Mama Nila never got to finish that sentence, for just then there was a crunching, rumbling noise as a great hand streaked with deepest scarlet tore a massive hole right through the roof of the brewing chamber. A stray piece of falling tile struck the beerwoman senseless on the floor as the blazing, eyeless face of Zarik, Lord of War, peered in, his many necklaces of swords and bones and spearheads clattering.

"Where is she?" he roared. Empty jugs burst apart like milkweed pods, full ones shivered with spiderweb cracks. "Where is my promised bride?" His head swayed slowly from side to side, his hairy nostrils snuffling, searching for Tareth's scent.

Kithi thought her heart had stopped. When she looked up into the face of the Lord of War and heard his awful voice battering her skull, her limbs turned to stone. She might have stood thus forever if not for one small, obstinate spark within her that flared into a full blaze of defiance. *Flesh or stone, what does it matter to Zarik?* it demanded. *He smashes both, indifferent. If you must die, at least die trying to live!*

It was like a slap in the face, a sudden sluicing of icy water. In one instant, Kithi shook off her terrified trance, and in the next she seized the nearest beer jug, dumping the contents all over herself and Tareth. The goddess screeched in shock as the reek of beer drenched the room. Before that scream ended, Kithi had picked up a second jug and used it in the same manner as the first. While Tareth gasped and spluttered, Zarik's blocky head with its thatch of gore-matted hair dipped lower into the house and turned toward the sound.

Nimble as a grasshopper, Kithi sprang onto Tareth's back, wrapping skinny limbs tightly around her neck and waist. Before Tareth could cast her off, she planted her lips close to the goddess' ear and urgently whispered, "Let me be your words, O Tareth, and maybe—just maybe—you'll leave here with your freedom and I'll stay here with my life. A bargain?"

Tareth shivered, her eyes fixed on the Lord of War, but Kithi saw her nod her head once, ever so slightly, giving consent. *A—a bargain,* came the unspoken words.

Good, Kithi replied, knowing that thoughts and words were all one between the two of them. *Now say exactly what I tell you.*

"Hail, O my beloved lord Zarik!" Tareth's sweet voice trembled only a little bit as she turned Kithi's thoughts to words. "My heart has hungered for you while you have dallied far from me. Is this how you show your love?"

"Love?" The Lord of War lowered and raised his eyelids, shuttering the gaping sockets in hideous parody of a puzzled blink. "What are you talking about? You are the one who ran away!"

"From you, O my treasure?" *Laugh!* Kithi ordered, and Tareth did as she was told. "Nonsense! If I hastened from your presence, it was only so that I might make all things ready for our wedding day."

The blind god smashed his fists down and demolished a goodly section of the brewing room wall, then stepped through the gap and seated himself on a throne of rubble. Kithi could hear the distant sound of panicky shrieks and prayers going up from every street and shrine in Agatash as the populace fled the presence of the war god.

"You lie," he said. "I'll teach you better ways once we are wed. All that our wedding requires is you and me, standing up before the other gods. I was ready months ago; where were you? *Hiding,* that's where!"

"Yes, my lord." *Sound sadder!* "I tremble before your wisdom. I *was* hiding: Hiding until your gift might be prepared."

Zarik's eyebrows rose. "Gift?"

Now we've got his interest. "Oh, yes, my lord!" Tareth clapped her hands together. "A gift of such splendor, such magnificence, such power that—!"

"Power, eh?" Zarik smiled and stroked his chin, streaking the ashes of immolated cities through the blood of slaughtered peoples. "What is this gift? Come here and tell me!"

Do as he says.

Tareth complied, growing in stature with every step she took until she was of the same majestic proportions as the Lord of War. Dislodged from her first hold, Kithi scrambled to get a fresh grasp on the goddess, coming to rest clinging inside a link of one of Tareth's necklaces.

Zarik brought his face close to Tareth's and sniffed mightily. "What's that I smell?" he demanded. "You stink of mortals and their trivial scurryings. Is this bitter stench part of the spell that hid you? Did your Mother scare one of her lickspittle worshipers into keeping you away from me?"

Tareth folded her hands protectively over Kithi. The girl could only see glimpses of the war god's face through the goddess' shielding fingers. Privately she prayed that her ruse would hold, that the smell of beer covering Tareth and herself would blunt Zarik's keen nose just enough.

"My lord is so quick to anger," Tareth said. *No, no, don't make it sound like a* bad *thing! Pretend you admire it!* "And so quick-witted, too! There's no hiding anything from you. If you smell a mortal here, it is only a poor old woman lying unconscious at your feet. I pray you be mindful of her."

"Mindful?" the god bawled. "When *she* is to blame for keeping us apart? I'll be mindful enough to crush her like a bug!" He raised himself partway from the rubble pile and began stamping around blindly with one huge, heavily sandaled foot. It was all Tareth could do to dart out her hand and remove the beerwoman's limp body to safety.

"My lord, as you love me, hear me! This woman is a great sorceress, mistress of wondrous magics! When I knew the unequaled joy of being your chosen bride, I flew to her at once so that she might bend her arts to the making of a wedding gift worthy of your excellence! *That* is what you smell and nothing more!"

Zarik looked suspicious. "So you say. And yet I think I also catch the scent of *another* mortal here."

Laugh! Laugh again, and this time give him a little kiss.

You want me to kiss *him? Are you mad, child? No!*

Kiss him now, or kiss your freedom good-bye.

The goddess gritted her teeth. The expression on the war god's face when her lips brushed his cheek was a jumble of surprise and delight, bewilderment and misgiving.

"My lord, you smell the mortal child whose blood was poured into the pot where the sorceress brewed my gift to you. It is a potion that binds heart to heart until the universe itself crawls back into the heavenly Egg that spawned it. When two drink it from one cup, he who drinks first becomes the master, she who drinks second his abject and absolute slave. *This* is the gift I offer you, freely and of my own will, because my love for you is greater than any wish to be myself."

The war god leaned back on the crumbled heap of bricks from Mama Nila's ruined wall. "Naturally," he said. "All right, pour it out and let us drink. I have other places to be and more important things to do."

"My lord . . . I can't."

"What?"

Speak as if your world had come to an end. "Because the potion is not yet complete. It only wants one last ingredient to assure its power over me."

"Well, then stir it in and be done! I'm in a hurry. What does it lack?"

A whisper, now; a meek and fearful whisper, O Tareth!

"Your tears."

Zarik's fist came down, smashing fallen bricks to brick dust. "I am the Lord of War! I shed no tears!"

"But my lord, you must, or else the potion has no virtue. I will still be your wife, but a wife like my Mother and the other goddesses. Not one of them has made herself utterly subject to her lord, not even those whose husbands are stronger than they. Those who can't stand up to their mates directly do so by trickery. Even your Father, the Lord of Storms, the mightiest among us, has never fully ruled his wife. She dupes him into thinking that her desires are his and has her own way in all things. The other gods look on and laugh, never suspecting that their wives do the same to them. Is *that* what you would have for us?"

"You would not dare." Zarik's scowl filled his empty eye sockets with lightning. "I would destroy you!"

"With respect, my dearest lord, you would only destroy me if you caught me at it. And until that time, you would not sleep well for wondering."

The Lord of War took a deep breath and let it out very slowly. "Tareth, you are wise. All the more reason to have you drink this potion with me, I suppose. Yet it may not be for, by the Egg of Worlds, do you dream there is anything in all the universe that ever *could* make me weep?"

The goddess stooped to pick up the largest brewpot left whole, standing, and full. She moved gracefully to stand behind Zarik, her arms around his neck, the pot held just beneath the lower lid of his right socket, and softly breathed into his ear the lone word: "Peace."

The tears rushed from Zarik's empty eyes and splashed everywhere. Kithi let out a whoop of triumph. "I have seen you weep, O Zarik! I, a mortal, have witnessed your tears! And now— now— Haste, O Tareth! Drink it and he is yours to rule!"

The goddess acted at the speed of thought, draining the brewpot in a single gulp just as the Lord of War realized how he had been gulled. His bellow of outrage was so loud it knocked Tareth from her feet. Kithi screamed as the goddess toppled backwards, screamed louder as her small hands lost their grip on Tareth's necklace, and kept on screaming up until the instant that she hit the ground headfirst and drank darkness.

* * *

"There you are, my dear." Mama Nila's face swam into sight through the parting clouds shrouding Kithi's eyes. The beerwoman changed the damp cloth on the girl's brow for a cooler one. "I was afraid that you wouldn't be coming back to us in time for the festival, and that would have been a great pity."

Kithi sat up and looked around. She was back in her room, lying on the leopard bed, but the coverlet beneath her had become a thick, soft, exquisitely quilted piece of purple silk embroidered with gold. A hundred questions filled her aching head, but the only one she could ask was: "What festival?"

"Why, the festival honoring the goddess Tareth, child. There have been great doings in the heavens and the earth since you last closed your eyes. All of the temple oracles have spoken, telling the king and the people of Agatash that they are to build a great shrine to the goddess and give her proper worship."

"Proper worship *if they value their lives.*" Tareth appeared at the beerwoman's back, grinning. "You left out the best part, Mama Nila; shame on you! It isn't every day that a mere half-mortal brings the Lord of War to heel. Now the safety of the boundaries that I guard is enforced by Zarik himself. His strength has become mine and looking after my business will keep him from starting quite so many great wars. Oh, I can't wait until they've built my temple! At last I'll have plenty of *real* work to do: Answering prayers, accepting offerings, conferring with my beloved high priestess." She winked meaningfully at Kithi.

The girl got out of bed and bowed low to the goddess. "O Tareth, I decline the honor. My father paid this good woman my bond-price and gave me into her service. I must respect that bargain."

"But I would make you my Voice!" the goddess protested. "You would live in luxury, with a thousand slaves to serve you! And you would rather stay here and learn to make beer?" Kithi nodded. "Well! I can't say I understand, but take my blessings anyhow. And

now I must be gone: The king of Agatash is invoking
me on the steps of the Lady's temple. If I don't appear
at once, Mother will say I have bad manners." She
slashed the air with flail and sickle and was gone.

Mama Nila looked at Kithi as if she'd dropped from
the sky. "I never thought I'd hear a girl turn down
such a great reward. But then again, I never thought
I'd live to see the truth behind the tales that claim a
god's power trickles from him with his tears."

"Truth is sometimes only what you believe it to be,"
Kithi said. "If Zarik hadn't also believed those old
tales, we might have been in trouble." She laughed.
"Thank all the gods it worked! I had too much to lose
if it hadn't."

"Your life and mine, yes. But what you just threw
away—"

"I don't want slaves or a temple or to be anyone's
Voice but my own. Oh, but there is one thing I do
want, what I fought for almost as much as for our
lives." Kithi took Mama Nila by the hand and led her
from the room, taking her across the courtyard to the
room of the stacked clay tablets.

"Here is true magic, Mama Nila. Here is *my* chosen
reward." She chose one and placed it in the beerwoman's hands. "Teach me."

GIFTS OF THE KAMI

by Carol E. Leever

Carol E. Leever currently works as a Computer Science Instructor at America River College. She is an avid reader and has been writing since she was a child. A student of the martial arts, she has been studying Kosho Shorei Kempo for years. She claims that she gets some of her best story ideas from lessons taught in class. Her stories have appeared in both *Sword and Sorceress* and in *Marion Zimmer Bradley's Fantasy Magazine*.

The lesson in this story reminds me of a button I saw at a convention once: "Oh, no! Not another learning experience!"

Muted sunlight slipped through the clouds and gleamed brightly off the slender dagger in Neko's hand. She stared at it in delight, her jade catlike eyes shining with pleasure. Over the years since she'd become the student of the Kami, the wild gods of the woodlands, they had given her gifts of clothing and food, but this was the first time they'd ever given her a weapon. A real weapon! Not a sword like the samurai carried, perhaps, but it was a beautiful dagger—a gracefully curved *tanto* from a sword set.

Her teachers, thirty golden temple cats, sat beside her in the tall grass upon a wind-stirred hillside. Shape-changers all of them, they preferred their natural feline forms and were sprawled lazily upon the grass, tails twitching in the rising breeze. Only one wore the Kami's more human form, her tall body clad in a golden kimono. But human shape or no, the face was still that of a cat, and her whiskers twitched in amusement as Neko examined the blade.

"Thank you," Neko exclaimed with youthful exuberance. She quickly rose to her feet so that she could bow to all the cats before her. "It's beautiful. I'll carry it with honor, and treasure it."

The kimono-clad Kami who'd given her the blade blinked slanted eyes in curiosity. Her thick fluffy tail flicked idly beneath the golden robes. "Treasure it? It's only a blade, Little Feline," the cat purred, calling Neko by the use-name all the Kami favored.

"It's a *tanto*!" Neko protested. "That's almost a *katana,* and the samurai carry their honor in their swords."

"Daggers and swords are nothing more than things," the cat informed her. "And things can be lost, or stolen, or broken. Honor, however, is a true possession and can only be given away. It should never be associated with a thing. Rather, you should treasure the knowledge we have given you and the lessons we have taught you—not the things. The things have no value."

"But it's a weapon," Neko attempted again, wondering why the Kami taught her the martial arts and yet seemed to hold weapons in such low esteem. She despaired of ever earning a sword from them.

"A weapon," the cat shrugged dismissively. "Trust to your own body and quick mind. Both will serve you far better than any weapon."

Neko's instinct was to protest the lesson in values and simply express her pleasure in the gift, but before she could speak, thunder rumbled far off in the distance. The sprawled cats stiffened suddenly and sat up, ears perked forward attentively. Several raised their noses to the air and sniffed the cool breeze. The wind was rising again. Far off down the hill Neko could see dark clouds rolling toward them, shadowing the wide river valley below the woodlands.

A storm was fast approaching, the angry billowing clouds promising rain and lightning. Like all cats, the

Kami hated being wet. Already Neko could see their golden fur bristling uncomfortably. One or two meowed plaintively, and they all rose and headed swiftly for the protection of the woods. They whisked behind flowering plants and green ferns, scrambled up trees, and raced along branches. The last flicking tail vanished swiftly from sight, and Neko was alone on the hillside.

Laughing softly at her teachers' behavior—they might be woodland gods, but they were first and foremost cats—Neko glanced around for her sandals. She'd removed them earlier to practice her martial-arts katas on the hillside. Spying them near the bottom of the hill, she set aside her new dagger and headed quickly down to retrieve them.

Eager to catch up to her teachers and return to the shelter of her camp to ride out the approaching storm, Neko slipped the sandals onto her feet and raced back up the hill to retrieve the dagger. She bent, hand outstretched, fingers poised to grab, only to realize, in some confusion, that the dagger was gone.

Neko frowned, stepping back one pace to scan the bent stalks of grass before her. Save for a few early autumn leaves, the ground was empty. Wondering if the dagger might have slipped farther down the hill, Neko searched the area swiftly. A sense of panic overtook her as she looked. Hadn't she told the Kami that she'd treasure their gift? It had been in her possession only a brief moment, and already she'd lost it! What would they say? What would they think of her? How could they ever trust her again with another such gift? She had to find that blade!

A sharp musky scent caught her attention, and she froze. A rustle of leaves and a chuckle of amusement drew her gaze upward to the trees. A man, clad in black robes with a sword stuck through his belt, watched her from the branches of a great elm—a man, or perhaps not, for there was something decidedly animallike about his shape. His feet were bare and his toes were too long, so much so that they literally gripped the branch upon which he stood. His skin was coated with a light dusting of grayish fur, his face oddly set with too wide a grin. And there was something else, something odd about the way he leaned forward, looking as if he should topple off the branch despite his gripping toes. Frowning, Neko cocked her head to one side, seeing then the strong prehensile tail that held him in place.

Neko's eyes widened. Briefly she thought that perhaps he was one of the Kami—a monkey-spirit. But there was something too earthy about him. The Kami gleamed with their own inner light, radiating a certain luminosity that could not be mistaken. This man or creature crouched in the trees was too mortal. A changeling, then, she decided, not unlike herself, human enough but with something of the Kami within him.

Then she noticed the dagger clutched tightly in one of the stranger's hands. "My dagger!" she exclaimed, taking a step forward.

"Yours?" the stranger said mockingly. "I found it lying on the grass. That makes it mine."

Outraged, Neko glared at him. He intended to steal her dagger! "That's mine and you know it!"

"Is it, now? And how am I supposed to know that? I think you are a liar."

Neko felt heat flush through her skin. No one had ever called her a liar before. The insult was not to be borne! "Who are you?" Neko demanded.

He grinned at that. "Saru-Oukou at your service. And would you perhaps be Neko-Butou-San, called Cat-Dancing by the Kami?"

"You've heard of me?" Neko nodded. Saru-Oukou, a self-titled Monkey-King. The Kami had warned her about monkey-kin. Thieves, tricksters, cunning warriors, they surrounded themselves with illusion. Only a fool fought a monkey. But that was her dagger, and foolish or not she intended to get it back—one way or another. "If you've heard of me, then you know I can take the dagger if I want to." She'd never actually tested her martial skill against another Kami-touched creature, but she saw no reason to let Saru know that.

"No, you can't," Saru laughed. "Truth is, I don't believe you're the great fighter everyone claims you are. And to prove it, I'm going to keep this dagger."

Neko glared at the creature. She knew her teachers would warn her against letting anyone goad her into such a challenge. They'd remind her that nothing was quite as it seemed; traps came in all forms. But she couldn't just let this creature get away with stealing her dagger! "Give it back now, and I won't hurt you!"

"Come and take it," he grinned insolently. He shot a quick glance at the angry storm rolling toward them. "Oh, I forgot. Cats don't like rain, do they?"

"You think a little storm is going to stop me?" Neko laughed. And with that she leaped, springing toward the branch Saru was perched upon. Monkeys might be masters at swinging through trees, but cats knew how to climb too. He'd find no escape that way.

Saru laughed and leaped backward, vacating the branch just as Neko caught it and swung herself up onto the perch. She steadied herself and looked for her opponent.

"Very good!" Saru laughed from the next tree over. "But how good are you at keeping your balance?" And with that he swung forward and landed on the far end of Neko's perch. Then grabbing the branch above him to brace himself, he proceeded to jump up and down, shaking the entire tree violently. Neko could feel her feet slipping, and she reached out to grasp another branch to steady herself. But the shaking only grew more violent, and her hand closed over empty air.

Knowing she was going to fall, she used her momentum to dive forward instead. Arms outstretched, she tackled the startled man, pulling them both to the earth. They hit the ground hard, Saru struggling to escape Neko's grasp. Their angry struggle sent them both rolling down the grassy slope of the hill.

Digging her heels into the loamy earth and clutching

at the long stalks of grass, Neko managed finally to slow her descent. She rolled swiftly to her feet just as Saru stopped and scrambled up. With no trees nearby to leap to, nothing to climb upon, Saru had no choice but to turn and face Neko. His body moved instinctively into a fighter's pose, but Neko was ready for him. She dropped low and kicked out one leg, sweeping his feet out from underneath him.

With a cry of surprise, Saru fell, but he kicked out as he did so, catching Neko a glancing blow to the shoulder. Grunting from pain, she caught hold of his foot and twisted. The bone should have broken, should have snapped in her hand, but somehow Saru succeeded in flipping his body around at an odd angle and freeing himself from Neko's grasp.

They faced off again, and this time Saru pressed the attack, lunging violently forward, his powerful hands moving in a series of blinding blows. But Neko sidestepped them all, kicking him once in the chest and then twice more in the head. He fell backward, and even as he dropped, Neko moved in for the kill, knocking the wind out of him with one well-placed punch. Then she trapped him in a grappling hold that held him immobile, his head bent at an odd, painful angle.

"Do you yield?" Neko demanded, seeing no reason to push the fight any further. All she wanted was her dagger, and save for the bruised ache in her shoulder from his kick, she held no other grudge against the man. Truthfully, she was rather surprised the fight had ended so quickly—she'd expected Saru to be a better fighter. The stories the Kami had told her about Monkey-spirits had suggested far more cunning and challenge.

"I yield!" he cried out, grimacing from her tight grip. "You can have the dagger."

"And an apology," Neko insisted. "For the theft in the first place—and for calling me a liar."

"Granted!" he agreed quickly. "I apologize. And

just to prove I am sincere, you may have my sword as well."

For a moment Neko froze. His sword? A real *katana*. She'd dreamed of owning one. Had her father not cast her out of her home on her naming day, she certainly would have earned one by now. She had hoped the Kami would see fit to give her one, but so far they had never even mentioned it. Perhaps they thought she was not yet ready for so noble a weapon? Whatever their reason, she saw no point in passing up the chance to gain one on her own.

"You would give up your blade?" she asked in amazement.

"I'm not a samurai," he replied, wincing again from the tight hold straining the muscles of his neck. "It's not a mark of honor for me. It's merely a possession."

And a valuable one at that—she could see gems gleaming from the hilt of the sword. What would the blade beneath the pale wooden sheath look like?

Making her decision, Neko released Saru, snatching her dagger from his belt as she did so. She stepped back, well out of the way should he decide instead to turn on her. Rather, he sighed in resignation, scratching ruefully at the gray fur coating his overstrained neck. "You are every bit the fighter people claim you are," he informed her sheepishly. "I should have known better than to steal from you. But it is in my nature to steal, you see . . . so hard to help myself."

Despite the situation, Neko found herself flushing from pride. Too often she heard criticism of her skill from her Kami teachers. Praise from another warrior like herself was unexpected and rather gratifying, especially since she suspected Saru was many years her senior.

"The sword," she prompted.

Saru smiled suddenly. "Ah, yes, the sword. Here . . . catch!" And he yanked the sword, sheath and all, from his belt and tossed it to her. Startled, Neko caught hold of the weapon and then stared after Saru in confusion as he raced up the hill. A moment later he vanished into the trees, leaving her completely alone on the hillside.

Bewildered, Neko glanced around, wondering what might have caused Saru's unexpected retreat. Their fight was over; it could not be fear that drove him away. And his amused smile had not suggested any trace of shame.

Shrugging she looked down at the weapon even as the first drops of rain from the storm struck her. The wooden sheath was white and oddly unadorned, but the hilt of the *katana* was finely wrought. Silver, and not the traditional ivory, it was etched with the images of lightning bolts, inlaid with fine gems of every hue. Closing her fist eagerly around the hilt, she grasped the sheath firmly and pulled, anxious to see the blade. Oddly, the sword did not budge.

Thinking perhaps there was a catch that held it firmly within its sheath, Neko turned it over, closely inspecting it. But search as she did, she could find no catch. Frowning, she tugged again, putting all her strength into the motion.

The sword did not budge.

Twice more she tried, bracing the blade at last against the rain-soaked ground and holding it rooted with her foot so that she could pull with both hands. Still the blade would not budge. She couldn't get it out of its sheath!

Glaring angrily up at the line of trees before her, Neko imagined the Saru was laughing at her efforts from some hidden perch. He'd given her a worthless sword! If she couldn't draw it from its sheath, she couldn't use it.

It was the scent that warned her of sudden danger— a scent that her catlike senses detected swiftly enough to save her life. A sharp, biting tang of rising brimstone filled the air. Instinct took over and she leaped away, diving and rolling to safety just as a blazing bolt of lightning arced through the heavens and struck the ground where she had been standing only moments earlier. As it was, the burning blast of lightning sent out a shock that knocked her down, and only fear alone allowed her to roll precariously to her feet. She stared in horror at the scorched patch of grass upon the drenched ground.

Lightning! She'd almost been struck by lightning! She'd heard of such things happening—heard also that lightning never struck the same place twice. But a moment later the rising scent hit her again, and with a cry of shock she leaped away once more. Again a white-hot bolt of lightning struck the place she'd been standing. This time the shock of power that filled the air completely knocked the wind out of her.

Hitting the ground with a teeth-rattling jolt, she gasped for breath even as she tried to scramble to her feet, the useless sword still clutched unnoticed in her hand. She shot a frightened look toward the safety of the trees. Panic took over. Warriors she could handle. Lightning from heaven was something else entirely. She turned and ran, racing desperately up the slippery hillside, wanting only to reach the relative safety of the forest.

The sharp scent rose again, this time directly in front of her. She dodged aside, but the blinding crack of lightning knocked her backward and sent her sliding down the streaming hill on her side. She was drenched now with rainwater, her clothes grass-stained and muddy, her long black braid tangled with bits of leaves and twigs.

Bruised from each near miss, she forced herself back onto her feet, and tried again to climb the now scorched hillside. But a deafening crack of thunder rumbled through the land, and a fourth flash of lightning delivered the inhumanly tall shape of a great, angry man.

Skidding to a halt, Neko stared at the stranger in horror. Clad in silk robes of sky-blue, he towered over Neko, nearly as tall as the trees themselves. Like the Kami, he glowed with a deep, inner light. But unlike

Neko's gentle teachers, there was nothing of peace or calm within this stranger. His eyes flashed with the contained power of the lightning and thunder, and his ageless face was twisted in rage.

Though they had never met, Neko knew him immediately, and she quickly bowed in frightened reverence. "Susanoo-Sama," she greeted the angry Storm God. "How have I angered you?"

Susanoo's frown deepened. "You are not Saru-Oukou!"

"No, Susanoo-Sama. I am Neko-Butou, student of the Kami." She could only hope that mentioning her connection to the angry god's gentle woodland cousins would save her from his wrath.

"That is my sword!" he growled, and thunder echoed through his voice. Around them the wind rose with his anger.

Neko's eyes widened with shock. His sword! Not Saru's! She'd kill the little thief. "Forgive me, Susanoo-Sama," she apologized quickly. "I did not know. Saru gave it to me. Here, take it back." She held out the weapon, hilt first, eager to appease his anger.

Somewhat mollified, he yanked the sword from her grasp and held it up. Clasping hold of the hilt, he yanked hard to pull the blade from the sheath. But as before, the sword did not budge.

Neko felt the blood drain from her face; she suspected now that Saru's treachery went farther than simply saddling her with his theft.

Susanoo's eyes darkened with anger as he pulled again. Again the sheath held fast, and he inspected the wooden sheath more intently. "This is not my sheath!" He held the sword out to her. "Remove it at once!"

Trembling, Neko gazed helplessly up at the angry god. "Forgive me, Susanoo-Sama, but I cannot. I've tried already. I could not pull the blade from the sheath either."

Susanoo's eyes flared with fury, and the wind rose

violently, buffeting Neko's shivering body. Lightning cracked across the sky, brilliant and terrifying. Unexpectedly Susanoo threw the weapon down at Neko's feet. "You have until nightfall to remove the sword from the sheath and return it to me! Do it, or I shall kill you, student of the Kami or not!" And in a flash, as quickly as he'd appeared, he was gone, leaving only a charred circle of grass upon the ground.

Until nightfall? Stunned, Neko glanced up at the streaming sky. The clouds were black and angry, and she could see no sign of the sun. Still, by the muted light all around her, she guessed she had no more than a couple of hours before nightfall. A couple of hours to figure out how to get the sword out of the sheath, or the Storm God would kill her. She had no doubt that her death would be swift, painful, and absolute.

Shivering from the cold, her clothing completely soaked with rainwater, Neko knelt in the muddy grass to retrieve the sword. Futilely she tried several more times to yank the weapon free. Finally, in desperation, she drew her dagger and used the blade to try to pry the weapon from the sheath. It was no use.

She tried instead to cut away the sheath, using the dagger to carve pieces off the wooden frame. But that, too, proved futile. Even the razor blade of the Kami's gift made no mark in the wooden sheath. If even a god's strength could not pry the sheath free of the sword, what hope did she have of doing so?

But there had to be some way—Susanoo had claimed that the sheath was not his. That suggested only one explanation—the sheath belonged to Saru. He'd stolen the sword. He'd then placed it in a sheath that no one could remove in order to make the weapon useless to anyone else, and then he'd given it to Neko to deflect the Storm God's wrath. Her teachers had been right. Nothing was as it seemed. She'd thought she'd won her battle against Saru, but she could see now that he'd intended her to win all along.

But why steal the sword in the first place unless he intended to gain some use from it? She had no doubt

he'd given it to her to throw Susanoo well off his
trail—the responsibility of returning the weapon now
rested solely on Neko's shoulders, leaving Saru in the
clear. Safe from the Storm God's wrath he might be,
but it still left him without the sword he desired.
Unless . . .

"Unless he intended to retrieve it," Neko murmured to herself. She frowned thoughtfully. What was
it Saru had said to her? 'It is in my nature to steal . . .
I can't help myself.'

A plan suggested itself to her, and she smiled
slowly. It might be in the monkey's nature to steal,
but cats had certain natures all their own. She could
see now that fighting Saru had been foolish, but there
were other ways around such creatures.

Rising to her feet, Neko slipped the *katana* through
her belt, fastening it securely at her side. Then pushing
her dripping hair out of her face, she made her way
resolutely up the hill and headed into the embracing
green of the woods. She walked deep into the forest,
glad of the dense foliage overhead that protected her
somewhat from the cold rain still pouring from the
sky. She forced herself to relax, forced her aching
body to move with a natural, easy grace despite the
constraint of time upon her life. Sunset was fast approaching. She could only hope she'd have time
enough to work her plan.

She'd walked for perhaps a quarter of an hour,
growing all the more nervous and panic-stricken as
the time passed without incident, when a noise alerted
her to another's presence. She stopped when Saru
dropped lightly from the treetops and landed calmly
in the mud in front of her. His damp, fur-covered face
was filled with curiosity, and his eyes took in the sword
attached firmly to Neko's belt.

"Still have my sword, I see?" he remarked.

Neko raised one eyebrow. "You mean the Storm
God's sword, don't you?"

His eyes widened. "You met him, then?"

She nodded, forcing herself to appear more smug than angry.

"And you're still alive to tell the tale?" Surprise tainted his voice.

Neko shrugged calmly. "He almost killed me. But then he realized at the last moment that I wasn't you. He was horribly contrite, and apologized profusely for the misunderstanding. And just to prove he had no hard feelings, he gave me the sword. Said I could keep it."

Saru's mouth opened in shock, his gaze incredulous. "He gave you the sword!"

Neko nodded. "It's a beautiful weapon with a deadly blade. And it has great powers, too—he showed me how to use it to call down lightning from the heavens. I won't ever need any other weapon. In fact . . ." she yanked the dagger from her belt and tossed it onto the ground at Saru's feet. "You might as well have that. I don't need it anymore. The sword is a lot better than a little dagger."

And with that she continued walking, moving swiftly past the speechless man. She glanced briefly over her shoulder as she walked, watching Saru out of the corner of her eye. She saw him bend and snatch up the dagger, gazing down at it in bewildered disappointment. When he turned to gaze after Neko, she dropped one hand possessively onto the hilt of the sword and continued walking, leaving Saru far behind. She heard his muffled curse as he leaped back into the trees and disappeared among the branches.

Smiling in satisfaction, Neko made her way toward a small rocky outcrop where she'd camped the night before with her Kami teachers. As she'd guessed, the cats were nowhere to be seen, off someplace where she was certain it was dryer, warmer, and far safer. But there was shelter enough by the rocks to shield a small fire from the rain and the wind, and Neko set about lighting a campfire to warm herself.

It was growing late by the time she'd finished setting

up her camp, and she knew she had only moments
perhaps until the fateful setting of the sun. Her nerves
were stretched thin. Her body trembled from the gam-
ble she was taking. It took every ounce of discipline
she'd possessed to retain her outward calm. She
couldn't give anything away. Couldn't appear nervous.
Cats were famed for their apparent indifference, and
she drew upon that feline aloofness to get through the
next few moments.

Finishing at last with her evening preparations,
Neko removed her sandals and set them aside. Then
drawing the sword carefully from her belt, she placed
it beside her on the ground. Her heart was pounding,
her throat tight with tension, but she forced herself to
calmly remove a towel from her small bag of supplies
and begin drying her bare feet.

The fire crackled before her, its light casting ever-
growing shadows against the stony outcrop that sheltered it from the storm. The deepening shadows warned
Neko of the approach of nightfall, and she gritted her
teeth to stop the scream of frustration building inside
her. It was growing late—too late, perhaps.

And then a noise, soft, barely discernible caught
her attention—she forced herself not to react. Even
forewarned, she barely made it, barely saw the gray
shape that moved almost silently along the stony outcrop, nearly missed the long hand that reached out
and closed around the sword's sheath. Neko's hand
shot out, her fingers closing tightly over the hilt of the
katana. She hung on with all her strength as Saru tried
to snatch the sword away from her.

She held the hilt; he held the sheath—the sheath he
had placed upon the sword, the sheath only he could
remove. He yanked and the gleaming, razor sharp
blade of the Storm God's *katana* slipped free and
flashed in the last light of day. Neko leaped back and
stood holding the naked blade before her.

"Hey!" Saru stared in shocked surprise at the empty
sheath in his hands.

Neko grinned at him. "Monkeys may be trickier, but cats are quicker. And Storm Gods are never contrite!"

Saru eyes widened in horror even as lightning cracked only steps away from both of them. Saru stared up in shock at the towering shape of the enraged Storm God. Quickly Neko handed over the *katana* to its rightful owner. Susanoo's eyes blazed with delight, seeing his sword returned and the thief before him.

Saru yelped in horror and bolted away. The Storm God raced after him, crashing through the woods and shouting with a voice that echoed with thunder. Neko watched in satisfaction, seeing the leaping form of Saru swinging from tree to tree while he dodged the brilliant flashes of lightning that raced after him. After a time they disappeared entirely from sight, and the storm rolled away with them. The sky cleared, the stars came out, and only the far-off sound of thunder gave any indication that the pursuit was not yet over.

The warmth of the fire drew the thirty temple cats at last from their hiding places, and they emerged from the darkness to gather around Neko. But the thirtieth again took human shape, and Neko saw her shadow across the fire. The Kami crouched in the starlight, her golden kimono shimmering in the soft breeze, and Neko found herself grateful that the radiant light shining from within her teachers was peaceful and calm and not the raging power of the Storm God.

"You lost your dagger, Little Feline," the cat informed her, the amusement in her slanted green eyes leaving Neko no doubt that her teachers were quite aware of all that had occurred. The other cats were watching her curiously, their fluffy tails flicking in gentle unison.

"Yes," Neko agreed. "But it was just a thing. And things can be lost, or stolen, or broken. Far better to trust to my own body and quick mind. Both will serve me far better than any weapon." She grinned at them.

"I gained something more valuable than any weapon in the end."

"And what was that, Little Feline?"

Neko winked sheepishly at her teachers. "A valuable lesson."

Around her the cats ruffled their fur. Deep rumbling purrs filled the air. The thirtieth just smiled, pleased. "Perhaps you are learning after all."

The approval Neko heard in her voice was all the gift she needed.

ONE IN TEN THOUSAND

by Aimee Kratts

Aimee Kratts has a M.A. in Science Writing from Johns Hopkins University. She earns a living as a technical writer in the computer software industry.

She loves ancient Egypt, and this story was inspired by an exhibit called "The Splendors of Ancient Egypt" which she saw in Richmond, Virginia.

She dedicates this story to her grandmothers, June and Lillian.

There were no such things as gods and goddesses, that much Mery-Sekhmet knew. She waded thigh-deep in the Nile harvesting papyrus stalks with her father's day-laborers as she considered the problem further. The only magic in the world belonged to people like herself and her father. They shouldered the burden of the gods.

Cool, muddy water swirled about her legs as she tied the last stalk to her bundle and lunged toward shore. She moved quickly because she would already be in trouble when her father heard she was wasting her time in a harvest.

As she had anticipated, her father met her at the door of their home. He followed her down the cool, dark hallway into the courtyard and berated her with his every stride.

"You were to stay here and lay out new strips in the pressing room. You know you aren't supposed to . . ."

"I do this for Inu," said Mery-Sekhmet under her breath.

Her father would not be stopped. "I gave you permission to give that old woman one of the best papyrus scrolls. Why would you want to make another when we have one ready for her?"

She is like my mother!" Mery-Sekhmet bit her lip and looked down at her feet. When her father made no reply, she continued more softly, "If you would let me find another one of us to help, we wouldn't have to worry about running out of scrolls."

"You know that anyone with the least amount of guile greed who understood the power they possessed, would use it for themselves."

"Isn't that what we're doing when we decide who recovers from an illness? Whose child lives or dies? Whose spirit continues on? Aren't we doing it for ourselves?"

"Daughter, you know it's not like that. Don't twist words to make our actions sound evil."

Mery-Sekhmet pressed her lips together and narrowed her eyes. She knew she was being unfair to her father. They always used their gifts for good, and yet . . . and yet she knew that somehow, somewhere, there were others out there who could handle the same burden of responsibility and not turn it into something evil.

"Father, if you'd just let me look for someone," pleaded Mery-Sekhmet, "you could judge the person's character before we told them what they possessed."

Tired of the old argument, Khaemhat put a hand on his daughter's shoulder and gave a dismissive squeeze before he turned away. "Even if I agreed, our kind of magic exists in only one of ten thousand. You'd never find anyone. The best you can do is to get yourself a body servant to help you with your own small needs so you have more time for yourself. Now I'm going to the workrooms to check on the others. With the counting coming up, our scrolls will be as precious to the scribes as fish in the dry season. I expect to see you there as soon as you set those reeds to soak."

Mery-Sekhmet nodded and wished so much she could tell someone the secret. It wasn't just the fact that she and her father had magic but also that she and her father could put their magic *into* the papyrus that they made. And if they cut the stalks themselves, the papyrus paper was even more powerful. Their magic, thus passed on by the scroll, helped anyone who owned it. The words written upon it meant nothing. It was only the scroll and the owner's innermost wishes that mattered. The pure innermost wishes only. It was as though the magic knew what was the right thing to do. Or did a piece of Mery-Sekhmet's soul go with each scroll and know what to do?

She shook her head. Concentrate on your task, she thought. Alone in the courtyard, Mery-Sekhmet began to peel the rinds off the papyrus stalks and cut them into long flat strips. She found that her hands were shaking and slowed her pace so she wouldn't make a wrong cut and ruin one of the piths.

There was too much to think about. Her father's rules, her growing unease with the burden her powerful magic conferred upon her and now Inu's approaching death. It was too much.

She had to make a scroll for the Book of the Dead to give to Inu before she died, or else Inu would not be reborn. Inu was already an old and precious soul. Everyone who knew the old priestess valued her friendship and leadership at the temple. But Mery-Sekhmet was the only one who really understood the value of an old soul. She was also the only one she knew of, besides her father, who could make certain that Inu was reborn again.

She smiled. As far as she knew, neither she nor her father had ever seen a baby with one of the souls they had caused to be reborn, but she did know when the rebirth happened. The sensation was a sweet shiver of happiness, like biting into a cellar-chilled apricot on a hot day.

Mery-Sekhmet cut the strips of white papyrus pith into cubit-lengths. She took a soaking pan that was leaning against the wall and put the strips in it, then carried the pan to her room and filled it with water from the courtyard pond, setting the strips to soak to dissolve the impurities. As she left her room, she silently thanked her father for being a wealthy businessman, so she could afford to have her own room. Then she gave a bitter laugh and thanked herself for having been blessed with the same magic as her father, so she could help the family fortune.

Filthy from her trip to the river and sweating from her work in the courtyard, Mery-Sekhmet cleaned her skin with fresh water and dressed in an immaculate linen tunic before she left to visit Inu at her house on the temple grounds.

As she walked through the narrow alleyways of the city, dodging children, dogs, vendors and livestock, she noticed the amulets around the necks of the citizens and shook her head in dismay. *Will you all never realize,* she thought, *worshiping creatures who do not exist and therefore can never answer your prayers is to indulge yourselves in a hopeless pursuit. Better to spend you money and energy on working harder to improve your own lives or giving your wealth to the poor instead of to the rich temples.* She shook her head again and hastened her steps.

The temple of Hathor was halfway across the city, but the trip went quickly as Mery-Sekhmet watched for the "one in ten thousand." She passed through one of the city's main markets near the riverside. Farmers wearing muddy rags were buying bread and beer. The strong smell of warm fish came from the ship anchored at the stone stairs leading down to the Nile. Cloth weavers pushed their wares into Mery-Sekhmet's path. Basket makers hawked their baskets. Old men sat in the shade and played senet. Containers of sugary-sweet figs were piled near her father's table, where the nonmagical scrolls were sold. As she passed by, Mery-Sekhmet waved to the shop girl who stood behind the table and was helping a customer.

The scrolls still brought a high price because of the quality, but no one ever knew that Mery-Sekhmet and Khaemhat made sure the special scrolls went to people with special problems, worthy people who needed to be reborn or needed an heir to live. *Yes,* she thought as she nodded to herself, *we need someone else to help us.* She had to find that one in ten thousand.

Ten thousand was a number so large that Mery-Sekhmet could barely comprehend seeing ten thousand different people in her lifetime, let alone finding one with her power. She had to believe it was as simple as seeing someone's soul-light. She and her father could see their own and each other's. Any person with power would have one, she reasoned. And if she could only find another and then train that person to help them make papyrus scrolls, then half again as many souls would be reborn as she and her father could make happen now.

Abruptly, Mery-Sekhmet felt a gentle pressure on her shoulder that made her stop and turn around. "Mery-Sekhmet," said a gruff voice.

Startled, Mery-Sekhmet turned to see the wood-carver's face. "Yes, Bakenptah, what is it?"

The man smiled kindly. "Didn't mean to scare you. Here." He placed a shabti into her hands. "Take this to Inu. It will be a faithful servant in the afterlife." The little statuette was inscribed in the usual fashion, "If one calls you at any time, you shall say, 'I will do it.'"

Bakenptah added earnestly, "Tell Inu that I thank her for all her help with my prayers to Hathor."

Mery-Sekhmet held the shabti in her hand for a moment. It was perfectly turned, carved and painted. It felt . . . it felt just right. She shook her head at the thought of being made comfortable by something that was a servant to the dead. Hastily, she said, "Thank you. And Inu thanks you, too." She turned toward the direction of the temple and started to walk along the alley. Then, she darted back to the river's edge for another look. Last season, she thought she'd seen a fisherman with the telltale blue soul-light that she and her father both gave off themselves. But then

Mery-Sekhmet thought that the fisherman's soul-light was probably a trick of the sun.

With her free hand, Mery-Sekhmet shielded her eyes from the sun, scanning the shoreline and the river for the blue soul-light. The inundation was receding, and fishing was good. Reed boats drifted along with the current until their owners raised the sails to tack upstream again. The smell of rich mud was thick in the air. And Mery-Sekhmet saw nothing but fishermen, reed boats, and fish.

Clutching the shabti, she wove her way back through the alleyways to the temple.

"Child," said Inu from her bed, "I'm so glad you came today." She held out her hand for Mery-Sekhmet to clasp. Even though the old woman's hand smelled of lotus skin cream, it still felt dry to the touch.

"What's that you've got there?" asked Inu.

It made Mery-Sekhmet slightly nauseated to see the grave goods piling up around Inu's bed. There was a new wig on the side table and Inu herself wore a necklace of gold, turquoise, and carnelian that Mery-Sekhmet had never seen before. And here she was, holding another gift for the pile.

She answered Inu, "It's a little servant from Bakenptah."

Inu held out her hand and took the shabti from Mery-Sekhmet. As she held it, a smile crossed her face and she seemed to breathe a sigh. Mery-Sekhmet had seen this before in people who were going to die soon after they started to receive grave gifts. She saw a lot when she delivered scrolls to the dying for their Books of the Dead.

"My first shabti," said Inu. "Bakenptah is so thoughtful. He was one of my regulars, you now. Prayers everyday." She lost herself in looking at the statuette again. "What a pleasant servant this will be. Tell him that I thank him."

"I will," said Mery-Sekhmet. "Now, tell me, how

do you feel? Is there anything I can do to make you more comfortable?"

"You could become a priestess in the temple," said Inu, smiling at the look on Mery-Sekhmet's face. It was a familiar request.

"I am not high-born as you were, and I am not married to a scribe."

"Ah, but not everyone need contribute in the same way. After all, you make papyrus scrolls. The temple always has need of them."

The comment felt like a taste of bitter beer in Mery-Sekhmet's mouth. If only she had been a priestess, then she would have had fifty scrolls ready for Inu's death and not had to fight her father for the time to make just one. But no. "Inu, my all-but-mother, you know I cannot leave my father alone in the business. Besides, someday it will be my business, and then I shall sell the temple my scrolls at below cost."

"Shush, girl, lower your voice," said Inu, but there was mirth in her whisper. "I should call my servants and have them throw you to the crocodiles for attempting to bribe a priestess!" The old woman's laughter turned to coughing, but her eyes gleamed.

Mery-Sekhmet shook her head. Inu was dying and laughing at the same time. She could be maddening.

Several days later, Mery-Sekhmet stripped to the waist to begin the task of making Inu's papyrus scroll. She took the strips that had been soaking in her room and laid them out on the worktable. First, she laid out a row of strips vertically, with the edges overlapping and then pounded them with a flat piece of wood. With the bottom layer of the page created, Mery-Sekhmet added her magic. She drew her palm across her sweaty forehead and then pressed her hand to the paper. "My mind knows your will," she whispered. Wiping her hand across her chest, she pressed the sweat of her heart into the papyrus. "My heart knows your wish." Last, placing both palms over her sweating navel, she touched the sweat of her spirit and placed it into the paper. "My soul will take you forward." The papyrus sheet now contained a shadow of a soul-light that would become stronger once it cured.

Having imparted her magic, Mery-Sekhmet finished the sheet of papyrus by laying a horizontal row of strips on top of the vertical strips. Her magic was sealed within as she beat the top layer with the flat piece of wood. She placed a flat stone on top of the papyrus sheet and started to make the next one. When she had twenty sheets and stones layered, she was done with the first step.

Days later, a servant from the temple found Mery-Sekhmet eating lunch in the market and told her about Inu. "She's near her time," said the woman. "She wants to see you before she goes."

"No!" Mery-Sekhmet whispered. "It's not done yet."

She gave her bread to a nearby beggar and ran to the temple, unbathed and wearing her work clothes, stained with sap and beer.

When she arrived, the old priestess was pale and shrunken, her voice nearly gone. The table at her bedside was filled with shabtis and jewelry. In her hand, she held Bakenptah's gift and was absently stroking it with a trembling finger.

"Child," she whispered. "Come closer."

Mery-Sekhmet knelt and put her ear near Inu's lips. "I leave you soon."

Mery-Sekhmet sobbed. "No." She put her hand on top of Inu's fingers. They were cold.

"I love you like a daughter," said Inu.

Mery-Sekhmet lay her head gently on Inu's chest. "I love you." Inu had been her mother, if not in body, then in spirit.

"Put this shabti on the table with the others."

Mery-Sekhmet sat up and did as Inu asked.

"Remember to thank Bakenptah for it."

Nodding, Mery-Sekhmet watched Inu's face for a smile or a wink, but her eyes were closed as she spoke.

"You are special, Mery-Sekhmet."

The young woman blinked. *Does Inu know?*

At this thought, Mery-Sekhmet swore she saw the corner of Inu's mouth twitch slightly.

"Don't worry about my spirit. Hathor and Anubis will lead me where I need to go."

At this, Mery-Sekhmet could taste her own desperation. *There are no gods!* she wanted to scream at Inu. *You can't depend on legends.* She raised Inu's hand to her own forehead and then placed it gently on the bed. "Wait for me," she whispered. "I have to get your scroll for the Book of the Dead."

Inu opened her eyes slowly and though her mouth was straight, the corners of her eyes crinkled with humor. "I know you don't believe in my gods, child, but all will be well. I will simply take a path other than the one you would prescribe."

Taking one step away from the bedside, Mery-Sekhmet bolted out of the room, pushing aside servants and priestesses alike. She had to get the scroll and bring it to Inu before she died.

When Mery-Sekhmet arrived home, she found slaves of the Pharaoh taking a large box of scrolls out of her fathers' house. Gasping, she raced inside and found the household servants packing a second box as her father supervised. He was holding the scroll for Inu in his hand.

"Father, no!" said Mery-Sekhmet. "Leave that for Inu!"

Mery-Sekhmet's father grabbed her upper arm and led her down the hallway to her bedroom. "The pharaoh's queen is sick and her doctors need this. I know you meant it for Inu, but the queen is more important. She has to live. The grand vizier has read the future and she must have children. She is mother to the next dynasty. If she dies, all of Egypt will suffer. How can you weigh that against the continuation of one old soul?"

Mery-Sekhmet put her hand on her father's fist that clenched the scroll. "What if Inu's old and worthless soul is supposed to be reborn into one of the queen's children? What then? Saving the queen now to bear life that will harbor an unworthy soul will make the act somewhat meaningless, don't you think?"

Making a sound of deep displeasure in his throat, Khaemhat removed her hand from his and unrolled the scroll to half its length. Taking a knife from his belt, he made a clean cut down the center and left the room with only his half.

Thanking the very gods that she did not believe in, Mery-Sekhmet snatched up the half-scroll and started for the temple. Before she reached the door to the priestesses' rooms, she heard wailing for the dead.

"No, no, no!"

She pushed her way past the mourners crowding the dark hallway that lead to Inu's room. The old woman's bed was surrounded by the leopard-skin clad Priestesses of Hathor who were praying aloud to their goddess. Mery-Sekhmet fell to her knees and squeezed between two women until she could see Inu. Her all-but-mother was dead. Mery-Sekhmet could feel the emptiness of Inu's body by touching her hand. Inu's spirit had gone. With hopelessness flooding her soul, Mery-Sekhmet gave Inu's scroll to the head priestess.

"Please use this for her Book of the Dead," said Mery-Sekhmet. "It is a personal gift from me. Inu knew I made it for her."

The priestess nodded sympathetically at Mery-Sekhmet and touched her head in blessing. Mery-Sekhmet flinched.

Mery-Sekhmet knocked softly at the door. A young girl answered.

"Yes?"

"My name is Mery-Sekhmet. I've come to thank Bakenptah for his gift to Inu."

The girl nodded and beckoned Mery-Sekhmet inside. "This is my father's new wife," she said, motioning to a woman as old as Mery-Sekhmet's father, who was making bread on a table in the corner. The woman's eyes flickered coldly over Mery-Sekhmet and she said nothing. Mery-Sekhmet instantly felt sorry for the little girl who had opened the door. She'd seen that look in the eyes of stepmothers before.

"Come with me to the roof," said the girl. "Father is up there."

Mery-Sekhmet followed the girl up the steep narrow stairs to the flat roof where they found Bakenptah sitting on a stool under a linen canopy that rippled in the breeze. He was carving a shabti, as were the girl and boy who sat near him. Another daughter and a son, thought Mery-Sekhmet. She had to chuckle inside. Their parentage would never be in question. They wore Bakenptah's face, both of them, as well as his pudgy body and thick hands. How the family had the dexterity to be such fine woodcarvers escaped her.

"Mery-Sekhmet! You know you've come too late," joked Bakenptah, "I've already remarried."

Despite herself, Mery-Sekhmet blushed.

"Well, now," continued Bakenptah, "How nice of you to come and finally visit me here in my home. How are you? I'm very sorry to hear that Inu has finally gone to the next life. Sit! Sit! You must be weary with all the work you are doing to provide scrolls to the queen's physicians."

Mery-Sekhmet paused at the comment and gathered her temper in before she answered. "Yes, we're very busy. No, I can't stay. I have to get back to my father. The pharaoh has purchased all our scrolls for the queen's doctors to use and we have no stock left. With the scribes' counting coming up, we have to make more as soon as possible. I just came by to express Inu's gratitude for the shabti you sent to her. She said I was to thank you for her."

"Ah, Inu," Bakenptah shook his head sadly. "Always thinking of others, even as she was leaving this life. Well, you have already thanked me for my work. I carved the piece. You may thank my son, here, for cutting the block of wood before me and my daughter for painting the shabti when I was done with it."

Mery-Sekhmet looked at each child and solemnly said, "Inu thanks you."

Both children nodded. Bakenptah rose heavily from his stool and gestured for Mery-Sekhmet to sit, but before he could speak, Mery-Sekhmet said, "I must be going. There's so much work to be . . ."

Bakenptah interrupted, "There's one more to thank. My daughter, Wen-shet. If you don't want to wait while I fetch her, follow me." He ambled to the second opening in the roof that led down to another room. Mery-Sekhmet followed.

As the man lumbered down the stairs like an ox through mud, he said, "The sun hurts her eyes, so she likes to stay in the workroom where it's not as bright."

Mery-Sekhmet took the stairs carefully in the dark. She could smell the burning oil and salt from the lamp in the corner of the room at the bottom of the stairs, but no one was sitting in its circle of light. Mery-Sekhmet turned and blinked as she saw in the opposite corner a girl her own age illuminated in her own bluish glow. She gasped. *The one in ten thousand! That was why Inu did not fear dying without one of my scrolls nearby. She had Wen-shet's magic in the shabti.*

Bakenptah thought Mery-Sekhmet gasped for a different reason. "Yes, it's true, poor Wen-shet is a half-wit, but we love her anyway. She is one of the rare people in this world who will love you unconditionally. She does not harbor an ounce of guile or greed. Come here, girl."

Wen-shet carefully set down the statuette she was polishing and ran to hug her father.

Bakenptah took his daughter by her shoulders and gently turned her around to face Mery-Sekhmet. In the circle of the lamplight, Mery-Sekhmet saw that Wen-shet's face carried in it all the signs of a half-wit: eyes too far apart, a flattened nose, thick lips, ears too small and set too low, and a hairline a little too low on the forehead.

The girl grinned then blinked and tilted her head

to the side like a bird. "Light," she said as she pointed to Mery-Sekhmet.

She can see my soul-light, thought Mery-Sekhmet. Bakenptah thought Wen-shet referred to the sunlight coming down the stairs.

"Yes, yes, you can go back to the cool dark and work," he said good-naturedly.

But Wen-shet stood transfixed and Mery-Sekhmet looked into her eyes. The old soul hidden in the eyes of the grinning simpleton caught at Mery-Sekhmet's own spirit. *Oh, you poor thing,* thought Mery-Sekhmet.

Proudly, Bakenptah said, "Wen-shet polished Inu's shabti. That's the most important part."

"I polished," said Wen-shet, pointing to herself and grinning.

As Mery-Sekhmet nodded and said, "Inu thanks you," she also looked the young woman over. Wen-shet was dressed as well as the other children and looked fed and healthy. Bakenptah was treating her no differently than his other children, which was much better than the lot of any half-wit that Mery-Sekhmet had seen on the street.

If only . . . but no, thought Mery-Sekhmet.

Nodding good-bye to Wen-shet, she climbed the stairs and heard Bakenptah behind her. When they gained the rooftop, Mery-Sekhmet saw that the other children had left to get bread and beer for their father's guest.

"It's a shame, really," said Bakenptah, shaking his head. "The new wife doesn't treat Wen-shet as well as I'd like, yet my daughter will be with us for the rest of her life. No one will have her as a wife, and I won't sell her into slavery.

Mery-Sekhmet waited a few moments as if considering the point, but she had already made up her mind. "Would you let her come work for me as my servant?"

Bakenptah laughed. "Now what kind of servant would she be, I ask you? I love the girl, but she's not smart. You could never send her out with money. She scares most people just by how she looks. What would you do with her as a servant?"

"I would teach her how to make papyrus scrolls."

Bakenptah seemed to consider the offer as he watched a family on the roof next door make preparations for dinner.

Mery-Sekhmet added, "What would happen to her if something happened to you? What you said about her new stepmother . . ."

Bakenptah rubbed his face, then stared at the ground. "You are a gift from the gods if you would do this for her." He paused, then said, "I could not have hoped for such an offer."

"I am no gift from the gods," said Mery-Sekhmet, "but I will treat Wen-shet well."

"I left offerings at the Temple for Hathor for Wen-shet's safety and happy life. Inu wrote special prayers for me. The shabti was my thanks to Inu. She requested one from me after I brought Wen-shet to the temple one day."

Mery-Sekhmet looked at Bakenptah, stunned by his tale. Then, she chuckled. It welled up from deep within her belly. The chuckle became laughter of the sort she'd never felt before. She thought the sound must be coming from not only herself, but from Inu, reborn into a squalling young baby, freshly received into the world because of Wen-shet's shabti. She laughed the laughter of her father that she knew would hear when she presented Wen-shet to him, the girl with life magic, the girl with neither guile nor greed. She laughed for Bakenptah, who would never appreciate the cleverness of Inu's manipulations because she couldn't tell him. Mostly, she laughed for herself, for her own foolishness that Inu had shown her after her own death, through the meeting of blessed Wen-shet. Mery-Sekhmet laughed because now she knew that there were gods and goddesses, the ones with magic such as she, Wen-shet, and her father, and the ones who worked magic through sheer wisdom.

Inu, what else have you done for the people of this city that I don't know about? That I will never know about? That no one will know about? What else have you done that people will take for the workings of a god?

Bakenptah looked at Mery-Sekhmet, perplexed. "Are you feeling well? he asked.

"Oh, yes!" said Mery-Sekhmet, "Hathor has given me a new sister, Wen-shet, to help me in my work for the rest of my life. She is my one in ten thousand!"

LORD OF THE EARTH

by Dorothy J. Heydt

Dorothy J. Heydt has been selling stories to MZB for years. In addition to her short stories in *Sword And Sorceress,* *Marion Zimmer Bradley's Fantasy Magazine,* and other markets, she has written two novels. She lives in Berkeley with her husband. They have two children, both of whom have professional writing sales to their credit—I guess writing is either hereditary or contagious.

This is another story of Cynthia, healer and witch. Dorothy has been writing them since the first *S&S* anthology, and she will have another Cynthia story in *S&S XX.* By then, she should have almost enough for the book she's planning.

As if the heavens themselves mourned Zeno's passing, the clouds had opened up over the old philosopher's funeral and poured. Cynthia had had to wait till the third day for the weather to dry up so that she could clean out the house. Now she sat on the doorstep, letting her body's aches blur the ongoing question of what she was to do next. The images of the bronze and silver coins sewn into her hem passed sluggishly before her closed eyelids: not nearly enough to take her to Neapolis, to search for Awornos, among whose shades she might at last find Komi's spirit.

As for the practice of magic, she had laid that aside as it were on some bottom shelf in her mind, as she had packed old Palamedes' three books into the bottom of her chest and laid old clothing over them. She probably had them by heart now anyway. But all her experiences had taught her how to answer the children's question: "Why aren't magicians all rich and powerful and living in palaces?" "Because, child, it is as hard to find a way to make a living with that skill as with any other." No, better to forget about magic, stick to medicine, with which she might occasionally earn an obol for curing a fever or a barley-cake for delivering a baby.

The sun was warm on her tired limbs. Slowly the knots in her back and shoulders began to loosen; slowly the warmth of the sunlight crept into her cold hands and feet. She was three parts asleep when a horrible scream ripped through the air.

And another, and a third, while Cynthia jerked awake as if a tub of cold water had been dumped over her head. It was the children, of course: three of them under the age of six next door, not counting the one in the cradle. They were playing Persians and Athenians again, fighting the Battle of Salamis all up and down the little street, enjoying the warm weather and their own rude good health and youthful energy.

"Yaaaah! Rise up, Athenians! Think of your country, think of your children and wives; now is the battle for everything!" The ghostly invocation trailed off in a long shuddering wail.

Cynthia let out a long sigh, mostly in pity for the children's mother who had to deal with them every day, plus the one in the cradle and the one in the womb. And a quiet voice murmured out of her memory:

"To drain the third part of another's strength for your own use, make the sign aforesaid and say 'Ramphis Ophobis Anubis.' "

"Well," Cynthia said. "Well, just this once." She raised her left hand and made the sign, she spoke the words; and a great surge of strength flooded her limbs, and in the street the children stopped, and giggled, and sat down to a quiet game of rock-paper-scissors. And that brought back memories.

Without warning a great shape loomed up to block out the sun. "Cynthia! There you are!"

She blinked. "Demetrios?" But Demetrios had never been so tall, so broad.

But it was Demetrios, grown from a skinny dandelion of a youth into full manhood, golden-haired and
-bearded, his face burned by wind and sun, his blue
eyes blazing—and, she noted with part of her mind,
dressed very fine. "I've found you at last! I thank
the gods!"

"Found me?"

"I've been looking for you forever," he said, "or at
least since you left Alexandria. Only last month I
found the captain who brought you to Athens, and I
hired his ship to bring us here. After that it only
needed buying a cup of wine for every loafer on the
Piraeus. They tell me you've been living with the philosopher Zeno, and now he's dead?"

"Yes."

"Peace to his ashes. Now you can come with me.
Arkhias, help the lady pack."

And a strong young slave she had not noticed before said, "Sir," and to Cynthia, "At your service,
lady."

"Everything's packed already," Cynthia said, and
went and found her chest. Arkhias hoisted it to his
shoulder, and they started down the hill.

"How is your father?" she asked, stepping carefully
over a loose stone in the street.

"Not very well," Demetrios said soberly. "He can't
walk anymore. When he speaks, it's not poetry, as he
used to do, but whatever's been said in his hearing
that same day. You'll take a look at him, I trust. But
the Ptolemy's doctors could do nothing. I'm taking
him to the shrine of Asklepios in Corinth, in hopes
he may be healed there—" he broke off in midsen-
tence, and for some minutes they walked in silence.

"And if not," Demetrios said at last, "then at least
he can die in his own city. What about you? How did
you come to be living with a philosopher?"

"You can stop talking as though I were his concu-
bine," Cynthia said. "We lived in the same house, he
was old and needed care. I kept his rooms, cooked

his pottages, doctored him with such skill as I had, and at the last laid the obols on his eyes."

"A pious act," Demetrios said. "Did he leave you anything?"

"Oh, no; an heir turned up, a cousin from Elea, who took away everything of value. I just finished tossing out the worthless things for the beggars this morning."

"Good, then you can come to Corinth with us. Can't you?"

"No reason why not. It's on my way to Neapolis."

"Up we go," Demetrios said, and gave Cynthia his hand while she stepped aboard the gangplank. The captain stepped forward and bowed, and it took Cynthia three heartbeats to recognize him: the same man, the same ship, that had brought her to Athens a few years back. She wondered whether Demetrios had hired him, or bought him out, and decided not to ask.

Palamedes lay on a litter on the deck, safely away from the path between the gangplank and the hold, with a slave-woman holding a fan over his face to keep off the sun. Cynthia brushed her aside and knelt to examine the old magician. His face was the color of tallow. His eyes were open, but did not appear to see her, but he said in a rattling whisper, "Cynthia, my dear, my dearest . . ." *(He repeats whatever's been said in his hearing.)*

She took a breath, and let it out again: she knew the signs of approaching death. But what she would tell Demetrios—

"Yes," he said before she could speak. "The Ptolemy's doctors said the same. They said he would probably last till Corinth, if we made haste. After that, it's in the hands of the god. Are we ready to go, Captain? Very well; we'll get out of your way."

He led the way to the ship's sole and only cabin, and Cynthia's mind was illuminated with a sudden memory, as a lightning-flash lights a darkened land-

scape for an instant: that cabin had held five from
Alexandria to Joppa, rubbing elbows all the way, but
they had all been women.

But Demetrios had caused a curtain to be hung
across the width of the cabin, and that brought back
another lightning-flash of memory: the curtain she had
hung in the Roman ship, to catch a murderer, while
Komi waited outside on the deck; and something like
a fist clenched hard above her heart.

The water of the Saraonic Gulf glittered in the sun,
and the white buildings of Isthmia and the great Sanctuary of Isthmian Poseidon lay like pearls scattered
on the shore. It was midafternoon, hot and still; the
winds died as they entered the crescent-shaped Cench-
reai Harbor, and the last few hundred fathoms were
done by rowing. The near-naked sailors gleamed all
over with sweat in the heavy air. The ship pulled in
and made fast to the dock, and the passengers made
their way to the road.

There were, astonishingly, ten in the party now: Demetrios and herself and Palamedes, and Arkhias, and
four more strong slaves to carry the litter, and the
woman to tend him, and another, marvelous to relate!
bought by Demetrios on speculation before they had
left Alexandria, to be a serving-maid to Cynthia if he
should find her. (Cynthia, long used to combing her
own hair and putting on her own clothes, had not the
slightest idea what to do with the girl. She would
have to teach her to grind powders and brew
draughts.) Demetrios had come out of Alexandria
covered with gold—more or less honestly, she understood, something about a work of engineering done
in the harbor that had added talents of profit to the
royal revenues.

"Cynthia, would you prefer to ride in the cart?"
Demetrios said now, touching her arm as if he were
afraid of breaking it. "It's only a few hours' walk, but
the day is getting hotter."

"I'll be all right," she said. "I've walked longer roads than this."

The heat was becoming oppressive, and a haze was beginning to thicken in the air that earlier had been as clear as glass; it hung like a patient vulture over men and beasts, waiting for them to die. Men cursed in a variety of tongues; draft-beasts tossed their heads uneasily and a pack of little street dogs ran about, barking and snapping.

Except for the low hills inland, they might almost have been able to see the Gulf of Corinth from where they stood: it was only a few hours' walk away. To their left the tall citadel, the Acrocorinth, rose high above the plain; to their right a deep-rutted road ran over the narrowest, flattest part of the Isthmus, and men were setting wheeled carts under a ship in order to drag it overland to the Gulf of Corinth. The Corinthians had been talking for several centuries now about digging a canal to link the two gulfs, like the one at Mytilene—perhaps Demetrios, with his new skills, would be the one to achieve it.

One of the roads out of Isthmia ran through the Sanctuary of Poseidon—in one end, out the other—and they took that road in order to do honor to the god on their way. Demetrios leading, Arkhias at his elbow, then the four men carrying the litter of Palamedes, with a canopy rigged to keep the heavy sun off his face; then Cynthia with the other women behind her, and the hired cart with the rest of the baggage. The procession halted in the middle of the temenos, while Demetrios and Cynthia went through a grove of pillars into the presence of the great chryselephantine statue of the god, twice as tall as a man.

Poseidon held a trident in his right hand, as master of the sea, and a water-serpent coiled around the tines and tried in vain to bite them. In his left, as Poseidon Hippios, master of horses, master of the earth and earthquakes, he held the reins of four plunging horses superbly cast in bronze. "Hail, Neptune," Cynthia said softly, and waited to see if the god would answer to his new name. But he was silent.

"What?" said the priest who had taken Demetrios' offering.

"He has a new name," Cynthia said. "In Roman lands he is worshiped with new vigor, and his name is Neptune."

"Really," said the priest. He was a man in middle years, mild, with the squint-eyed look of a scholar. "His old name is very old, older than the Hellenic: in an ancient tongue he was called 'the husband of the earth,' *posis-dama*. Yet I dare say that if a Roman came here with a pious heart, the god would listen to whatever name he called him by. Ah, thank you again, good sir. May the god be friendly to you."

"The Sanctuary of Demeter is way up the hill, halfway to the Acrocorinth," Demetrios said as they came out of the temenos. It was almost as hot outside as in, the air unmoving, thick and still: what the peasant folk called earthquake weather. "Sad, when man and wife choose to live so far apart. There must have been trouble between them, though I don't recall any hymn or story that tells why."

"Perhaps they just tired of each other, after so many years," Cynthia said. "I have thought from time to time that being immortal isn't such a good thing as it's made out to be." A little fly buzzed up to investigate her face, and she fanned it away with her hand.

The Asklepeion was outside the city proper, as such shrines always were: healthy living conditions, and especially pure water, were an important part of the cure. From the steps leading up to the sanctuary they could look down on the sparkling waters of the Gulf or Corinth and across to the snowy peaks of Arkadia far away, or turning southward, see the Acrocorinth rising steeply above the hills of the city, making them look like no more than gentle slopes. The sun's heat and the haze lay thick and heavy over them.

The priest who met them at the entrance looked

grave as he examined Palamedes, but said, "Well, we'll see what may come. He should have bathed first in the sea, and next in the basins here, but since he can't walk—" They brought him inside, and the priest poured a few drops of sea water over Palamedes' head, and then a dipperful of fresh water from the basin. The slaves carried his litter through the temple enclosure, where Demetrios offered honey cakes at the altar. They visited the temple where clay images of human body parts hung from all the walls: votive offerings from grateful patients. They could be bought from any of half a dozen merchants whose stalls lined the city wall.

Behind the temple was a hall called the abaton, where the patients lay. They put the litter down between the pallet of a man who twitched at intervals, his arm thrust over his face to keep the light from his eyes, and another man who did not move at all. "He will remain the night here," the priest said, "under our care and the god's. If fortune is favorable, he will receive a vision in a dream, telling him how he can be healed. You may return in the morning."

Arkhias found them rooms in a well-kept guest-house, and after some acceptable food and excellent wine they went to their beds. Cynthia lay awake till the wheezing and muttering of Palamedes' attendant, on her pallet by the door, had settled into a steady and rhythmic snore. Then she rose out of bed and slipped into her clothes, fumbled for her sandals. There was her stole, hanging over the back of a chair—

"Lady," a voice whispered, "where are you going?"

Cynthia squinted in the dim light. The maid Demetrios had given her had risen and was wrapping her own clothes around her. "Can you keep a secret? What was your name, again?"

"Rhodopë," the woman said, and grinned. She had one dog-tooth missing, and her freckled nose wrinkled. "I can keep some secrets, not all—only yours, lady."

"Good enough," Cynthia said. "I'm going to the Temple of Demeter. Perhaps you'd better come along."

Overhead, the inky bulk of the Acrocorinth blotted out a quarter of the stars. The Sanctuary of Demeter and Persephonë/Korë was made up of many buildings, but the pillars of the temple itself shone in the faint light, reaching halfway toward the stars. Inside, lamps burned steadily in the motionless air; even now, two hours after sunset, the heat was oppressive, and the whole city seemed to be holding its breath. A priestess sat at the foot of a little altar, but she paid no attention as Cynthia and Rhodopë went by. It was the sort of thing Cynthia had come to take for granted—

—perhaps unwisely. Deep in the shadows something moved. Cynthia put her hand on Rhodope's shoulder, pushing firmly downward, and the maid fell to the ground and covered her face. "Hail, Ceres," Cynthia said softly. "How is it with you?"

The goddess had taken a form only a little taller than a mortal's, and mortallike she shrugged and shook her head. "My daughter and I are still sorting things out between us," she said, and Cynthia nodded sympathetically. "It's a long road."

"What brings you here tonight?" the goddess asked. "Is it this air of bad omen that lies over the city?"

"I came only to greet you, lady," Cynthia said politely. "But I've felt the air, too, that hangs heavily as a curse over this land, as far as the harbor's mouth. Has someone called upon you for a curse? Surely not upon the whole city?"

"Oh, no, it is no curse of mine." The goddess looked troubled. "Cynthia, it was a brave thing you did, saving that girl of Jupiter's from the vengeance of my sister his Queen. And a clever thing, too, to guess what was needed when no one could tell you."

Cynthia put her hand over her eyes. "Oh, thank you, lady, let me take my cue. This is from some other god and you can't tell me about it. Will it pass soon? Can you tell me that?"

"Oh, yes, very soon," Ceres said. "I wish I could avert it, for it will cause great sorrow, and I have become fond of this city and of you. I cannot even see whether you will survive it. If you do, take this advice: Go as quickly as you can to Italy. You are waited for there." And she was gone, leaving only a fading patch of dusty light where she had stood.

Cynthia stood there for a moment, and drew in her breath. "Rhodopë, get up; we're finished here."

At daybreak they went back to the Asklepeion. Morning rounds were going on, the priest-physicians going from patient to patient, hearing the dreams and visions they had seen of the divine Asklepios, son of Apollo, curing them or telling them how they might be cured. ". . . The god seemed to boil some kind of medicine over a little brazier. Then he pried the lids of my blind eye with his thumb and fingers and poured it in, and now . . ." Cynthia looked at the man closely as they went by. Certainly he looked as if both his eyes could see, as both together looked now at one priest, now the next.

They found Palamedes lying quietly on his litter, seemingly unchanged. Three priests stood by him, two in ordinary robes and one wearing a band threaded with gold over his breast and one shoulder. The two juniors began to chatter, "You must take him away, you must take him out of here, it is not lawful—" but the senior priest raised a hand to quiet them.

"Lord Demetrios, your father indeed received a vision of the god in the night," he said. "And his wits are restored, as you hoped for: but he is dying. He may not last the day. You must take him away at once. It is not lawful for him to profane the sanctuary by dying in it."

Demetrios stared at the man for a long, shocked moment, and the tears burst forth from his eyes. While he stood weeping, Cynthia stepped forward. "We shall obey. You four, take up the litter. Palamedes, can you hear me?"

The old wizard opened his eyes. "Oh, yes. You're Cynthia. Now, where did I meet you?"

"In Margaron," said Cynthia. "Come, we'll have a little while to talk over old times today; we must leave this place now. Ready? Up!" The men raised the litter. "Arkhias, see to your master. No, wait." She opened the pouch of red leather tucked into Demetrios' belt, and found a gold piece among the silver and bronze. This she gave to the priest. "Offer our thanks to the god," she said. "He has given Palamedes a chance to say good-bye to his family. And we will have a votive offering made, as soon as we can decide what shape it should take." And to the others, "Let's go."

The litter went forth out of the sanctuary, the others trailing behind it, Arkhias leading Demetrios by one hand while he wiped his eyes with the other, and Cynthia thought, *Now if I had stayed the night here, could I have talked to Asklepios myself and cut a better deal for Palamedes? And is this any part of the curse that Ceres spoke of?*

"You are right," Demetrios said, more or less his own man again, when they reached the outer wall. "The god has given us that much. Let's get back to the inn."

"No," Palamedes said, his voice surprisingly strong. "I want to go home."

Demetrios started to protest, then changed his mind. "Very well, Father; we'll go home." The litter set off again, and Demetrios fell into step behind the off-fore bearer, talking quietly to the old man. Cynthia and Arkhias tactfully fell behind a little, out of earshot.

"Is his old home still there?" Cynthia asked.

"Oh, yes, I believe so, lady," Arkhias said. "But of course it belongs to somebody else now, I don't know who. I know if I were a householder and someone came to my door asking room for an old man to die in his old home, I wouldn't refuse him. For all I knew, it could be a god; and even if it weren't, hospitality is sacred."

"We'll hope the present tenant is a pious man, then," Cynthia said, and tucked her skirt up a trifle as they began to ascend the slope into the town.

The air grew steadily hotter and more oppressive, as the sun rose; they could feel its beams heavy against their backs. They climbed to the broad shelf of the agora, lined with many temples, and crossed it and climbed again into wide streets, and narrow ones, and great houses gave way to smaller ones.

The house was one of the small ones, but it had a small garden where low-growing thyme gave out a pleasant smell underfoot and three old pear trees leaned on the high wall as if for support. The house-holder was a shipbuilder, and after a long moment's look at the party of visitors he seemed to decide that they were either what they seemed or a visitation of wandering gods (and that besides, if he forbade them the house, they could easily overpower him and walk in anyway), and let them in.

The house was even smaller inside than it had looked, and very dark, and everyone agreed it would be well to take the litter into the garden. The slaves put it down and, seeing Demetrios was paying no attention to them, sat down with their backs to the wall and went to sleep. Rhodopë and the other woman sat at the foot of the litter.

Demetrios looked toward the small building at the far end of the garden, where a curtain fluttered in the one small window: the gynaikeon, the women's quarters, and no business of his now, even though he had undoubtedly been born in it. After a moment he turned his back on it and sat down beside his father. "How long do we have?"

Cynthia stepped up to the litter and knelt down to look closely at Palamedes. His breathing was labored, but steady, and his eyes were clear. "I remember now," he said. "In Margaron, you were the physician's daughter. You came to the city walls, and you used the spell of the three *daimonia* to turn the Romans away. That was well done."

"Thank you," Cynthia said. "It gave us time to escape, at least."

"Do you still have my books of magic? You must keep them and study them. You have the gift. You must practice my art, and take care of my son. I love Demetrios, but he never inherited the gift. He'd make a better engineer than a magician, if he could find anyone to train him."

"He has," Cynthia said. "He studied under Eratosthenes in Alexandria. He earned lavish fees from the Ptolemy; he can provide for himself wherever he goes. You need not fear for him."

"Good," Palamedes said, and closed his eyes again. Cynthia and Demetrios looked at each other across the litter, and were silent.

For an hour or more they sat there, while the dappled shade of the pear trees crept over Palamedes where he lay, and the air thickened like barley-gruel not quite at the boil, and Cynthia searched her memory for tales of someone who had ignored the behest of a dying man and *not* suffered for it. She could think of none.

"Oh, that's wonderful," Palamedes said suddenly. He opened his eyes and actually turned his head toward Demetrios and Cynthia. "Good-bye, my son, I am going now. Weep a little for me, but not too much. I can see everything now: it will be very well for you, and you and Cynthia will give me grandchildren."

Cynthia found herself on her feet, her mouth open but unable to speak: no, now this was entirely too much—

And the ground under her feet began to tremble; there was a distant sound as of lions roaring, and the earth shook harder and harder, till she must step back and forth to keep her balance, as if on a ship's deck in a storm, a Maenad's dance with Mother Earth.

The dance slowed and stopped, but the roaring went

on, walls falling, stones tumbling, hills sliding a little
farther away from the Acrocorinth. The garden wall
had fallen over onto the four slaves who had been
sitting there. Demetrios lay sprawled across his father's breast, as if trying to shield him. From within
the gynaikeon, someone screamed.

And her heart knew what had happened, what had
been foretold, maybe even why, before her lips could
shape a word. And she felt herself fill with rage as a
cup is filled with wine.

She raised her left hand and said, *"Ramphis
Ophobis Anubis,"* and felt strength flow into her, and
she raised her right hand and said other words and
saw the stones of the walls rise up into place again.
The men underneath were unconscious, but alive; one
had a broken shoulder, and she touched it and said
certain other words and healed it.

Palamedes was dead. Demetrios had fainted, and
would be some time rousing since Cynthia had drained
most of his strength. The two slave-women were the
same: they had clutched at each other in their terror
and now lay curled up together like two sleeping cats.
They would keep.

She turned toward the gynaikeon, and seemed to
reach the door without taking a step, such was the
power she still contained. She touched the door and it
opened; inside, two young women and several children
were gathered around an old woman who lay on the
tiled floor, moaning. She had broken her hip. Cynthia
said the words again and healed her.

Outside, the rumble of falling stones was subsiding,
and she could hear cries and groans from every part
of the city. But she was down to her own allotment
of power again, and dared not drain her companions
any further, nor those who were wounded. She ran
into the house, where the owner lay on the floor calling on all the gods at once, and out into the street.

It was not (she would learn later) the worst earthquake Corinth had ever had, even in living memory.
But walls and roofs lay tumbled in the streets every-

where, from where she stood down the slopes to the
sparkling waters of the Gulf, and the Sanctuary of
Poseidon that lay upon the shore like a cluster of
fallen pearls. She raised her hand and said, "*Ramphis
Ophobis Anubis.*"

It was like taking into herself a wave of the sea,
like being possessed by it or rather like possessing it,
for she contained it and commanded it. The power of
immeasurable depths of water, heavy and salt, advanc-
ing upon the shore as inevitably as tomorrow's sunrise,
flowed into her left hand and out again from her right,
raising stones, clearing rubble, healing wounds. This
was what it was like to be a god, to take hold of
the reins of the sea, to hold a city in the palm of
one's hand.

And she knew where the power had come from, of
course, and after she had cast her spells across the city
and made it whole, she turned her hand again toward
the distant sanctuary and pointed her finger, and she
was there, stepping between the tall columns into the
shadow of the temple, and blinked; for she was seeing
two things at once. The great figure of Poseidon Hippios still stood in its place, but Neptune himself lay at
the statue's foot, on a couch like a great white shell,
cushioned with drifts of sea-foam, attended by nymphs
with silver scales for skin and webs between their
fingers.

"Now, why should you have done that?" the god
said, in a soft voice that made the floor tremble under
Cynthia's feet.

"Surely it's obvious?" she said. "For my friends and
my fellow human beings. The riddle is: Why should
you have done what you did? To do me harm, perhaps, or this city, for having the favor of my lady
your wife?"

"Oh, that old bitch," he said, dismissing the thought
of his wife with a wave of his hand. "No, I was
cramped, that's all, and felt the need to stretch. You
wait till you've spent a hundred myriads of years,
watching Africa shoulder its way up into Europe, and

the Midworld Sea close its gates and dry up and break open and fill up again: see if you don't want to get up and stretch."

"I'm unlikely to see these things," Cynthia said, "unless they happen much more quickly than you describe. It will not have escaped your notice that I'm mortal."

"That can be dealt with," Neptune said, and crooked a finger at one of his nymphs, who stepped forward with something in her hands.

"I'm not inclined to harm you, girl, no matter what the old bitch may think," he said. "I like you. You've got guts. I like a man, or woman, who's willing to stand up and fight for her own folk—even if it means earth and sea will be as calm as a lily pond for months to come. I have a gift for you."

The nymph held it out. A green flower, lying in a white scallop-shell dish: no, the green flesh of a melon-half, carved into flower shape. Or a jelly made of the deep green sea-water . . . And it smelled like the fresh sea air. It smelled delicious.

"Eat it, and be one of us," Neptune said. "Spend the next few centuries with me, maybe more, and be a goddess in your own right."

Ahhhhh. So this was why young Aretë had forbidden her to taste any of the food of the gods, why Mercury had served himself and her with separate cups and plates. It was simple: eat the green sea-flower, and gain immortality, and lose . . .

But she might as well be polite about it. "No, my lord, I thank you," she said. "I'll take it as a compliment: but I will remain with my own people for whom I've fought."

The god looked at her for a long moment, and she felt very cold. Then he shrugged. "Fair enough," he said. "In that case, the old bitch was right: get yourself to Italy as soon as you can. You'll find—well, let's say you'll find most of what you seek. You can go now." And Cynthia bowed politely, and went.

*   *   *

As if the heavens themselves mourned for Palamedes, the heavy air gathered itself up into thunderclouds over the old magician's funeral and poured. After Demetrios had done his duty to the dead, they had to wait till the third day for the weather to dry up and to find another ship that would take them to Italy, for war was in the air and the Punic captain thought it best not to go where he might suddenly be taken for an enemy alien at best, if not a spy. So Demetrios hired an Athenian ship, bound for Neapolis in any case, and hung the curtain up in its cabin. He had sold the litter-bearers, no longer needing them, but Cynthia would sleep behind her curtain with two waiting-women in attendance.

"It's for the sake of your reputation," he told her. "Of course, you don't have to travel as my sister-in-law any more; you could always travel as my wife."

"I'll travel as what I am," she said tartly, "a respectable widow going to Awornos to make sacrifices on behalf of my late husband."

"That will do to start with," Demetrios agreed, and grinned, and leaned on his elbows upon the stern-rail, watching Corinth dwindle into the sea. Cynthia turned away to look forward, into the northwest where Italy would one day rise up from the horizon, where she would perform her own duty to the dead.

LADY OF LIGHT

by Jennifer Ashley

Jennifer Ashley lives in Arizona with a husband and the semi-obligatory writer's cat. She plays classical guitar, is a member of the Phoenix Filk Circle, and has been known to write the occasional filk song (filk songs are science-fiction fans' version of folk songs, and the work "filk" is, of course, a typo for "folk"). She has sold short stories in several genres, but her first published short story appeared in issue 25 of *Marion Zimmer Bradley's Fantasy Magazine*.

This story is an example of the moment when all the things you have been studying come together, and you realize just what it is you've learned. If you're lucky, it makes the remainder of your studies easier to bear, if not easier to learn.

She heard a clear note, sweet and loud, as the spell completed.

Mirinda sat back on her heels, exhaustion filling every pore of her body. This spell had been the most difficult she'd ever worked. She'd had to draw every line, speak every word, exactly, or the spell would have bound her to it until another mage came to free her.

Chalk lines snaked around her body just beyond the folds of her linen trousers, every one perfect. Mirinda had practiced in secret for months until she'd been brave enough to trace the lines with the stub of chalk in the patterns of clarity.

The risk had been worth it. The spell would help free her from the cruel woman who'd held her for five years, and it would give Mirinda the power that was rightfully hers.

Mirinda waited, eyes closed, throat aching, for the manifestation of the spell to take. To combat her tiredness she whispered the words of the meditation chant, the one the sorceress always forced Mirinda to repeat as the sharp reed came down again and again on Mirinda's back.

The words soothed her. After five years of torture, Mirinda had learned to stand firm under the lash, controlling her fear and pain.

The air in the room grew sweet. Mirinda inhaled, but strangely, she smelled only the dry desert air outside the shed and the pungent bristle-bush that grew out by the well. Over that was the burned smell of her grease lamp and the fresh aroma of crushed herbs.

But the sweetness grew, and Mirinda realized she was smelling it from the *inside,* rather than breathing it in.

Mirinda heard a soft spread of chimes on the wind, and knew it did not come from the room or the night outside. The sound grew louder, and then over them, she heard her name.

Mirinda unfolded her stiff limbs and climbed to her feet. Moonlight spilled through the open door of the shed, turning the spell lines silver. The lines glowed faintly as Mirinda stepped over them.

She slipped out of the shed. Across the dusty junk-strewn yard was the small house the sorceress had built out of *caliche,* the granitelike slabs that littered the desert floor. The sorceress slept there now, soundly as always.

Mirinda had been a child when the sorceress had plucked her from the streets of the high desert town and brought her to this desolate land five years before. They lived in isolation, eking out a living from the arid soil Mirinda tilled. The sorceress used Mirinda like a slave and beat her with the thin reeds that Mirinda gathered from the dry riverbed. The sorceress taught Mirinda minor spells, and made Mirinda weave them while she worked deeper magics.

From child, Mirinda had grown to woman, and always she had one thought, one goal—freedom.

Mirinda knew she had power. She felt it deep inside her, like a live thing that waited to thrive once winter snows were melted away. And she knew that the only way to freedom was to find and release that power.

Mirinda thought of freedom now as she searched for the source of the summons. It had come from the dry riverbed, which ran with water only after the summer storms.

The black brush that lined the dry wash seemed undisturbed. Mirinda moved around a stand of withering reeds and saw a light in the river bed.

A woman stood alone. Light surrounded her, not white light, but red and yellow and blue and all shades of the spectrum. The woman was tall. She had muscular shoulders and a stern face, her hair close-cropped and dark.

It was from her that the sweet, fresh scent drifted. She turned and looked at Mirinda, and the chiming music grew louder.

Mirinda stepped out from the shadow of the brush and into the moonlight.

The chimes took on a different, almost surprised note. "*You* summoned me?" The woman's lips didn't move, but the music seemed to express the words.

"Yes," Mirinda whispered.

"Why?"

"To gain my power. And my freedom."

"How?"

"By freeing you."

The chimes rose in crescendo, then took on a merry note. "You have already proved yourself to have great power. How did you learn the spell?"

"I copied it from the book. Onto prepared vellum with the right kind of stylus. Then I learned it by heart. Tonight, I attempted it."

The chimes laughed. "If you had gotten only one thing wrong, little sorceress, you would have been bound forever, as I am."

"I know."

"Brave heart. Shall we free ourselves?"

The woman moved toward her, light and chimes accompanying every step. She swept past Mirinda and moved out of the river bed, seeming to float on light.

Mirinda scrambled behind her, dusting reed pollen and river sand from her trousers. Together, they approached the house.

"Can you make a light, little sorceress?"

Mirinda wet her dry lips, then chanted the words. She knew the light spell by heart, and quickly summoned a white light to hover above them.

The woman pushed open the door of the house. Stuffy, warm air met them as they went inside. The old sorceress snored on a pallet near the cold oven. When the light touched her, she snorted and awoke.

Mirinda had known she'd have to face the sorceress in order to free herself, but when the sorceress rolled to her feet, Mirinda's heart pulsed in fear. Her sorceress was strong, the strongest in the known world, and she suddenly wondered if it were possible to defeat her.

The chimes sang out. "Your brave apprentice has freed me."

"Not yet, she hasn't, Kierav." The old sorceress' voice was like grating sand on rock, harsh next to the beautiful chimes that rippled from Kierav.

"True." Kierav turned to Mirinda. "You must kill her, little brave one. I am sorry, but it's the only way."

Mirinda clenched her hands. "How can I?"

"You have power, little sorceress. You feel it, don't you? She has given you all the keys, whether she's meant to or no. All you must do is unlock the locks."

The sorceress tried to hold Mirinda with her gaze. It was a trick she had for taking the fight out of any who dared oppose her. Mirinda forced herself to close her eyes.

She felt her own power, sensed it sharp and clear

like the colors that surrounded the conjured woman. The years of withstanding brutality, of piercing together the little bits of knowledge the sorceress let fall, came together at last. Mirinda touched her power, felt it raw and pulsing through her limbs, and she opened her eyes, smiling her triumph.

The sorceress glared at her. "Don't be a fool, girl."

The chimes crashed. "You have done it. Now, little one!"

Mirinda drew her power forth. It sparkled and crackled around her, a live thing, and she took courage from it.

The old woman faced her. Her lips moved, and Mirinda braced for an attack. But one didn't come. Puzzled, Mirinda listened a moment, then realized the sorceress murmured not a spell, but the words of meditation, the same that Mirinda used to confine her fear and pain.

"Do not wait!" the chimes jangled. "Free us!"

"Why do you not strike me down?" Mirinda asked the sorceress.

"Why do you not strike me?"

Mirinda brought her hands down to her sides, but she did not suppress her power. "You are not even defending yourself."

The sorceress shrugged. "What matter? You are more powerful than I. I could not withstand you."

Mirinda laughed. "*I* am more powerful than *you*?"

"You see?" Kierav's colors swirled and flashed. "She fears you."

The sorceress showed no fear. And yet, she had begun the chant to retain courage in the face of fear.

"There isn't much time," Kierav said. "You must choose."

Mirinda's thoughts wandered back over the five years of back-breaking work in the hot, dust-laden desert. The sorceress had shown her how to make a strange, pungent drink that would cool her throat and let her stand the heat longer as she labored. She'd made Mirinda learn the painstaking process of preparing vellum to take a spell. A spell couldn't simply be copied from one book to another, because it was bound to the vellum on which it had been originally written. Copying it would change its nature, rendering it useless at best, deadly at worst.

Mirinda had learned the precise way to draw a spell, then how to learn it so that the spell lines were no longer necessary. She could now mind-cast the light spell, which had become as natural to her as breathing. And she could stand and look calmly into the face of pain, as calmly as the sorceress looked at her now.

"I choose," Mirinda said. She released the tension in her body, letting the power ebb away until it rested deep inside her once more.

The lights surrounding Kierav flickered red, then black, obscuring the stern face. "No!"

The sorceress smiled slowly. "It is not your time yet, Kierav."

Kierav swung to Mirinda. "She is wrong. Free me!"

Mirinda felt the push of the old sorceress' spell against the lights. She reached out and added her own power to the spell.

The chimes clanged and a foul odor spread through the room. Kierav screamed. The lights went red again, then winked out. Kierav vanished.

The room fell silent. A breeze drifted through the open door, bringing with it the dry, sharp scent of the desert night.

Mirinda let out a breath. "Who was she?"

"A bitter enemy." The sorceress turned, raking her fingers through her iron-gray hair. "A cruel and evil woman. It took four of us to bind her. That you partially unbound her, and still remain alive, attests to your power."

"Then you admit I have power."

The sorceress nodded. "Of course I admit it. I knew it the first time I saw you, when you were a child. I saw that you had a great power, and that it must be contained before it destroyed you. So I brought you here."

"To use me and hurt me and cow me."

"Which is nothing to what you will face when I am gone. When every sorceress tries to challenge you to steal your great power. When leaders try to use you to conquer others, when greedy apprentices try to trick you into revealing your greatest secrets, when those who fear you imprison your body in effort to capture your soul. That is what you will face, girl." She gentled her gravel voice. "All your life, all will want what you have. You must learn that. When there is no one to trust, you will always have yourself. When knowledge of yourself is firm inside you, as hard as the desert *caliche,* then none will be able to destroy you—ever."

Her words fell into silence. From outside came the sound of a rodent skittering across the yard. The faint breeze sighed through the reeds on the river, bringing with it a touch of chill.

"You have taught me that," Mirinda said softly. "You taught me to stand firm and unafraid."

"And you have learned more swiftly than I ever dreamed. It was a hard choice you made tonight, but it shows what you're made of. You chose compassion over power, compassion even for one you hated."

"What would have happened," Mirinda asked, "if I had killed you? If I had freed Kierav?"

The sorceress shrugged. "Who knows? You are much stronger than she; you could have dealt with her if she caused trouble. But who knows if you could have dealt with yourself?" She turned away and limped back toward her pallet. "In the morning, you will begin some new lessons. You will not like them. But they will serve you well." She sank down onto the pallet and shivered. "First, bring in some wood and make a fire in the stove. The night's turned chill."

Mirinda turned away. Her body felt numb and strange, yet she still sensed the power coursing through her.

The sorceress grunted. "Hurry up, girl. I'm cold."

Mirinda smiled quietly to herself and left the house, making her way through the littered yard to the wood pile.

ALL TOO FAMILIAR

by P. Andrew Miller

This story marks P. Andrew Miller's second appearance in the *Sword and Sorceress* series. His first story, "Patchwork Magic" appeared in S&S XIII. He has also had stories appear in *Dragon Magazine, Twice Upon a Time,* and many other venues. He lives in Cincinnati, where he teaches creative writing and literature at a local university.

In between grading, he still manages to squeeze out a story or two. A bit of advice he tells his students is that most writers he knows own cats. (True, but I'm not certain that a causal relationship has been scientifically established). Debo and Hex are based on his own cats, Circe, who died before the story was finished, and Medea, who still reigns over the house. Judging by this story, he's very fond of animals.

"You've got to be kidding. A bear? There was a wizard out there with a bear as a familiar?"

Dora stared at the black, shaggy creature that now sat on its haunches just inside her clearing. She still gripped an ax in her right hand, the only weapon she could find when she first saw the bear come out of the bushes. It met her gaze, then lowered its head, wiping its paw across its face.

"Don't you try to be cute at me," Dora said, though she did have to admit, she was softening.

Her own familiar, Debo, a small, and traditional, black cat, licked a paw before answering.

:Luga belonged to Edgar of the Mountains. And remember, not everyone has your good taste. :

Dora snorted; she recognized the compliment as simple cat ego. "Is Luga male or female?" she asked.

Female. : Debo responded.

"You told her the rules? No harassing the others, or eating them? And in her case, she'll have to sleep outside, at least until we get the barn finished."

:I've told her. :

Dora finally relaxed her grip on the ax. "All right, Luga, you can stay. Though the Green Lady only knows how I'm going to feed you."

Debo didn't respond. Instead he glanced back at Luga and started walking around the edge of the clearing, toward the back of the cottage, back toward the garden and the berry patch. Dora sighed. So much for having that pie this week.

The first of them had shown up over three months ago. That had been Hex, the tortoiseshell cat and former familiar to Duncan of the Marshes. She had followed Debo home. At first glance, Dora thought that Debo had just found a mate. Then he explained that Hex's master had died, and she needed a home. That was all Debo had said, no matter how many questions Dora put to him. She had finally given up and just accepted the new cat into the house.

Two weeks later, Keekaw the crow flew into the clearing. And then two weeks after that, Soonie the ferret slunk into the house. Then Fluffy, a tiny white poodle. ("Fluffy? A familiar named Fluffy?" She had belonged to Gloriana, the Good Witch of the North-Northwest, Debo explained.) And just a fortnight before the bear showed up, she had nearly stepped on the large scaly lizard sitting on her doorstep. She had screamed, then caught her breath.

"Let me guess," she had said. She had been right. His name was Igor and he was actually an iguana.

Dora guessed that perhaps the Green Lady herself had shown the animals to her door. She had no other explanation, since she was nothing more than a simple herb witch who barely qualified for a familiar of her own, though now she had a houseful of them. Even so, she felt like putting up a sign proclaiming her cottage Dora's Home for Lost Familiars.

Dora watched out the back window as Luga ate the raspberries from the vine. Debo sat curled in the sun nearby. Now was her chance.

She reached under the bed and pulled out the silver bowl she used for scrying. It was currently a dark shade of gray from a thick layer of dust. Dora wiped it out and noticed that the bottom was starting to tarnish. She didn't have time to polish it but promised herself she would take care of it.

She carried the bowl to the kitchen and placed it on the table. She filled it with water from a pitcher. Then she went to her shelf to get a few of the herbs that would help her spell as well as the powder she would need for the headache she would have later. She hated scrying for that reason and the fact that she simply wasn't very good at it. But five dead mages in three months was more than mere coincidence, and since Debo was not forthcoming about answers, she had to try.

She turned back to the table and Soonie was drinking out of the bowl.

"No, you stupid ferret, get out of there! Didn't your master teach you any manners?"

Soonie ducked from the bowl and scampered out of the room.

The ferret was almost as bad as Debo. She had tried a few other minor divination spells when the animals starting showing up but Debo had interfered in most of them. She had to finish the attempt before he came in.

She crushed the dried lemongrass in her right hand and let it drift into the water. Then she closed her eyes, called on her meager Talent, and cast the spell onto the water. She opened her eyes.

The water in the bowl shimmered, and the reflection started to change. She saw a man appear in the bowl, featureless so far. She leaned closer when she heard

a bark and a meow. Hex came racing from the storage
room, Fluffy yapping behind her. The cat jumped onto
the table and slid into the bowl. The water sloshed
and the beginning image vanished.

Dora glared at the cat as Fluffy cowered under the
table. Hex simply stared back at her.

"Fine," Dora muttered. "Be that way. I can take
a hint."

But the worst thing was, she could still feel her
headache starting.

The headache powders had barely taken effect
when the familiars went crazy. Keekaw flew toward
the door cawing and scratching at the wood. Fluffy
started yapping, and Hex stood by the door hissing.
Soonie joined her, his back arched and his neck hairs
bristling. Even Igor waddled towards the door. Outside, Dora could hear Luga roar and then Debo
jumped through the window.

"What's happening?" Dora asked.

:No time to explain. You have to hide. : The black
cat hit the floor and raced into the bedroom and then
the storage room.

"Debo! What do you mean?"

*:There's no place to hide in here! Not for you. We'll
have to run. :*

Dora looked at all the animals gathered before the
door. "What are you talking about? Why should I run?"

:No questions! Please! Just run. NOW! :

The urgency and force of Debo's mindshout moved
her toward the door. And brought her headache back
as well.

She gripped the knob and flung the door open. The
animals rushed into the yard. Even Igor sped past her.
She watched as they advanced a few feet and then
stopped, frozen. Even Luga, who had come back into
the front yard and was standing on her back legs,
was immobile.

"Debo?" Dora called, walking into the yard. She
didn't get an answer. At least not from her familiar.

"They won't be able to help you, little witch, just like they couldn't help any of their previous owners."

Dora looked around trying to find the source of the voice. Her fingers flexed, summoning a protective charm. Laughter erupted from the air before her.

"That won't help you either," the voice said.

She was about to shout "show yourself" when the air fifteen feet in front of her shimmered. In a few seconds, she could see the man clearly as the invisibility spell ended.

He was of average height and looks. His hair was blond, his eyes blue. He had a goatee that accentuated his pointy chin. He wore a tan tunic and black breeches and boots. Dora thought he looked very ordinary, except for the pig that he had tucked under his arm.

He smiled at her and put the small pig down on the ground. It stayed put, staring at her.

"My name is Corwin the Clever," the man said. "This is my familiar, Butch."

Dora rolled her eyes. That was worse than Fluffy.

The wizard's smile vanished. "I assure you, witch, you are not in a place to judge me or my choice of names."

Dora had already recognized that. The spell of invisibility he had used was beyond her knowledge. She knew he commanded far more power than she had. She might have had a slight chance if she had stayed in the house, where most of her wards were. But then she noticed that her geraniums and snapdragons, both planted for protection, had wilted upon Corwin's arrival. She was in big trouble.

She decided to at least try to bluff her way forward into hopeful survival.

"What do you want from me? As you've already pointed out, I'm no threat to you."

He leaned over and scratched the pig behind the ear. Butch closed his eyes and grunted softly. Corwin continued with his scratching for several minutes with-

out answering. Dora knew he was deliberately trying
to upset her. She refused to give in. Instead, she
started humming. That annoyed him.

The wizard straightened, and looked at her again.
She stopped her humming. Butch rubbed against his
master's leg.

"Threats can come in all shapes, just like familiars,"
he replied. "I've been doing a very efficient job of
eliminating my magical competition. Soon I will be
the strongest wizard in the realm. No one will be able
to stop me."

He stopped talking and stared into space, watching
a scene of his own dreaming. Dora noticed the change
in his voice, though. She recognized it. This wizard
had given in to the Mage Lust, seduced by his own
power. As he continued to gaze at visions, she started
humming again. He snapped out of his reverie and
glared at her.

"You are no threat to me in terms of power. But
you are curious. I felt the beginnings of a scrying spell
trying to find me. I traced that to you."

So that's why the animals stopped her.

"I can't have anyone know what I'm doing until I'm
done. There are still a few wizards to kill, you see. I
don't want them warned."

Dora thought about protesting. She could tell him
she would never tell, that she didn't know any wizards,
which was true. She knew he was expecting her to
plead for her life. She wasn't going to give him the
satisfaction.

"Well, get on with it, then," she snapped.

Her tone and answer startled the mage. Even the
pig grunted in a questioning tone. Then Corwin bowed
slightly. "Very well," he said.

He held his hand above his head and it started to
glow with magefire.

He's taking his own sweet time about it, Dora
thought.

:Dora! Get ready. :

:Debo? But . . . :

:We may be frozen in body, but not in mind. I had to wait until he was occupied. :

:Wait for what? :

:Wait for the moment to stop him. :

:Stop him? I don't know how to stop him. :

:No, but we do. :

Behind Debo's thoughts, Dora could sense the others. She could sense their anger and resentment at this man who had taken their partners from them.

:I still think we should try a Firestorm. :

:I vote for Clouds of Carnivorous Gnats. :

:I don't know that one. :

She had no idea what they were arguing about, but she did know that Corwin's fist glowed like a hot coal.

You better hurry. : she thought at Debo.

:We go with Dante's Portal. Now! :

Dora staggered as the spell and the power to use it burst into her mind. Corwin even paused, his fist still in the air

"What are you doing? Can't you hold still long enough for me to kill you?" he said.

Dora smiled and spread out her arms. "Why don't you just go to hell?" she said.

His eyes showed his shock at her tone, then he looked even angrier. She didn't care.

She let the spell flow from the familiars through her like cool water. Her hands suddenly glowed with blue light.

"What are you doing? How are you doing that?" Corwin called out, his own spell seemingly forgotten.

Dora didn't answer as she watched the air behind the man rip open, creating a portal to another realm. A realm of fire and darkness from what she could see of it.

The wizard must have noted her attention. He turned his head to gaze at the opening. "No!" he yelled, and tried to bring his hand down, striking her with the spell. But he couldn't. A scaly, taloned eight-fingered hand, its origins in the portal, had already seized his wrist. The wizard looked back up and tried to pull away. The creature held him fast. And then, the hand pulled him through. The portal snapped shut with a thunderclap. Butch squealed.

Dora had time to feel relief, and then the power from the familiars left her and she collapsed.

She awoke when something wet hit her face. She twitched and opened her eyes to see Fluffy licking her. The dog's breath struck her and she almost gagged. She sat up quickly.

"Thanks, Fluffy," she said, scratching the poodle behind the ears.

The rest of the animals surrounded her, and she thanked each one of them. Soonie, Igor, and Keekaw looked pleased. The two cats looked like cats. She even scratched Luga's furry belly.

"What exactly did you do?" she asked.

:None of us had the knowledge to defeat him alone. But he failed to take into account that our collective knowledge and power was enough to vanquish him, if we had the proper familiar. :

"Excuse me?"

Debo licked his paw.

:You know what I mean. :

Dora nodded and suppressed her grin.

"Well, at least that's over with. We've seen the last of him."

:Well . . . :

Her stomach jumped. "He is gone, right?"

:Yes. We won't see the wizard again. But . . . :

Something grunted, and Butch came walking out of the bushes.

:The pig wants to know if he can stay. :

Dora sighed. What was one more?

"Welcome to the group, Butch."

ARTISTIC LICENSE

by Deborah Burros

Deborah Burros has sold stories to *S&S VIII, S&S XV,* and
Marion Zimmer Bradley's Fantasy Magazine. She has a
Master's Degree in Library Science and has worked as a
copy editor and copywriter.

Her mother is an artist, and Deborah occasionally draws
or makes jewelry. She has also worked in an art gallery,
so she had plenty of background to draw upon for this story.

Mindful of what Duke Verdigris had done to the
last court painter to disagree with him, I kept
my voice as smooth and blank as a freshly primed
canvas: "How may I make this portrait more pleasing
to you, Your Grace?"

The painting was not of Duke Verdigris. To best
represent him would require a mosaic's array of hard,
cold stone. (A charcoal sketch would best represent
me—all jagged lines, dark and a bit rough.) The portrait was of his betrothed, the Lady Gemma. For her,
I had needed the depth and richness of oils.

The theme was Winter, so Lady Gemma had posed
in a gown of velvet as black and lush as sable, heavy
enough to muffle the rustlings of her snowdrift petti-
coats. A frost of lace draped her proud shoulders.
Holly berries studded the coils of her midnight hair—
*although I had been understandably reluctant to use
any red.* Icy diamonds—a gift from Duke Verdigris—
hung from her neck and earlobes and weighed down
her hands.

In her right hand, she displayed a silk fan embroidered with violets. I had not needed artistic license to use the same hue from my palette for her eyes; the only artistic license I had taken, for Lady Gemma's sake as well as my own, was to sentimentalize their expression. Had I dared to be completely truthful, I would have shown her with a stormy gaze: purple, brooding with sorrow, and about to flash with anger.

Duke Verdigris pointed at the fan in the portrait. (My mother had taught me, as a little girl in the provinces, that pointing was impolite; Duke Verdigris had taught me, as a young artist newly arrived at court six months ago, that rules of etiquette and rules of law did not have to apply to him. Even my guild, the Artists' Guild, had seemed powerless against him.)

Tossing back his coppery mane, Duke Verdigris shifted his blue-green glare to me, then back to the offending picture. "*Spring* flowers—even embroidered on a fan—do not belong with the *winter* theme! Others may not, Aiglentine, but *I do* notice transgressions against the proper order of nature."

Lady Gemma and I had counted on that.

I curtsied deeply. "Your pardon, Your Grace. Allow me to redo the fan in the portrait; let me replace it with one whose decoration does not clash with the season."

A week later, I returned with the corrected painting. Its reek of turpentine was sweetened by the candles also providing light from a grove of candelabra. Duke Verdigris eyed my work. "Nicely done, Aiglentine." I forced myself to simper at his crumb of praise.

He scrutinized the repainted section. "*This* fan—it appears to be a map . . . most unusual!"

"Indeed, Your Grace. I found it hidden in the back of the sandalwood cabinet where Lady Gemma keeps her fans." Right where she and I had decided she would keep it.

"*Hidden?* What is this a map *of*? Some treasure unaccounted for in the marriage contract?" Duke Verdigris said, gripping my arms. "At our betrothal three

months ago, all she declared to be bringing to this
marriage was her vineyards, merchant ships, and her
family's old villa. . . .

"I will see this map and the Lady Gemma.
Immediately!"

Duke Verdigris and Lady Gemma were alone in
his private chambers. Not completely: his bodyguard,
Bruno, lurked in the background to make sure no as-
sassins lurked among the hunting trophies of panther,
wild boar, and stag; I discreetly attended Lady
Gemma. Scarcely allowed a sip of wine or a moment
to warm herself by the fire, Lady Gemma told her tale.

"Generations ago, two of my ancestors—*another*
Lady Gemma and a Lord Coruscati— were wed. The
Artists' Guild was commissioned to make a wedding
gift: an especial challenge, for Lord Coruscati was
colorblind and Lady Gemma disliked the grayness of
chiaroscuro, so how could they *both* appreciate any
one work of art?

"Aiglentine's predecessors met the challenge. The
wedding gift was a bower of crystal roses: colorless,
so the groom was not slighted, yet sparkling with rainbows to please the bride.

"This treasure was too special to be gawked at or
gossiped about—even the knowledge of its existence
was to be cherished by being closely kept. It was hidden in my family's villa for safekeeping; the map to
this treasure was disguised as a fan for safekeeping,
too."

Lady Gemma drew the fan from her sash, managing
to indicate me without actually pointing it at me.
"Safe," she said, "until Aiglentine copied it into the
portrait!"

I hung my head. "Your pardon, My Lady, I meant
no harm, only to improve the painting—as Our Duke
commanded—and this fan was so intriguing. . . . And
I had heard only the vaguest of rumors in the guild
about that bower."

"Enough!" snapped Duke Verdigris. He snatched
the fan from Lady Gemma, but opened it as gently as

if it were a wing of a prized falcon that he was examining.

The fan was of yellowed parchment trimmed with crystals. Remnants of gilt threaded a path through the faded-sepia outlines of passageways.

Just after sunrise, we followed the map.

Duke Verdigris, his bodyguard, Lady Gemma, and I began in her old villa. "So, my sweet, you finally invite me into your bedchamber." Smirking, Duke Verdigris surveyed Lady Gemma's room—and stopped short at his portrait: "I see you have already made me welcome here, but why did you pick that *unfinished* painting?"

It had been the last painting done by Angelo, a previous court painter. He had died six months ago, leaving it uncompleted. In it, Duke Verdigris, cape aswirl, speared a unicorn through the heart. Angelo had argued with Duke Verdigris about whether blood was *crimson* or *scarlet;* to settle the issue, Duke Verdigris had examined fresh blood by stabbing the artist through the heart.

"This painting is suitable here," said Lady Gemma. She slid it aside to reveal an archway.

We were soon in deserted corridors in a closed-off wing of the villa. Frescoes of nymphs gave way to frescoes of goddesses. Finally, by the image of Nemesis, we reached the end of the path. On the other side of a locked door awaited the treasure.

Lady Gemma and I entered first; Duke Verdigris and his bodyguard followed us into the whitewashed room. I opened the shutters, then extinguished our lantern.

Morning sunlight glowed through the dusty air, glinting on the violet brocade draped across one corner of the room.

Lady Gemma pushed aside that curtain.

Rainbows bloomed. Crystal roses were twined into an arch, each blossom filled with fragments of light; however, only the light was fragmented—every petal, every leaf, and every thorn was intact.

"Exquisite," whispered Duke Verdigris.

Lady Gemma smiled. "You need not be concerned about sound shattering the crystal, nor anything else damaging the bower: to protect it, especially from overeager admirers who would pick it bare, it was wrought to be almost unbreakable."

"Almost?" Duke Verdigris tapped a bud with the dagger that had slain Angelo; the rose chimed softly, uncracked and unchipped. "Ah, I have never heard such a sweet note," he said, "even from my best castrato. . . ."

Lady Gemma silenced the rose with a touch. Carefully withdrawing her hand, she explained, "To pluck a rose, you first must pay for it—"

"—with a kiss?" He tried to embrace her, but she drew back.

"No—with your blood."

Scowling, Duke Verdigris turned to his bodyguard and commanded him to fetch Lady Gemma a rose. Bruno bowed, squared his shoulders, and marched toward the crystal flowers, stripping the leather gauntlet off one hand.

"Stop! I will not accept flower from a *lackey*," said Lady Gemma. "Should such uncommon blooms be gathered by a commoner in your stead?"

She arched an eyebrow already as perfectly curved as a black swan's neck. "What *else* would you have him do for me in your stead?"

The bodyguard blushed. I deliberately giggled. Lady Gemma indignantly fanned herself.

Duke Verdigris shook his head. "Very well, my sweet, I will indulge you in this. He ungloved a hand, dropping the suede in the dust as he sauntered over to the bower. Grasping a crystalline stem, he let the thorns sink in; as blood oozed, the rose began resonating to his pulse, petals clinking softly. The stem snapped.

Duke Verdigris handed Lady Gemma the rose; accepting it, she took care to avoid its thorns. It sparkled like the tears she had shed in secret over the murder of Angelo, her lover. She smiled as Duke Verdigris reached for another rose.

Like a goblet's rim stroked by a blood-moistened finger, the crystal hummed, siren sweet. Again, Duke Verdigris gave the bower some blood and received a flower. And again. The crystal clinked like bead curtains in an opium den. The blood welled up from his hand at each sharp kiss from the crystal; rainbows welled up from the bower, overflowing the crystal flowers and splattering the crystal leaves with orange, yellow, green, blue, indigo, and violet.

And red.

Bestirring himself, the bodyguard reached to pull his master away from the crystal. Bruno had the over-muscled build that looked magnificent in a sculpture but excessive in the flesh; nevertheless, Lady Gemma restrained him from his duty with a tap of the fan, resting its diamond-sharp edge against his throat.

He, Lady Gemma, and I made a tableau as Duke Verdigris continued to pluck the roses and heap them at her feet.

The bower clashed and clattered like a maenad's tambourine, faster and louder; its colors flashed, faster and brighter. Laughing and weeping, Duke Verdigris flung himself into the crystal thorns' thirsty embrace.

The last rose fell from his hand.

The crystal bower quieted and dimmed. Duke Verdigris' blood-drained corpse, released, slid to the floor. It no longer mattered to him whether blood was crimson or scarlet.

Lady Gemma apologized to Bruno, who was too dumbfounded to reply. She snapped the fan closed and handed it to me; I had drawn the map as part of the revenge that my guild and I—with Lady Gemma—had crafted, so it belonged to my guild. The Artists' Guild would also repair the bower of crystal roses and return it to the guild's secret treasury, until we needed to avenge another artist.

EARTH, WIND, AND WATER

by Bob Dennis

Bob Dennis sold his first story to *Marion Zimmer Bradley's Fantasy Magazine;* it appeared in issue 24. He says that in her tradition of paying forward, he is grateful to be in her ledger book as a "payee." (Actually, she always called them "my writers"—she was very proud of the number of writers whose first sale was to her. I think, in a way, she considered all of us to be her children.)

Bob lives in Washoe Valley, Nevada, on the east side of the Sierra Nevada mountains, and he studied geology in college, so he probably has a pretty good knowledge of earth. From there, one needs only a good imagination to come up with a system of earth-magic.

Around the last turn on the trail out of the mountains, the darkening sea spread out before Kemrae and she almost turned back. The unending rise and fall of the waves was frighteningly different from all that she'd learned in a lifelong apprenticeship to the earth-sign sorceress Teryxia. The two had never left the land because an earth-sign sorceress' power flowed from the earth, channeled by her stones. Teryxia's stones were tied in a leather bag at Kemrae's waist. They were all that remained of her teacher. The weight jouncing at her hip was a constant reminder that Teryxia was given back to the earth now, too suddenly and too soon. There had been no time for Teryxia to pass the stones on to Kemrae, and they had to be given from a sorceress to an apprentice or else they were useless.

The trail went out on a spit of land that narrowed

to the dock. When Kemrae arrived, a cold rain was slanting in from the sea. Her horse startled as its hooves clattered on the planking. At the end of the dock a ship waited, tugging at its lines in rough swells. Across the sea a sorceress who could properly pass the stones to Kemrae had offered to complete her apprenticeship. But it was across the sea, and a true earth-sign sorceress would not choose to leave the land any more than a tree would choose to uproot itself. Kemrae wondered if she even deserved the stones.

At the dock her horse backed and shook its head as if to say: this is the end of the land, there is no place left to go. Kemrae agreed with all her being, but dismounted anyway. An old man who lived under the dock came up and took the reins along with her directions for returning her horse to the stables in the mountains.

She started walking out to the ship. The sea slapped and splashed at her from both sides. She could feel her strength pulling away from her. There was a tearing inside her heart almost as bad as the morning she'd found Teryxia as peaceful and cold as rock.

Sailors in glistening oilskins helped her up a swaying gangplank. The lines were thrown off. Kemrae watched the severance from the land, from her apprenticeship, from Teryxia and felt only dread. She placed her hands in the bag of stones, small comforts of solid earth.

When the squall line rose on the horizon like a cliff of gray slate, the crew did the only thing they could to protect their passenger: they battened Kemrae below in a hold. The storm was tearing the old ship apart, and she could do nothing. Even a full earth-sign sorceress could neither quiet the wind nor calm the sea. She heard the sailors yelling, the snap and tearing of sails. When a roar like a landslide shook the hull, she instinctively ordered the earth to be still.

But the waves were not stone, and they washed over the ship, taking the crew with them.

The keel shuddered beneath her feet. In the yellow glow of an oil lamp, Kemrae saw black water weeping through the wood. She chanted a binding spell to the ship, but it would not listen to her. Its beams and planks once had roots tied to the earth, but after one hundred years of seawater and whale song it did not remember. Now the ship belonged to the sea, and Kemrae could cast no spell upon it. Her young powers worked on nothing but earth and the nearest was a bed of sand at the bottom of the sea, beyond her reach.

Cold seawater washed across her sandaled feet and she wrapped her arms around herself feeling helpless. She'd watched Teryxia harvest slabs of granite from a mountainside for a queen's castle with a single word. For a land cursed with famine, her teacher had created fertile soil with a touch of her hand, but Teryxia's greatest spells could do nothing for Kemrae. She thought back to simpler charms, finding precious stones and binding rock walls. Kemrae could sense what was out of place, the gem in the dirt or the loose stone in the middle, but when she reached out with that sense, she found only herself. The simple blessings on farmers' plows to open the earth gently and roads to stay free from ruts were no help. Kemrae vowed her feet would never leave the comfort of earth again.

Rain lashed the deck above her head. The hull groaned, giving into the sea. The water was coming for her; she should have never left the land. Tears welled up in her eyes. "There is enough salt water in this sea!" she cried out. She wiped the tears away, but could not stop them. How many crying babies had she quieted with the simple spell of placing a pebble in a baby's hand and whispering the words, "Sleep like a stone." She'd tell the mothers, "When it's time for them to wake up, just take the pebble out of their hand." Little did they know how protective a charm it really was, for nothing could wake or hurt a child while they slept like a stone.

A warm rush of hope coursed through Kemrae as she thought about the spell. Could she cast it upon herself? She had Teryxia's bag of stones, any stone would do. But if it worked, who would break the spell? Would she sleep forever, drifting in the sea? Someone would have to take the stone out of her hand. How would they know? There was no time to think about these questions. She pulled a small stone out of Teryxia's bag. It was the heart stone, a drop of rose quartz warm in the palm of her hand. She closed here fingers around it and whispered to herself, "Sleep like a stone."

The ship came apart into pieces like a half-forgotten dream and the lamp went out and the water came over her like a blanket just as she fell sleep.

She washed up on an island in the far western reaches of the sea. Above the beach on a barren headland of sandstone the exiled wind-sign sorcerer Arkizan slept in his keep. All night long he had cast squall nets out to sea at a passing ship. When his catch broke apart in the waves he cursed in thunder. The morning tide would bring him broken pieces of decking and rope, nothing to help him escape from the island.

He awoke from a nightmare in which the sea turned into earth and rose around his keep like a tide. Outside the sea was still only water and salt and fish, but he smelled earth. Then he saw Kemrae lying down on the beach and the wind told him the scent of earth was coming from her. He drifted down from his keep quiet as a breeze. The waves hissed at him and the seagulls screeched high above, keeping one eye on him.

"What has the sea brought me this morning?" Arkizan asked himself. Years in exile had taught him the habit of speaking to himself. He saw Kemrae's long green dress spread out and drifting, still caught in the foamy wash at the sea's edge. Her black hair lay

twisted across the white sand like seaweed. He studied
her pale face turned up to the pink morning sky and
brushed sand off her cheek. A memory from years
before and half a world away from his exile surfaced
in his mind.

"I know you, don't I? Young Kemrae, isn't it? Apprenticed to Teryxia, I think. Yes. Well no wonder
the fish threw you out, you're probably stinking up
their sea with that scent of earth."

He pulled her higher up on the beach by the wrists.
As her dress came free of the water, silvery arrow-
shaped fish spilled out of her skirts onto the sand and
the seagulls descended in a spiral storm on the catch.

Arkizan laughed, "Oh that's a good spell, turning
me into a fisherman. What are you doing in the sea
anyway? An earth-sign sorceress sailing the seas." He
sang the tongue-twister out loud, watching the seagulls
swoop and pick and fight.

"Anyone knows water and stone don't mix," he
scolded Kemrae. "The stones, I nearly forgot!" He
found the bag tied around her waist and opened it.
Counting the stones, he spread them out on the sand.
"Four? Even a wind-sign sorcerer knows you always
carry five stones. Where is the fifth?" He saw her left
hand was closed and opened her fingers one by one.
"There you are, number five," he said taking the stone
out of her hand.

Kemrae awoke and smiled, feeling the comfort of
the earth's curve against her back. Silently she
thanked the memory of Teryxia for the spell that had
saved her life. She sat up and saw Arkizan bent over
the stones, talking to himself. "Thank you," she said
to him.

The sorcerer started, making a quick warding sign
in the air between them to keep her away. "I know
little of earth-sign sorcery, but I should have guessed
what that stone was for," he said placing the rose
quartz back in the bag. "A little sleep spell to get you
through the storm. But I need something stronger to

get me off this island; which one of these stones can do that?"

Kemrae sighed. "Out of the sea and onto the Isle of Arkizan," she said quietly to herself. When she was younger she'd heard stories about him. How he had used his power over the wind as a weapon. How he used the wind to kill. She would not help him escape exile. "The stones do not belong to you."

"Such gratitude! Whatever washes up on my island belongs to me. It's a simple right of salvage."

"But you can't use them," she pointed out, angry at the thought of Teryxia's stones in his hands.

"No, but you can," he answered her.

Kemrae was about to tell him she could not use the stones either, but then decided it would be better if he believed she had some power with the stones.

He held up a clear quartz crystal to the sky letting sunlight flash prisms on the sand. "This one cleaves sunlight like a sword, it must be very powerful."

"The crystal only shows the true nature of light, Arkizan. Quartz crystals are the eyes of the earth. They see all. They are for finding truth."

He dropped it in the bag with a frown. "A lot of good truth does me on this sand pile." He picked up a pink stone. "What power could there be in this plain stone?"

"Feldspar exists from the mountains to the sand beneath your feet. It is the bone of the earth. Feldspar brings strength."

Arkizan paused, rubbing his thumb over the feldspar. "But strength and power are not always one and the same, sorceress. Are they?"

Kemrae shook her head.

"My bones may be old, but are strong enough," he decided putting the stone back in the bag. "What about this one?" He showed her a piece of gray pumice.

"Beauty stone."

"Beauty? This ugly rock? I don't believe you."

Kemrae reached for it, asking, "Would you like to see how it is used?"

"Ach! Of course not," he answered placing it with the others. "Last one," he said, holding out in his hand a worn piece of red basalt.

"That is basalt, dried blood of the earth."

"A blood stone! Surely this must have some power."

"It is very powerful," she answered him.

"Tell me how it works."

Kemrae smiled slowly at him. "You place it in the left hand of a woman in labor to squeeze and ease the pain of childbirth."

"A birthing stone!" Arkizan yelled, discarding the last stone into the bag. He wiped his hand on his robe with disgust. "Dirty earth-sign sorcery. Beauty is the eye of a cyclone; truth is wind that never stops. Your silly stones are useless to me," he said to her, throwing the bag down on the sand beside her.

"Are you giving me the stones?" she asked.

"Yes and a whole lot of good they will do you when you're back in the sea." He turned toward the water. "I will show you strength. My winds will gather a wave to wash you clean off my island." He whistled and a whirlwind swept him into the air, spitting sand into Kemrae's face.

She watched him fly back to his keep and picked up the bag of stones. Arkizan had given them to her! They had been passed from a sorcerer to an apprentice. Without knowing it, he had just made her a full sorceress, completing her apprenticeship. She stood up and faced a strong onshore wind. A line of dark green appeared out at sea. Sunlight glinted from its crest. She took the birthing stone to the edge of the water and pushed it into the wet sand. She'd told him the truth, it was a birthing stone, but helping bring babies into the world was only one use. A birthing stone could bring many things into the world.

"Sand, be rock again, for Teryxia," she whispered. The sand trembled beneath her feet as a vein of rock flowed out beneath the water. A wall of white granite broke up through the sea rising in front of Arkizan's wave. The two forces met with a crash that showered the beach with a fine mist of salt water. Kemrae laughed in the salty spray, licking it off her lips. The stones worked for her. "Anyone knows water and stone do not mix!" she yelled up at the sorcerer's keep.

An angry wind blasted down from the keep, knocking her to her knees. The wind shrieked in her ears. She stood up, but was pushed back into the sea, splashing in the surf up to her waist. She had to keep her feet on the bottom to draw power to fight him. In her bag of stones she found the feldspar and clasped it between both hands. "Solid as a rock," she chanted to herself. The spell gave her the strength to hold her ground, but she could not move forward. Arkizan drove the wind harder against her, but she channeled more power from the earth into her spell.

"Arkizan, we could go on like this forever!" she screamed into the wind. The battle between wind and stone was as ancient as the earth itself. Kemrae realized they were at an impasse, but Arkizan did not. He coiled a hurricane around his keep and then hurled it at her. She rooted herself to the core of the earth. She saw the water receding from around her. He was blowing the sea back from the shore! Choppy waves were streaming away from the island and piling up in a white-capped wall of seawater behind her. When he stopped the wind, the released sea would crush her.

As she waited for the wind to die, Kemrae suddenly realized she was standing on a plain of glistening seabed that had once been a mountaintop. She knelt and laid her hands on the seabed, ordering it to rise up. The earth pushed up against her hands as Arkizan ceased his wind. For a moment she was bathed in the green light cast by the translucent wall of sea hanging over her, but then her mountain thrust up into the sunlight. A cataract of pent-up sea split around her mountain and rushed over the little island below her.

She saw a whirlpool spinning frantically over the keep, holding back the crashing sea, but the column of air collapsed with a gurgle and a pop. The sea swirled one more time over the spot and then was quiet. Kemrae looked out from the new mountaintop and saw sails on the horizon. She knew it would not be long before ships came to discover the new island. She knew that when they did, she would tell the sailors the name of the island was Teryxia.

FIRE FOR THE SENJEN TIGER

by Stephen Crane Davidson

Stephen Crane Davidson lives near Atlanta with his wife and children. His sword and sorcery adventure novel, *Far From The Warring Lands,* was published by the internet book publisher VirtuaBooks.com and will soon be available through another publisher. He has previously published short stories in *Marion Zimmer Bradley's Fantasy Magazine, Transversions, Millennium Science Fiction,* and a number of other magazines and anthologies. His work can be found on the internet at Fables.org and Alternaterealitieszine.com, among other sites. He is currently the fantasy editor for the e-zine www.WritersHood.com, and an excerpt from *Far From The Warring Lands* is available there.

Some schools simply have tests and report cards, but in others, the student evaluation process is much more challenging.

The stench of sulfur bit at Princess Li's nostrils and burned in her lungs. She joined the pain. Neera. Illusion.

Screaming in rage, the Senjen tiger spewed fire, engulfing Li in flames. She sat motionless, a living wick, one with the fire. The whirling yellow eyes gleamed and then dulled. The beast turned its massive head away. The dull gray of hard-cut granite replaced the bizarre image of a fire-spewing tiger.

The fog of incense stung the princess' nose. Sitting in a cross-legged posture. Li began again the novice exercise she had practiced daily for two years. Chi, she named the breath she inhaled. Her awareness of the word burned in the palm of her left hand and burrowed into the pit of her stomach, a tight ball of leashed power.

The cold stone against her knees, the pungent scent of the incense, the illusory tiger rhykyas that frequently attacked her senses, all disappeared in the word. The word began outside, became inside, subsumed the void and devoured all substance.

A clear note from a bell shivered through her awareness. Bowing, she enjoyed the surge of hot pleasure that traveled down her spine as she stretched to touch the floor with her forehead. Behind her, silk robes whispered across the floor.

Li stiffened.

A touch on her shoulder signaled her to stand. Hands cupped and face now burning with shame, she paced to the Senai's chamber. A gray-robed master opened the door and stepped aside to let the princess enter. With her white-robed novice status, Li could not even open the door.

One candle burned on the right arm of the Senai's wooden chair. Shadows filled the small room. In the dim light, the old woman's wrinkled face floated above a mass of darkness. White streaks wove through the black of her hair. She neither moved nor spoke. On the left arm of her chair, a second candle remained unlit.

Li approached to within seven steps before stopping. Focusing, she made her breath the word and the word a vision of the unlit candle igniting. Energy flowed from her. A flame sputtered to life. Li bowed in respect for the power. The Senai nodded back. Ritual complete, Li sat.

Straining to keep the desire from her voice, she began the petition she had already made too many times. "Honorable Senai, the breath is the word in me. My energy turns to substance. I seek to shed my white robe, be tested for the gray—"

"No."

The blood drained from Li's cheeks.

"I did not call you here to listen to your desires," the Senai said.

"But I—"

"No!"

Li sank back, devastated. "Then let me leave, Senai, for I have brought great shame to my family and myself."

"Your shame is no more than clouds hiding sky. The sky, as you are, is still there. But that is as none."

The Senai shifted in her chair though she continued to stare intently at Li. "The rebellion of the Ch'an power shapers has turned violent," she said. "Three of your elder brothers have been killed. You are now second to the heir."

"What?" Li scrambled to her feet.

The Senai leaned forward, staring at the Princess. "On the New Year festival, the Ch'an Prince swore over the tomb of his ancestors to kill every member of your family until their land is free. Your elder brother is where the Ch'an will not find him. You are here now as you have been here these two years to be kept alive, not to learn to wield the power. Practice the word as you wish, you will not be tested."

I must learn in order to fight the Ch'an," Li said.

"To live, Princess, that is all, enough."

Li stared at the floor.

"You were close to your brothers?" the Senai asked.

Rather than lie, Li did not reply. Born of the king's second wife, she had never been close to her half-brothers. She pressed her hands together and bowed. "I must make ready then, go to my family, to help defend them and mourn our deaths as is right."

"No! You stay here."

Li stopped mid-step, shaking her head. "I must go. To be a Princess and still a novice after this time spent is already great shame. To then not stand with my family or mourn for the dead is unworthy of my ancestors and more than can be asked."

"Must not? Cannot?" the Senai said and snorted. "What would you protect them with—the feeble flame you make to light a candle?" She pointed a withered finger at the candle, and it exploded with a thunderous clap that slammed Li against the wall.

"Will your puny flame set the Ch'an's robes on fire? Hah. Black-robed masters are there to protect your family already. You stay here. I have spoken too much. You will not leave the fortress. Go. Continue your practice. Learn nothing . . . as you have already done so well."

The Senai drew back, her face now obscured by darkness.

Stung and dazed, Li forced herself to hold her head upright. She turned and walked stiff-legged out the wooden door and down the narrow. shadowed halls.

The slapping echoes of her sandals taunted her as she trod down the three hundred steps and seven curved landings to the library, her place of work, the work of a white-robed novice.

She finally reached the library and stopped to scowl at the two black-robed clay figurines that guarded the entrance. They stared back unmoved. Li opened the door, walked in, and stopped. The novice she was to replace was not there.

"Chang?" Li called out. Her voice echoed amidst the stone walls and stacks of silk and paper and then died. Li shrugged, deciding that Chang must have left early. It was just as well. Li did not feel like seeing anyone. Her face still burned. She closed the heavy door behind her.

The dim flickering of the candles set near the door threw only wavering edges of illumination into the darkness beyond. From that gloom strode a robed figure. The man stopped in front of Li. Surprised and frightened, Li backed up a step. A cold chill ran down her back.

Tall, with an angular, thin face, the black-robed master stood motionless. "Princess Li?" the man said.

Masters frequently came to the library for their researches, yet Li hesitated before responding. The man looked threatening.

The Master became taller, filling the room with his presence. "You are Li, white-robe?"

"Yes," Li said, the words dragged from her unwillingly. With the recognition that her voice had been forced from her, came a thought—assassin—and the thought crushed the breath from Li's lungs. Heart pounding against her chest, she edged toward the door, hoping the Master would not notice the slight movement. Unarmed, Li had few choices. She could feel the other's power tugging at her as the wind would tug at her robe. Sweat ran down her sides. "Who are you?" she asked.

"Tian," the man said as he walked forward and pushed Li from the doorway. Tian now blocked the only exit.

"What are you doing here?" Li asked.

The Master narrowed his eyes. "You will come quietly with me. Do not be as your brothers. You could be as useful alive as dead."

"What about my brothers?" Li began to inch toward the darkness of the stacks, her last hope of escape.

"Your brothers were fools. They sought to fight. I killed them. Their swords were as nothing to the shaping of Gy. Do not make the same mistake."

"But why?" Li continued to sidle back and to the side. From memory, she knew one of the stacks was no more than ten feet in that direction. The Master didn't seem to be noticing Li's slight movements. If she could get behind the stack . . .

"The Land of Plains must be returned. No more questions. Go out in front of me."

Li steeled herself. "No," she said and glanced behind her, looking for the stack and not seeing it.

Tian scowled. Then a smile inched across his face. "You make it easier. Perhaps your body will fire some of these worthless stacks of scrolls."

Tian's face went blank and fire flashed from his

hand. Diving back and sideways, Li landed and rolled behind the aisle. The fire singed her hair. She struggled to her feet, twisted around, and darted away just as another bolt seared by her face, bursting stacks of silk rolls into flames. The heat knocked Li back into another stack that toppled down behind her. The fire spread. She rolled to put out her smoldering clothing.

Tian extinguished the candles at the front. The only light now came from the flaming stacks. Smoke billowed, and Li coughed as she twisted and ran to put another stack between herself and Tian.

With the doorway the only exit, Li had to slip around the deadly Ch'an Master. The smoke thickened. Sweat broke out on Li's face. She got to her knees and crawled down the aisle. She had to lure the Ch'an farther into the stacks. It seemed impossible. There had to be another way.

She had no knife or even a kira. She did have the word and its power. For a moment, Li stopped and considered trying to attack with the fire she could create. She thought of the tiny flame with which she lit the candle and the derision of the Senai. Worse, the first move she made with her hand as if to direct a flame, the Ch'an would know that Li had at least some power. The Ch'an would no longer toy with small, careful bolts of flame. He would incinerate Li with one massive surge of energy. Li wished for her knife. How could she, a white-robe not even worthy of testing, fight a master?

The books behind Li blocked the light of the fire. She crawled through darkness, still hoping to circle around the Master. Reaching ahead, Li found another aisle.

She stopped again, then slid down until her body rested on the cold rock. Inching forward on her belly, she turned back to the left in what she assumed was the path to the closed door. The smoke swirled lower as she moved.

Suddenly, Tian appeared out of the darkness. A glowing bubble of clear air surrounded his body, a sign of his utter contempt for a white-robe's power. The Master pushed his hand through the bubble to marshal a last deadly bolt.

Li felt the inrush of power. Blood pounded in her ears. In near panic, she looked to either side, and saw nothing but stacks piled high leaving no route of escape. She started to back away.

Tian laughed, a hollow croak of a sound. He pointed to Li. "Run, white-robe, as all your feeble blood will soon."

The scornful words knifed into Li's mind. Muscle clenching rage drove through her body. The image of the strange, fire-spouting tiger grew in her mind. The beast snarled with anger.

Breathing in, Li's breath became the word and the word became the tiger. She filled her lungs with an all-consuming blast. The word became tiger's fire. The Master's eyes widened.

Li roared a flame that burst from her mouth and overwhelmed Tian's bolt with a thunderous crack. The Ch'an Master crashed against the wall. The bubble of air exploded into fire. Tian's body burst into a white hot blaze. The man screamed once, stepped forward, and crumpled into the roaring fire that enveloped him.

Blasted by the explosion, Li flew backward. Her skin seared from the heat. She gasped in smoke. Choking, she tried to crawl, but with each breath she inhaled more smoke, and her arms collapsed under her. Racked with coughing, she curled away from the flame that licked across the rolls of silk. Her lungs burned. Blackness took her.

The darkness faded into pain. It hurt to breathe. For a moment, as memory flooded back, she was surprised she breathed at all.

Covered by a wool blanket, she lay in a bed, her head propped up on a cushion. She looked around in confusion. A small window let in a dazzling shaft of light that struck and sparkled on the rough rock walls. A Master's gray robe hung on a hook nailed into a rough wooden wardrobe. Li breathed in again, and this time cried out. Her movement brought another wave of intense pain. Her chest was bandaged, skin sensitive to the slightest movement against the cloth.

Soundlessly, the door opened. The Senai entered wearing a black robe tied at the waist and carrying a white robe across her arm.

"What happened?" Li managed to croak out.

"Do not speak. You killed the Ch'an and nearly died yourself. That robe," the Senai pointed to the gray robe on the wall, "is yours. To create is the first level of mastery. By lighting the candle on my chair, you have created, but because of the white robe you have worn, the Ch'an, a man of formidable power, did not think to protect himself from you. No one looks for a tiger's fangs in a white-robed mouse. Thus you live.

"Will you wear this gray robe now, or will you continue to wear the white of the rank and shameful beginner?" The Senai held up the white robe.

Li stared at the novice's robe with disgust. She thought of the Ch'an Master who had left himself undefended. "White," she said.

The Senai smiled. "Wisdom is one sign of the blackrobe, and you tread toward it."

FIGHTING SPIRIT

by Karen Magon

Karen Magon works as a teacher's aide in an intermediate school, which has motivated her to go back to college. She is the proud mother of three talented daughters and the wife of a wonderful husband. In addition to writing, she is interested in history, astronomy, and anthropology.

This story is her second sale; her first was to *Marion Zimmer Bradley's Fantasy Magazine*.

Tahn thrust the sword high above her head, her arm trembling as she fought to hold it steady.

"There is still time to stop the spell," whispered Ophidae. Though the sun shone mirror-bright, the sorceress seemed wreathed in shadows. "It's not gone too far yet."

"No," Tahn gasped. "I must force Lord Sem to release my father. Give my sword an animal's strength and bravery."

"You know I cannot control which animal takes your sword for its own."

Ophidae's voice was a whispered hiss as she swayed to and fro. Tahn guessed she'd mingled her spirit with a snake's.

The thought must have communicated itself to Ophidae. The sorceress smiled, her eyes like marbles gleaming in the shadows. "The snake chose me," she said. "As it might choose your sword."

Tahn shuddered at the thought, but the reflex went unnoticed because the trembling in her arm was spreading to her body. "No snake," she said, putting as much force as she could behind the words. "A wolf or a bear. Even a great eagle will do. My sword must have a strong spirit."

Ophidae said, "I cannot control—"

"Begin the spell!" Sweat stung her eyes and her shoulder felt as if it would break.

The sorceress raised her arms and her sleeves fell back. Light welled up in her palms as she clapped them together and flung the light at Tahn's sword.

The popping and spitting of her chant sounded like fire consuming wood, but already more light grew in the sorceress' hands, and she flung the bright streamers out and brought her hands back again to fill with light.

Shapes appeared in the light around her sword; a bear, an eagle, a wolf. Other animals joined them, their images reflecting back from the blade: a lion, its mane shedding sparks like comets, a great fish, its teeth like jagged razors, a fierce raven, its feathers shiny as black water, and a snake—surely Ophidae's snake—enormous in length and girth. Still more creatures circled her sword; finches and turtles, a scurrying fox and a tiny bat.

Tahn ignored them all, focusing on the lion as it wound its way around her sword. Its massive paws, its long, curved teeth, its eyes devoid of pity for others' suffering. With this animal to lend its strength to her sword, it wouldn't matter how meager her skill in swordplay.

Tahn felt a thud against her sword and saw the pommel burn as if with inner fire. At last an animal spirit had claimed her sword for its own. She craned her neck to see which, but saw only a flash of fur.

The sorceress lowered her arms and her chanting rose to a shriek as the animals swarmed towards her, their rush like a tornado swirling her hair and robe.

She saw the lion swing past the sorceress' head, its tail flicking Ophidae's ear before he vanished with the others.

Tahn panted as if she had run for miles, but marveled that she could already feel a difference in her sword. It was lighter than before, and she gripped the hilt as if the sword were part of her. The relief in her arm and shoulder was so sudden that she cried out with wonder.

Tahn swung her sword around her head in glee. For the animal to meld so perfectly with her sword, she knew it was a creature of great fighting merit.

The sorceress smiled at her with approval. "Don't you wish to see which animal has taken your sword?" she asked. "Or will you stand there until winter comes?"

Tahn knelt on the ground and laid the sword across her lap. She examined the blade, hoping for a lion's regal countenance to appear. At first she saw nothing, and then large, teardrop-shaped eyes came into focus, blinking at her.

With a snarl she threw the sword, not caring when it clattered against stones.

"Which animal loaned its spirit to the blade's?" asked Ophidae.

Tahn could hardly bear to say the words. "A rabbit," she said, snorting with disgust. "How can I defeat Lord Sem with a rabbit?"

"Rabbits are fine animals. Rabbits survive and thrive in—"

"You keep it, then," Tahn shouted. "A rabbit is useless for what I need."

"I cannot," said the sorceress.

"You can. I give it to you."

"You would give a rabbit to a snake?" Her voice held only contempt.

"No." Tahn buried her head in her hands and mourned the wasted sword. She should have tried to get the sword to her father. She wished now that she'd never left him at all.

Tahn felt the sorceress' fingers, cool against her cheek. "A rabbit is not such a bad thing," she said.

"I would agree with you," said Tahn, "had I wanted a cloak or a stew."

*   *   *

When she sought their help, her father's supporters turned her away; some with sympathy, some with laughter.

Lord Sparrow's wife caught her sleeve as she left their hall, her breath smelling of onions. "You'll never get the help you seek if you tell them Ophidae empowered your sword with a rabbit," she said, her voice low.

Tahn sat on the beggar's bench, her body aching with exhaustion. "The lie would soon be known for what it was," she said. "And I can't betray supporters the way Lord Sem betrayed us. I would be no better than he, perhaps even worse."

"What are you going to do?"

Tahn leaned against the wall and closed her eyes. "Somehow," she said, "I'll try to force Lord Sem to release my father and abandon his hold on our property and lands."

Walking as if on important business, Tahn skirted her family keep's outer walls until she saw the configuration of stones that signaled the section she sought.

She pushed on the hidden lever. When the narrow door didn't open, she pushed again. Nothing happened. She jabbed at all the stones, not believing that Lord Sem had discovered and blocked the hidden entrance.

She clenched her jaw, knowing she had one option left. She turned and made her way to the hill that held another entrance, one nobody but she knew about.

Pushing aside the thistles that obscured the entrance, she heard footsteps behind her.

As she reached for her scabbard, her hand met only cloth. The rabbit in her sword had wrapped her skirt around itself, and when she tugged on the cloth, it wrapped tighter. She turned to face whoever was behind her, defenseless because her rabbity sword hid from her.

"What are you looking for, girl?"

The man before her was tall, his fur collar meant for decoration rather than warmth, his doublet and hose of perfect cut, and his shoes encrusted with jewels.

Tahn bowed, keeping her head down so he couldn't recognize her. "Oh, Lord Sem. I wanted to climb this hill to watch for attacking armies. I was hoping if I saw them first, you would give me a reward."

His thin cheeks iifted in a smile and a glimmer of amusement lightened his eyes. "And have you discovered any attackers?"

Tahn bowed her head lower, and reminded herself that his charm was a sham. "No, though there may be one some day."

He reached for his purse and tossed her a silver coin. "This is for your trouble," he said. He turned and walked away, picking through rocks and thistles.

Tahn made sure he was gone before she reached for the thistles.

She hesitated before slipping into the passage. She knew she must hurry, but could hardly face the thought of the close, narrow tunnel leading to the keep's inner chambers. She'd always hated small spaces, and this passage was the worst of all.

As she held her breath and lowered herself down, Tahn noticed her rabbit had released her skirts so they swung free around her legs.

"Oh, so now you show yourself, coward," she muttered.

Her breathing seemed overloud as she felt her way along the rough rocks, tripping over uneven places. She stretched her eyes wide, but there was no relief from the darkness.

The rabbit at her side pressed into her knee and the scabbard rubbed her leg. "What, then?" she said. Her voice sounded hollow.

Tahn feared to take her hands off the wall, lest she lose her way, but her sword danced in its scabbard, its gyrations so demanding that she drew it out. "So? Now that there is no need for you, you want to come out and fight?"

Before she had spit out the last word, Tahn suddenly realized she could see in the darkness. What was more, she felt comfortable and secure in the small tunnel.

In her sword, she could make out an eye's liquid gleam and the rabbit's long ears. "At least you're good for something."

A rustling sound nearby made her stiffen. "Please, not rats," she muttered. Then the sword pushed hard against her, forcing her against the wall. She fought against the sword, but looking beyond it, saw Lord Sem not far away.

Tahn stood still, her breathing shallow, stunned that he had followed her.

Lord Sem took a hesitant step and cracked his knee against an outcrop of rock. His curses were so vicious she almost laughed out loud.

As he passed by, Tahn tried to raise her sword to strike him, but couldn't lift it. She wanted to throw down the sword and attack Lord Sem with her bare hands. She shifted her weight and heard gravel crunch beneath her heel.

"Girl, is that you?" Lord Sem's voice echoed.

Instead of answering, all she could do was remain quiet and hope the world, which was a very big place, wouldn't notice her. There was much to fear, and it was best to stay small and tucked and wait. . . .

Tahn shuddered and shook her head. These were not her thoughts. They were the rabbit's. She hated what the creature was doing to her.

She cast a quick glance to where Lord Sem stood, realizing with a shock that he had moved on.

She brought her sword close to her face. "Don't you ever do that to me again," she whispered harshly to the rabbit.

She could feel the rabbit urging caution like a tide rising in her head. *We are together,* she thought, *and together we can be safe and strong.* There was a moment's hesitation, and then it no longer blocked her from following Lord Sem.

She saw a crack of light ahead, and realized that

Lord Sem was letting himself into her father's old quarters.

She broke into a run, but was too far behind to catch the door before it closed. If she opened the door now, he would see her. She rested her forehead against it, not sure what to do.

"How did you find the passage?" she heard her father ask.

Tahn was so relieved to hear him that it was a few heartbeats before she realized her ears couldn't have heard through the thick door, but rabbit's ears could.

Sending the rabbit a message of thankfulness, she pressed the side of her head against the door so she wouldn't miss a word.

"For the price of a silver coin your daughter showed me the entrance," he gloated. "I know she's somewhere here now, and soon I'll have both of you."

"Tahn would never betray me."

She moaned when she heard the weariness in his voice.

"But you have been betrayed in every way possible," Lord Sem said. "You have no supporters, no one to rally around your banner."

"Yet still you allow me to live."

"Do you think I've forgotten how you humiliated me so many years ago? My pleasure in watching you squirm is the only reason you are still alive. However, with your daughter loose somewhere, this foolishness must come to an end."

Tahn heard the snick of a knife withdrawn from its sheath, and flung the door wide. She leaped into the room, sword at the ready.

She cried out when she saw her father resting on a bed, his frame wasted and feeble.

Her sight was washed in a red glaze as she turned to face Lord Sem. She raised her sword to block his knife as it slashed down. It clattered on her sword and dropped form his hand.

In one smooth motion, his sword was drawn and resting easy in his hand, his weight forward on the balls of his feet. "Don't be foolish girl," he said. His smile was a thin curl on his face. "You cannot hope to best me."

As he spoke the last word, his sword flashed toward her, and she leaped, slashing downward.

He grunted, surprised rather than pained from the blow, circled, and jabbed again.

She met his sword with a brief parry, but her strength was no match for his. Disengaging, she backed up and stood paralyzed with fear. He moved to hit the sword from her hand, but with a leap she was away from him. her feet had springs as she danced from his blows, escaping his attacks by inches.

Tahn sensed the rabbit's terror, but she drove it and herself mercilessly, working her way closer to Lord Sem even as he thought victory was imminent.

Lord Sem's smile stiffened to a grimace, sweat running down his face. With a final roll and swerve, she slipped under his guard and swiped her sword, hitting Lord Sem broadside on his calves. He shrieked as he fell, and she held her sword point against his throat, forcing him to remain flat.

Her father struggled to sit and then leaned back, too weak to rise. "Well done, Tahn," he said. "Ophidae must have empowered your sword with a formidable beast."

Tahn laughed as she saw the rabbit preen itself at her father's words. "Oh, yes," she agreed. "My rabbit and I are a match for anything."

PRIDE, PREJUDICE, AND PARANOIA

by Michael Spence

This story is an interesting example of literary evolution. Elisabeth Waters wrote a short story called "The Blade of Unmaking" in 1996. It was published in *S&S XIV*. Unfortunately, it was the last piece of fiction that Elisabeth ever wrote by herself; she developed writer's block later that year. But as long as she was living in MZB's household, she was expected to produce stories, so she and Michael collaborated on a story—"Salt and Sorcery"—for *S&S XVI*. They were friends when they were in high school, and the intervening years apart (until the 1997 Worldcon) had not changed their ability to work together.

At that time Michael was studying for his comprehensive exams for his PhD in Systematic Theology. He has since passed them and is now completing his dissertation: "Secular Theology in the Fiction of Harlan Ellison" (formerly "Author and Reader-based Hermeneutics for Imaginative Literature as an Aid to Analyzing Popular World-views, with a Focus on the Fiction of Harlan Ellison").

As a change of pace from his dissertation, he wrote this story, a sequel to "Salt and Sorcery." It is dedicated to his long-suffering wife Ramona, who shares Melisande's distress over the amount of living space occupied by her husband's books.

Michael, Ramona, and Michael's books currently reside in Dallas, Texas, but by the time this book is in print, he should have been awarded his degree, which means that they will be free to go wherever God sends them.

It was a good thing, Melisande decided, that she had spent as much time as she had in the front rooms of the student union recently, drowning her frustrations in mugs of minimead. Otherwise she'd probably break her neck tripping over the furniture in this dim light. At least it would be warm in here, after she managed to lose the bitter chill of the snow-covered quadrangle outside.

"And just think," Laurel was saying, coming up behind her and peering through the murk. Behind the seventeen-year-old blonde was her friend Edward, who negotiated the various obstacles with the skill typical of a first-year student in his third trimester. "With Stephen passing his Ordeal, I don't have to coach him any more, so Grandmother's *geas* on me is nullified and I'll be out of your apartment. And then he'll graduate, so you can get out of there, too!"

"Don't I know it! I've been dreaming about getting out of that little box for several days now," Melisande answered as they passed a posted handbill that read, REMEMBER: McCHEYNE APPLICATIONS DUE THIS WEDNESDAY. FORMS CAN BE PICKED UP FROM THE SYSTEMATIC THAUMATURGY DEPARTMENT SECRETARY BEFORE MONDAY. At the bottom someone had scrawled, *The Sys-Thaum secretary can be picked up on Tuesday.* Melisande continued, "Please don't think I've minded having you as a house guest this past week. But there comes a time . . . Where *is* he? And why in the name of heaven and earth do they have to keep it so *dark* in here?"

"Who knows?" her sister-in-law said, maneuvering around the strands of a beaded veil that might have garroted a less attentive patron. "I think it's supposed to be romantic. Which might work, if romance depended upon never actually having to look at your date. Melisande, are you sure this is when he was going to be here?"

"Oh, yes," Melisande replied. "That's what we agreed on this morning: meet at the BBC at Nones for snacks and celebration. That would allow time for both of us to complete our Ordeals without undue hurry. I checked the department office and they said Lord Logas is back in his workroom, so he and Alyssa must have finished with Stephen a while ago. But where could that man be?"

"Well, we've checked out most of the rooms. The only one left is the Abyss. And if you think the rest of the place is dark—" Laurel stepped through the doorway into the back room. "Hm. Only five table lights on. Start with the first . . ."

Life must be governed by a dramatic formula, Melisande thought: they found him at the last booth they investigated. Despite the moderate temperature typical of the Bell, Book, & Canteen, Stephen hadn't taken off his coat or scarf. He sat swaddled in the booth, staring down at the mug in front of him. He didn't even seem to notice that his wife and sister had arrived. Only when Melisande sat down beside him and picked up his mug did he show signs of life. "Hi, Mel. Hi, sis."

Melisande took a small sip of the mug's contents and made a face. "Eeeyugghh! What in the world is that?"

"A Mefisto-in-Byronics," he said. "I felt like ordering something dark and foul. Matches my mood at the moment." He looked up at his wife's expression and added, "Your eyes are shining; I'm guessing you passed it. Congratulations to a new Senior Thaumaturge!"

"Thank you, kind sir," Melisande said, and, pushing her raven hair out of the way, leaned over to kiss her husband. Then, as she sat beside him and Laurel and Edward took seats opposite the couple, she continued, "But this doesn't make sense. I thought you'd be pleased that we both passed our Ordeals. Unless—"

"Ah, yes, the 'unless.'" He slumped further in his seat. 'Unless' it is, beloved new wizard. I failed the Ordeal."

"Failed?" Melisande said. "How? You were all ready for this! Lord Logas said you were ready. Lady

Sarras said you were ready. And *I've* known you were
ready for years. I don't understand.''

Stephen scowled. ''Yes, yes, you all said I was ready.
But you left out one voice. I, you recall, said all that
time that I *wasn't* ready.'' His hand reached out from
the overcoat to pick up the mug; he took a pull from
the MiB, choked it down, and coughed wetly. He sat
further into the coat as if it were a shroud. ''It seems
that in this case,'' he said softly, ''the minority opinion
was the correct one.''

''So?'' said Edward. ''So you take it again in eight
months. What's the problem?''

Laurel punched him on the arm. Leaning close to
him, she muttered, ''Listen, buster; you're charming
as all get out, but you can be so *dense* sometimes!''

''Eight *months?*'' Melisande said. ''I don't remember that in the catalog.''

From within his overcoat Stephen *hmph*'d. ''Lots of
stuff not in the catalog. The Spouse's Ordeal wasn't in
the catalog, you remember. Don't overlook any potential
wizards, but don't let students think they can just come
in and qualify two Seniors for only one tuition. But
the mandatory waiting period was in the student hand-
book. Just not in very big print. Eight years or eighty
thousand kilometers, whichever comes first.''

Laurel stared at her brother. ''Kilometers? Eight
years? What are you talking about?''

Stephen returned the stare. ''What do you mean,
what am I talking about? Two trimesters, eight months.
The waiting period. What Edward said.''

Laurel looked down at the table and shook her head
as if to clear it. Melisande sat up. ''No. I don't believe
it. I *know* you were ready to take this.'' Her jaw stiffened. ''Something's not right. I'm going to see Logas
about it and find out what's going on.''

''Please, Mel,'' her husband said. ''Don't make it
any more awkward than it is. He's already disappointed, I can tell. It won't help if he has to deal with
our paranoia, too.''

At least you didn't say your *paranoia,* she thought.

Thank you for that. "Perhaps I am paranoid. Or perhaps I know my husband better than he thinks I do. But I just know something is wrong here."

"Are you talking as a Sensitive or as a spouse? Mel, I love you dearly, but sometimes we just have to know when to quit."

"No," said Edward suddenly. "Stephen, she's right. If something peculiar is going on, we need to find out. And if there's something my Weak talent can add to your and Laurel's Strong talents, I want to help."

Melisande looked at him with gratitude. "Why, thank you, Edward. I appreciate having *someone* on my side."

Laurel broke in. "I think the two of us need to talk, and I know you guys do. Edward, why don't we go check out the Pollock exhibit in the library?"

He stood up. "I guess so. Let me know what you find out from Lord Logas." He helped Laurel out of the booth. As the two shrugged into their outer coats and started to leave, Melisande said, "Wait a minute, if you would." She edged out of the booth and went over to them. "I need to say something."

She turned to Edward. "I want to apologize. I know we got off on the wrong foot when Laurel first introduced you, and I'm afraid my initial, well, dislike came out as rudeness. I don't like prejudice, and it's hard for me to realize I'm as guilty of it as anyone else—I guess I just care about Laurel enough that I was skeptical of a young man I hadn't met. It was inexcusable. And I just want you to know that I appreciate your offer to help Stephen. I really do."

He coughed and glanced at his feet. "I'm, uh, glad to do it. I'm sorry if I was abrasive as well. I hope something good comes of this." He smiled, and Laurel tugged at his elbow.

"Come on, Mister Congeniality," she said. "We have a date with some paintings. And I have an idea on how we might strengthen your talent for a while." Turning to leave, she asked, "Have you ever heard of linkstones?"

They hadn't gone five steps toward the door when Laurel stopped and wailed, "Oh, no! I'm going to be stuck here another eight *months!*"

Melisande froze in horror. *Oh, my sweet Lord—so am I.*

The next hour was slow and painful. Melisande tried her utmost to cheer her husband up, and he just as energetically refused to be cheered. Finally, as they were leaving, she said, "All right, you win. I promise I won't go to Logas."

"*Or* Lady Sarras."

Damn. "Or Lady Sarras," she sighed. "But I won't promise to believe that your Ordeal went the way it was supposed to. Call me paranoid, but I just won't. You're good at your magic; I've watched you." They made their way toward the door—it was easier with her eyes used to the dark—and as they passed the handbill again, she nodded toward it and added, "And Lord Logas has said he thinks you're good enough for him to recommend you for that McCheyne Fellowship. So he obviously doesn't think you'd normally fail the Ordeal either."

They opened the BBC's carved oaken door and stepped out into a sea of cold white light. Although the snow had been shoveled and swept from the walkways, the untouched expanses in the quadrangle and elsewhere took the rare January sun and scattered it abroad in its full blinding glory. They shielded their eyes, wool-scarved their necks and faces against the chilly gusts, and set out in the direction of the married students' rooms.

Stephen's spirits seemed to revive somewhat in the chill air. As they turned a corner, he caught his wife's elbow, spun her toward him, and kissed her. "The McCheyne would help pay quite a few bills, wouldn't it?" he said. "Look, I love you and I appreciate your faith in me more than I can say. But I just don't want us to make a big noise about this. I don't know what Mother and Papa would make of it; I especially don't know what *Grandmother* would make of it. And Edward is right: I can retake it in eight months. I'll review continually until then. Who knows? It may well go better then."

"You're darn tootin' it'll go better then," Melisande retorted. "You'll do so well that Logas and Alyssa will wish they could hand you your diploma, the McCheyne, and six job offers on the spot." She stopped suddenly. "You go ahead—I'll meet you at the apartment. I have to get something for dinner."

Fortunately, Stephen was still depressed enough not to ask questions. He slogged on homeward, while Melisande, in addition to a quick stop at the grocer's, stopped by the Student Message Service's office, then continued home, very nervous about what she had just done. *It would have been so much easier if he'd let me go to Logas or Sarras,* she thought. *There are days when obeying your husband makes things really difficult.*

Back at the married-student apartments, she climbed the stairs to the third floor. But when she reached their front door, she found it standing open. Stephen was slumped on the sofa, and Laurel stood just inside the doorway, staring down at something in her hand. It was one of those new instant-delivery forms, the kind that once written on would disappear and reappear elsewhere, even hundreds of miles away—what they were calling "post-it notes." Laurel looked up at Melisande with eyes filled with a mixture of guilt and terror. "She's coming."

Stephen looked up, and his face went gray. "Oh, no."

Melisande didn't have to ask to whom they were referring. And for the sake of her marriage, she hoped it wouldn't occur to either of them to ask why she was coming—or rather, how she had found out.

"It was obviously nerves," Stephen told the other four, assembled in their apartment. Melisande sat in one chair, and Edward had taken the other, with Laurel seated on its arm. Stephen sat on the floor, his elbow resting on an ad hoc hassock made of stacked books. First-year books, as it happened; to Melisande's perpetual frustration, her husband didn't seem able to give, sell, or throw away any of his accumulated library. "I could have told you all about Michelangelo's 'David,' Rodin and 'Amphibienne,' Krazny's 'Epiphany,' even the history of the Junipero Serra pioneer missals—and yet I couldn't tell Logas and Alyssa about magic, the nonhuman intelligences, or any of the recognized divination/analysis techniques. I wanted to be anywhere but there, I can tell you."

"I doubt that not at all," said the tall, regal woman seated at the center of the sofa. She wore a long, full-skirted dress of midnight blue that accented her bound silver hair; around her neck, a tartan stole fastened with a brooch bearing an opal that blazed with elemental fire. The way she carried herself, however, the Lady Wizard Ysenda would have looked like royalty even had she gone barefoot and worn rough homespun. Which, decades ago, she had done. Those days were long past, however; now she was the matriarch of the most respected clerical-wizardly clan in half the country.

Privately, Melisande would sometimes call Stephen's grandmother "the Tsarina." Very privately. With the door locked and the windows shuttered.

Her carriage, emblazoned with the clan's coat of arms, had touched down on the mossy ground in front of the main gate, which adjoined the school's main administration wing. Within the building it was as if someone had kicked over an anthill. Faces appeared and disappeared at windows every other second. One could hear the sounds of feet rushing down corridors. Heavy armoire doors were opened and ceremonial gowns hurriedly donned by officials wondering why their visitor was here and grousing that she had to choose *today* of all days to come (although, truth to tell, they would have said the same any day). The Chancellor had not even reached the front portals, however, when the carriage door opened and the Lady

Ysenda stepped out. He finally made it out into the entranceway only to stare open-mouthed at her retreating back as she strode briskly into the distance, toward the married students' rooms.

He shrugged and turned back toward the tall, carved doors. One of these days she would *slow down* for a change. Yes, indeed—and on that day pigs would do aerobatics and auld Nessie herself would drop by for tea.

Now the Lady sat upright on a sofa almost as old as herself in Stephen and Melisande's apartment, her gaze fixed on her grandson, who looked rather like a moth pinned to a board. Ysenda spoke in a calm, melodic, but unrelenting voice. "And the information didna surface at any time during the Ordeal?"

"No, ma'am, not until I was back at the student union and able to relax somewhat. When I thought back on it, I could have kicked myself a dozen times. I could even tell you how to set up the kinetic vectors to do it, too. But in front of Logas and Alyssa I drew a complete blank."

He said no more. Nor did any of the other students. They knew who was entitled to the next word.

"Wi' some people I know, I would think this quite normal." Her gray eyes regarded him carefully. "But no' you, Stephen. Your father may be a Weak talent, but he was never a scatterbrain. Neither is his Strong son. Certainly ye've taken enough years to get to this point"—Melisande and Stephen winced in unison—"but it's no' been because ye lacked either the magical talent or the mental ability. And tha' includes being subject to 'nerves,' as you put it."

"I don't know what else to call it," Stephen replied. "There I was, at the table in the examining room, relaxing in luxurious comfort on the finest leather—"

Laurel and Melisande exchanged startled glances. The examination chairs were wood.

"—and Lord Logas and Lady Alyssa asked me their questions, and the sky itself welcomes you! The answers just weren't there. I simply couldn't find a better deal if you scoured the whole land. It was humiliating, to say the least."

By now Laurel's expression was creeping steadily up the scale from "bemused" to "horrified." Edward sat listening intently. Melisande was numb. Stephen appeared not to notice.

"And now I can't seem to work the magic at all," he said quietly.

Both Laurel's and Edward's eyes opened wide.

"This afternoon, when you met me in the Abyss— I had wanted to meet you in the graduate students' taproom, but I couldn't get in. The admission spell wouldn't work—and I couldn't even see the wards in order to aim it. As though the universe were adding insult to injury." Stephen chuckled without humor. "I've found a few cases in my reading where a strong emotional shock produced a kind of magical blindness, so to speak. I suppose that's what's happened here. I can only hope it passes quickly."

His grandmother appeared to be considering it. "Perhaps. Tell me what you meant by 'scouring the land' and 'sky welcoming' a moment ago."

He looked puzzled. "When did I ever say *that*?"

"Never you mind. Stand up," she said, herself rising from the sofa to face him. "Give me your hands." He stood and held his arms out forward. She took his left hand in her right hand and his right in her left, holding them with her fingertips in his palms. Her eyes stared into his . . . and then it was as if she was looking *through* them to somewhere else. Melisande felt a tingling she had only recently learned to identify: Power was being expended. And received, and processed.

Ysenda's gaze returned to the room. "No," she said. "Your wife is correct. The two of ye come wi' me. We are going to see Logas."

"Balderdash."

The Lord High Wizard Logas, chairman of the Division of Systematic and Historical Thaumaturgy, Head of the Order of Wizards, and Adviser to the King, bustled about his sparsely decorated workroom, attending to various experiments and works-in-progress, his gray beard drifting behind him like a windsock on a mildly breezy day. "Yes, yes, I've heard of—Melisande, is it?—Melisande's idea. Not an hour ago Laurel managed to sweet-talk one of my graduate assistants into lending her those linkstones of yours to help a friend with an investigation. I've told him I am seriously contemplating using his head for a bookend. Anyway, I've had great expectations for the boy, and I was disappointed and frustrated when we had no choice but to give him a failing grade. Most unfortunate. But this talk of tampering with the Ordeal . . . it's unheard of."

Lady Ysenda was not even fazed, let alone deterred. From the chair he had offered her, she watched in mild amusement as he scurried around the room. Stephen and Melisande stood off to the side, against the wall.

"Unheard of, aye," said the Lady. "But would ye be so arrogant as to claim to have heard of everything that happens within these walls?"

"Of course not," he said, as he leaned over a workstation, spread the two middle fingers of his right hand at a measured angle, and waved them in a lissajous pattern between two posts wrapped with silver and copper wires. He examined the fingertips and made some notes. That task done, he reached for a laboratory stool, swept the hem of his robe behind it, and sat down. He wore violet trousers that clashed horribly with the brown robe, and if he weren't careful there would soon be a hole in the knee. "Omniscience is, alas, an attribute still reserved by the Almighty. But it has been a long time, a mighty long time, since I was surprised by anything here. Much as I hate to say it, the Ordeal proceeded just as one would expect, given a candidate who was unprepared."

"Indeed. And from all the work ye've done with

Stephen, would ye have supposed he'd be so very unprepared? Does that truly make the least bit o'
sense?"

Logan chewed a few stray hairs of his mustache.
Then he looked over at Stephen, and then at Stephen's grandmother again. "No, it does not. Hence my
frustration. But have you an alternate hypothesis?"

She stood and walked over toward one of Logas'
emptier workbenches. "I do. It is yet unproven but I
would like to test it here, if ye'd allow me."

Logas smiled. "By all means. Stephen, would you
help me clear off this bench?"

When they had done so, Ysenda said, "All right,
Stephen, lie here." Melisande thought, *My mother
would have said, Lie here,* please. *Who does this
woman think she is?* But when the Lady then said,
"Come over here, child," she found herself obeying
without hesitation.

Ysenda took her hand and guided her to the workbench, where she stood looking down at Stephen's
face. He grinned and winked. She gave him an I-hope-
you-know what's-going-on look and kept quiet.

"Now, then," said Ysenda. "Logas, have ye a
brazier?"

"Of course," he replied, fetching one from a corner.
"They're standard issue with these workrooms. You
should tour the department facilities sometime."

"I might just do that. Choose a suitable incense—it
need not be aromatic, but we do want a fair bit o'
smoke here."

Logas pulled a drawer in another bench. "This
should do." He lighted three cubes, blew out the
flame, and set them in the brazier. Smoke rose into
the air above the workbench, and as Ysenda gestured,
it began to coalesce into a translucent, contained mass.

After putting Stephen in a moderate trance, she resumed her seat and steepled her fingers. To Melisande
she said, "Now, child, this is one way ye can put your
Sensitivity to good use. I want ye to close your eyes
and try to see, not through your eyes, but through

Stephen's. Dinna worry about seeing clearly; we won't expect ye to, and it's not necessary. It's just a way to get the right frame of mind for this procedure."

Melisande closed her eyes and tried to do as she was instructed. She imagined herself lying on the bench, wearing Stephen's face—with those strands of light brown hair lying across her forehead, her nose at more of a downward point, her chin somewhat retracted. For a moment she thought something might be happening, but . . . "My lady, I don't see anything at all."

Ysenda's voice said, "Oh?" Then it said sharply, "Stephen! It would help if ye'd open your eyes!"

"Sorry," his voice whispered. Suddenly Melisande's senses were assaulted with light! At first it was a blast of pure white, which reminded her of their recent visit to the BBC. After a few seconds the white light became tinted, with patches taking on different hues, blue and green in a delicate ballet with yellow and red. Soon bright swirls of color swooped across her vision, slowly resolving themselves into blurred patches that tried but failed again and again to attain more definition.

Her grandmother-in-law's voice sounded again, and for the first time in Ysenda's visit she sounded taken aback. "Logas! D'ye see that?"

The wizard's voice was hushed, awe-struck. "I do, indeed. I apologize—it appears I can be surprised after all. She is actually *seeing*, or trying to. It's as an infant sees, before it learns to differentiate colors and recognize objects. I wonder how long it will be before she learns to sort out all the visual input she's getting?"

"It would be interesting to see. For now, though, let's move on. Stephen, close your eyes now. We've built the bridge. Child, keep that perspective ye've established; strengthen it as ye have the opportunity. But don't try to see anything—just let whatever tries to come to your mind do so."

All right, if it will accomplish something . . . Melisande relaxed and continued repeating those thoughts she had used to link with her husband and reviewing the images she had seen as a result. A moment later, Stephen's grandmother said, "There. D'ye see that? There's the flow from the visual cortex, and just to that side there's where the extra perceptual talents have set up shop."

Logas's voice was a trifle impatient. "I know thought patterns when I see them, Ysenda. Please explain what this has to do with your hypothesis."

"A moment. Below and to the left—d'ye have some more o' that incense? Put it on—there. There's where I'm thinking his technical memory resides."

"Indeed, and I see nothing amiss there. No one has taken away anything, nor inserted anything foreign. He has the knowledge he had before, no more and no less—allowing for everyday growth and increase in complexity, of course."

"Of course," she said. The chair creaked, and the sound of her voice moved across to the workbench. "Now look here—here, where I have ma finger—these Kirkpatrick nodes. D'ye see them?"

Logas's tone changed abruptly to one of wonderment. "Indeed . . . I do. Interesting . . . they appear to be *almost* normal . . . but not quite. Had I not looked closely—"

"Exactly!" Ysenda's voice was triumphant. "The knowledge and the memories are there, but his ability to reference different items was subtly jiggered. Something, some sensory impression or other, was corralled and pushed into a closed loop, so that it would distract him from thinking about anything else!"

"Blessed Son in heaven," said Logas. "And there, some more of them, and there, and there, and over there, and . . . This is hard to believe. Or rather, I would prefer not to believe it."

Me, too, thought Melisande, almost opening her eyes.

"Happily, the nodes are merely bruised," Ysenda noted. "But right beside them—the Isthmus of DuMont—several lesions there."

Melisande couldn't stay quiet one second longer. "Is

he hurt? Please tell me; I don't see what you're seeing. I don't see *anything,* really.''

Ysenda sighed. "I fear he is indeed injured, child. The reverberating loop was strong enough to strain those parts of him that sense the erg-currents and interact wi' them. They tried to compensate and couldn't; and in the trying they crippled themselves."

Melisande's heart sank. Logas cut in. "It isn't necessarily permanent. We can help Stephen regain the use of those senses and his magical abilities. It will require some intensive therapy—about a year's worth, I would say—but it can be done."

Just then someone else spoke—a man's voice, gentle but insistent. "Just picture yourself relaxing in luxurious comfort on the finest leather upholstery made by human or other hands—" The sentence was cut off. Silence followed.

"What was that?" said Logas' voice. Melisande heard soft, retreating footsteps and, "I thought I shut the news-speaker down before you got here." A moment later, from some distance away, he went on, "No, it's dormant. I did shut it down."

The new voice sounded again. "—kilometers, whichever comes first—the most comprehensive limited warranty you can find. Marrakesh: The Sky Itself Welc—"

Again all sound ceased. No one spoke for several breaths. Then Logas said, "Now *that's* interesting. Should I assume we're not picking up a signal from an outside source?"

Stephen's grandmother answered, "Indeed we are not. This is coming from Stephen himself—"

The voice broke in. "—down today to your Marrakesh Aerial Rugs Showroom—"

"Enough!" Ysenda snapped. "Melisande, open your eyes." As Melisande looked around her, Ysenda brought Stephen out of trance. "Well," she said, "I think now we know wha' was in that memory loop."

Logas sat on his stool and fiddled with his beard. "We also know why it disabled Stephen. It wasn't the

existence of the memory loop, but its content. Stephen
would have emerged with no damage at all, and whoever did this would probably have gotten away with
it, had the memory-spell not ensnared that broadcast
advertisement in the loop. Really, I'm impressed that
Stephen survived." He snorted. "Broadcast media.
I've always said it would turn your brain to mush."

As Ysenda told her grandson what had occurred
during his trance, Melisande's nascent despair hard-
ened into anger. "My lord, my lady, I said I couldn't
see—but I could *feel* something while I was joined
with Stephen's thoughts. It's different, and it's faint.
I've never felt it when I'm around Stephen, but I have
sensed it somewhere else."

As she explained, Logas added an occasional *hm,*
until she was finished. He then said, "I see. It appears,
then, that we have a second problem in addition to
this one. What do you suggest, Lady?"

Ysenda thought for a minute, but it was Melisande
who spoke up. "My lord, I think there is a way. It
may be somewhat extreme; I defer to your wisdom.
But I think you can understand why I want to do
something."

She elaborated on her idea. The expressions she saw
in response were varied: Stephen, sitting up on the
bench, looked pained; Logas, perched on his stool,
looked pensive; Ysenda, enthroned in the center of
the room, looked as though she were about to laugh
out loud. "Child," she said, her eyes twinkling, "I like
your way of thinking. You and I need to talk some
more."

She said something else to the group, but Melisande
didn't hear. She stood frozen in shock.

She likes *my* way of thinking?

She *likes* my way of thinking?

She likes my way of thinking?

The thoughts threatened to forge an endless loop
of their own, but fortunately Ysenda's voice finally
broke into them as she said, "I think we may be able
to deal with this after all. And for good and all."

"Very well, then," said Logas. "All of you, come with me. It appears we need to summon your friend and your relation." He opened the workroom door and ushered the two younger people out. He and Ysenda followed some distance behind them.

As they made their way back to Stephen and Melisande's apartment, she could barely hear Logas saying, "I am impressed. That was the most vivid display of diagnostic capnomancy I've yet seen."

Ysenda replied, just as quietly, "Ye can thank Melisande for that—especially the sound samples. I've no' met a Sensitive before who could produce sound as well as light. But Wolfie, you and your people would have done something like this, no?"

"My area of concentration is econometrics and you know it. I leave neurothaumaturgy to you specialists. Besides, my Lily . . . I confess it did not occur to me to do so."

Ysenda clucked her tongue. "Poor Wolfie. All those afternoons we played doctor and you still canna diagnose worth a plugged ha'penny."

Laurel and Edward were still at the apartment talking over strategies when Melisande and Stephen came through the door. Edward tried to get to his feet quickly, but only succeeded in scattering books across the floor. Stephen said dryly, "Don't get up. I just wanted to give you a message from Grandmother: Don't use the magic."

"I beg your pardon?" said Edward.

"Oh, I'm not offended. This time, anyway. Don't use the magic you've stolen. It will be healthier for you. In fact, it would be better if you just gave me your stone now."

Edward pushed away from the sofa and this time made it to his feet. "That's ridiculous," he spluttered. "What do you mean, stolen? And what do you mean, healthier?"

"I mean just that. You obtained those linkstones under false pretenses. You told Laurel you wanted to use them to help me, but you merely wanted to use them for yourself. I'm telling you, don't."

Edward raised his hands. "I did no such thing!" Stephen and Melisande immediately shielded themselves—but Edward's gestures weren't a magical attack, merely part of an address-retrieval routine.

Nonetheless the effect was the same. A bolt of brilliant lightning jumped between his hands, and a loud *boom* shook the apartment. Stacks of books fell; two framed prints fell off the wall; and in the kitchen three cupboards spilled their contents onto the floor. Edward himself was knocked backward several feet, and fell to the floor . . . right on top of the massive *Bierce's Unabridged.*

"Ooh, that's got to hurt," said Stephen. "He who lives by the books . . ." Melisande told herself it wasn't polite to laugh at someone else's misfortune. Herself disagreed, and proceeded to giggle.

Edward shook his head to clear it. "How—?"

Ysenda entered the room. "Did ye think those stones were the only way to establish links? And did ye think they were the only linkstones in existence? What Stephen said is true. From now on, whenever ye use Power, ye won't be drawing on Laurel's skills alone, but on the four of us as well. And the feedback reaction will happen again and again, until it finally burns ye out, leaving ye with no ability at all. And perhaps a few IQ points lower, too."

Edward counted those in the apartment and was about to say, "The four of you—?" when Logas stepped through the door. Pointing a gilded rod toward Edward in a formal summoning gesture, he said in a firm voice, *"Advocamus te."*

They had convened in the Assembly Chamber in the central administration section: the room normally used for hearings, trials, and the occasionally polite verbal brawls known as "faculty meetings." It was a long room, with tiers of seats on either side of a slate floor, not unlike the choir loft in the chapel. At one end were two tall, massive doors of carved oak; at the other end was a rostrum with the table where the Chancellor, the Academic Dean, and the Dean of Student Affairs normally presided. In front of the rostrum sat the school's heavy ceremonial (most of the time) rod, encased in a parallelepiped of rose quartz.

The room was empty but for the six of them. Edward, Melisande, and Stephen stood at the far end, the quartz-cradled rod between them and the rostrum. At the table sat Logas, Ysenda, and Laurel. ("But why me?" Laurel had asked plaintively. To which Logas had replied, "We could summon Lady Sarras as our third judge, to be sure; but a Senior Thaumaturge may also serve. Your youth notwithstanding, you have passed the Senior Ordeal. And so, your youth notwithstanding, you must begin learning some of the responsibilities that go with the rank.")

Logas, acting as chairman, was saying, ". . . and thus we will consider charges against you not only for the fraudulent acquisition of thaumaturgical equipment, but also on the charge of black magic."

The blood drained from Edward's face as Logas went on. "The procedure you used on Stephen was done without his consent. Nor do we believe he would have given it had you asked."

"But what," Edward said in a quivering voice, "about the Lady Ysenda's *geas* on Laurel and Stephen? Was that consensual?"

Logas sighed. "First, Lady Ysenda is clan chief, which gives her certain administrative powers with regard to clan members. Second, do you recall the phrase *'Caritas non quaerit quae sua sunt'*?"

Edward's face fell. Melisande leaned over and whispered, "That rings a bell, but—"

Stephen whispered back, " 'Love does not seek after its own things.' Saint Paul."

Melisande said, "Oh. right. Ouch."

Logas was saying, ". . . and therefore, to speed

things along and hasten Stephen's graduation, the *geas* was laid. The principal beneficiary was Stephen, not Ysenda. Hence the distinction."

Laurel spoke up at this point. She scrutinized Edward—evidently trying to view him objectively as a man rather than as some lower life-form that scavenged its dinner from the sewers—and said, "Why? I just don't understand."

He shot back, "Of course not! You do all things perfectly! I've watched! *You* don't have to hear all the time—" His voice took on a nasty whine. " 'You'll never make it. You just don't have what it takes to turn a crowd.' *Do* you?!"

Suddenly his face fell. The anger and sarcasm vanished as quickly as it had appeared. He squeezed his eyes shut for a moment, and then spoke in a different voice altogether. "Laurel. Please forgive me. I had no right to say that, and to you of all people. I am sorry." He glanced about him, suddenly remembering the others watching. "My lord, my lady, I apologize for my— "

"Wait, wait," said Laurel. "Your dad said that, didn't he?"

"Well . . . yes, he did. But not often."

"How often would it have to be?" she said.

Logas took up the questioning. "And your father is—?"

"Alexander, my lord. Magistrate of Dunbar Parish."

"Has he held many posts?"

"Several, my lord."

Logas took a seat. He was silent a moment, and then said, "How many of those positions involved referenda?"

"Almost all of them, my lord. He hasn't lost a one."

Laurel said to Logas, "It's a hard example to follow."

Logas sighed, a different sort of sigh this time. "I suspect it is more than that." He made a note and glanced at Ysenda. She nodded. "Soon," he said. She nodded again.

Edward resumed his earlier statement. "I apologize for my outburst. I just . . . I came here determined to become an expert mage, someone they'd . . . well, they'd pay attention to back home. I'm a Weak talent, and when Laurel lent me the stone and the power that came with it, and then when you all came in demanding it and accusing me of something I didn't do . . . I guess I panicked. I didn't want to give it up." His hand went to his throat and came away holding the coruscating sphere, which he lay on the table in front of Laurel. She placed her own stone beside it, saying nothing.

Ysenda raised an eyebrow and said coldly, "Something you 'didna do'? Are you telling us you *didna* assault ma grandson?"

"No, my lady. I did that." He fell silent.

Laurel spoke up, "The linkstones! He didn't know about the linkstones when Stephen took the Ordeal!"

Ysenda said to Edward, "Is this true?"

"Yes, my lady," he replied. "I didn't know. They didn't come into it until later—and when I saw what they did, I hoped they would allow me to heal Stephen before this went any further. But that didn't happen." He said nothing more.

Stephen spoke up. "My lord and ladies, I personally accept that the linkstones were not the motivation behind Edward's actions but an unrelated factor. As to what the motive actually was, I think I know. What's more, I suspect Lord Logas knows, too."

Logas too raised an eyebrow. "Indeed?" Then, "Ah. I see. The McCheyne Fellowship."

Edward said, barely audibly, "Yes. The McCheyne would have let me study with some of the most powerful wizards in the kingdom, perhaps on the continent. If anything would look good at home, that would."

A few seconds passed, but Edward said nothing further. Logas said, "And . . .?"

Stephen said, without animosity, "And so he had to deal with the one he considered his main opposition, and then perhaps others." He glanced over at Edward for confirmation, and the other glumly nodded. He went on, "I also understand that the enduring physiological results are not the result of the spell but of external factors."

Logas replied, "A distinction that is no distinction at all, in this case. The damage to you resulted from Edward's actions. Had it not occurred, those actions would be no less evil."

Turning to the other two judges, he said, "Is there further discussion concerning the respondent's guilt or innocence on the charge of fraudulent acquisition of thaumaturgical equipment?"

The others both replied, "No."

"Declare!" Logas said.

"Not guilty," Ysenda said. Laurel said firmly, "Not guilty."

Logas turned to face Edward. "And I: abstain. On the charge of fraudulent acquisition of thaumaturgical equipment, the respondent is declared to be not guilty." He turned back to the others. "Is there further discussion concerning the respondent's guilt or innocence on the charge of personal violation by magical means?"

Ysenda said, "No." Laurel glumly shook her head.

"Declare!"

"Guilty," said Ysenda. Laurel answered, quietly, "Guilty."

"And I: guilty." He faced Edward again. "On the charge of personal violation by magical means, then, the respondent is declared to be guilty. Stephen."

Stephen stepped forward. "Yes, my lord."

Logas recited, "You have heard the charges, the responses of the accused, and the panel's declarations. I ask you now for a choice. Two options exist for sentencing. The first: cautery. The three of us would focus our blended powers with the result of burning away those areas of the condemned party's brain that facilitate the use of Power. The operation produces considerable pain over the short term. Over the long term, however, the condemned party is protected from further involvement in the dark varieties of magic, as are his prospective victims."

Edward's eyes closed again. He stood as if turned into granite.

"The second: coequal impairment. The condemned party would be subjected to the treatment he himself inflicted on you, to the extent that it produced comparable damage, requiring comparable healing operations. He would thus be restrained from doing further harm for the duration of healing, and it would be hoped that the process would produce rehabilitation. On the other hand, the long-term future remains in question." With that, he fell silent.

Edward looked at Stephen, without expression. Stephen went to Melisande and said in a low voice, "How can I possibly decide this?"

She said, just as quietly, "Between 'an eye for an eye' and preemptive erasure? My love, this is your decision. It must be. You are capable of it, and worthy of it. And you know I will support you in whatever you decide." She kissed his cheek.

He smiled mirthlessly. "Capable of it, agreed," he said. "Thank you." He turned to face the rostrum. "My lord, my ladies, may I have a couple of minutes?"

Logas bowed his head in a single nod. The others also gave their assent.

"Thank you." He walked over to one of the faculty benches and sat down. For two minutes he sat there, facing the floor beneath him, his lips barely moving. The others stood where they were: uncertain, suspended.

He rose and returned to the group. "My lord and ladies," he said, "I request a third alternative."

Logas raised his eyebrows; the other two appeared similarly surprised. "A third?"

"Yes, sir. I wish to register my consent to Edward's operation retroactively. 'I declare with unfettered mind and unbound spirit' that I understand Edward's actions to have been initiated by my desire, expressed prior to the Ordeal, for a spell that would improve

my memory. My sister will confirm the statement."
Logas and Ysenda looked at Laurel, who nodded
slowly, still bewildered. "He misunderstood my casual
comment, it is true, and his spell produced results different from what he intended"—he glanced at Edward, who nodded vacantly—"but I do reject that it
was undertaken unilaterally."

He paused. Logas *harrumphed* and said, "Would
that the problem were as easily solved. However, I
think you know better, Stephen. Declaring without co-
ercion that something which flies, has feathers, and
quacks is a horse does not make it one—"

Stephen could not resist it. "Well, there *is* Kennea-
ly's work with genotypic transmutation . . ."

"That's right, you did have that on your biblio-
graphy," Logas said. "Nonetheless, I say unto thee:
Don't push it."

He cleared his throat again. "All right, declaring
that it is a horse *without* three weeks' work and five
lab assistants certified in chromosomal telekinetics,
doesn't make it one. I dare say you'd need consider-
ably more in this case. The dark magic, and the inher-
ent risk both to yourself *and* to Edward, depend on
his attitudes and intents at the time, and cannot be
wished away by a simple *ex post facto* declaration, no
matter how uncoerced."

"I yield, my lord. Still, I do ask the judges if, in
light of what has been said here concerning Edward's
background, you would consider withholding judg-
ment on this aspect of Edward's guilt or innocence
until a specified period of study."

"Study in general?" said Laurel, "or do you have
something specific in mind?"

Stephen was silent for four seconds and said, "I
propose an independent-study project, with myself as
principal investigator, to determine the nature and effects of darker magics in the early stages of a prac-
titioner's development; specifically, whether the course
of such magics is truly irreversible. All elements to be

approved by the SysThaum departmental faculty, who will assign whatever safeguards they believe necessary."

Logas shook his head. "That seems merely to be burdening yourself while letting Edward off the hook rather easily. I fail to see why *your* work should substitute for *his* punishment, assuming that he is found guilty."

"Well, for one thing, my lord, this project will have a staff of two: myself and Edward. His participation in this project would be in addition to his other duty."

"Making it substantially his project. I see. That 'other duty' being . . .?"

"I understand that I will require one year's therapeutic treatment in order to recover from my injuries. I would request that Edward be excused from his regular studies for that period and, in addition to the project already discussed, that he be assigned to work on my therapy."

The panel was still. Edward stared at Stephen, completely unaware that his own mouth had fallen open and that a fly was trying to decide whether to mount an expedition. Then his grandmother said, "Hm. Is this part of your 'object all sublime'?"

Stephen smiled. "Only if you delete the part about 'innocent merriment.' "

Ysenda considered this a moment, and then said, "My fellow tribunes, I recommend that we accept this request."

Logas was about to say something, but just then something happened which Melisande had never seen in her admittedly few encounters with her grandmother-in-law. She had seen the face of Ysenda in repose, Ysenda annoyed, Ysenda angry, Ysenda with full dignity cutting an impertinent upstart down with a stare, and even—on extremely rare occasions—Ysenda graciously approving. But she had never, ever, seen the face of Ysenda *asking*.

Logas said, "Well." Then, to Laurel, "How do you recommend?"

She answered, "My lord, I agree with Lady Ysenda's recommendation." She shot a look at Melisande: What in heaven's name are you guys *doing?*

Again Logas was about to speak, but Ysenda said sharply, "I have one further recommendation. I further recommend that in order to complement whatever weaknesses exist in Edward's talent and understanding, that he be assisted in the execution of this assignment by Senior Thaumaturge Laurel."

Logas smiled—"Agreed!"—while Laurel gasped.

Cutting off her protest in mid-syllable, Ysenda quietly said to her, "Child, we can either make this unanimous, or we can register our two votes against your one. I am of the opinion that this experience will improve your magic skills significantly, as well as your knowledge of people—a valuable resource for a magician. I do hope ye agree." As Laurel began her reply, her grandmother added, "Would it make things easier if I provided another *geas?*"

Laurel's eyes opened wide. "*No!* Uh, er . . . I agree also." She faced forward again, her expression totally blank.

Logas announced, "I agree. Both recommendations are carried. So mote it be." He clapped his hands once. The hearing was over.

Still, no one moved. Melisande finally broke the tableau by going to her husband and embracing him. In his ear she whispered, "Are you certain you want to do this?"

He replied, "It's what you would do. And don't try to tell me differently. I know better." She started to protest, but he placed a finger over her mouth. "And we do have two Seniors in the family." He withdrew his finger, kissed its tip, then placed it back on her lips.

Laurel sat in her chair, stunned. Melisande caught her eye and mouthed the words *I'll help.* Laurel smiled feebly, with a touch of relief.

Logas announced, "In the meantime, Stephen will be unavailable for teaching duties and others normally performed by a Junior Thaumaturge. As it happens, I am told by the Office of the Dean of Student Affairs that we have need of adviser/arbiters for the first-year students. Stephen, your performance today suggests that you and Melisande together might do well in this position. Are you interested?"

Stephen and Melisande were dumbstruck. They looked at each other, and then Stephen said, "My lord, we are."

"Report to the Dean's office tomorrow at Terce. I shall join you there." Turning to Melisande, Logas added, "I believe you will find the staff quarters significantly different from those of the married students. The apartments have four rooms, with a garden plot in back. One of the rooms is outfitted as a study, with extensive bookshelves. Rather capacious bookshelves at that."

Melisande couldn't believe her ears. To escape from the Slough of the Bibliophile? At long last, to be able to entertain, or simply to move around without tripping over a grimoire?

She said to Stephen, "Will you promise me that you'll keep your books in that room only, and not let them overflow into the other rooms?"

Stephen paused. Then, recognizing defeat, he said, "Yes. I promise."

Laurel, coming down from the rostrum, said, "Yeah, right. Don't worry, Melisande. Between you and me, we can see that he keeps his word. Painful though it'll be for him."

Stephen shuddered in anticipation. "By the way, sis, thank you for helping me not to launch into selling flying carpets in the middle of the hearing. I don't think that would've helped things at all."

She grinned. "My pleasure."

Edward chose that moment to grab his arm. "*Why?* Why not just let them cauterize me and have done with it? What's in this for you?"

Stephen replied, "A healer with a vested interest in my health, I suppose. Also, you're not the only one who's had to deal with a family situation in which the dominant personality isn't you." He looked guiltily at his grandmother, still sitting quietly on the rostrum. She only arched an eyebrow in response—but the corner of her mouth turned upward just a little, noticeable bit.

Logas joined them on the main floor. "Stephen, Melisande, I shall see you tomorrow. By the way, what was that 'object all sublime' business all about?"

Melisande answered, " 'My object all sublime / I shall achieve in time, / To let the punishment fit the crime, / The punishment fit the crime.' We all have our tastes, my lord. I like opera. My husband prefers Gilbert and Sullivan."

"Ah," he said. "I see. Well, Stephen, my congratulations on passing."

He turned to leave, but as he did a befuddled Stephen asked, "Passing, my lord?"

"Of course," Logas answered. "What, did you think Edward was the only one being evaluated here?"

His exit was spoiled by Laurel this time. "Wait a second," she demanded. "Are you saying that everything that goes on at this place is an *examination?*"

Logas chuckled. "Isn't everything in life? Remember, tomorrow." With that, he was out the door and headed back to his workroom.

Ysenda descended from the rostrum and glided toward them. They stood respectfully as she looked at each one and said, "A fair day's work. Remember what happened here today."

To Stephen she said, "An interesting proposal. Wha' was your thinking?"

"It just seemed to me," he replied, "that there was more than one way to let the punishment fit the crime."

"Aye, tha' there is. Laurel. Melisande." She fixed her gaze on each of them. "First impressions, daughters." To Melisande she said, "You are a Sensitive. Remember it." To Laurel she said, "You are not. Remember it."

Laurel looked abashed. Melisande simply felt bewildered.

"And *you,*" Ysenda said to Edward, who stood rigid. "A moment ago ye said, 'I'm a Weak talent.' "

She stabbed his chest with a rigid forefinger. "No! Ye *possess* a Weak talent. You are yourself. Remember the difference. I wish ye well."

She turned to leave, but then turned back and said, "Stephen, Laurel, Melisande. I shall expect ye at Eastertide."

Sister and brother mumbled their promises to visit. Melisande, however, stepped forward and took the Lady Ysenda by the elbow. "Grandmother?" Ysenda turned to regard her, and she said, "We're going to the BBC for some refreshment. Would you join us?"

Ysenda's eyebrows rose in surprise. But then, for the first time since her arrival, she smiled broadly. "Why, thank ye, child. I should like that very much."

The four of them started to leave, but when they were halfway to the doors Ysenda said, "Hold."

She turned to where Edward stood at the end of the room, motionless, beside the ceremonial rod. "Are ye coming, then?" she said.

Edward stepped warily forward, then came to join them.

The five departed the room, and Stephen closed the doors behind them.

A SIMPLE SPELL

by Marilyn A. Racette

Marilyn A. Racette lives in Waltham, Massachusetts, with her son—an in-house computer consultant—Sean and her cat Midnight. She has a day job in a computer bookstore, and this is her second professional sale. (Her first was to *Marion Zimmer Bradley's Fantasy Magazine*.)

She says that this story is about her fascination with the consequence of getting what you wish for. MZB always used to say, "Be careful what you wish for, because you will almost certainly get it."

Celi, my latest apprentice, had reminded me that she would be leaving in three months. I pushed that thought and its attendant vision of a mountain of undone work from my mind to concentrate on the clients before me. The spell they required was a simple one to cast, and though I am not a prophetess I knew what the results would be. So I asked once more, "Are you certain that this is what you want?"

The girl before me nodded emphatically, and her mother looked at me as if my brains were addled.

"Well, then, I will need some strands of your hair, or some nail clippings . . ." The girl dutifully plucked three long strands of her golden hair and handed them to me, her liquid brown eyes shining in happy anticipation of the results of my work.

". . . and payment in advance." Her mother frowned, the wrinkles marring an otherwise lovely and carefully made-up face. With a clatter of golden bangles she drew forth an old and elaborately embroidered purse and carefully counted out the coins for my fee.

"The change will be gradual," I cautioned, "but as you requested, by the next full moon you will see the completed results of the spell."

"And you guarantee satisfaction," the mother said sharply.

I chose my words carefully, contractual laws being what they are. I could ill afford a lawsuit, or the mutterings of an unhappy client, particularly one attached to a noble house, even if that house had come to less prosperous times.

"I guarantee that the spell will produce the physical change that you have requested. I cannot guarantee that the change itself will be all that I think you or the young lady expect it to be."

The girl looked at me quizzically, and then at her mother, the first sign I had seen of some intelligence behind her fair features. There might be hope for her. The mother was a different matter—wouldn't have seen a wart on her nose if you handed her a mirror. She harumphed and rose stiffly, and her daughter, long and leggy as a young fawn, followed her out the door.

They returned sooner than I had expected, just before the second full moon. A commotion in the street below drew me to the window of my small studio above the glass blower's shop. I watched them alight from a modest carriage and cross the street, the girl trailing after her mother, eyes downcast, avoiding the stares and smiles of the men on the street. I could not help smiling myself, but I had shoved the clutter on my desk into a drawer—Celi had returned home just last week—and was all business by the time they had reached my door at the top of the stairs.

"Good day, Madam, young mistress. How may I be of service to you today?"

Mother and daughter seated themselves while I poured tea. The mother was just as cold and stiff and formal as she had been before, but the daughter's

fawnlike grace had been replaced by the shy awkward-
ness that sometimes accompanies an early flowering
of the cuves of womanhood. And curves she had, by
the goddess. I had outdone myself.

"My daughter is unhappy with the results of this
spell. We wish a reversal."

"I'm not surprised at the sentiment." Indeed, I had
heard some stories regarding the amorous behavior of
several young lords at last month's festival ball, all
revolving around their desire to engage the attentions
of a certain young lady. She must have been quite
overwhelmed and over pinched.

I addressed the girl. "You wish a reversal of the
spell?"

She nodded, gaze locked on the floor, while her
mother looked on disapprovingly.

To that worthy matron I said, "It is quite difficult
to undo the spell without some risk of marring the
young lady's looks, and it takes much longer."

"How much, and how long?" the mother inquired
irritably.

"Three moons, at the least, possibly six. As for the
cost . . ." In a flash of inspiration, I named an exorbi-
tant figure.

"That's ridiculous!" she exclaimed, rising out of her
chair, bangles jangling.

"However," I added quickly, "I can suggest an alternate arrangement. One of my young apprentices
has returned home for several months, possibly longer.
The young lady may remain here and trade her labor
for the desired results. This will allow me to monitor
the changes and make any needed adjustments. And
she will learn a few simple spells that any young
woman with some expectations of a household to run
would find useful."

I faced the girl. "If your mother allows this, would
you find it acceptable?"

The girl smiled, the first time she'd done so since
her last visit. She really did have a lovely face, finely
formed, and her eager smile was the perfect adornment.

"Madam?"

"How long did you say?"

"I think we should plan on six months. At that point, you and your daughter can decide if you would like her to continue the apprenticeship."

Mother considered briefly.

"Perhaps you're wondering what to tell the young lady's father?"

She nodded.

"I suggest you say you've decided to send her abroad for her education. There's no need to worry about anyone recognizing her. Anyone who might know her will think that she looks remarkably like your daughter, but couldn't possibly be her. I can make certain of that."

We made a few further arrangements. As they rose to go, I felt quite satisfied. As I said before, I am no prophetess, but I expected things to turn out this way. And I had needed a new apprentice.

SWORD OF QUEENS

by Bunnie Bessel

Bunnie Bessel says of herself: "I live in Arlington, Texas with my best friend and husband of 26 years, a fanatically energetic border collie, a lethargic golden retriever, a bossy cat, and two lovely gentlemanly horses with avarice for carrots. All of the above (and a full time job) keep my days filled with various challenges, thrills, and joys. I can honestly say that I have a pretty neat life. Writing is like icing on the cake. Characters, plots, scenes come out of nowhere and snatch me up and send me off on unplanned journeys. Writing, like reading, is full of wonderful images and unexpected surprises as the characters live in your mind and on the pages. Only writing is better, because there are no limitations on time, setting or action—everything is possible!"

This is her third sale to *Sword and Sorceress;* she had stories in *S&S XI* and *S&S XVII*. She has also sold to *Marion Zimmer Bradley's Fantasy Magazine* and *Dragon*. She hopes to publish her first book soon. I think she has an excellent chance.

Brianne pressed her heel into Gilly's side and sent the horse galloping across the Queen's Field. As his heavy hooves thudded into the turf, Brianne kept her eyes fixed on the flame at the center of the clearing. A single tongue of fire, it reached taller than Brianne's head, even on horseback. A flame that burned with no fuel, and at its center hung the Sword.

Her jaw tightened at the sight of the blade. She had never planned, never thought, that she would be here seeking this Sword. The last Sword Mistress, Queen Wilmere, had claimed the blade from the flame when

Brianne was nine. By all rights, the Queen should have lived another twenty years. It should have been Brianne's daughter, not Brianne, who entered the field.

But fate had taken an odd twist. All of Standfield had been caught off-guard when Wilmere returned the Sword of Queens to the field, set the flame, and had gone to her bed, surrendering to a wasting illness. The timing couldn't have been worse. Standfield was besieged with both internal conflicts and encroaching armies on her borders. The country needed the Queen and her Sword.

Gilly's ears pricked forward uneasily as he neared the flame and he veered slightly away from it. Brianne allowed the horse to slow but nudged him with her knee until he came to a halt beside the blaze. Heat rippled around her, warming her arm and face.

The fire flickered yellow, with tinges of amber. Brianne felt a wash of relief at the colors. As long as the flame remained yellow, the Queen lived. The blaze would deepen to cobalt blue at her death. Then the Sword would be available for claiming.

Within the flame, the blade hung tip down, gleaming like molten gold. It looked to be more of air and heat than solid steel.

Brianne stared at it, her thoughts racing. Given a choice, she'd leave the Sword where it was and return to her quiet life on her father's lands. Too much history, though, hung with the blade. A history laced inescapably with the names of Brianne's ancestors. She did not want Wilmere's title or the Sword. Yet, wanted or not, she might have to take the thing.

She flinched at the thought of Wilmere's death, and a familiar grief welled within her. The Queen was her friend as well as her ruler. Brianne had been unprepared when her father brought the news of Wilmere's illness.

"The Queen will be dead before winter," Lord Favirn had told Brianne in a voice tight with annoyance. "Pack. We are going to court."

The order surprised Brianne. Her father seldom left Lakerealm, and Brianne didn't believe he cared enough for the Queen to want to attend her funeral.

In fact, Wilmere's death would cause a lot of inconvenience for Favirn. Over the last few years, he had cultivated the friendship of Wilmere's husband. Favirn and the Prince Regent spent many a night plotting one profitable enterprise or another. Now the partnership was useless and Favirn would have to cultivate the new Queen's spouse.

As she thought of that, Brianne realized why her father was taking her to court. Not for the funeral, but for the crowning. He planned for Brianne to contend for the throne.

The thought dismayed her. She was eligible, of course. She was First Daughter, in an unbroken line of First Daughters, all the way back to Standfield's founding families. As such, she was one of the few who could claim the Sword of Queens from within the flame.

But she had never expected to be a contender. And she wasn't sure she would be the best person to lead Standfield at this time. Surely, her father knew that. But one look at Favirn's face had convinced her that discussing the matter would be futile. She knew his mind was already whirling with visions of being the power behind the throne.

She had packed as Favirn ordered and spent the trip trying to recall the names of the other First Daughters eligible to contend for the Sword. She could name six at least. Surely one among them, she thought hopefully, would be better qualified to be Queen. One of them would know enough about leadership, politics, and war to help Standfield recover from these bad times.

Even now, sitting on Gilly with the Sword gleaming like a jewel within the flame, Brianne did not crave the crown. Standfield needed someone of courage and experience. Brianne did not believe she had enough of either.

She wasn't even sure if she had the nerve to reach into the fire. Legend said the fire would melt the flesh from the bone of any Daughter it found unworthy. This was why Brianne had come here now, before the flame was ready to release the Sword. Best to find out if the flame would reject her before the public ceremony. Better to face the flame here and alone than to race the other contenders across the field and then learn she was too frightened to touch the fire.

With a deep breath, she reached forward, feeling the heat intensify. She bit her lip, expecting to stifle a cry of pain.

Instead, she gasped. She felt no searing heat, but a silken touch. A caress as smooth as satin wrapped around her fingers. In the same instant, a yearning washed through her, drawing her near the fire. She leaned forward, reaching deeper into the flame until her fingers were a mere hair's-breath from the Sword.

A voice whispered within her mind, *You have come.*

Brianne straightened in the saddle, looking at the Sword in amazement. Had she heard something or imagined it? The words echoed in her mind. Three soft words, yet she felt them coil around her, biding her to come back to the fire, back to the Sword.

She brought her fingers to her lips and found the tips surprisingly cool. She wanted to reach back into the fire, to wrap her hand around the Sword, even though it wasn't time yet. She wanted that blade, more than she had ever wanted anything.

The sound of hoofbeats from behind broke her concentration. For an instant she fought a mixture of annoyance and relief. She had never expected the lure of the Sword to catch her so strongly. She hated being interrupted and yet at the same time felt a sense of reprieve.

Still, she turned with a frown to look over her shoulder. Although not forbidden, it was irregular for a contender to come to the flame before the Sword was ready to be claimed. She wondered who else had the audacity to cross the Queen's Field.

Another horse cantered across the clearing, the woman on its back wearing light armor and leathers.

Brianne knew the rider instantly: Caliste, Lady General of the Queen's Cavalry. They had never met, but Brianne had seen the General once when she had led the cavalry across the edge of Lakerealm to fight a battle on the plains to the west. Her name was spoken with respect throughout the country.

The Lady General rode, not at the breakneck gallop that Brianne had chosen, but in an elegantly controlled piaffe. Her horse's hooves touched the grass lightly, as if dancing, and Caliste sat the saddle as slim as a reed.

Even across the distance, Brianne could feel the intensity of the Lady General's blue eyes. As she watched the woman approach, Brianne tried to remember if Caliste had been a contender for the Sword when Wilmere had taken the blade. A First Daughter could only be a contender once. If Caliste had not tried before, then she could claim the Sword this time. "And Caliste," Brianne told herself softly, "would be a Queen worth following."

She felt an instant flush of relief. There was someone to lead Standfield. Brianne wouldn't have to take the crown. Even so, Caliste's first words startled her.

"The Sword will select me," the General told her curtly, drawing her horse beside Gilly. "Not you."

Brianne would have agreed, except she found herself suddenly reluctant to give up all rights to the blade. She could still feel the touch of the flame and hear the echo of the words in her mind.

Caliste went on, "Do you really think running a small estate like Lakerealm qualifies you to rule the country? Do you know anything about our problems at court? Or the armies at our borders?" Caliste persisted. "Have you ever held a blade?"

No, Brianne thought honestly. She was good with a bow, but she had never been taught swordplay.

Caliste gave her no chance to reply though. "The

country needs a strong Queen. Standfield does not have time for someone to learn to rule."

Brianne agreed with Caliste. But she had been in enough discussions like this with her father to know that responding in any way would lead to more argument. Instead, she took the path that always worked best for her. "Excuse me," she said softly, "I have other commitments." She turned Gilly and withdrew.

She did not look back, but Brianne could imagine the Lady General's blink of surprise as she rode away. Caliste would look a fool if she followed after Brianne, shouting at her back. And Brianne doubted that the Lady would risk looking a fool, even with no one watching.

She allowed herself a small smile, but then sobered immediately. Behind her, she could feel the pull of the Sword. It called to her.

She shook her head, trying to clear her mind. She had entered the field seeing the Sword as a burden. Now it had become a temptation. After barely touching the flame, did she desire the Sword's power like everyone else?

No, she told herself firmly. Power was not something she coveted. She still wasn't sure if she would be the best Queen for Standfield at this time. She'd seen Wilmere struggle to make the right decisions. Ruling was not a task anyone should take lightly.

No, Brianne didn't want the crown. But the Sword was something else. She'd like to hold it, just for a moment, to have it whisper within her mind again.

Did that mean the Sword wanted her? Or did the blade speak to every First Daughter? She looked back toward the flame. Caliste waited near the fire, watching Brianne, but not following.

The woman seemed incredibly sure of herself, incredibly intense. Were those qualities that Standfield needed in a Queen?

A memory flickered across Brianne's mind, something Wilmere had said once. "General Caliste has courage,"

Wilmere had told her. "More than I do. I have to drag up the energy to keep up with her." There had been admiration in Wilmere's voice, not envy. "But she is impatient. If there is a long way and a short way to reach any goal, Caliste will always pick the short way. Even when the long way would be more prudent."

Caliste had certainly just proven Wilmere right. She had definitely taken the short, curt approach to Brianne. What would Wilmere think of Caliste as Queen? Would she approve of the General? Unable to even guess as the answer, Brianne rode to the castle with a dozen questions crowding her thoughts.

As she crossed under the narrow inner gate of the courtyard, she turned automatically to her left and rode to the ivy-covered buildings of the Queen's Quarters.

A servant stepped forward, taking Gilly as Brianne dismounted. No one spoke to her as she crossed the vast entry foyer and went up the stairs to the Queen's bedroom.

Two priestesses sat on prayer mats outside Wilmere's door, their hoods drawn over their faces, their soft chants filling the hallways. Not a good sign, Brianne thought. They sang the Song of Release. Wilmere's time was near.

Brianne slipped inside the room, and paused with her back to the doorway. The Queen lay with the covers tucked neatly about her. Her dark hair fanned out around her pale face. She seemed to be sleeping.

As Brianne drew nearer, though, she saw the telltale shadows under Wilmere's eyes. The skin stretched like parchment across the delicate bones of her face. The Queen would never sit up, smile, or speak again. "Oh, Wilmere," Brianne whispered, a tightness knotting her chest.

Another priestess, standing near the bed, looked up at Brianne's words. "She can't hear you," she told Brianne softly. "The Queen's mind has already reached for the afterlife. Her body will soon follow." She bowed, and left the room, closing the door behind her.

Brianne looked down at the Queen and realized

that although they had spent time together, there was much she didn't know about Wilmere. When the Queen visited Lakerealm, the two women talked of plants and raising sheep. Wilmere seldom spoke of the duties of her office or the problems of the country. The Queen's time at Lakerealm had been her respite from the trials of leadership, and Brianne had given Wilmere the peace she needed.

They had never spoken about the Sword, although Wilmere wore it constantly. Brianne didn't know if Wilmere had wanted the power or had gone to the field as reluctantly as Brianne now faced it.

Wilmere's rule had not been an easy one with the country pulled apart by both internal struggles and foreign armies harrying their borders. Territories had been lost, some to war and others negotiated away. Brianne did not know how Wilmere felt about the loss of those lands.

She couldn't even say if Wilmere had been the best Queen for Standfield during the times of so much strife. But she knew that Wilmere had always tried her best.

Brianne heard the door open behind her and turned to see who had entered. Caliste stepped into the room and Brianne felt a flush of anger. "Are you following me?"

"No," Caliste replied. She strode across the room, stopping beside Brianne and looked down at the Queen.

Emotions Brianne could not read flickered across the General's face.

Then Caliste corrected herself softly. "Yes, I did follow you." She glanced toward Brianne. "What I said in the field was badly done. I wanted to speak with you, but I didn't mean to do it that way."

Brianne knew apologizing could not come easily to Caliste. Still she wanted no part of the woman and wanted her out of Wilmere's bedchamber. "Fine. We'll talk later," she tried to brush her off. "I'll meet you—"

"No," Caliste objected. "There isn't much time. We have to talk now." She hesitated and then rushed on.

"If the Sword doesn't choose me, you are the only other one it will take."

"There are six other contenders," Brianne reminded her.

"Those," Caliste snorted. "They are pampered children. They'll be lucky if they don't fall off their horses riding across the field. None of them should even be contenders for the Sword. They don't deserve it. Their only ambition has been to catch well-born husbands."

"I never planned to be a contender either," Brianne told her.

"I did," Caliste said fiercely, then looked away. "From the time I was a small child, all I thought about was the Sword. I knew I would have a chance to claim it. I was determined it would come to me." She paused and looked down at the bed. "I was three months too young when Wilmere became Queen. They wouldn't let me onto the field. I thought my opportunity was lost. So I served the Queen instead." She glanced up. "Now, I can try again. And I will claim the Sword." She paused again and added. "If you don't."

Brianne started to protest, but Caliste waved her to silence. "I've asked about you. People say you are fair and caring. And you have done a good job of running Lakerealm despite your father's interference."

Her gaze held Brianne. "But are you strong? Standfield needs a strong Queen. We will not survive with another weak one."

"Wilmere was a good Queen," Brianne said in an instant defense of her friend.

"No," Caliste said firmly. "Wilmere was not a good Queen. She tried her best. But she cared too much for her husband, and he cared too much for his own profit." Her face tightened with a hatred that startled Brianne. "He's sold half the kingdom to line his own pockets. I'd have him hanged as a traitor."

Brianne heard the coldness in the General's tone. Killing was something Caliste knew well. But where was her compassion? Shouldn't a Queen have as much compassion as strength?

"Could you?" Caliste asked, her eyes narrowing. "Could you hang a traitor? Someone you knew? Someone who had eaten at your table?"

Brianne answered carefully. "Yes," she said, hating the truth of her words. "If the evidence was convincing and I was sure of his guilt, I could hang a traitor." She just hoped that she would never have to face that situation.

A grim smile crossed Caliste's lips. "What if it was someone close to you? Even your father?"

Brianne straightened as if slapped. "My father is no traitor."

"Not yet," Caliste agreed. "But if you take the Sword, he will seek to use you, just as Wilmere's husband used her."

"He won't," Brianne replied stiffly.

Caliste snorted again. "He already plans to marry you off to his advantage. He has potential suitors lined up in the hallway while he dickers with them."

"Every father seeks an advantageous marriage for his daughter," Brianne reminded her.

"Which do you really think your father cares more for," Caliste challenged, "Standfield or his own wealth?"

Brianne felt her heart thudding with despair. Caliste's words were too close to the truth. She knew her father. Greed could easily overcome any concern for the country.

"Think hard, Lady Brianne," Caliste whispered, "before you reach for that Sword. Know the choice you are making. Know the life you will have to live if you become Queen." She tossed another glance toward the bed. "That's what I needed to tell you. I tried to warn Wilmere, but she was already Queen and it was too late." Her sharp eyes came back to Brianne. "Think about it before you cross that field."

Brianne's mouth felt dry, but she lifted her chin and met Caliste's gaze. "Do you think to scare me away?"

"No," Caliste said softly. "I saw you reach into the flame today. You don't scare easily."

For an instant Brianne's breath left her. She wondered if Caliste had reached into the fire, too. Had
she heard the whisper of the Sword? An unexpected
jealousy flashed through Brianne.

"You have the courage," Caliste said. "But do you
have the wisdom?"

Brianne took a deep, steadying breath. Too many
thoughts and feelings were rolling within her. She
needed a little distance to think. "This is not the
place," she told Caliste.

She saw annoyance cross the other's features. "You
can't just—" Caliste began.

"I will not argue with you any longer at the foot of
Wilmere's deathbed," Brianne said firmly. She turned
and headed out the door with Caliste dogging her
heels.

Once in the hall, Caliste caught up to her. "Is this
how you deal with all confrontations, by running
away?"

"No," Brianne told her as she led down the stairs.
"I will fight when I need to." She turned and faced
the woman. "I saw no reason, though, to waste time
arguing with someone who is unreasonable."

"I'm not unreasonable."

Brianne had to laugh. She couldn't help it. Caliste
looked so completely affronted. Shaking her head,
Brianne started down the stairs again. "Not unreasonable?" she asked softly. "You just tracked me down
at the field and followed me to a dying Queen's bed.
All to tell me why I shouldn't contend for the Sword
that you want desperately. And, you allow me little
opportunity to get a word in edgewise." She glanced
sideways at the General. "Not unreasonable at all."

Caliste blinked at her, a flicker of a grin on her lips.
"Well, when put that way—"

The heavy peal of a bell interrupted her. Both of
them turned toward the sound. The bell pealed again.

"The fire is changing color," Caliste whispered.
"The bluing has begun."

"Wilmere." Brianne started back up the stairs.

Caliste caught her arm. "You can't do anything for her. We need to go to the field."

"She's alone," Brianne told the woman.

"She has always been alone," Caliste replied softly.

"I thought you didn't want me to contend," Brianne challenged, trying to jerk free.

Still holding Brianne's arm, Caliste replied, "If the Sword does not choose me, then you have to be there. Standfield needs one of us." She tugged Brianne down the stairs and into the courtyard. The servant still held Gilly at the bottom of the stairs and Caliste shoved her toward the horse.

Around them, people were scurrying out of the castle. The courtyard was crowded with carts, horsemen, and people on foot.

As Brianne swung onto Gilly, Caliste drew her mount up beside her. "Follow me," she ordered, then plunged into the crowd. "Make way!" she shouted.

A path opened in front of them and Caliste led them through. They continued that way to the field, with the General's authoritative voice clearing a pathway for them.

At the edge of the field, Caliste left Brianne. The perimeter was thick with people, their voices rising to a roar of excitement. Over their heads, Brianne looked toward the flame. It had turned a pale blue with the blade glowing golden within it. "Not blue enough," Brianne told herself, and wondered instantly how she knew.

With just that glance, she could feel the Sword's pull again and the depth of her dilemma settled on her like a heavy weight. Caliste was so certain of her ability to be Queen that she was unaware of her limitations. Brianne was so aware of her limitations that she was uncertain of her ability to rule. Which Queen was right for Standfield? Did the country need someone who could order decisions instantly or someone who needed to think about them first?

What do you want? She whispered in her mind to
the Sword. She got no answer—she expected none.
She knew the decision rested solely with her.

With a sigh, she accepted her fate. Right or wrong,
she was a contender for the Sword. She would do her
best and trust that it would turn out right.

Spotting her father's banners along one side of the
circle, she frowned. Caliste was right about him. If
Brianne became Queen, Lord Favirn would be a problem. He would try to use his daughter for his own
profit.

With another sigh, she accepted that, too. She would
have to stand up to him. She would learn from Wilmere's mistakes, and put the country before her
family.

As she approached her father's camp, Favirn's face
was tight with anger. "Where have you been?" he
demanded. He didn't wait for an answer. "Get off that
nag," he ordered her, catching Gilly's bridle. "Martin
has a better horse for you."

One of her brothers held a high-strung bay at the
perimeter of the circle. Dancing sideways at the end
of the reins, the animal was already sweating with
excitement.

"I'll stay on Gilly," Brianne told her father.

"Don't be a fool," Favirn snapped. "The other one
is faster."

"This isn't a race," she replied evenly. "The first one
to reach the flame doesn't always claim the Sword."

"Isn't it?" he snapped back. "Do you think the
Lady General will dawdle on the way to the fire? You
need to get there as fast as you can."

Brianne glanced toward Caliste, and realized her
father was probably right. This time it would be a
race. But she shook her head. "Put me on that brute,"
she told Favirn, nodding toward the other horse, "and
he's liable to pitch me off before I reach the flame."

Her father glanced toward the bay as it pranced
sideways again.

"I'll stay on Gilly," she told him.

He scowled, but relented. "At least change into a decent gown. You look like a peasant. The maids have brought more appropriate attire for you."

Surprised, Brianne glanced down at her loose blouse, split skirt and dark girdle. Nothing fancy, she admitted, but serviceable. To her father, though, appearances always mattered.

She started to do as he asked, but the flame drew her attention. It had darkened to almost blue-black. The Sword glowed within its dark core. She felt her chest tightening.

In a moment it would begin to throw out sparks and the contenders could enter the field.

"No time for fancy clothes," she told her father, and edged Gilly toward the edge of the clearing. She paused there, waiting. She could feel the Sword tugging at her like a strong tide. Her heart seemed to slow and the noise of the crowd receded.

Directly across the circle, Caliste faced her. The Lady General's face was tight with concentration.

Brianne glanced sideways, noticing the other contenders for the first time. Only three other first daughters waited at the edge of the field. They were all elegantly dressed and sitting sidesaddle on high-spirited horse. Brianne found herself agreeing with Caliste, none of them would stay on their mounts long enough to get anywhere near the flame. She dismissed them from her thoughts.

She leaned forward and whispered in Gilly's ear. "It's up to you now, boy." His ears flicked back at her voice and then forward again.

Brianne picked up the reins and felt the horse gather beneath her, his muscles tense.

Suddenly, sparks exploded from the fire, showering the field in blue-and-golden embers. Gilly exploded at the same moment, shooting out with a speed that took Brianne's breath away. She flattened along his neck and clung to his mane.

On the other side of the field, she saw Caliste thundering toward her at the same incredible speed. They

were like two stars rushing toward collision. Brianne
leaned closer to Gilly, squeezing, urging even more
speed. He responded, surging forward again.

Brianne barely felt the horse beneath her any
longer. She felt as if she rode the wind. Incredibly,
she reached the flame a moment before Caliste. She
pulled Gilly to a lunging halt and plunged her hand
into the fire.

The silken blaze caressed her. Her fingers slipped
through it and began to curl around the hilt of the
golden Sword. Then she stopped.

A whisper trickled through her mind, *The Sword
decides.*

It took all Brianne's strength to pause. Her aching
fingers poised above the Sword.

On the other side of the fire, she saw Caliste reach
into the dark flame. The General's eyes flickered as
hot as the blaze as her fingers stretched to touch the
blade. In that instant, Brianne knew that she had lost.
The Sword would go to Caliste.

Amazingly, the Sword turned, shifted slightly, and
dropped into Brianne's palm.

With a gasp she drew it to her. The blue blaze vanished, leaving a blade that glowed like liquid fire. Brianne curled it to her chest, hugging it to her as
extraordinary emotion flashed through her.

The history of the Queens flooded her mind. The
strife of every battle, the birth of every child—all of
their lives were with her. The memories rushed at her
with a strength that made her dizzy. She clutched at
Gilly's mane to keep from falling off.

Strong hands eased her from the saddle and Brianne
slid down until her feet numbly touched the ground.
Then she leaned against Gilly's shoulder, closed her
eyes, and let the Sword take her.

The story of Standfield as seen through the hearts
of those who ruled washed through her like an ocean.
Some had achieved wonders; others had known only
failures. For most, though, it was a mixture of both.
Through it all, through the triumphs and tribulations,

Standfield had survived. Now it was Brianne's turn and her task. She would have to make the choices.

As she opened her eyes, she wondered how she could rule burdened with so many voices in her head. But the lives of the past Queens receded. Brianne still knew their stories, but not with the intimacy of just moments before. The choices she made, good or bad, would be her own. Standfield now rested in her hands.

She looked down at the blade still clutched to her chest, and then up to find Caliste standing in front of her, a dazed look in the General's wide eyes.

"The Sword chose you," Caliste whispered in a hollow tone. Bowing her head, she sank to her knees. "I am your servant. Whatever you need of me, I will do."

"I don't need a servant," Brianne told her and pulled her to her feet. She looked into the woman's intense blue eyes. "I need a friend."

Brianne could feel the General hesitate, and she remembered that Caliste had to make this choice before when Wilmere took the Sword.

"You have one," Caliste replied, her voice gruff.

The words were sincere, but they lacked the passion that Brianne had come to know in the General. Something was fading within Caliste, and Brianne couldn't let that die. The woman's intensity and her drive were too important to Standfield.

An unthinkable thought flashed through Brianne, and her blood froze. She caught her breath and then slowly let it out as the idea flowed through her. It was the only thing to do.

No, the Sword objected.

Yes, Brianne whispered. Then she opened her mind, pouring her own visions into the Sword. She showed the Sword who she was and who she would be. She laid it all bare, visualizing her strengths and her weaknesses. Then she added an image of Caliste. She painted a picture of the General's courage, her knowledge, and her dedication. *This is the way it has to be,* Brianne insisted. *The country needs this woman.*

For a moment Brianne felt a chill, as though the
Sword had withdrawn from her mind. Then it returned
glowing with a new strength.

Agreed.

Brianne shivered. Even though it was her idea, she
wasn't sure she had the courage to do this.

You are my daughter, the Sword reminded her.

Without allowing herself time to consider, Brianne
uncurled her fingers and shoved the Sword into Caliste's hands.

The Lady General's eyes widened in alarm. No one
except the Queen could hold the blade. To touch it
meant death.

But Caliste didn't die. Instead, the blade took her.

Brianne watched enviously as the lives of the
Queens surged through Caliste just as they swirled
through her. She watched the woman's eyes widen
and steadied her as she swayed with the force of the
transformation.

When Caliste's gaze cleared, she whispered to Brianne, "What have you done?"

"What had to be done," Brianne replied. The prize
here, she reminded herself, was not the Sword but the
country. She reached forward and wrapped her fingers
above Caliste's on the hilt of the Sword. She watched
the other woman's eyes widened again and then slow
understanding filled them.

Brianne had not given the Sword to Caliste, but had
chosen to share it. "Two Queens," Brianne told her.

"Can we do this?" Caliste asked, as much to herself
as Brianne.

Yes, the Sword responded in both of their minds.

"It won't be easy," Brianne told the General with
a sigh. "I don't think we will always agree."

Caliste's lips lifted in a smile. "You don't think so?"

Their eyes met and held. For the first time in history
the Sword had two mistresses and the land two rulers.
Between them they might just rebuild a country worthy of the Sword of Queens.

BETTER SEEN THAN HEARD

by Emily C. A. Snyder

Emily Snyder is a recent graduate of the Franciscan University of Steubenville, Ohio, where she earned her degree in English: Literature and Drama. True to her stomach, if not her craft, she has temporarily abandoned the customary plan of starving in garrets and is currently working in the exciting world of power suits and cubicles as a cover for her true vocation. Her credits include a story in *Marion Zimmer Bradley's Fantasy Magazine,* the production of her play "The French Butler—An Evening's Diversion," and various essays, reviews, and poems in literary magazines. She also has a novel or two under her bed, as well as an academic thesis on Fantastic Fiction.

Her interests in fairy tales led her to write "Better Seen Than Heard." It always seemed more than a little improbable to her that not *one* princess would realize the simplicity of ameliorating traditional verbal curses.

She would like to dedicate this story to all those who assisted her in the mad dash to write this piece, with especial thanks to Annie McAndrew, sister, editor and punster extraordinaire.

The Princess Melliandra had been in the middle of what was shaping up to be a historically thrilling denunciation of the treacherous Jarl Raznikov to the court of King Andrzej of Jolveg when she was suddenly struck dumb.

Literally.

But a little thing like muteness is easily remedied when one is a princess who has had a good education, Melli thought, grinning wickedly at the Jarl Raznikov, who had just burst unceremoniously into the Skellic, his fingers still crackling with power and his heavy coat littering the Great Hall with snow.

"I object, Your Majesty," he said in a tone more icy than the white drifts that settled on the floor. "The foreigner . . . has spoken out of turn."

Melliandra shivered, longing briefly for the sunlit valleys and warm plains of her own Aurelia. She had not come a willing victim to this hinterland, to court a barbarian monarch—even if he was the nicest royalty she had ever met, and rather handsome too, in a dark, barbarian way—but willing or not, she had no intention of allowing this petty Jarl to overthrow a prospective bridegroom . . . especially when her own vociferous charms had scared off several eligible bachelor princes already.

So, curtsying deeply to the King (who had been acting unaccountably obtuse ever since he had opened court that afternoon), she graced the wondering audience with a smile every bit as dazzling as the ivory-gilded floor and pillars of the Great Hall.

Snapping beringed fingers, she called her maidservant Belinda to her side. The young girl, dressed less flamboyantly if no less richly than her mistress, had been with Melliandra through several curses now: insomnia, hibernation, shapechanging, statuettes and many more too numerous or too embarrassing to print here. She had even taken a part in alleviating (although not entirely removing) Melli's latest curse of speaking backward—laid on her by a wall-eyed witch who had been aiming for another princess altogether.

Together they had studied the means of thwarting the most common spells any disgruntled majicker might hurl at a princess—a study that had proved more than rewarding during their numerous ambassadorial journeys.

Belinda's appearance interrupted Melliandra's haphazard thoughts, which was just as well. The maid, thinking quickly, had brought with her ink, quill, and paper, along with two pageboys in the bright parti-colored uniforms of the Jolven Court, who carried a small writing table and an ornate chair.

Then, stepping up to the low dais, and curtsying modestly, Belinda said, "Majesty, I beg of you a boon. My mistress has been . . ." She hesitated, glancing at Princess Melliandra who shook her honey curls and glanced significantly at the Jarl. She could not afford to have her maid struck dumb as well! Belinda nodded and continued, ". . . *overcome* with the import of her news, and begs leave to address you by means of the written rather than the spoken word."

Andrzej nodded slowly, as if the gesture entailed great sacrifice. Encouraged, Belinda continued. "But, being thus overwhelmed, she asks that the Great Hall be cleared until her missive is complete."

"She might retire to another room, if she desires solitude," the Jarl retorted.

"Gladly would she consent to a private meeting with King Andrzej. In the Solar, perhaps?"

Raznikov laughed, although he appeared troubled. "His Majesty could not possibly quit his throne just yet. He is attentive to his duties. He is most . . . attached."

"Then I pray," Belinda said despite Melliandra's previous warning, "on behalf of my mistress, that the Jarl Raznikov remove himself."

The court gasped as sparks shivered and wound around the Jarl's hands, and even Belinda skipped backward in fright. Melliandra gripped the table edge, ready to launch herself across the room and into the sorcerer should he aim at her maidservant.

Only Andrzej did not flinch: his face remained strangely impassive. Slowly, painfully, he raised his hand and shifted his eyes to glance sharply at the Jarl.

Raznikov recollected himself, dark brows lowering as he muttered, "Impossible, my King. This well-dressed vermin speaks falsehood and slander, and her mistress speaks not at all—a wonder in and of itself, for we all have heard nothing but a month of her *mellifluous* voice."

Melliandra clenched her fists and scowled at Raznikov—vermin, indeed!

"Forgive me," Belinda said, lowering her lashes in a show of practiced humility, "I am but a stranger and a servant here. And yet, is there not a whispered tale that in no other court but the court of Jolveg are all women treated with the dignity afforded every human by the grace of God? Is it not whispered that here is a court, here is a King who does not subscribe to the age-old axiom . . ."

"Better seen than heard?" Raznikov chuckled. "Majesty, the Princess is, by her maidservant's own admission, overwhelmed. If she in her reason had taken a dislike to me, I would leave the court at once. But Her Highness is clearly distracted. Far better she were removed for a time until she . . . recovers."

The smile Raznikov gave the Princess was as bleak as cold Hintev's endless nights, and Melliandra blessed the curse that kept her silent.

Andrzej's sleepy eyes blinked once, causing Raznikov to settle his shoulders more comfortably and Melli to dig her fingernails into her knuckles. The court held its breath as it waited for Andrzej to speak, for all knew that the throne was enchanted so that whatsoever the King said must be done.

"He may stay," Andrzej intoned like an automaton. He seemed to struggle for a moment before saying, "But neither he, nor any other courtier assembled now in this room, will offer harm." Letting out a long sigh, Andrzej slumped in his throne, oblivious to Raznikov's tightened lips or Melliandra's joyful eyes.

Flourishing the long peacock quill and swirling her lacy headdress, Princess Melliandra sat, noticing smugly that Raznikov resembled nothing so much as a thwarted stormcloud. *Well, as long as he doesn't do something to my hands,* Melli thought as she dipped the quill point into the ink.

The intricate calligraphy gave her ample time to consider the rest of her letter . . . no small matter, since she was still thinking backward (in order for her

words to come out frontward. Sadly, it was the only
remedy Belinda could find on that particular curse—
blast all wall-eyed witches) and that she had only
learned Jolvič a year ago. But her facility with words
soon took over and she wrote without listening to the
sounds around her, narrating how she had overheard
Raznikov (*"whose mode of entrance cannot help but
be suspicious"*) conferring with one of his retainers
regarding the Jarl's army, which was even now
marching on the Skellic. The army was not, appar-
ently, very large, but Raznikov had promised his re-
tainer that he had taken certain precautions to ensure
victory. Melliandra could only suppose this wretched
curse to be that "precaution." If so, she thought, Raznikov had chosen poorly indeed. Such a trick might
have debilitated a . . . a merfolk, perhaps . . . but
never an enlightened Aurelian.

A good half hour passed as the Princess concentrated on each symbol. By the time she had finished,
the light from huge stained-glass windows depicting
the Hunting of the Muchlin Boar had slipped from the
floor to the far wall. Melli motioned to Belinda, who
skimmed the letter for mistakes, made one or two
corrections, and then dripped red wax on the bottom
of the page. The Princess pressed the sunburst seal of
her own kingdom firmly on the paper, then nodded
to the maid to deliver the letter.

The room grew silent as Andrzej murmured thanks
and took the missive. Satisfied that her story had been
delivered without further mishap, Melliandra turned her
attention from the King's stern face to peek at the
sorcerer. His hands were behind his back and no harm
immediately proffered, but his dark eyes flitted
casually—too casually—to the letter, then back to
Melliandra. Andrzej's brows were pulled together,
Melli realized, and his lips were inexplicably mouthing
each syllable. But . . . but Andrzej was literate . . .
was not barbaric like his people! Then why . . .?

"You should have offered *me* your hand, Highness,
if you intended to marry a King," the Jarl said, sud-

denly beside the Princess. "Although there is still
time. May I take your silence as a yes? I do so
enjoy docility."

She glared at him and pulled away.

"Oh, no, Highness. Fear not. I know the rules. No
harm from those in this room . . . *now*." He chuckled
and passed by, the bottom of his furred cloak brushing
her like a tail.

Melli rubbed her arms as though to wash them.
Without waiting to see where Raznikov went, she hurried to the throne. Andrzej must have read the letter
three times by now. Had she written it backward? Did
her muteness extend to her hands as well?

Squinting her eyes and taking a step or two toward
the dais, she noticed the faint stench of brimstone
around the iron throne. The small hairs on her arms
tingled as she approached; her useless tongue felt thick
and heavy between her teeth. He did not react to
her coming, not even with his usual smile. Melliandra
glanced behind, but Raznikov had gone. He *couldn't*
have charmed *Andrzej* . . . could he?

She reached out for the King's wrist, hoping to feel
the movement of his blood, and didn't see when a
legion of men crashed through the tall windows and
into the Skellic, slashing at any who stood in their
path to the dais.

Andrzej's eyes remained fixed on the carnage before him, although the tendons on his neck were pulling and straining as though against invisible bonds.
Soon his whole body was shivering and twitching and,
despite her royal upbringing, Melliandra took a step
back. Andrzej's hand shot out and grabbed her by the
waist before she could retreat further. He pulled her in
and tugged her down, kissing her hard upon the lips.

Then he was standing, shuddering, running his fingers through his hair and saying, "Oh good. It
worked." He smiled and drew his sword, slicing neatly
through one of the invaders who had reached the
throne. He pierced two more soldiers before he found
a moment to thank Melliandra with another kiss, add-

ing as he jumped into the thick of the fray, "We'll discuss the marriage plans later. Oh, and don't sit on that."

Melli nodded, working her mouth in the hopes that the kiss that had cured Andrzej might also have worked for her. It hadn't.

Belinda was beside her a moment later, taking her by the elbow and leading her out of the room by means of a set of stairs behind the dais. "Forgive me, Highness," she said as soon as they were clear. "I only realized that Raznikov had enchanted the *throne* too late. That must have been the precaution he had meant. I'm afraid I have become so used to *your* curses that I have forgotten that inanimate objects might be spelled as well. Truly fascinating, though. I imagine it took a great deal of willpower for Andrzej to overcome immobilization; perhaps he found the cure alluring?" Melli blushed and Belinda continued, "Forgive me. I had thought the Captive Monarch an obsolete spell. But in such a country where the grimoires are centuries out of date, I should have thought of it sooner."

Princess Melliandra shook her head as if to say that the mistake was mutual. Her head was still reeling from the past five minutes, wondering over and over again at Andrzej's proposal. At least she *thought* it had been a proposal. She really ought to listen more closely from now on.

The sounds of fighting echoed down the hall, growing distant as the two women hurried to their rooms. "What shall we do now, Princess?" Belinda asked, heaving the saddlebags over her shoulders as if to answer the question.

Melli leaned against the wall. What to do? Motioning for pen and paper, she wrote, *Tiaw dna rood eht rab.*

"What?"

Squinting, Melliandra looked at what she had written and quickly corrected it. *Bar the door and wait.*

Belinda nodded nervously, biting her lip, and put

down the saddlebags. "Well, in the meantime, I'll check the grimoire to see if I can't find a reversal that only calls for herbs or candles or something."

Melliandra grinned, giving her maid a quick hug. The girl blushed, muttering that Melli ought to act more proper, but said nothing more about her misgivings.

Belatedly, Melli remembered Andrzej's words on the throne, *"none assembled shall offer harm,"* and, except that Belinda had barred the door already, she would have fled back through the corridors to his side. She needn't have feared, of course, for Andrzej had a sharp mind (when not under enchantment) and had touched his foot upon the throne, yelling something to the effect that Raznikov's men would promptly run from the Skellic and the Jarl himself offer no resistance to arrest. As a result of touching the enchanted throne again, his foot gained something of permanent pins-and-needles, but since the invading army was shoving its way out and Raznikov himself was under compulsion, the discomfort was but little payment.

Princess Melliandra only learned this much later, of course, for while Andrzej ordered Raznikov to explain himself, she was taking pleasure in the small sounds of the snowfall and the firecrackle. The kingdom of Aurelia was one of those nations given to flowery speeches and subsequent glassy stares, and Melliandra had been brought up accustomed to both characteristics. But now she heard with much joy Belinda humming an ancient tune as she pored over the neat columns and figures, and she heard the cheers that rang up from the Great Hall, punctuated by the softer sounds of mourning. A hesitant knock, made familiar by the month spent in the King's court, sounded at the door, followed by the frou-frou of Belinda's skirts and the rattle at the latch. It was really surprising how much sound the world could hold.

"King Andrzej, your Highness," Belinda said unnecessarily.

Melliandra turned, smiling and extending her hand

for Andrzej to kiss. She was surprised when he stuck a small flask into her palm instead.

"Drink it," he said, accepting a damp towel from Belinda and rubbing his face and neck free of sweat and blood. "Raznikov promises it's the antidote. And it would be an awful shame for you to write the wedding vows rather than reciting them. My nation may be backward, by your standards, but we do have some dignity."

Melli raised one eyebrow, blushing nonetheless. The potion was thick and sour, as all potions should be, but did indeed seem to loosen her tongue. It took a few minutes to manage anything beyond vague noises, but eventually she said, "Thank you," and handed the flask back to Andrzej who was gaping at her, as was Belinda.

She patted herself to make sure she had the correct number of hands and heads, and realized belatedly that she could see neither leg nor limb. Princess Melliandra had become invisible. "Oh, bother," she said, making Andrzej reach for his sword and Belinda rush back to her books. She smiled grimly, although neither of them could see it, and said, "Will you settle for better heard than seen?"

OPENINGS

by Meg Heydt

Meg Heydt has been active in the Society for Creative Anachronism all her life, and in SF fandom for a large part of it. She designs and makes costumes for both venues (sometimes winning in convention categories), taking advantage of her employee's discount at the local fabric store.

She sold her first story to *Marion Zimmer Bradley's Fantasy Magazine* when she was still young enough that her mother (Dorothy J. Heydt) had to cosign her contract. Meg says, "Most people think I'm trying to follow in Dorothy's footsteps; I'm not. I'm just a cynic who occasionally has a good idea."

The stink of the dungeon competed fiercely with the guard's foul breath on her face. Even though she had lived with worse smells, their presence was never so apparent as now. It didn't help that her hands were held by her captor's, and were put in manacles shortly thereafter; either way, she couldn't bury her nose in her sleeve.

"That will hold you now," he grunted. Fortunately, he was bored, and she was far too small to be interesting to any man. She counted only twelve summers, and sometimes had been mistaken for a boy. One of those times was the start of the mess she now found herself in.

Curse the man for his weak stomach, she thought.

She had counted the rotation of the guards around the smaller warehouse just outside the gates to the tower. It wasn't large enough to hold animals in, but it was perfect for holding grain for the farmers, or fodder for shepherds. Tired of picking through the rubbish piles outside for things to eat, she had chanced the building for something, anything, more sustaining. After all, the older street-children usually found the good pieces first.

The guards would always rest and talk for a few minutes before their replacements arrived at sundown; and in fall, the sky darkened before the sun set, letting night in even sooner. In that time, she crept toward the door and set to pick the lock. She thought she had a good five minutes to open the door, steal some food, and make a run for it.

She didn't.

A strangled cry and hoarse dry laughter erupted from around the corner just as she opened the door. One of the guards, green both in age and in face, appeared and promptly became sick not four feet from the door. His companion, a grizzled red-face, followed behind.

"Ah, boy. How do expect to stay long in this commission if you can't hold dinner? My leg isn't *that* . . . Hold there! You can't be in there!"

*　　*　　*

Dumb luck had caused her capture then; but carelessness had caused it now. The guard finished fixing the manacles to her wrists, and they hung just above her head while she sat on the floor. From the dim torchlight she could see several pairs, all in stages of decay, attached to other walls. The dampness from the stone clung to her back through her tunic. She wished again for the comfort of her hood; but it, along with all her tools, sat in the mess they called a guardroom.

As the guard left, the smell lessened. Unfortunately, so did the light. One lonely torch cast shadows along the walls of her prison. A window set into the wall

outside the door let in more light from the courtyard.
Noises, laughter and music, floated in and reminded
her of the situation.

                    *   *   *

The guards dropped her, a pile of rags, skin, and
bones, onto the carpet without any ceremony. They
looked upon her as trash to be dealt with, and then
thrown out. But human life called for human judges
with more authority than these two; and so she came
before the tower's lord.

They called him a Warden. His actual title set him
high up in court, where such things mattered; but in
his role here, he simply kept an eye on the borders of
his land. He was no more than a watchdog, faithfully
collecting tithes for his masters; and she thought him
no different from any other rich man.

She sat there while the guards laid out her crimes
to him with all the vigor of a great saga. He listened,
never keeping his eyes off her for more than a minute.
The one time she dared to meet them, she felt as
though his eyes looked right through her to some object beyond. She closed her eyes, and shook her head
to clear it, but the gaze still held her as easily as
chains.

"Can you pick any lock or just doors?" The question caught her by surprise. She blinked and shrugged
in answer.

He rose, collected a small box from the shelf behind, then placed it upon the table between them. The
lid sparkled with polished jewels, but the edges were
worn and reddened with rust and age.

"I have lost the key and cannot open it. It would
not matter much, but a keepsake is inside that I want
back. Can you open it?"

She picked up the box and turned it over. The in-
sides tumbled and thudded against the lid and sides,
making her all the more curious to see. The lock

showed great care in its making, and great neglect. She found herself thinking in unkind ways about a man who let this beautiful object go to rot.

"Need my tools," she finally said; and set the box down, giving him a sour look. He merely glanced at one of the guards and raised his eyebrows for the command. She heard him sigh, fumble with his pouch, and produce the needed object.

Her picks consisted of twigs, pieces of bone, some with teeth, and her prize: an old bent cloak pin. Some lordling's brat had made the mistake of tangling with her before his nurse could haul him away. She had kept the pin when she pulled off his clasp in the struggle. He left sporting a bloody nose and a bruise over one eye. The bit of iron opened more and larger boxes than any of her other tools, including the door that got her into this mess.

She studied the lock again. The pin was too large, so she chose a small bird bone with a knob at one end. Feeling around the inside of the lock, she tested for a spring or clasp. She eased carefully against the catch, mindful that if she broke this pick, her neck might follow. All the while, her captors watched.

To her relief, the lock clicked, and she opened the lid to find a simple amulet of stone wrapped in leather. The lord lifted it out and smiled to himself. Then he waved the guards away and sent them to bring food for himself and his guest.

*   *   *

The rattling of keys broke her out of her reverie. A man swaggered in with all the bravado of one who truly commands no one. His hair thinned at the crown and pulled back into a braid no bigger than a rat-tail. His eyes bulged out even as they squinted in the torchlight and his lips, though set in a disdainful frown, made his face look even more like a fish. His shoulders were too narrow for the great cloak that he

wore, and his belly too large to make his stance anything more than pathetic. She thought even less of her
current captor than her last one.

"Look, my dears, at this miserable cur I have
caught. She thought to rob you of your treasures, but
my men have seen to her proper punishment." The
three women huddled around him as though she were
a wild animal ready to tear them to pieces. Two shared
the same dark-gold hair, and clutched to either side;
the third sported dark brown and stood behind. The
youngest of the three begged her lord to protect her,
letting her gold locks frame her face with deceptive
innocence. Her sister, feeling his attention stray,
pulled at his arm and pleaded for his comfort. The
third just watched with empty eyes, clutching her
belly.

"There is no danger to you now, you are all quite
safe. She could even be trained to be a maid for you."
She felt his eyes wander over her body. It left her
feeling more filthy than years of living wild had made
her. She struggled against her chains and snarled at
them, sending them back to the door. He shuffled the
women out the door, then turned back, trying to hide
his fear with lechery.

"You won't be the first I have broken, but if you
submit, I would make you as favored as the others.
What do you say?"

She spat in his face.

As he left, she cursed the man who had given her
this mission.

*   *   *

"I want you to steal something."

She looked up from her bread, puzzled by the statement. For a moment, she thought he might be joking,
but his face showed only sobriety.

"Something big, something small . . .?"

"It doesn't matter so much '*what,*' as 'from where.'
There is a band of outlaws denned somewhere north

of here, about two hours ride. I need something they
have stolen, or better yet, something personal, to find
them." He gestured over to a small mirror hanging on
the wall. It glowed and visions of life outside would
appear and change like a dream. She looked back,
even more confused.

"There are many in the world who have some small
talent: mine is to use a mirror to look at places and
people far away. Just as yours is to . . ." he paused,
looking for the right words, ". . . open things. But I
can't always pinpoint their location without something
to guide me. Most of those visions there are from the
surrounding farms and village, and I have a collection
of small items to help me. Until I have something from
them, I cannot find the bandits; and they may move on
soon, with no way to track them. Will you help me?"

A part of her wanted to help. Some small voice
even told her to; but old habits set in and she asked
the familiar question from the streets.

"What do I get?"

They settled on a deal that gave her a new set of
iron picks, a new set of clothes and shoes, and a full
pardon; providing she left the area after she brought
back the requested item. So she left the tower well-
fed, clean, and warmly dressed and rested after two
days' lodging.

She found them, about half a day away, in an old
keep that remained from the last conqueror. It was
little more than a quarry now; but the lowest floor,
and as she found, the jail, were still intact. She had
not realized the tunic she wore was visible even at
night, and the bandits spotted her as she tried to sneak
in under a wagon.

They took her picks, her hood and her food, and
locked her away.

*   *   *

And now they offered her a selection of choices
that made hanging almost welcome. She knew that if

she didn't return, that thrice-blasted guard-dog that
called himself a lord would just send some other poor
soul after this goose.

What they didn't know, was that she wasn't out of
tricks. Secured in her hair, nestled in the braid, hid
her precious cloak pin. Now that her bandit captors
had seen her safely locked away, they would not come
again until daybreak, by which time she hoped to be
far away.

Slipping the pin out of her hair, she set to work on
the manacles at her wrists. One by one the locks gave
way, and she stood up, rubbing at the skin. She stood
at the door and listened for any movement, but the
only sounds came from outside. That gave her hope.

The lock took it away. She had access to the key-
hole from her side of the door, but the tool she needed
did not match the tool she had. Her task looked for
all the world like plowing a field with a blade of grass.

Still she tried, and went to work on the lock with
the hope that her luck would turn for her. She worked
for hours, as the torch burned down and the sky began
to brighten with the predawn.

Tired, hungry and desperate to be rid of the place,
she put the pin to the door again. But the pick was too
small to reach, let alone move the bolt in the door. Finally,
pulling her pin out, she slammed her fist at the lock.

"Open, damn you!" she cursed.

And sat amazed as the bolt drew back with an audi-
ble *click* and the door swung open into the room.

I must have picked it hours ago, she thought, and
slipped into the hall.

The noises had long since ceased, save one lone
drunken voice outside. She made her way to the
guardroom and found the door off its hinges and rotted mostly away. The bodies of men lay about, some
lying on benches, some leaning up against walls. Her
goods had been placed up on a ledge, away from wine.
She collected them and picked her way back through
the bodies to the outside.

And there, slumped over in what remained of a

nobleman's chair, sat her host; barely aware of what
was around him and smelling like a brewery. Anger
flashed through her, and then disgust, that she might
have ended her life like one of his chattel: with a
broken will and a broken spirit. She slipped the dagger
from one of the sleeping guards and crept toward him,
ready to kill him if he dared touch her.

His head nodded around on his neck and fell forward, with the rest of his body following onto the
floor. He did not look regal, nor beautiful, nor dangerous. He looked old, without wisdom, and even a little
sad. She found she didn't hate him enough to want to
kill him, she just wanted to be rid of him. *If that means
helping the tower-lord,* she thought, *I might as well do
the deed.*

*   *   *

"You made it back! I worried that they might catch
you and . . ." The silence made the unthinkable that
much more hideous. He waved away the thought
and continued.

"Did you manage to retrieve anything from them?
Or if you didn't, could you show us how to get there?"

She nodded and pulled out her small trophy.

"This was more trouble than it's worth, but it'll do,"
and threw it across the table into his lap. He picked
it up gingerly and stared at it. It was a small skinny
braid of hair.

"Call it the tail of the rat," and she turned to go.

"Wait," he called. She stopped and turned, wondering what he could possibly want her to do now.

"Did you kill him?"

"Not unless he died of fright when he woke up."

The Warden smiled. "Good. Very good," and tossed
the tail into the fire.

While she was still staring at it, he went on, "Would
you like to consider staying on here? This place could
be your home, and you wouldn't have to live on the
streets anymore."

"Why should I?" She knew this sort of talk could lead one into bigger trouble.

"Because I know something that you don't even know." He picked up the box from the shelf and turned it over in his hands, then said levelly:

"This lock was rusted shut. No one could open it with key or lock, and yet you could make the lock open. You have a talent, a gift, to open what others close. Right now, you need your tools to focus your thoughts; but in time, I could teach you to do without them."

She thought of the lock in the cell, how it opened when she commanded. She thought of her life on the streets, the days of hunger and the nights full of cold. She weighed his words in her mind. He offered a chance to break away from the life she knew, to become caged in one she had always despised.

"I don't want to be your pet, so I'll make a bargain with you. I'll stay here, and work in the stables or the yard or something. You can teach me whatever you can, and when I've learned all I can, I'll leave and never come back, deal?"

"On one condition . . ." She groaned inwardly, for she wondered what she would have to give in to now.

"Tell me your name."

She blinked, and for the first time in who knew how long, she smiled.

"It's Kel."

"I'm called Richard. We can start tomorrow."

A LITTLE MAGIC

by P. E. Cunningham

Pat Cunningham's last appearance in *Sword and Sorceress* was in volume XIV; not much has changed since then. She still lives in Pennsylvania, is still female, and still uses her initials for brevity (the P. E. stands for Patricia Elizabeth). She works at home and is happy not to have to commute anymore.

She would like to dedicate this story to the ants that invaded her kitchen last summer, and provided the inspiration.

The valley wasn't large, but it was clearly rich. A pleasant, placid river watered fields of soil so deep that plowing oxen sank to the hocks in it. Crops grew tall and green, in the case of the corn, or tall and golden for the wheat. Apple, peach, and cherry orchards stretched their regimented lines up the hillsides while vineyards writhed along the river. Every homestead had a well-tended garden plot bulging with vegetables. Goats and cattle grazed in pastures of lush emerald grass. In the gentle sunlight of midmorning the land sparkled like a polished jewel.

Hervokk the Conqueror surveyed it from a hilltop and vowed he would add it to his crown.

Without taking his eyes from the opulent prize, he spoke to the young man sitting a milk-pale mare beside his sturdy gelding. "Well, Vinn? What do you know of this place?"

The wizard rubbed his bold and hairless chin. You could tell he was a wizard because he wore the traditional voluminous robes, even though such garb was impractical when traveling with an army on the march.

The robes were dyed a stormy blue and black, in a pattern guaranteed to catch the eye, announcing to all this was a man of powerful magics and not to be trifled with. "I've heard of this valley," he said. "The King's Breadbasket, they call it. It's got quite a reputation for such a little place."

"Good or bad?"

"Good, on the whole. Their produce is superb; they make a healthy profit for the King through sale of exports. It's situated just far enough off the major trade routes that no war's bothered it yet. Probably why it's never been conquered. Too small and remote to trouble with."

"You'd think someone would take the trouble, a well-off place like this." Hervokk licked his lips. Seven baronies, two fiefdoms, and a seaside port had already fallen to his raiders. This valley would make an ample larder, on which he could feed and build an army fit for a conqueror . . . and more than a match for the King.

He eyed the small castle seated at the valley's mouth. It didn't look strong enough to withstand an attack, or a brisk wind for that matter. But Hervokk the Conqueror hadn't become master of seven baronies, two fiefdoms, and a seaside port by being reckless. "Who's governor here?" he asked Vinn.

"A duke named Pettil, I believe. An unambitious sort. Loyal down to the roots. You won't shake him free of the King too easily."

"Any regular royal patrols?"

"Too far off the beaten track."

"Standing army?"

"None that I'm aware of."

"Have they a magician?"

Vinn's lip curled. "In a place this small? Be serious. They'll be lucky if they've got a village witch. Nothing I can't handle."

Hervokk snorted. He might be lacking in years, this hired wizard too young for a beard, but he wasn't short in arrogance. Or skill: three of the baronies and one of the fiefdoms had fallen largely due to Vinn's magics. And this plum did look ripe enough to fall into somebody's hand. Why not a conqueror's?

His decision made, Hervokk turned his horse so that he stood broadside to his army, a dramatic effect he'd spent years perfecting. He surveyed his forces: two hundred horsemen strong, armed with bow and ax and sword, fronted by his special corps of fifty trained pikemen. He spotted the three supply wagons in the distance, only now trundling over the last set of hills. All would be in place by nightfall, then. Excellent.

He drew their attention with the famous shout that heartened his horde and struck terror into the hearts of rulers and peasants alike. "I want twenty horsemen to ride with me to the castle yonder." Immediately arguments broke out among the men as they vied for the honor. "The rest of you, make camp along the river. Make sure you're seen and your strength noted. And I don't want any fighting with the locals."

The men swore over that. Vinn raised an eyebrow. "It's a profitable area," Hervokk said. "Be a shame to ruin it if we don't have to. Is this Duke Pettil a practical sort?"

"I've never heard it said."

"He'd better be." The brief contention in the ranks, with the aid of daggers and a couple of kicks, had sorted itself out. The twenty victors pranced their horses forward to present themselves to Hervokk. He surveyed his honor guard and nodded. All were big and fierce and blooded warriors. The duke would be a fool to resist. Hervokk waved his arm. "Let's ride."

The Conqueror and his entourage did not quite make the intended impression on the valley folk. Oh, there were stares and pointing fingers and even some looks of apprehension, but precious little fear. Hervokk liked fear; it fought his battles for him, sharp as any sword. He didn't like this. Simple farmers ought to be terrified at the sight of a foreign warlord. "Are you sure this Duke Pettil has no defenses?" he asked Vinn.

"None that I've heard of, and none that I can see. Look, they don't even have guards on the castle walls. The trusting fools."

Hervokk squinted at the castle. From where it squatted on the plain, it commanded a clear view of all that went on in the valley. Thus, by the time the invaders neared the gates, a crowd already lined the walls. Hervokk scanned for weapons. He saw only that Vinn was right: no archers, no spearmen or pikemen, not even any daggers hanging from belts. The castle folk appeared armed, at best, with only mild curiosity.

Hervokk smiled. This would be a canter down the path.

He brought his party to a halt before the gates, Vinn beside him, the men lined up smartly behind. A peasant working a garden plot just outside the walls stopped for a moment to stare, then went on with his weeding.

"Ho, the castle!" Hervokk shouted. "I would speak with your lord."

There was a bit of shuffling up on the wall, and a plump man in green linen appeared. His thick brush of a mustache, cinnamon with a liberal flecking of gray, bristled at them. "I'm Duke Pettil," he announced himself. "What can I do for you fellows?"

"I'll make this easy on you," Hervokk said. "We're here to take your valley. I want your lands, your goods, and any able-bodied man who wants to join my army. In return, I'll let you and your people live and not burn this castle down around your ears. You will surrender to me immediately."

The Duke harrumphed. "Well, someone's got quite a high opinion of himself. Are you aware you're on the King's lands, my boy?"

"I don't see any King around. But I'm sure you can see them." Hervokk waved a mighty arm. As if on cue, his army poured over the rise and headed for the river to make camp. As per instructions, they were making a boisterous production of it.

Mutterings broke out on the castle wall, and were silenced by a scowl from the Duke. "They may look a bit disorganized now," Hervokk went on pleasantly, "but they drop into ranks fast enough when battle's joined. Believe me, you don't want to buck them." He beamed a smile at the walls. "Your answer, lord Duke?"

A young woman, her hair restrained in twin blonde plaits, appeared beside the Duke. She wore a light robe similar to Vinn's, though hers was spring-leaf green. "What's going on?"

"This ruffian and his mob just rode up and demanded our surrender." The Duke's eyes flashed. "We're being invaded. Can you believe the nerve?"

"I'm waiting for your answer," Hervokk said.

"It's no, of course." The Duke drew his bulk upright, chins jiggling in outrage. "You want to camp for the night, all right. You may bargain with the farmers for food. But this is King's land, and I'll not give it up. I want you and your army out of here in the morning."

"Perhaps you didn't hear us." Vinn stepped his mare forward. The air around him trembled with his might. "Hervokk the Conqueror has asked for your surrender. You'd be well advised to—"

"Vinn?" The blonde woman leaned over the wall. "Vinn Mousetussle, is that you?"

Vinn's jaw dropped. The woman waved her arm at him like some rustic maid. "It *is* you! Vinn! Remember me? Carmany, from school?" She peered down at Hervokk and his horsemen, then dismissed them with a shake of her plaits. "Don't tell me this is the 'great destiny' you were always going on about."

Hervokk fought off a smirk. "You know the wench?"

Vinn's face had gone scarlet, his eyes stormy. "We trained together," he said tightly.

"She's a mage, you mean?" A brown wasp hummed around Hervokk's nose. He swatted it away with a callused hand. "You told me they had no magician!"

"They don't." Vinn's expression made way for a sneer. "She had a little talent, only good for little magics. She could never stand against a real wizard. You'd have to be a total fool to put any faith in her."

"It's not the amount of magic you've got, it's what you can do with it," the woman recited. "Didn't you listen in school? Elemental wizard," she explained to Duke Pettil. "They always get a bit blustery."

"Likes to muck about with the weather, does he?" The Duke addressed the Conqueror. "See here. You take your threats and your wind machine there and you ride right out of here, or things will go badly for you."

"Maybe we haven't made ourselves clear." Vinn raised his arm, which suddenly burst into fierce and powerful flame. "I can blast your pitiful castle to bits, and your little witch hasn't the magic to—"

A wasp swung by his eyes, arrowing right at his nose. Vinn yelped and took a swing at it, forgetting for an instant that his arm was alight. The fire leaped onto his robe and hair. He beat at it frantically for almost half a minute before he remembered the snuffing spell. The people on the walls roared with laughter.

"Rather careless, your wizard," the Duke remarked. "That how he lost his beard?"

"Enough of this!" Hervokk roared. This wasn't going well at all. "Here are our terms: surrender or die. You have no other options."

Carmany snorted. "Don't be too sure about that."

Hervokk gauged his own options. The castle was small, its people unarmed. He had twenty warriors with him, and a smoldering magician. They could probably take the place right now.

He was about to order a rush at the gates when a horse behind his squealed. The next instant his gelding jumped and plunged. He hauled on the reins, while equine shrieks and human shouts erupted from his guard.

The air was full of wasps. They dove and dipped at Hervokk's force like a hail of tiny arrows. Yet none seemed to rise high enough to bother the watchers on the walls. The man in the garden, scant yards away, also seemed immune. "You have until sunrise to be on your way," the Duke called over the screams. "If you're still here, I promise you, things will get ugly."

Hervokk fought to keep his seat on his bucking horse. "You'll regret those words, I promise *you!*" he flung up at the Duke. He waved to his men, and the riders fled in a line far more ragged than their arrival. The wasps pursued with vigor. Vinn finally managed to whip up a gale that sent the insects spinning, and gave the invaders a chance to escape.

They rejoined the body of the army at the river, where tents and cookfires had already bloomed like some martial garden. The escort went stomping down to the riverbank for mud to slap on their stings. "Damned bugs," Hervokk muttered. A wasp perched on his shoulder, trying to work its way inside his breastplate. He crushed it in his fist, then wiped his hand on his leather-clad thigh and turned to Vinn. "Tell me about the Duke's magician."

"Magician? Oh, you mean Carmany." Vinn snorted. "I wouldn't call her a magician. More like an untalented amateur. If old Shekkim hadn't taken a shine to her, she never would have finished her training." He dismissed her, and a last clinging wasp, with a casual flick of his hand. "She's no threat to you or your plans. And if that Duke is keeping her on, it doesn't say much for him either."

"That Duke," Hervokk snarled. "A man with no army and a half-baked witch shouldn't speak that way to a conqueror. What he needs is a good, swift arrow between the eyes. Or a good, swift zap." He looked at Vinn hopefully. "I don't suppose you could . . .?"

Vinn shook his head. "I've told you before: the magic can't be used to directly harm another living

thing. It just fizzles out if you try. It keeps us wizards
from blasting each other, and anyone else for that
matter." He aimed a thoughtful gaze at the distant
castle. "Although, with a little time, I could probably
weaken the stones. If a wall collapsed and fell on him,
that wouldn't be considered direct."

"Maybe later. Let's let the boys have some fun."
At their leader's return the army had started to gather,
and now watched Hervokk expectantly. "Men," he addressed them, "I requested a surrender from this valley's governing Duke. He refused. You know what
that means."

The army voiced a rowdy cheer, like some great
hungry beast. "No prisoners," Hervokk ordered. The
cheer dropped a couple of decibels. "And try not to
trample too much of the fields. I want this land intact.
Other than that . . ." He waved his arm at the inviting
green. "It's all yours."

The men whooped and dove for their horses, to ride
forth and do what invading armies do best.

The horde returned at dusk, tired, well-fed, and in
quite a few cases well-liquored; a land with this much
fruit and grain produced a wide variety of spirits. Only
a few grumbled that they hadn't been able to indulge
in their favorite pursuit. But the valley was small, and
word spread quickly. By the time the army swept up
from the river, there wasn't so much as a girl or
granny to be found. The few men they'd seen had
simply stood aside and let the invaders ride by.

"An' the Duke watched it all," a semi-sober pike-
man reported to Hervokk and Vinn. "We seen 'im up
there on the castle wall, him and his witch. Just like
you wanted, right?"

"Right." Hervokk was grinning. "Find a couple of men
who aren't quite so potted and post them as perimeter
guards. Tell them to watch for riders bearing a white flag.
I imagine we'll be hearing from the castle shortly."

But dusk deepened to nightfall and then to full
night, and still no word came from the Duke. "The

fool!" Vinn spat. "He doesn't actually think he can resist us, does he?"

"Let him," Hervokk said. He munched on an apple brought to him by one of the raiders. Sweet, sticky juice ran into his beard. "This is a lovely place, plenty of water and food. The men could do with a holiday, and I've always enjoyed a good siege." He scratched idly beneath his breastplate. "So the little farmer-bunnies have fled. Probably ran right to the castle. That'll eat into their stores. What about water? Could you foul their supply?"

"I don't like to. Wells are tricky. I could ruin the valley's whole water table, and I'm sure you don't want that."

"Not if I can help it. All right, let them drink. When the food runs out and the babies start squalling, then they'll change their tune." His scratching turned more vigorous. He tossed the apple aside to devote both hands to it. "We'll make the usual runs at the walls, pick off a few of their men, throw the fear of invasion into— hell's teeth!"

The itching had grown to a burn. Hervokk tore off his breastplate, then the padded shirt underneath. The dark, matted forest of hair on his chest writhed with crawling life. He raked his fingers through the thickest of it, and came up with a tiny invader.

"What—" Vinn started.

"Fleas." Hervokk cursed and crushed the flea between his fingertips. With his other hand he tried to eradicate its brethren. "We must have camped on a nest of them. I hope you've got some powder in that sack of herbs you carry."

"I'm sure I can find—" Vinn broke off. His arm prickled. He thrust a hand up his sleeve. A second prickle started at his ankles. He balanced precariously on one foot while furiously rubbing with the other. "Something."

They returned to a flea-infested camp, with men and animals swatting, scratching, stamping, snorting, and swearing, according to inclination and species. The men were used to fleas, but not in these great numbers. Vinn scurried for his sack of medicines, while Hervokk cast a black look at the castle. "If I didn't know better—" he said.

"Don't be silly. Who'd attack an army with fleas? Now hold still." Vinn dusted the Conqueror with a chalky powder that cast up evil yellow puffs.

Hervokk coughed fit to choke. "Gods, that's vile!"

"Think how it smells to the fleas." Vinn dispensed powder between his own furious scratchings. "If this doesn't work, I've got a lotion that—"

"I don't want to hear about it."

Neither did the men, but they had little choice. It was either bear the odor, or the bites. They opted for odor. At some point the tiny pests abruptly abandoned their hosts, leaving welts and a reek like rotted cheese behind. It left the men grumpy and irritated, and nobody slept very well.

With the dawn came heat and stillness. And the flies.

Hervokk awoke to the screams of horses and a burr like the rumble of trolls. He flung back the flap of his tent. The sky was nearly black with flies—great hairy monsters the size of his thumbnail, with huge bulbous eyes and a taste for horseflesh. The horses tore loose from their pickets and fled in a mad attempt to escape the swarm. The men ran after them and found themselves targets. The buzzing cloud fell on the camp like a multilegged blanket. Almost as one, the army abandoned the horse chase and made a frantic dash for the river.

A fly tried to crawl into Hervokk's ear. He slapped it away. "Vinn!" he bellowed. "Do something!"

Vinn stood just outside his own tent, swinging his arms at the air. Black designs that weren't part of the pattern crawled across his robe. Then he held his arms still. A mighty wind rose and whirled about him. It scooped up the flies and sent them tumbling over the fields, away from the river and the camp.

Vinn slowly lowered his arms, panting in time to the dying gusts of breeze. "That," he gasped, "was not natural."

"Aren't you the bright fellow," Hervokk snarled. "Looks to me like you underestimated the witch."

"Nonsense! I trained with her. She was nothing then, and she's nothing now." He shook a few stray flies out of his sleeves. The groggy insects spun away. "This is nothing. A minor irritation. She won't be able to— OW!"

Vinn leaped a foot straight up. Hervokk managed half that height and a comment that was twice as juicy. Ants were boiling out of the ground, red as embers, and long-pincered. They poured like a wave over the men's naked feet. Vinn hopped and cursed, and Hervokk kicked and cursed. The army, wading back to shore, plunged into the water again.

Their leader and his wizard quickly joined them.

From the river Vinn called up a driving rain that pounded the earth and drove the ants back into their nests. It also drenched Hervokk's already-soaking army. It was a sodden invasion force that finally dragged itself out of the river and plodded back to camp.

"I want a fire," Hervokk commanded, "and a cup of *chaka. Now.*"

Building fires wasn't easy; Vinn's rain had saturated everything. And even the bitter comfort of *chaka* was denied them. The aide who had gone to the nearest supply wagon suddenly shrieked like a girl. Hervokk and Vinn rushed to his side. "*Now* what?" Hervokk snapped.

The aide choked and stumbled away from the wagon. Hervokk glanced inside, and nearly gagged. Maggots had got into everything. Thick clumps of the sightless, squirming things had made themselves at home in every sack and crate. They'd also brought their friends. Hervokk spotted roaches skittering in the corners, waiting for the humans to leave so they could get back to breakfast.

Hervokk backed away. "Burn the foodstuffs," he told Vinn. "And you," he ordered the heaving aide, "choose a party to fetch fresh water and food from those farms." Slowly, but with confidence, the conqueror's smirk returned. "We're not licked yet."

The men brought water from the farmers' wells, as well as fruits and squashes and corn, untouched by mite or maggot. It took a while; they had to go afoot. A few of the horses had ambled back into camp, but the rest found the succulent grass to their liking and loped away from the men sent to recapture them. "We'll round them up later," Hervokk said. "It's not a pressing task. We're going to be here a while."

Recovered now, the army strapped on their armor, hefted their weapons, and waited. The sun stood high, and the air lay still. Hervokk scented ambush. But from where? "Stay alert," he told his men. "We must be ready for—"

One of the wagons crashed into kindling. Someone in the ranks let out a yelp. Hervokk and Vinn exchanged a look, then sidled over to investigate the remains.

The wagon's wooden frame was riddled with termites. The insects seemed to blink up at the massive fleshy creatures gawking at them, before they shrugged their wings and returned to their meal. Seconds later the other two wagons collapsed.

Meanwhile, the remains of Vinn's magical rains had collected into puddles in the fields. The standing water congealed around grasses and weeds, forming soupy little swamps and doll-sized fens, which soon grew warm and stagnant.

The mosquitoes were ecstatic.

By the time Vinn recognized the glow on the pondlets as a miniature time field, the first generation had hatched, matured, and now descended thirstily on the warrior buffet. The men slapped and shouted and ran down the now well-worn path to the river. The few horses back in camp fled again, tails lashing behind them like desperate brooms.

Hervokk snatched up a blanket and flapped it madly at the humming horde. His bare forearms and the exposed bits of his legs acquired great clusters of bites. "Do something!" he howled at Vinn. "Kill them! Why don't you just kill them?"

"I can't!" The magician's robe protected all but his face, and the mosquitoes had zeroed in on it. "They're lives. Tiny, but still lives. The magic doesn't work."

"Then find something that does. And *no more rain!*"

Vinn's eyes frosted. So did the temperature. Within minutes the air was thick with swirling snowflakes. Mosquitoes hit the ground like miniature ice pellets. The bulk of the swarm turned torpidly toward the hills and buzzed away in search of warmer climes.

Hervokk clawed at the bites on his cheek. The expression in his eyes could have blasted brick to powder. "That's *it*," he announced. "We're storming the castle and we're storming it *now*."

Vinn sagged to his knees. Working so hard against Nature's pattern left him drained, but not so weak he couldn't summon a snarl. "The witch is mine," he wheezed.

Hervokk drew his sword with a hand as red as a radish. "You can have what's left of her."

It wasn't an intimidating charge—a horde of sopping, bug-bit horsemen minus the horses—but it was loud. Hervokk gave orders for the army to yell like three times their number. Tired and irritable and covered with welts as they were, looking and sounding dangerous wasn't a problem. They ran at the castle, brandishing swords and axes and pikes, and howled for blood, anyone's blood.

Because of their howls, they did not hear at first the ominous drone all around them. But they couldn't miss the slow-moving clouds rising out of the orchards and gardens and fields of wildflowers, to melt into one huge buzzing thunderhead. Hervokk, in the lead, slammed to a halt, creating an abrupt and noisy army-sized collision at his back. "Vinn!" he yelled. "What the hell's that?"

Vinn staggered, heaving for air, to his side. Full-speed foot charges were rarely required of wizards. He bent double, hands on knees, and squinted at the approaching cloud while he got his breath back. His eyes stretched to plate size. "Oh, bokkers."

"What?" Hervokk peered at the swarm. Surely not flies again. Or mosquitoes. No, these were louder. And larger. He saw what Vinn had seen, and his curse was blunt and ripe. *"Bees!"*

The army saw them, too, and turned to make their now-familiar dash to the river. Except this time the way was blocked by the mass of bees. The only open path led back up the line of their charge. Without waiting for orders they about-faced and raced back to camp.

Hervokk didn't lead the rout, but he was near the forefront. His face was white, his eyes panicked. "Do something!" he shrieked at Vinn. "Don't let them get on me!"

Even winded, Vinn managed a shadow of his customary sneer. "What's this? The mighty Hervokk, scared of bees?"

"I'm *allergic,* you idiot! One or two stings—the tents!" he screeched. "Take cover in the tents!"

The men reached camp ahead of their leader and dove into their tents. Seconds later, screaming, they dove right out again. Heedless of the bees, many chose to make a run for the river anyway.

Hervokk slid to a stop in the grass and grabbed the arm of he wheezing Vinn. "Vinn," the conqueror said tightly, "why are the walls of my tent moving?"

With a sick feeling in the pit of his stomach, Vinn gingerly approached the tent, Hervokk at his side. The wizard peeled back the flap, and made a strangled noise.

The tent was literally crawling with every form of

centipede, millipede, and spider the valley had to offer. Not a square inch of tent wall could be seen beneath the writhing mass. The living carpet on the ground scuttled back from the sudden light. A curious spider dropped on its thread from the ceiling and peered at Vinn with sparkling compound eyes. Vinn hastily dropped the flap, just as the bees descended.

Screams of pain and panic arose from the army. The warriors valiantly swung sword and ax at the enemy, for all the good it did. Hervokk found a discarded blanket and cocooned himself inside it. Bees landed and stalked its surface, seeking entrance. The blanket shuddered.

Vinn felt a sharp prick on the back of his hand. A narrow-tailed yellowjacket regarded him nastily before it zigzagged away.

Rubbing his hand, Vinn glared across the plain, beyond the mass of bees, at the distant lump of the castle. He imagined he saw Carmany on the battlements, laughing at him.

Rage engulfed him. He snapped his hands in a fluid pattern. Fires leaped to life throughout the camp. The flames burned sluggishly, hampered by damp fuel, and vomited clouds of thick smoke into the path of the attacking bees. The swarm hit the smoke; their drone turned lethargic. The bees lost altitude as well as aggression, but they didn't disperse. The few men remaining in camp were more than happy to abandon it to them.

Vinn swayed on wobbly knees with arms dangling and fists clenched. Though his energy was all but depleted, his anger was still raw, hot, and soaring. With fury to bolster him, he was confident he could call up enough power to set off an earthquake, and crack that damned castle—and the witch within it—like a nutshell.

He strode determinedly across the plain, the castle fixed in his sight. The ground seemed mushy underfoot, but he ignored it . . . right up until the earth crumbled out from under him, and sent him sprawling facedown in the dirt. His body sank into soil loose as water, and his panicked flailing only hastened the process. Within minutes he sank out of sight.

Unhampered by rain, smoke, fire, or wind, the beetles and worms had been busy.

After that, things quieted down. The bees hummed at the perimeter of the camp, but did not attack. In sodden, sheepish clumps, the wary fighters crept out of the river and back to their tents, though no one went inside. After about twenty minutes or so a soggy, dirt-caked Vinn hauled himself out of the ground. Long he glared at the castle; but at last his expression broke. Gathering his muddy robes about him, he trudged back to camp, where he sat with his back to the castle, apart from the rest of the horde.

At some point Hervokk crawled out from under his blanket. He looked at the valley, then he looked at his men. Then he sat with the blanket around his knees and did not move for hours, not even when the sun slipped down behind the hills. A few fireflies flitted up to circle the camp, blinking their taillight codes.

No noises issued from the camp throughout the night. Toward morning, however, a vigilant passerby might have picked up many furtive sounds: the flap of hide tents, the rustle of leather, the muffled clink of metal. The fireflies signaled to each other and slipped away into the dark.

By dawn the riverbank was clear. Only scuffed earth, charred grass, and the splintered detritus of three wagons remained to mark the army's stay.

When word came down from the Duke's magician that all was safe once more, the people left the castle's safety and returned to their cottages and farms. Little had been ruined, and only food stolen. As compensation, they discovered a herd of marvelous horses placidly grazing in their fields. All were large, healthy, muscular animals, bred to carry armed and armored warriors. They would make excellent draft beasts.

Some boys got together and rounded them up and drove them in with the valley's stock.

About the middle of the afternoon a forlorn figure in a soiled magician's robe appeared at the crest of the slope. It paused there, as if debating, then tramped down the hill to the castle.

Just outside the castle gates, Vinn paused again. He looked to the right and left—at the rich, well-aerated soil, at the bees humming their work song among blossoms and crops, at the trilling of fat and happy birds. When he looked up again, Carmany was leaning over the wall and grinning down at him.

"Hi, Vinn," she said cheerfully. "What can I do for you?"

"Carmany." His hands twitched. He forced them to his sides. "I've come to tell you Hervokk's army has, um, chosen to withdraw. You've nothing more to fear from them. Or from me. The army and I have parted company."

"I'm sorry to hear that. I know you always said you wanted to have a job like that—"

"Don't you feel sorry for me. I'm a mighty wizard. I have power. I don't need—I don't—" His hands shook. The last of his arrogance popped. "I don't know how you did it. You barely made it through training. All you ever had was—"

"A little magic. Yes, I know. You boys made sure I knew." Carmany shrugged. "Lucky for me Shekkim saw potential. He felt it was his duty to help us all achieve our best. You should have listened to him more."

"Yes," Vinn agreed. "Perhaps I should have. I may just go back and do that. It's not as if I have anything else lined up." He stood silent a moment, summoning his courage, then bowed to her, stiffly, from the waist.

"There's no need for that," Carmany said. "I was just doing my job. Oh, Duke Pettil and I have something for you. If you can wait a minute—"

She disappeared from the wall. A few minutes later

the gate creaked open and Vinn's milk-colored mare
ambled out. "She got into the garden," Carmany explained from the gate." She's nice and all, but the
Duke's too heavy and I don't ride much, so—"

"Thank you." Vinn approached the mare and
mounted. She'd been well cared for, watered, and
groomed. He patted her neck and she whickered gently. There wasn't a tick or flea on her.

He clucked to the mare and she trotted off, away
from the castle and the valley and the ambitions of
wizards and conquerors. Partway up the slope he half-
turned in the saddle, and after much deliberation,
waved. Carmany waved back.

Color flashed at the edge of his vision. Vinn found
himself surrounded by butterflies. They swirled around
his head, lighting briefly on his shoulder and the saddle's pommel and between the mare's ears, then flitting off again. They swooped beside him as he rode,
and cheered him on his way.

ELOMA'S SECOND CAREER

by Lorie Calkins

Lorie was raised in New York State, but lived in several states before finding a true home in the Seattle area. Her "wonderful husband and four incredible kids" are very supportive of her writing, and very good about jumping up and down with her when she makes a sale. "Eloma's Second Career" is her second professional sale; the first was to *Marion Zimmer Bradley's Fantasy Magazine* (not counting a poem in the local newspaper, when she was in second grade). She has been writing and submitting (and collecting rejection slips) for 12 years.

Her hobbies include reading (all kinds of fiction; and science, especially space science, physics, and cosmology), woodcarving, genealogy, birding, crocheting, puzzles, and collecting pewter dragons. If she's not in the "writing room" or the kitchen, she's probably at Starbucks or the horseshoe pits.

She has no pets because she's allergic to everything, but she says that if a stray dragon turns up in her yard, she'll be quick to adopt it.

Eloma presented herself at Wizard Bartholliver's door, burdened only by the small bundle of clothing and few keepsakes she could carry. It had been painful in some ways, to part with the home and possessions of a lifetime, especially her healing herbs and implements for cooking. But what elation that freedom had brought her! At last her path would be her own. From her father's charge to her husband's, she'd never had the responsibility to make her own way in the world. Until now. Sartha, with his wife and young family, had been happy to have the house, although they had begged her to stay on with them. Waiting, she noticed that the wizard's wooden porch badly needed sweeping, and two of its planks had nearly rotted through.

At last one of the wizard's young apprentices opened the door. "No donations this day, His Wisdom bade me tell you, and I'm not to buy peddled goods, neither." He quickly shut the door in her face. Eloma rapped again, this time with the handle of her walking stick.

"Who taught you your manners, you little pip?" she said when the same green-robed lad cracked the door open. "Do I *look* like a beggar?! Let me speak with your master, boy, before I tan your hide for insulting a guest!"

A panic of indecision swept the boy's countenance. He must have deemed his master's wrath less formidable than the old woman's, perhaps unsure whether she might be a sorceress incognito, for he gestured her into the receiving room and fled through a doorway at the back, curtained with coruscating orange, yellow, and blue light. The wizard himself soon retraced the boy's steps. "What is it you want, old woman? We have plenty of rags, and need no housekeeping help!"

"Oh, you don't?" Eloma crossed to a low table in front of two loose-jointed wooden chairs, raising puffs of dust from the carpet with her wooden clogs. She picked up a carved bowl from the floor under the table and showed the fur-blue contents to the old wizard. "Is this one of your spells, then?"

Embarrassed irritation made the wizard's frown stormy, but Eloma had known her husband's frown for too many years to be put off by that of a stranger, even one she hoped to learn from. "How-be-it, I'm not applying for a housekeeping position. I am applying as an apprentice." There, she'd said it. "I want to become a sorceress."

The old man stared at her as if she had suddenly shape-changed into a chamber pot, rather the same way Sartha had looked when she'd shared her plan with him. Then the wizard snorted and guffawed. He laughed, chuckled, giggled, and guffawed again, holding his sides and shuddering with abandon, until he had to drop onto one of the rickety chairs for support. The groaning creak of the wood sobered him enough to sit upright. A dozen apprentice boys and girls had slipped past the coruscating curtain, and gaped in amazement at the spectacle of their master, laughing. "Old woman," he said, still smiling, "thank you. That was the best laugh I've had since I turned His Wisdom Lasordu's chair into a rotten roc's egg, back in school. I'll buy anything you're selling. It was worth it."

It was Eloma's turn to frown. But she glared instead, willing the pompous magician to become a block of lake ice in the coldest winter of the land. She straightened, admittedly no taller than the young lad who first opened the door, but as tall as her old bones would allow. "I am selling nothing," she repeated, in tones a block of lake ice could understand. "I came to indenture myself as an apprentice. I wish to become a sorceress." With a flick of one gnarled hand, the wizard sent the various-aged children scrambling back through the doorway. Bartholliver rose, rerobing himself in hauteur. "Old woman, I cannot bargain with you. You have obligations to attend to, a husband, a family, or such. I would not accept you anyway, even were your father here to barter for the apprenticeship. You are too old to learn the vast knowledge required to do magic." Another arrogant flick of the hand was intended to dispose of her.

"Well, *old man,* if we are to dispense with courtesy here, I can do that. See how quickly I learn? My face may be wrinkled, but my *mind* is not! How much I can learn, or how well, only time will tell about me, just as it is with your more youthful charges, I am sure. My father is long dead, and so is my husband. No one must barter on my behalf, for I own myself. As for obligations, I have none. My children are grown, with families of their own. I have given away

my house and all that is in it. All of my possessions
are in this sack." She nudged the brown cloth bag
with one foot. "And none of them are *rags*."

"I can't accept a grown woman as an apprentice.
The townsfolk would gossip. Both of our reputations
would be ruined."

"My reputation with the cackling hens at the village
well is of no concern to me. As for yours, well, I
doubt it could be any more unsavory." She raised her
eyebrows at his fleeting smile. "The rumor-mongers
say you use your magic to satisfy all of your desires,
but after seeing you, I think you merely convince
yourself you have none."

Wearing the frown of an ogre with a headache, Bartholliver raised his nose a twig higher in the air. "Ma-
dame," he uttered with pained civility. "My
apprentices toil for their upkeep, as well as studying
their lessons. How do you propose to merit your
keep?"

Now Eloma smiled. She had won a concession of
courtesy as well as tacit victory on his earlier points,
and the answer to the current question was obvious.
"You have already denied a need for the services I
am most competent to offer in trade, Your Wisdom,
but I am strong and healthy, and will chop wood or
carry water, hoe the garden or run errands, just as
your other apprentices do." She smiled, but carefully
looked away from the curious faces that poked
through the magic curtain.

"Oh, Master!" the boldest blurted, "Ask her can
she cook!" The others nodded in eager agreement,
but all of them disappeared when the wizard swung
around.

Looking angry, then thoughtful, he said, "It is true
that our recent meals have lacked, er-"

"Edibility!" shouted a voice from behind the curtained doorway.

Bartholliver growled as if to clear his throat. "Well
then, can you cook?"

Eloma grinned. "I'm a good cook, if I must say so.

And I can give you some advice on teaching those youngsters some manners, too."

"Done!" Bartholliver said, glancing back at the doorway. "The kitchen is out that way." He waved toward an ordinary doorway. "I will expect dinner at sunset and breakfast at dawn. I give you permission to press any idle apprentice into service to help you cook and clean," he clarified her job description. "And you may sleep in the kitchen, or make a pallet in the female apprentices' sleeping room."

"Fine. When should I report for my first lesson?"

"My apprentices must prove their mettle before they may learn magic," he smirked. "I will let you know when I deem you ready to learn." With a hiss of his embroidered black robes, he vanished through the curtained doorway.

Dinners and breakfasts passed, and Eloma settled in. She reorganized the household, prepared the meals, made the garden flourish, cleaned and repaired the entire house, and taught the youngsters how to do everything as she went. One morning as she perused the market stalls for fresh fish for dinner and some yardage for a new apprentice's cloak, she passed Sartha's stall, and he stopped her with a reproach. "Mother, why don't you come home now? You're just a housekeeper in that place, without even the title. You could do the same for us, and at least you'd be among family!"

"I'm not a housekeeper. I'm an indentured apprentice to the wizard."

"You're not apprenticed to that magician any more than I am. What magic has he taught you? Come home, where you can sit in the sun and mind your grandchildren."

"I'm too young to sit in the sun and let my mind rot, grandchildren or no. I love the little ones, Sartha, but I want an interesting life. I want a second career, and I'm going to have it. I'm done with raising children and keeping house!'

"Are you, then?" Sartha simply nodded, pursed his lips and said nothing.

Angered by the truth of Sartha's words, Eloma dickered more shrewishly than usual for the fish and yard goods. After three months, despite frequent requests, the wizard had taught her nothing but a few parlor tricks. She wanted to learn more than just delusion and misdirection. She had become so engrossed in setting the house to rights, doing the things she knew so well, that she had lost sight of her dreams. *I'm already very good at self-delusion,* she thought.

"Valmar!" she called to a green-robed boy in the garden. "Come and prepare this fish. You are cooking tonight!" Then she pulled her brown cloth sack from beneath the bed she had built, thinking to pack her belongings, but something nagged at her mind. *If I leave now, even to go on to something more interesting, or something I might do well, he will have won. And I will never know whether I could have been a sorceress.* Also, there were the terms of the indenture. In her anger, she had thought to accuse the wizard of failing to teach her, thereby breaking the contract. But now she recognized that the Wizard's Guild might consider illusions enough instruction for a beginning apprentice, and find *her* to be the party in breach. She pushed the sack under the bed again, and turned her hand to dinner.

"Never mind, Valmar. I will prepare the fish myself. But light the stove for me before you go out, please." Eloma stared at the dead fish on the table, too discouraged to do more. Cooking seemed to be too much trouble now. Nothing seemed worth while, if she was going to be stuck here as a servant for the rest of her life. On the other side of the table, Valmar hurried to the stove, as if to do the smaller chore quickly, before she changed her mind, and her gaze wandered to him. The boy opened the firebox, but instead of taking a match, he made a gesture with his fingers and tossed an imaginary scrap at the neatly-laid tinder. At once, the flame caught. A smug grin had replaced the chore-weary sulk on his face when he turned. "Anything else?"

The housekeeper's face showed a new expression as well—determination. "Yes. Teach me that spell."

Valmar looked flustered. "I—I can't teach you. You're just an old woman."

Nothing could have stiffened her resolve more than those words. "I am an apprentice, just as you are. I am paying my way the same as you. Or don't you think that cooking and cleaning are worthy payments?" Valmar had been conscripted for enough household chores to know that they were hard work. He stared down at the floor.

"I'll take that as agreement. Why shouldn't I learn the spells you've learned, if I'm paying the same price?"

"But you're old!" He hunched into himself, ashamed of what he'd said, and expecting a blow that never came.

"So I am. You are older than the other apprentices, too. Yet you wear the novice robe."

He gulped and said in a soft voice, "I was apprenticed first to a butcher, but the killing gave me nightmares."

"So it was the wrong trade for you. No shame should follow you for that." The boy looked up at her in surprise. "Now you are older than the other beginners. Does that make you incapable of learning what they do?"

"Of course not!" he said, then, "Oh." He thought for a long time, his face weighing things first to one side, then to the other. Eloma waited. At last he said, "The fire spell is not the first. You should learn in the same order that we do, for magic can be dangerous to experiment with." It sounded like one of the wizard's lectures, but Eloma saw that was exactly what she needed.

"What is the first lesson, then?"

Dinner was a trifle late that night, but Eloma had

learned her first taste of real magic. Thereafter, she extracted a spell for every darned sock, a lesson in magic theory for every snack. Clean clothing cost a divining spell. Fresh straw in the mattress ticking cost apprentices the loan of their books overnight. A new robe cost the senior apprentice an entire evening of tutoring. One swaggering fellow had threatened to tell the wizard of her deals, but the others had painfully and memorably made clear to him that if Eloma were sent away, they would be back to cleaning their own clothes and eating their own cooking. Despite Eloma's attempts to teach each one the basics of washing, sewing, and meal preparation, no one was eager to give up her delicious stews and delectable desserts. Her magic skills grew quickly, since she didn't have to learn to read and write, as the young ones did. The apprentices took pride in the success of their student.

Late one evening, she was studying "The Book of Changing" at the rough wooden table in the kitchen by candleglow. The wizard seldom entered the kitchen, but it was only when everyone had gone to bed that Eloma's time was truly her own. Shumy, one of the young beginners, entered the kitchen shyly. "Eloma, Ma'am, could you help me with this spell? I've been trying to get it right for three days, and His Wisdom will be awfully angry if I still haven't got it tomorrow, but nobody else is awake."

"Sit down, Shumy, and we'll look at it together." The spell was one Eloma had struggled with herself, until she'd finally thought of it in reverse, from the result to the spell, as if it were a garment she wished to copy. Then she had understood that she needed to see the result exactly in her mind, in order to make the gestures match it. She helped Shumy figure that out for herself, and the little girl was able to perform the spell perfectly. She must have told others, for ensuing weeks brought Eloma her own little class of beginners in the kitchen late at night. They came to her for the explanations the wizard was too hurried to give, and the way of seeing that, from his lofty perspective, he didn't see a need for, or no longer knew how to share.

As the months passed, the older students came to Eloma as well. Her eagerness to learn had put her ahead of them in many areas. But still she craved more knowledge.

The senior apprentice shook his head. "I can't think of anything else to teach you, Ma'am, to pay for a tonic for my mother's cough. I've taught you everything I know."

"I'll make the tonic for your mother all the same, Teddeth. Perhaps you will think of a suitable payment later." Teddeth watched as she set about mixing the proper herbs and boiling the water to steep them.

"Ma'am," he said hesitantly, "why don't you ask His Wisdom to give you the examination for Journey Sorcerer? I've taught you everything I know, and I'm to take the test next week."

Eloma was surprised to hear this, thinking always that she must still be among the lowliest students, for every time she learned some new magic, she saw how much more there must be to discover. She said nothing as she puttered about, finishing the potion and capping the vial, but as she handed it to him she said, "I think you have paid me full value for this tonic, Teddeth. Good health to your mother, and good luck to you on your examination."

"To you as well, Ma'am."

Eloma waited. When Teddeth's voice resounded with joy as he received the Journey Robe of fine blue silk from Bartholliver, she smiled. That evening, after the celebration was over and the wizard and his apprentices had gone to bed, Eloma offered Teddeth the last piece of blueberry cake she had made in honor of his new robe. Smiling, he accepted, saying, "What do you want to know?"

"What was the test like, if it isn't a secret?"

"No secret. Every test is different. The Master Wizard is free to make the test easy or hard, but mostly, they always make it hard. They don't want unqualified sorcerers in the trade, making us all look bad. The Journey Robe test usually includes seven problems: Making Fire and Unmaking of Fire, Matter In Motion, a Gateway spell of some sort, Scrying, Casting an Illusion, and Levitation."

"Self-levitation?"

"No, no. That's too hard for the Journey test. Self-levitation is in the test for the Master's Black Robe. Levitation of any inanimate object is enough for the Journey examination."

"I see." She ushered him out of the kitchen, so she could study a bit more. "Thank you, Your Wisdom," she said with a smile.

The next day, she went to the wizard in his study. "I would like to take the examination for Journey Sorceress, Your Wisdom. I believe I am ready."

The wizard was to stunned to reply for a moment, and then he burst into laughs that shook his massive oaken workbench and threatened to spill him off his high stool. Expecting his rudeness this time, Eloma merely crossed her arms and tapped her foot until he was done.

"What makes you think you can demand to be tested?" he asked, wiping his eyes on the deep, belled sleeve of his robe.

"I have read the Guild Bylaws. A student may request testing at any time, if he, *or she*," she emphasized, "believes she has been unfairly passed over. And I do. I believe you have unfairly neglected my training, and failed to test my knowledge. Now I request examination for my Journey Robe."

Bartholliver's mouth opened to laugh again, but the ice-dragon stare Eloma gave him smothered the chuckle in his throat. So certain was he that she knew no magic worth testing, that he sneered at her in contempt. "All right, then. You'll have it immediately. Show me one spell, one single incantation of substance, and I will grant your Journey Robe. Not a card trick, mind you! Not a lovers' posset! A real spell worthy of a serious sorcerer."

Just one spell? That didn't seem like much of a challenge. But Eloma smiled. It was the opportunity she had only received in daydreams. After several perfectly formed hand movements, and an incantation in the ancient language of magic, she crushed a pinch of herbs from her pocket and blew them at Bartholliver himself. She stepped out of the way as he rose from his seat, a shocked expression on his face. When he reached the doorway, she remembered that the Gateway, the coruscating curtain the wizard had erected in place of a door, would not allow her spell to leave the room. Quickly, she chanted the words to collapse the Gateway, so the bespelled wizard could pass through. Knowing it was an important safeguard to protect the students' projects from escaping, she focused her strength and erected a new one, in a pattern of white, maroon, and deep green that complemented the room's furnishings. "Gateway. That's one," she said to herself.

She hurried after the wizard, tossing Fire spells to light the candles in the sconces along the hall ahead of him, so he could see his way. Being thrifty as well, she left Snuff spells behind her to put them out. By now the young apprentices had begun to gather behind her. "Two and Three," was all she said, following Bartholliver silently as he made his way toward the kitchen. In the eating room, a chair had been left out from the table, and with a Gesture and a Word, she spirited it out of the wizard's path. "Four—Matter in Motion," she ticked off the problems on her mental list. As Bartholliver entered the kitchen, Eloma made curling gestures with her hands, and the sleeves of his black robe began to roll themselves up for work. He squeezed between two of the youngest students, and plunged his hands into the hot, soapy dishwater. With a look of horror, he lifted a cooking pot from the depths of the sink, and started to scour burned food from its bowl. "What have you done?!" he roared. "What evil spell is this?!"

"No evil," she said, reassuring the young ones with a smile. "It's a simple Volition spell. You would have protected against it, if you had any respect for my ability to learn magic."

"What is this?!" he roared again, as an image began to color the rinse water in his pot.

"Scrying, that's five," she muttered, before assuring the wizard, "It is merely a Future-vision I cast for you. But I *have* been considering a third career, that of *teaching* magic."

"This can't be my future! I see a sorceress helping me teach magic to my apprentices!"

"It is one of the real futures that is possible. The choice is still yours to make." Eloma would not force his hand, but the many grinning faces and eagerly nodding heads of the students assured her that he would have plenty of help making the decision.

"All right, all right! I don't know how you learned so much, but if you can make me behave as a kitchen drudge, you are certainly a proficient Sorceress. You can have your Journey Robe! You can have anything you want, but break this spell!"

Eloma waved her hands in a cut-off movement, speaking the last words of the spell in reverse order, and it was broken. While the wizard reached for a rag to dry his hands, she concentrated and waved her hands up and down herself, whispering an Illusion spell, and smiled as her robe appeared to change from Apprentice Green to Journey Blue. "Six. Illusion." She muttered some more and gathered all her power for one last problem on the examination she had set for herself. When Bartholliver turned to face her, his mouth gaped with shock as he saw that her eyes were level with his. He stared mutely at the hand-span of empty space between her feet and the floor. After a moment, he blushed with embarrassment, finally recognizing how much he had underestimated her.

When he looked up, though, his face expressed the respect due a new member of his Guild. "A new-won Journey Sorcerer, or *Sorceress,* is permitted to ask one boon of her former Master."

"Ah, then, I would dearly like for someone else to cook dinner. Magic can be even more tiring than housekeeping, I think." She settled gently to the floor.

Bartholliver nodded in tactfully silent agreement, as he scanned the room, reckoning the students' cooking skills. "I shall take you out to the tavern for dinner." With a grimace that showed the pain to his purse, he added, "We'll all go."

While smiling agreement, Eloma had to shake her head in bafflement. There was still so much to teach him.

SYLVIA

by A. Hall

Ms. Hall is a native of Washington State and currently lives in Lakewood (near Tacoma) where she works in the family business as a resident apartment manager. She majored in math and Spanish at the University of Washington.

Judging by this story, she must have come into contact with poets at some point in her academic career. We traditionally end each volume of *Sword and Sorceress* with something short and funny. We hope that you enjoy this story as much as we do.

> "*When Sylvia smiles, the dappled sea*
> *Dreams softly in tranquility . . ."*

I pushed myself up from the plunging gunwale, wiping my mouth with the back of my hand. "Can't you think of anything but poetry, Elmo?"

"Or would 'serenity' be a better choice, friend Deirdre?" he continued, not quite losing his far-away look, I bet. "For the alliterative effect you know."

At least that's what I think he said. I can still recall every detail of the fried egg sandwich I ate for breakfast that morning. Conversation, on the other hand, I remember only in patches.

"It won't be long," he added companionably. "We'll make port in about an hour. We can buy horses and be well on our way by nightfall."

Elmo was the seventh son—and thirteenth child—of Edric of Long Glen. I suppose he must have thought that if he couldn't be Lord of the Long Glen, the next best thing, surely, was to be a poet. God save us from lords' sons and poets in equal measure.

Lord Edric had sent me to accompany him to Selkirk Abbey so he could join the good Brothers. It
seemed we would never get there.

We had climbed to the "mountain's snowy breast."
We had rescued Selina of the White Hand from the
wizard Suleiman. And at every turn of the road, Elmo
stopped to play marbles with hedge wizards or to
trade sonnets with mermaids and walruses.

"This time we really need to get going," I said later.
We were jogging our horses inland and I was again in
my right stomach. "We're almost there, and I'll have
to make excuses for our delay as it is."

He was murmuring something about Sylvia and the
golden apples of the Hesperides. He had that distracted look he sometimes got when unable to come
up with a rhyme.

"What is it about this Sylvia, anyway?" I asked, a
little exasperated.

He drew up his horse. "Don't you know anything?"
he said, spluttering. "Sylvia is . . . a poetic ideal of
womanhood. A nymph. A muse. Any poet worth his
salt has dedicated verses to the divine Sylvia."

"Trust a poet to waste verses on an idea," I grumbled, urging my horse to a canter.

"Anyway," he said later, when we had slowed to
give them a breather, "we can't go straight to Selkirk.
Don't you remember? A troll has been killing off livestock to the east in Stamford."

This was how it always started.

We stopped in Stamford that night. It was a village
of maybe ten hearths. There was no inn. Tossing and
turning in the hay of someone's loft that evening, I
thought about the lonely road home from Selkirk
Abbey. And I decided I was not about to let the Brothers have him.

I felt around for his flask. Opening it, I measured
in four drops from a crystal vial. They glowed a weak
amber in the unlit loft. Clammy steam from the flask
condensed on my fingers as I closed it. It was a love
potion I'd stolen from the witch-queen Ragnarad the

time I saved Elmo from the snake pit. I'd saved him more than once since, and if anyone deserved him, it was me.

In the morning, we followed the river into hilly country reminiscent of my childhood. Troll haunts for sure; once you've seen them, you never forget the look of them.

We had heavy axes, sharpened and ready, and had polished our shields to a high gloss. The idea was to temporarily blind the creature. Trolls don't really turn to stone in the light of day, more's the pity.

We hunted along the river's edge for an hour with no sign of troll. I suggested we break for lunch and tapped my flask suggestively. It was a mistake. Elmo had just taken a good gulp when the troll crashed into view with a rumble of stony feet.

His horse threw him. He looked up at the approaching creature with a dawning wonder. His eyes lingered on the angles of her stumpy figure, on the piece of gristle stuck rakishly between her teeth. "Sylvia!" he breathed.

I sent them billygoats for the wedding.

MARION ZIMMER BRADLEY

THE DARKOVER NOVELS

EXILE'S SONG

A Novel of Darkover

by Marion Zimmer Bradley

Margaret Alton is the daughter of Lew Alton, Darkover's Senator to the Terran Federation, but her morose, uncommunicative father is secretive about the obscure planet of her birth. So when her university job sends her to Darkover, she has only fleeting, haunting memories of a tumultuous childhood. But once in the light of the Red Sun, as her veiled and mysterious heritage becomes manifest, she finds herself trapped by a destiny more terrifying than any nightmare!

- A direct sequel to *The Heritage of Hastur* and *Sharra's Exile*
- With cover art by Romas Kukalis

☐ **Hardcover Edition**   UE2705-$21.95

Mercedes Lackey

The Novels of Valdemar

Eluki bes Shahar

THE HELLFLOWER SERIES

☐ **HELLFLOWER (Book 1)**   UE2475—$3.99

Butterfly St. Cyr had a well-deserved reputation as an honest
and dependable smuggler. But when she and her partner, a
highly illegal artificial intelligence, rescued Tiggy, the son and
heir to one of the most powerful of the hellflower mercenary
leaders, it looked like they'd finally taken on more than they
could handle. For his father's enemies had sworn to see that
Tiggy and Butterfly never reached his home planet alive. . . .

☐ **DARKTRADERS (Book 2)**   UE2507—$4.50

With her former partner Paladin—the death-to-possess Old
Federation artificial intelligence—gone off on a private mission,
Butterfly didn't have anybody to back her up when Tiggy's
enemies decided to give the word "ambush" a whole new and
all-too-final meaning.

☐ **ARCHANGEL BLUES (Book 3)**   UE2543—$4.50

Darktrader Butterfly St. Cyr and her partner Tiggy seek to complete the mission they started in DARKTRADERS, to find and
destroy the real Archangel, Governor-General of the Empire,
the being who is determined to wield A.I. powers to become
the master of the entire universe.

Science Fiction Anthologies